MOTHER CAN YOU HEAR ME?

Margaret Forster is the author of many successful novels, including *Lady's Maid, Have the Men Had Enough?* and *The Memory Box*, two memoirs, *Hidden Lives* and *Precious Lives*, and several acclaimed biographies, including *Good Wives*.

Margaret Forster

MOTHER CAN YOU HEAR ME?

VINTAGE

Published by Vintage 2004

2 4 6 8 10 9 7 5 3 1

First published in Great Britain in 1979 by
Secker & Warburg

Vintage
Random House, 20 Vauxhall Bridge Road,
London SW1V 2SA

Random House Australia (Pty) Limited
20 Alfred Street, Milsons Point, Sydney
New South Wales 2061, Australia

Random House New Zealand Limited
18 Poland Road, Glenfield,
Auckland 10, New Zealand

Random House (Pty) Limited
Endulini, 5A Jubilee Road, Parktown 2193,
South Africa

The Random House Group Limited Reg. No. 954009
www.randomhouse.co.uk

A CIP catalogue record for this book
is available from the British Library

ISBN 0 09 945558 7

Papers used by Random House are natural, recyclable
products made from wood grown in sustainable forests.
The manufacturing processes conform to the environ-
mental regulations of the country of origin

Printed and bound in Great Britain by
Bookmarque Ltd, Croydon, Surrey

For Theodora Joy Ooms,
sixteen years too late.

One

Angela Bradbury waited many years to tell her daughter Sadie the story of how she came to exist. It was, she thought, a beautiful story, full of romance and passion, and Angela had many times imagined, with tears of happiness in her eyes, how she would tell it. 'It was a lovely day,' she would begin, her voice low and quiet, 'a hot, still day even though it was only March, and we went to the seaside, your Father and I, on bicycles, with a picnic in the basket on my handlebars, and when we got there we swam even though the water was freezing cold and then we crouched among the sand dunes and ate our picnic and then—' her voice would surely break '—and then we made love and you were conceived.' Sadie would ask why she had wanted a baby and Angela had a touching explanation—honest but tender. 'I worried so much whether it was the right thing to do,' she would say, 'I didn't know if I wanted to be a Mother with all it meant but your Father persuaded me—wanting a baby so badly was enough, he said, and it did not need justifying. It would be visible evidence of our love for each other, he said, part of an inevitable natural pattern, and I should not be afraid. And as soon as I knew you were on the way I was so happy I knew he had been right.'

But unfortunately Sadie never asked, not once, ever, not a hint of curiosity and if Angela tried to foist the charming tale upon her she groaned and said 'For chrissake, Mum.'

On Mondays, Wednesdays and Fridays Angela was in the habit of ringing her Mother, who lived in St Erick, a country town in north-west Cornwall. She rang her at six thirty precisely. If for some reason she was delayed, her Mother rang her to see what was the matter. They rarely rang each other apart from these rigidly fixed times that were as much part of Angela's life as getting up or going to bed. The 'phone calls hung over her but were essential to her peace of mind. After she had chattered to Mother for at least five minutes she would make some acceptable excuse and hang up, feeling immediately relieved and, if Mother had been in good spirits, which was rare, even happy.

To answer the telephone on a Sunday afternoon and hear her Father's voice was alarming and meant disaster. She gave the number and he said, 'Is that you, Angela?' which irritated her. Who else could it be since her voice was surely that of an adult female and no other adult female lived in the house? In ways like that she was cruel to him.

'Yes, of course,' she said, curtly, though she had caught the despondency in his voice and interpreted it correctly with great speed. 'Is anything wrong?' Because she was a Trewick by birth, Angela knew that this was the expected thing to assume.

'It's your Mam.'

Naturally. It always was. Nothing else made the stomach lurch with such violence.

'What's happened?'

'She's took bad. I took her breakfast in, bran and that, got her up, got her dressed and nice, said she wouldn't bother with her hair but I said oh no we're not starting that game and I did it, best I could like, anyways I got her going and I thought hello her mouth's a bit funny but she says she's all right, bad tempered like, and anyways when I came from getting a loaf—I had to get a loaf or I wouldn't have left her—anyways she says she wants to lie down so I took off her slippers and she lay down on the settee, but her colour was bad mind'—

He had to be heard out. Even if she could have brought herself to, Angela would never have interrupted. She listened almost dreamily, absent minded, picking at a bit of fluff on her sleeve. Perhaps he would go on forever and nothing need be done.

—'anyways she tries to get up to go to the doings and she was away, down in a flash, head missed the fender by an inch, like a log, couldn't move her and she's shaking and her face all screwed up—what a business—oh dear—so I grabbed the poker and banged on the wall for Mrs Collins and luckily she was in and got the message—anyways she came in and between us we got her

2

back on the settee—she's a deadweight, you'd never think, till you come to lift her—and Mrs Collins says straight away "she's had a stroke, Mr Trewick" and by god she was damned right, the doctor said "she's had a stroke" soon as he'd seen her, and I must say he came quick, just a young fellow but very nice, "she's had a stroke" he says, but that was yesterday—what a night—and now this morning she's worse, a bit of pneumonia got into her the doctor says—'

'How awful,' Angela said. He had paused too long for breath for her to ignore the break. 'Poor Mother.'

'Poor Mother all right,' Father said, 'you're dead right there—thought she was a goner—but anyways I'm managing and we'll see how she goes—the doctor's coming back this afternoon and he's given her pills and everything, course she can't hardly swallow, can't speak either, it's a job getting anything into her but I'm managing and Mrs Collins is very good'—

'I'd better come down,' Angela said. There was no alternative. She despised herself for the grudging way in which she said it, but Father did that to her.

'Valerie's coming,' Father said, his voice rising with triumph. 'I didn't ring her first, mind, only she rings Sunday afternoon and I couldn't keep it from her, now could I, so she knew first.'

Angela ignored that part. The assumption that she might be offended at Valerie being told first was too crass to go along with. He did it deliberately, fostering, he thought, a spirit of rivalry that would breed closer contact, quite unable to fathom that there was no competitive relationship at all between his daughters in this respect. Angela would have been grateful if only Valerie had been told. Valerie would have been grateful if only Angela had been told.

'I'll get an early train tomorrow from Paddington,' Angela said. 'Gives me time to get organized.'

'I don't think it will be a wasted journey, lass,' Father said. 'Thanks very much.'

Father's humility was never convincing. He wasn't really thanking her. He understood very well that thanks were inappropriate, but he liked to cast himself in the role of the pathetic old man who needed help. Till she got there, at least.

There had been other journeys like this one over the last five years, other calls to rush to Mother's bedside because she was sinking fast. Only she never sank. She recovered miraculously from her many and various ailments and berated Father for presuming to summon the family. Each time she went, Angela packed a suit for the funeral, carried away by Father's gloom. She packed a black suit and a cream silk shirt and a black and silver necklace because Father didn't like bare open necks. He would want her to look smart, would not allow grief to be an excuse for slovenliness. He and Mother both disliked Angela's clothes—they frequently reminisced about how neat and well turned out she used to look before she went to London. They said her clothes now were like dressing-up clothes, completely ridiculous for a teacher and mother of four children. There was no need for it, they said. Both of them paid great attention to their own clothes and were immaculate whatever the time of day. Especially Mother. Every afternoon of Angela's childhood Mother had changed from her morning skirt to her afternoon skirt even when they were both threadbare. The distinction was extremely important to her—pride in her appearance was not due to vanity but to the importance of keeping up morale.

The first time Father had summoned her, when Mother, aged seventy, had a severe attack of influenza, Angela had travelled first class with Max, her new-born son, in a carrycot. She could remember the snow outside and the light it reflected into the grey, dusty compartment where she sat huddled in a corner breast-feeding her baby, wondering if her milk would survive the strain of getting up from bed to make a three-hundred-mile journey. She had hoped Max, ten days old, and winter—it was January— would excuse her from going at all but Father's voice was so bleak. 'She's sinking fast,' he said, and there seemed no alternative, not unless one had a heart of stone, not unless one wished to be entirely selfish. She had arrived. Mother rallied. She opened her eyes to look at Max, her first grandson, and smiled and stretched out a finger to touch him where he lay on the bed. It was like a miracle watching the baby grip the finger and watching the life blood flow back into Mother. 'I knew it would do the trick,' Father had said, boastfully. Angela was home in a week, drained by all the emotion, leaving Mother a little radiant with the drama of it all and Father ebullient. She survived again and again and again, though never growing immune to the horror of it all.

This time, she travelled second class. The fares had shot up, the cost was exorbitant. The train, as ever, was packed with the deprived of the entire country. Nobody affluent ever seemed to travel by train, not from Paddington to Penzance, or if they did their affluence was obliterated by the crushing mass of people. There were children everywhere, sweets stuck in their hot hands in the most ridiculous fashion, no thought given to how they were to amuse themselves when the sucking palled. It wearied her to see it. Even when the children squabbled and yelled she could not bring herself to feel sorry for the harassed mothers. They had brought it upon themselves. They had neglected their duty as mothers. Angela glared at them furiously. Sit nicely, they said, sit quietly, sit straight, sit, sit and look out of the window—it was sickening. Proper mothers would have brought crayons and paper and story books and puzzles. Proper mothers would have played with their offspring. Proper mothers would have understood the children's frustration. Angela tried not to look. She sat and thought how determined she had been to be a proper Mother. Like Mother, she thought, without ever having defined what that meant.

The baby was beautiful, after an agonizing birth—ordinary, but agonizing. Angela felt no ecstasy. They had done so many awful things to her—shoved tubes up her nose, yelled at her to push when she didn't want to push and the pain had been all the more terrible because it was unexpected. 'What am I doing wrong?' Angela had shouted back at them, but nobody seemed to know. She had done all the right exercises, she had been calm and kept her head, and then quite suddenly there had been an explosion of pain and they were forcing her to take the gas and air she did not want. So there was no ecstasy, or even relief—only a deep shame and misery. She lay on the high bed while they mopped up the blood that seemed to be everywhere—'All over the floor,' the nurse who was cleaning it said crossly—feeling utterly sad and even frightened. She had no strength. She could not lift an arm or move her head. Her face was stiff with dried tears and her hair stuck to her forehead with sweat. They brought the baby over to her, tightly wrapped in a blanket. The shock revived her. It struck her as magical—a face she did not know but which she had created. And the pity of it engulfed her, bringing the tears again fast and furious. So pitiful—such a pathetic scrap and she herself so battered and exhausted. It was all too much to understand and yet all night

*she lay puzzling it out when all she craved was sleep. I am a Mother,
she said to herself over and over again. What does it mean? And into her
poor tired head swam pictures of her own Mother who had gone through
all this before and never spoken of it.*

She saw the bright orange door opening before the taxi had
stopped. Father had recently painted it—'Two coats, inside and
out, best Dulux, no messing'—and would want it noticed. What
a joke taxis were outside London, such slow friendly cheap
things with drivers carrying luggage for you so quaintly. Father
would have seen it coming round the corner, on the look out for
half an hour. Trewicks were always on the look out. There was
a mirror in the corner over the television so that the front door
and gate could be seen from anywhere in the room. Nobody
ever needed to knock on a Trewick door—it always opened,
sometimes alarmingly, as soon as the startled caller's hand moved
towards the bell. If the visitor had not been seen by Father, he
would have been heard, yet the bell was piercing as though the
small house had secret wings and corridors not visible.

'Good journey,' Father said. He rarely asked questions. He
made statements which you either contradicted or agreed with.

'Not bad.'

'Get yourself in then. Come and see her. Take your coat off
first. Don't want wet coats near your Mother, not in her state.'

He stood and watched her remove her coat, frowning hard.
Briskly, he shook all two raindrops off it and hung it up correctly
on a hanger.

Valerie, sister Valerie, was sitting on the bed, a tin bowl of
water in one hand and a piece of cotton wool in the other. 'Just
moistening Mother's lips,' she murmured. Her spectacles were
filmed over with the steam rising from the water. '*Hot* water?'
Angela said. 'She seems so cold,' Valerie said, moving the cotton
wool with exaggerated care over Mother's cracked and swollen
lips. Angela sat down, on the other side of the bed. Mother was
propped up on three pillows, her white bushy hair pushed in
weird directions. Her eyes were closed, her skin grey. Angela
took her hand, lying limply on top of the blue coverlet, and said,
'Mother, can you hear me? It's Angela.' Slowly, slowly, with
enormous effort Mother's eyes opened and tried to focus—eyes
drugged and bloodshot but still bright blue. Her lips moved but

6

no sound came from them. Angela squeezed her hand again and bent right over Mother's face. 'Mother, can you hear me? It's Angela—Angela.' And this time Mother smiled and managed to whisper 'Angela' and to return the faintest of pressures with her hand. The smile was the same wistful slip of a smile for which Angela had striven all her life.

'She prayed to God you would come,' Father said from the foot of the bed. 'Didn't you Mam? Eh?' He came round to where Angela sat and leant over her and shook his head. 'Bad,' he said solemnly, 'very bad.' Too quickly, Angela jumped up, shaking the rackety old bed enough to spray Valerie with her own hot water, and went out of the stifling room and upstairs to the bath/room where she buried her face in the same blue and white striped towel that once she had taken for swimming on Thursdays after school. It smelled peculiar, but would have been washed vigorously in the dolly tub last week. Her Father would not have a washing machine—no need. He would not send things to the laundry either—no need. He said that he had to have something to do and that he could manage and went on breaking Mother's houseproud heart by ruining her treasured scraps of linen.

She washed her face, battling with the usual claustrophobia the house gave her. The bath had a strange contraption across it to help Mother get in and out since arthritis had begun to cripple her. A large green rubber mat lay in the bottom of it so that she would not slip. Father frequently pointed it out. 'That's her mat,' he would say, taking you into the bathroom so he could point, 'so she won't slip. And her special thingamebob for getting in and out—but I still stay near, oh yes.'

She went back downstairs, relatively composed but surly. Father made her surly, with suppressed fury. He was sitting in front of the fire, arms crossed, legs thrust out, right in front of it in his patched leather armchair. She stood in front of the window, watching the rain fall on the privet hedge, making it glossy and a darker green than it really was. It was a viciously neat hedge, cut as soon as it showed any signs of growth. She did not want to sit down, shunned even the intimacy of sharing the fire. But Father said, 'Sit yourself down' and she had to obey. She sat primly on the edge of a hard upright dining/table chair, as far away as it was possible to get in that small cramped room.

'What do you think of her?' Father said. 'Eh?'

'She seems pretty ill.'

'Oh, she's that all right. I don't think you'll have had a wasted journey.'

'It doesn't matter about the journey.'

'Children all right?'

'Fine.'

Valerie came out of the downstairs sitting room that had been turned into a bedroom. She was tip-toeing and had her finger to her lips. She sat down beside Father and sighed, passing a hand over her forehead.

'Have you changed her?' Father asked.

'She wasn't wet,' Valerie said, 'I've just looked. I've washed her face and rubbed some salve on her lips. I've taken the quilt off and put a heavier one on instead and another blanket. But I've opened the side window just a crack to let some air in and—'

'Oh no,' Father said, and got up. 'No, no, no—not an open window. Definitely not.'

'But it's so hot and stuffy,' Valerie protested, 'it's not healthy to—'

'I'll say what's healthy,' Father said. 'In this rain—and her so cold—you'll kill her,' and he went towards Mother's door.

'Don't go in now,' Valerie said, 'you'll waken her—I'll creep in and do it if you insist.'

'I can creep myself,' Father said.

He opened the door, watched by both daughters, who knew his clumsiness. He stepped carefully inside, leaving it open, and began to move round the bed in the narrow space between wardrobe and dressing table, but with his eyes fixed on the offending window towards which he edged his way he forgot the little stool that jutted out from beneath the washstand and tripped over it. Putting out his liver-spotted old hand to steady himself he pulled the lace mat off the chest of drawers and brought down the tin-framed photograph of Mother's mother. 'Goddam,' he said, and looked towards the bed. Mother did not stir. He got to the window and closed it and stood for a while fussing with the curtains. Then he went over to the bed and twitched the blankets and felt Mother's head, and shook his own.

'I think I'll go for a quick walk,' Angela said, when they had all taken up their positions again and the silence grew.

'In this rain,' Father said.

'I don't mind rain.'

'It was wet coats and shoes I was thinking of,' Father said, 'not you minding the rain. Wet things in the house—that was what I was meaning. At a time like this, in her condition.'

'I'll hang my coat in the washhouse when I come back.'

'And wet hair?'

'I'll dry it.'

Father pursed his lips and started jabbing with the poker at a big piece of coal on the fire.

'No consideration,' he said, 'always the same.'

'Want some coal brought in when I've got my coat on?' Angela asked.

'There's plenty coal in the bin.'

'Coming, Valerie?'

'Oh no—I'll stay with Mother,' Valerie said with a tired martyred smile. 'I'm exhausted anyway.'

She walked to the cemetery. There wasn't much choice. Two slabs of land owned by the council, one for the dead and one for a huge sprawling estate where she had spent half her life. Her bedroom window had overlooked the cemetery—it was the first thing she saw each day, those white tombstones and the long rows of yew trees leading upwards to the new crematorium. She had a great affection for it, not finding it in the least morbid or depressing to spend hours walking in it. It was extremely well laid out, very formal, with broad poplar-lined paths and little iron-work bridges over thin trickling streams which appeared to irrigate the dead. There were flowers everywhere—not just wreaths, poor shrivelled things, but rows and rows of blazing geraniums beneath the trees and enormous square beds of vulgar, vivid dahlias at all the intersections. All her relations, both the Trewicks and the Nancarrows, both sides were buried there. Father used to take them round all the graves every Sunday morning and she had never thought it the least odd. Indeed, the tombs of her ancestors had always impressed and satisfied her. James George Trewick, her great-grandfather, was the oldest of them all, buried in the only overgrown corner of the cemetery where the trees and bushes had thickened around the graves to form an almost impenetrable wall. She knew the dates off by heart—born 23 January 1832, died 1 November 1894. Her favourite was her great uncle William's because he was born and died on the same day with exactly fifty years between, but the prettiest grave was her Mother's mother. Of pale grey stone, an angel stood with spread wings above the oblong of turf where Beatrice Nancarrow lay beneath a giant sycamore tree. The wings from the tree were deemed a menace every year and as a child she had been set to gather them up and put them in the green grass-clippings box beside the stream. She would come with her Mother and Valerie on a Tuesday afternoon when they were little and Mother would take a small pair of shears out of her shopping basket—wrapped in a thick cloth for fear of accidents—and a cushion to kneel on—for fear of rheumatics—and she would laboriously cut the grass on the six feet by four feet oblong grave. Angela would be sent to get water from the trough and then she and Valerie would dip small scrubbing brushes into the water and dab them with scouring powder and scrub the stone angel, who was encrusted with scaly black stuff. They never got much of it off, but the sight of it distressed Mother so much they always tried very hard. Most of Mother's distress was about things like that, out of proportion and puzzling to a child, but none the less distressing. When they had done all they could, they would find a bench in a shady place and have a drink and a biscuit. The atmosphere came back to Angela strongly as she followed the twisting narrow paths that connected the main thoroughfares. Of contentment, of basking in Mother's approbation and enjoying a job shared with her. It had bound them very close. It had been easy, sitting there, to curb her vitality and control her exuberance the way all of them tried to do with Mother. To súit Mother, to gain her approbation.

The beautiful baby cried a great deal. Angela took it home and looked after it devotedly, enjoying the need to wash so many nappies and clothes, enjoying the slavery and the chance to prove how anxious she was to do the right thing, but the baby cried and drove her frantic. It gained weight, it was pronounced fit and well, it was not sick but it cried. She seemed to have no natural instinct that told her what was wrong and no natural ability to deal with the problem. And the crying was so heartbreaking, so desperate and insistent. She tried putting the baby where she could not hear it but then worry forced her to go and listen. Mother said, 'You can't expect perfection' and the clinic said, 'Babies do cry' but neither source of wisdom consoled her. She felt it was her fault when the baby cried and could not forgive it. She cried herself with self-pity and resented the hours spent walking up and down, up and down, holding the small sweaty bundle of unhappiness that was her baby. She loved it so much, she had tried so hard, it was so unfair. The neighbourhood was full of neglected babies who slept all day and night and never caused a twinge of concern. She felt terrified, sure that she had taken on—wilfully—a role she could not fulfil. She wasn't like Mother. She wasn't patient and tender and quiet. Her poor baby would notice the difference.

'Mother, can you hear me? It's Angela.' She sat where Valerie had sat, her wet hair wrapped in a towel to appease Father. Mother opened her eyes and tried to smile. It was hard to know whether to talk to her. My voice will come from a long way off, Angela thought, and it will not be clear to her. All she can appreciate is my physical presence, my being there. The hugs, the strangling hugs she had once given Mother—oh, the crushing, bruising kisses, the tight gripped hand-holds, the all-embracing cuddles so that Mother cried out for breath and Father shouted, Stop that. And the caresses, the endearments—'I love you so much, so so much, I love love love you—oh I love you best in the whole world'—on and on until Father was goaded into a fury. She had never wondered why. Mother did not object. Mother remained passive but allowed the demonstrative display to continue. But to take Mother in her arms now was impossible. It was hard even to kiss her convincingly, though it was not physical distaste that prevented an embrace—it was fear that Mother would find her out, would sense the difference between what had been and what now was. Even if it was what Mother most wanted and needed it was the last thing she could give.

Valerie crept in, revived by the revolting milky sugary drink she had made herself. She sat on the other side of the bed, her face solemn and lugubrious. She spoke to Mother in a sickening creepy whisper that Angela found patronizing. She wanted to say to her sister 'Oh for christ's sake shut up' but didn't. Valerie crumbled too easily. She was the youngest child, a wartime baby, a clear mistake yet loved more freely by Mother than any of the four of them. Once, when Valerie aged two had been in hospital with scarlet fever and had just returned home, weak in the legs, Mother had cried out to Angela, 'Oh look at her—the darling!' and Angela had hated her.

The hatred, over the years, had been distilled into irritation and lately into indifference. Valerie was welcome to Mother.

'What do you think?' Valerie whispered, leaning over the bed and peering into Angela's face. 'What are you smiling at?'

'You.'

'I don't see why. What have I said?'

'Nothing.'

'You aren't very nice, Angela, in the circumstances.'

'No, I'm not.'

'All I asked was what you thought about Mother—about whether you thought—you know—if she'll—'

'Die?'

'Sssh!' Valerie put a hand over her own mouth, and gestured towards Mother, an expression of the greatest anguish on her face.

'No,' said Angela, 'I don't think she will. Unfortunately.'

'Oh, Angela!'

'Oh, Valerie. She's old and tired and unhappy. Why want it prolonged?'

'You used to cry when Mother was ill—you used to have nightmares that she would die—you used to wake up screaming, I remember you did, and that was why, and now you're so callous, it's horrible.'

The room used to swim with blood—everything that was brown became blood—the chest of drawers, the wardrobe, the end of the bed, the door, the window ledge, the linoleum surrounds on the floor—blood everywhere and Mother dead. And she did scream, until Mother came and held her tightly and kissed her brow and soothed her sobbing. 'I dreamed you d-d-died,' she wailed and Mother said, 'Well, I'm not dead. I'm alive,' and the reassurance was bliss, almost worth the horror of the dream that had gone before. Mother was alive. She would fall asleep happy and comforted totally. Nothing else in the whole world mattered except that Mother was not dead.

'Just think,' Valerie said, breathing heavily and flushed with anger, 'just think what it feels like to be Mother.'

'You know, do you?'

'I try—even if I'm not a Mother myself—I try—and I can't imagine anything worse than lying in bed desperately ill feeling—'

'Oh shut up, Valerie. You don't know what you're talking about.'

Valerie began to weep. Her shoulders shook alarmingly: the

large tears plopped onto the blue nylon eiderdown, staining it. Making Valerie cry was so easy. Mother used to get so cross—'Leave the poor little thing alone,' she would say, as Valerie's fat, tear-streaked face came into view—'Don't torment her so.' *She* torments *me*,' Angela had cried, but Mother didn't believe it. Watching Valerie yet again on Mother's knee being cuddled and petted Angela would vow secret vengeance. She forced Valerie to play games she did not want to play and terrorized her when Mother was out of the house. They were never allies, except against Father.

Angela got off the bed and sat on the only chair. She picked up Mother's Bible, full of texts and cuttings from the Parish Magazine, and held it in front of her face so Valerie would feel ignored. Mother read the Bible every day with self-conscious virtue. Father, who did not believe a word of it, quite liked her to do it and if she was low would push it upon her—'Here, Mother, see what the good book can do for you.' Valerie alone of the four of them had followed in her footsteps. In the part of Manchester where she lived she was a pillar of the church, never away from the place—so much so that Father cruelly alleged she had her eye on the curate. The two older brothers, Tom and Harry, never went near any religious establishment but since they were in Australia it was Angela's defection that hurt most.

Cautiously, after a few minutes flicking, Angela lowered the book. Valerie had composed herself. Her nose was red and shiny and her eyes still swam behind the huge spectacles but she was quiet.

'I'll stay up tonight if you like,' Angela said, 'I haven't done it yet.'

Valerie nodded. 'You won't keep Father out,' she said, 'he comes and goes all night—never settles.' They stayed silent for a while, the silly squabble forgotten. Mother's gasping filled the tiny cramped room, up and down, up and down, with a rumbling, rough sound every few breaths that was most alarming of all. With nothing to do they were acutely aware of each other.

'How are the children?' Valerie said, eventually, and Angela knew she must be kind.

'Fine. Sadie thinks of nothing but boys and pop music, Max is all football, Saul loves school and Tim loves me. That's about it.'

'You are lucky,' and Valerie sighed. A familiar theme. 'Just like Mother,' Valerie went on, 'four children—except only one girl.'

'Fortunately,' Angela said.

'What?'

'That I only have one girl.'

'But why—Mother preferred girls—do you remember how thrilled we were when she said she loved her boys but she liked girls best? And only recently she said to me boys were a washout, never came near after they were grown up, just grew away from you, but girls grew closer.'

'Oh god,' Angela said.

'What's the matter? It was a compliment—you and I have stayed close.'

'Speak for yourself,' Angela said, 'I feel a million miles away. Boys have the right idea.'

'I don't understand you,' Valerie said, 'I don't really. Don't you like Mother? Don't you like Sadie? What's wrong with you?'

'I think you should go to bed,' Angela said.

Father took a long time pretending to settle down for the night. He reappeared twice after he had officially retired upstairs to say, 'Aren't you going to ring them up at home? Eh?' 'No,' said Angela carelessly. 'Why should I?' 'Oh, you're not like your Mother,' Father muttered, shuffling off, 'not like her at all—she'd have fussed and fretted about you all, worrying herself sick.' And worrying us with her incessant worrying, Angela thought. I won't do it. I don't want that kind of relationship—I want to cut through it, I want no guilt or remorse, I want Sadie to be as free as air. All the long uncomfortable night she sat thinking about her vow never to tie her children to her apron strings, never to give them cause to want rid of her. She had intended to cut the knots herself before they were tightened. She must not need her children too much. They must not need her too much. But that kind of balance was proving so hard to maintain.

Towards morning she woke from a doze to see the light coming through the thin curtains. There was something different about the room. With a start of alarm she realized she could no longer hear Mother's awful breathing. Jumping up, she bent over the sleeping form in the bed thinking only that Father would never forgive her if he had not been called and Mother had died. But she wasn't dead. Her breathing had simply become normal, or near normal, and to hear it one had to go closer and listen. Angela felt Mother's forehead and looked critically at her complexion. There was no doubt she was improving. Smiling, Angela went quietly into the kitchen and made herself some tea. She took it back into the bedroom, relieved that she had not woken Valerie or Father, and sat sipping it feeling amused. Another sinking fast journey over. Mother's resilience was staggering—one could not help being amazed by it.

'Hello, Angela,' Mother said, and Angela was so startled she spilled some of the tea. Mother's eyes were fully open and clear. She smiled and raised her hand slightly and Angela felt extraordinarily happy.

Two

They put on a marvellous show for the District Nurse when she arrived, neat and punctual, in her red Mini.

'In my day,' Father said, with a smirk, 'in my day the nurse—if you could get one, like—she had a bike, an old push bike and lucky to have that. Cycled miles in all weathers and thought nothing of it—no cars in them days, not for nurses.'

But it was all part of Father's patter and the District Nurse was familiar with it. 'I'll go away again and come back on a bike if it'll please you, Mr Trewick.' 'Want a cup of tea?' Father said, pleased.

They clustered round Mother's bed while the District Nurse pronounced herself astonished—Mother's progress was remarkable. Phrases like 'over the worst' and 'on the mend' flew through the stifling air and when the District Nurse said the room could do with being a little less hot Father had the window open in a flash, only saying, 'You're taking a chance, mind.' He leaned against the wardrobe watching the application of ointments and creams. 'Had a perm over the weekend, then,' he said. The District Nurse smiled slightly but Mother was improved enough to let out a little moan of distress at Father's familiarity.

'Yes, I have, as a matter of fact,' she said.

'Going to a wedding or something?'

'You're very cheeky for an old gentleman,' Angela said, and squeezed Mother's hand to show her she knew how she felt.

'I'm not cheeky,' Father said, 'just showing an interest, that's all, something you could do with doing. Anyways, I'm not old, is I Mam?' Mother shuddered at his grammar, but Father was enjoying himself too much to care. 'How old do you think I am?' he said to the District Nurse. 'Go on, take a guess.'

'Don't spare his blushes,' Angela said. Valerie winced. Mother might be better but not so much better that facetious conversations across her bed were in order.

The District Nurse was perfectly willing to humour him—it was almost as if she considered it part of her job. 'Well,' she said, sticking a thermometer under Mother's tongue, 'you must be retired, so I know for a start you're over sixty-five, don't I?'

'You do indeed,' Father said. 'Correct. I'm all of sixty-five as the song says.'

'What song?' Angela said, rudely, but Father ignored her and pressed his victim for an answer.

'Let's see,' the District Nurse said, pretending careful deliberation, 'well, sixty-nine I'd say—seventy next birthday, eh?'

'Ten years out,' Father said, triumphant. 'Eighty next birthday. Now then.'

The District Nurse's astonishment was clearly genuine. She repeated 'never' and 'eighty next birthday' several times as she busied herself with Mother.

'Give him a medal,' Angela said, but nothing would dampen Father's sudden high spirits, until the District Nurse said she would like some more hot water and he and Valerie collided in the doorway in their haste to be the first to get it. Angela laughed.

Father turned on her furiously, all good humour gone, and held up a warning finger. She went on smiling steadily at him, refusing to give in, but to her disgust her heart pounded and her face felt hot. She still could not taunt him without fear of swift retribution. She carried in her head the memory of thrashings and ugly scenes and the inevitable humiliations that followed and though he was now powerless to hurt her, she had never quite stopped trembling. He couldn't, of course, help it, any more than she could herself.

At two years old, the baby became Sadie, indisputably a person and a wayward person at that. Angela looked back to Sadie's babyhood and wondered why she had found it difficult—why had she wanted her baby to talk so much, why had she wanted her independent? At every turn, Sadie crossed her. She would not eat her food, she threw appalling tantrums for no apparent reason, she was cross and difficult about the most simple things. Angela remembered how Mother had never lost her temper—only Father. Mother never shouted or smacked—only Father. With horror she began to realize that struggling to be like Mother was useless. Despair and depression made her so angry she frequently slapped Sadie or pushed her hard into her room, and then wept tears of remorse. 'I'm sorry,' she would say afterwards, 'I'm sorry, sorry, I'm a horrible awful Mother.' Miraculously, Sadie did not seem to hold it against her. Within half an hour after some appalling screaming match between them she would be humming cheerfully and only Angela would be gloomy. Will Sadie grow up afraid of me, she wondered, and the question haunted her. She had never been afraid of Mother, who was all sweetness and light, a constant haven from all the storms of childhood. With great patience Ben, her husband, explained that not every mother had to be like Mother. Sadie would take the rough with the smooth. But Mother was all smooth, Angela said. I am no use.

None of them wanted the District Nurse to go. Valerie made more tea and they all sat around drinking it in the sitting room, Mother left to sleep after the exertion of being washed. The District Nurse said she was quite sure Mrs Trewick would now go from strength to strength and complimented them all on the care they had taken. The crisis was over, she said. 'Thank god,' Valerie said. 'Good,' Father said, emphatically. Angela said nothing, knowing her silence was noted and held against her.

'We'll wait and see what the doctor says this afternoon,' Father said, 'then these lasses will want to get off home, but I'll manage. They work, you know, can't just drop everything, but that's the way the world is these days. One's a teacher, and the other's a probation officer—what do you think of that?'

'Haven't they done well?' the District Nurse said. 'You must be very proud of them.'

'And I've two sons,' Father said, 'in Australia, both of them, or they'd be here too.'

'I doubt it,' Angela murmured.

'What?' Father said. 'Course they would. You watch your tongue, miss.' Again, the warning finger.

'I think I'll have to be going,' the District Nurse said. They were all fulsome in their gratitude, overpowering in their appreciation.

'What did you say that for, about Tom and Harry? Eh?

Daftness—course they would come to their Mother's sick bed if they could—deliberately letting folk think they wouldn't care—wickedness—what did you say it for?'

'What do any of us say anything for?' Angela said, knowing such affected talk enraged him.

'You keep that sort of silly remark for London,' Father said, 'it won't wash down here. We talk sense here. I don't know what gets into you.'

'You never did.'

'You're right there—damned right. All a waste of time. You struggle and sweat and do your best and what for? Nothing. Get away with you, go on. See what you can do for your poor Mother before she goes.'

'She isn't "going" anywhere,' Angela said, but he had lumbered off on one of his invented important errands.

Mother fully recovered the use of her voice that afternoon, shortly after the doctor had been. It moved Angela to tears to hear her Mother speak, in a rough, husky whisper quite different from her usual light voice. The glory of someone returning from the almost-dead struck her as blinding—she could not but admire the determination, the love of life itself, that had kept Mother's frail body and soul together. Her rejoicing at such a recovery was as genuine as Valerie's and Father's, though only a little while ago she had wished Mother finally dead to save her from future misery. In the evening, she sat with her while Valerie cooked and Father made endless telephone calls, booming out the good news to all and sundry, and kept to herself her vision of the grim months ahead. Better to forget that things were far from rosy—Mother's lungs were still congested, her heart weak, her arthritis crippling, her sight fading, her hearing impaired. It would be weeks till she was up, weeks till she might stagger out, and meanwhile she would remain locked in mortal combat with Father pushing and domineering and fussing and annoying all at once.

'You shouldn't have come,' were almost Mother's first proper words, addressed to Angela. 'Those poor children—left—all this way—'

'The children are fine,' Angela said, 'and I wanted to come.'

'It was good of you. I'm sorry you had to—I'm such an old nuisance—'

'No,' Angela said, 'you are not. You're not a nuisance at all—

you're my poor Mother and you're not to worry about anything. Just relax and get better.'

Protecting Mother had been a lifelong occupation—from herself, from the cruel world. 'Don't tell your Mother' was one of the first instructions Angela learned. It applied to anything whatsoever that might be considered disturbing news. Mother mustn't be told anything nasty or distressing and that covered a wide variety of topics which grew ever more extensive.

Obediently, not wanting to be the one who made Mother sorrowful, who brought to her face that pitiful expression, Angela learnt to swallow her own fears, anxieties, worries, nightmares the better to shield Mother. Mother would embrace her and dry her tears without ever knowing what they were about, and soon Angela learned to control even those signals of distress. Mother never knew how at ten she was wrongly accused of stealing at school and subjected to terrifying interrogations by an over-zealous headmistress who did not even apologize for them when the real culprit was found. Mother never knew swimming lessons were purgatory. Off she would go, twice a week, to the public baths to have lessons, paid for by Grandma, from a brute called Mr Shropshire who roared at her and poked her in the back with a long pole that had a nasty sharp hook on the end. 'Enjoyed yourself, dear?' Mother would ask, smiling, pleased that Angela was learning to swim because she could not swim herself and had always wanted to, and Angela would say 'yes' because she did not want to wipe the smile from Mother's face.

'I don't know why God spares me each time,' Mother was saying. 'Sometimes I think it's just to give your Father something to do.' She looked hopefully at Angela, who evaded the issue. Conversations about what God did or did not intend were doomed to failure. Religion was Mother's greatest comfort and it would be cruel to attack it—cruel and unnecessary. Lately, they had all encouraged Mother in her devotion to God and Jesus because it was such a relief to feel that she had something to put her faith in. Instead of mocking the texts pinned up round the house and deriding the religious messages in the printed pamphlets Mother collected Angela found herself nodding sagely at them and welcoming more. The last thing any of them wanted, at this stage, was for Mother to start querying Christianity and its meaning.

Father came in and stood at the bedside looking down at Mother with a maddeningly proprietorial air.

'How are you feeling, Mam?' he asked, head on one side.

Mother was too weak to give vent to irritation but there was no mistaking the beseeching look she cast in Angela's direction.

'She's tired,' Angela said, 'obviously.'

'Do you want propped up, Mam?' Father asked, already dragging out another pillow and preparing to heave Mother around.

'Don't be ridiculous,' Angela said, 'she doesn't want to move a finger.'

'Oh, she has to move,' Father said. 'Must get her moving, soon as possible, that's the way, or we'll have her bedridden—oh no, she has to be got moving'—and with rough, hurried movements he shoved the other pillow under Mother's shoulders so that her head flopped forward at the most uncomfortable of angles.

'We have to get her moving,' he said again, 'and up to the bathroom. Do you want to do anything now, Mam? Do you need the pan, eh?'

Mother mutely shook her head and directed that look of appeal at Angela again, but Angela said nothing. She could not take on that burden again—it was no use Mother electing her as her champion to enter the lists against Father's insensitivity and coarseness. When Father left the room to fuss over something else, Mother whispered, 'You don't know what I have to put up with.'

'But I do,' Angela said. 'I know exactly—but he doesn't mean it that way—he can't help himself—that's just the way he is.'

It was not what she should have said. It was not what Mother wanted her to say. It was not what she used to say when she lived at home and lashed Father with her tongue in Mother's defence, steeling herself to take the brunt of his rage. Father only attacked Mother through being what he was, what he couldn't help—since he worshipped her, he could never even shout at her let alone strike her. But he could shout at Angela and hit her when she went too far and on the sidelines would be Mother, the cause of it all and yet innocent.

It was always the little things that caused the scenes, the refinements. Mother would sit at the neatly set table eating her meal with great delicacy, cutting up her meat into small pieces and popping it daintily into her mouth, which she would then close while she chewed thoroughly. Father sloshed his food with gravy and drowned it in great dollops of sauce and walloped it into his mouth with half a slice of bread, losing half of it on the way up from the plate. A tiny shiver of distaste from Mother and Angela would say, 'I think I'll eat in the back kitchen. I don't like eating with pigs—it makes me sick watching him.' Things like that, silly, absurd, unforgivable things. Mother used her, and regretted it.

'I think I'll have to go home tomorrow,' she said, 'though I would like to stay.'

'It was good of you to come,' Mother said.

'I can come again, soon.'

'No, no—you mustn't leave the children—I don't like to think about it.' The little tick in the corner of Mother's eye, that nervous twitch she had had ever since Angela could remember, began to work again, feebly, overcoming the drugs that had stilled it during her illness.

'The children are fine,' Angela said, 'Ben is so good they don't even miss me.'

'Oh, they do,' Mother said. 'All children miss their Mother.'

'Well, mine don't,' Angela said firmly. 'I've trained them not to. I'm not a Mother like you were.'

Leaving Sadie was always hard. Angela could hardly bring herself to go out in the evening when Sadie was asleep—suppose she woke and needed her?—never mind during the day when she was awake. The casual way in which other Mothers left their small children appalled her. Only with Ben in charge could she relax. On his day off she would sometimes dash into town and shop and when she came back Sadie was often standing with her nose pressed against the window, forlorn and sad: 'Be sensible,' Ben said, 'you know perfectly well she's quite happy with me—we have great games—it's just when you come back she cries.' But Mother never left me, Angela thought, not when I was tiny. Mother was always there. Small children were so pathetic, their understanding so physical. She promised herself that when Sadie could talk and understand, everything would be different, she would leave her without a qualm. But leaving her now, at two years old, was a betrayal. She had no right to want freedom from Sadie. Mother had never wanted it.

Ben rang up, sounding depressed, urging her to come home that day.

'Wants you home, eh?' said Father.

'Poor man,' Mother said, 'he's very good letting you come, very good. Some men wouldn't.'

Angela laughed. 'He doesn't have much say in the matter,' she said. 'I do what I like and he has to put up with it, I'm afraid.'

'Oh, Angela,' protested Mother, but she smiled slightly. Angela's independent spirit had always thrilled her. She was convinced she had bred, by some fluke, a strong powerful fearless daughter in the image not of her craven self but of her dreams. It made up for the loathing she felt for her own weak character. Nothing pleased her more than a display of Angela's strength. 'Right from a little thing,' she was given to saying, 'you knew what you wanted and you were determined to get it. Not a bit like me.' Every strident boast Angela came out with received Mother's silent approval until she felt any hesitancy, any uncertainty, would be unthinkable. Often, Mother would openly admire her resolution just as her nerve was failing and then it was impossible to give up. 'I couldn't have gone abroad like this,' Mother said, as they sat waiting for the taxi to take Angela, fifteen, to the station where she would begin her journey alone, to stay with a family in Avignon. 'I couldn't even have coped with London,' Mother said, 'I would have been far too frightened. And as for catching a boat train—and getting the right connection the other side—' One by one she listed Angela's fears. 'Oh, it's nothing,' Angela said, 'I'm looking forward to it.'

Valerie said she would stay a few more days, make a week of it, see Mother properly over the hump. They went to the shops together before Angela left and stocked up with tins and dried goods, things Father would use if they were provided. It was the only way to combat partially his frugal housekeeping.

'It's good of you to stay longer,' Angela said, 'it makes it so much easier for me to leave. I appreciate it.' She hadn't meant to be so abrupt and clipped. Valerie's sloppiness made her abrasive.

'Well, you've got the children to think about,' Valerie said, but with no edge to her voice.

'A wonderful let out. A job isn't nearly as convincing, though it can't be easy for you.'

'No,' Valerie said, 'but I couldn't put work before Mother's health. It wouldn't be right. If anything happened, I would never forgive myself.'

Quickly, Angela banged four tins of soup into the trolley they were pushing round the supermarket. It was like talking to Father and about as realistic.

'What would we do,' Angela said, 'if Father dies or falls ill? Have you thought of that one? I wake up at night sometimes sweating with the fear of it. Mother would have to be put in a home.'

'Oh no,' Valerie said, hand poised above a packet of jelly, 'never. I wouldn't allow it. We would work something out.'

'What?' Angela asked. 'I couldn't have her, I just couldn't.'

'Then she would come to me.'

'I couldn't have Mother—it would kill me. We've got the space and the money and I only work part time but I couldn't—I would go mad. I'd disintegrate.'

Valerie picked a tin of beans off the shelf and put it carefully in the almost full trolley. She was a little flushed. Together, they walked towards the checkout point. 'You used to say Mother would come and live with you when you were grown up, Angela,' she said. 'You used to get her to promise she would. Don't you remember?'

They had fought over it. They had walked down the road pulling at Mother's coat sleeves and shouting 'Me! She's going to live with me!' and each of them clamoured for Mother's agreement. Dancing and skipping along, five and seven, fighting over her, desperate to get her to commit herself but she would give nothing away. 'When I'm old,' she said, 'you won't want me.' 'We will! We will!' 'When you grow up,' she said, 'you'll have husbands and you won't love me any more.' 'We will! We will!' they cried. 'All right,' Mother said, an arm round each of them as they turned up their adoring faces, 'I'll come and live with whoever wants me most when they are grown up.' 'That will be me,' Angela shouted, and Valerie wept, because it sounded so final.

Father insisted on coming to the station with her, which prolonged the ordeal of departing. In some ways, it was worse than saying goodbye to Mother, who was much better about it than anyone had a right to expect. Mother in some strange way had always seemed to crave the arrival of long dreaded painful moments—she was impatient to have done with them when the time came. She lay back on the white pillows looking frail and tired but also pretty in her pink nightdress with the lace edging round the neck, a last Christmas present from Angela. The sun came through the net curtains and lit up the whiteness of her thick hair and the vivid blue of those large eyes neither daughter had inherited. There was a little more colour in her face and her expression, though weary, was free from pain, her forehead quite smooth and unfurrowed. She let Angela go with a smile and a willing pressure of the hand whereas Father, stern and unyielding in his dark trilby hat and stiff winter overcoat, was reluctant to let her escape.

They were always much too early for the train. All Trewicks traditionally stood on freezing station platforms half an hour before there was any likelihood whatsoever of their train approaching, and if, as often happened, that train was delayed then their early arrival became even more absurd. Angela stood, ramrod straight, beside Father, knowing it was no use suggesting the waiting room or the buffet for a cup of tea. Trewicks did not have wanton cups of tea at all hours of the day—a cup at breakfast, a cup at lunch, a cup at teatime and that was quite sufficient thank you very much. The wind snaked in through the arch at the end of the platform, blowing the litter along with it and stinging the eyes that strained to see the express that still had not come. Father stamped his huge army style shoes. 'Perishing,' he said. Angela said nothing. She turned up the collar of her coat partly to keep out the wind but also to hide from Father's scrutiny. Any minute he would begin.

'I just hope she'll be all right,' Father said at last, shaking his head doubtfully. 'I don't like the look of her at all, not at all. It'll be a long job.'

'Well, don't rush her,' Angela said, weakly. The faintest hoot of a train's whistle was only her imagination.

'Oh, I won't rush her, no fear, but if she stays in that bed much longer anything could happen. And of course you leaving will bring her low, bound to, but it can't be helped, we'll get over it, no choice.'

'I'll keep in touch,' Angela said. 'I'll ring every day.'

'When will you be down again, then?'

'I don't know.'

'Not coming for Easter, eh?'

'I don't think so. Not this year.'

'It disappoints your Mother, but there you are. Easter isn't what it was, I keep telling her but she doesn't see it that way, she can be cantankerous at times about things like that.'

Still the train did not come. Numb with cold and dread, Angela found herself wondering what in Father's opinion Easter had once been. All she could recall were new clothes and a procession in a church filled with heavily scented lilies, and at home brightly coloured eggs that looked exciting and tasted dull.

'What did you think of her?' Father was saying.

'Well, she's been very ill. I thought she seemed amazingly recovered, considering.'

'Course, *you* don't see what she's like when you aren't there—plays up something chronic on occasions—doesn't like this and that, just wants left—it's shocking. I have to humour her out of it.'

'Yes,' Angela said.

'She misses all of you, that's half the trouble,' Father said, 'not having any of you anywhere near.'

'We aren't that far away,' Angela said, 'Valerie and I.'

'Hundreds of miles,' Father said, 'couldn't be further away if you'd tried.'

The train sped into the station like an angel of deliverance. Father was immediately taken up with procuring her a seat as though she was incapable of getting one herself. He pushed and shoved on her account and shot perfectly innocent passengers venomous glances for presuming to sit on a seat he had had his eye on. 'Here you are, Angela,' he bawled from the end of the carriage, 'look lively or somebody'll snatch this one too, they're that eager.' To please him, she took the badly positioned seat he had selected. 'I'm not stopping,' he said, 'I'll get back to your Mother. A good journey now—all the best.' It was his one endearment, a euphemism for all the hundreds of loving remarks he could not condone. Angela was careful to control her strong desire to clap her hands and laugh at her approaching freedom and instead went with him to the door and waved until he was out of sight. She immediately felt sick with relief.

Listless and with an aching head she slumped in the corner seat she had moved to and watched the countryside flash past. It had always been the same—she had always wanted to leave even though the chain that bound her to home was the tender one of her Mother's love which she must not fail. Why else had Mother lived? All of them, all four of them, were her life's blood, literally. Nobody could be cruel to Mother, nobody could find it in them to be callous and to be truthful would involve both. The fields gave way to moorland as she tried to rid herself of all the images that stayed so firmly in her head. Mother, lying in that awful stuffy crowded little room without even a view—without a glimpse of sky or trees, all day staring at the shrouded window bothered by that clumsy fool, dependent upon him for every mortifying service, with only death ahead and until then the terrible necessity of dressing and eating and dragging herself around at his querulous insistence. And Father, a strong powerful working man reduced to making messes on trays and buying half pounds of corned beef and washing tea towels, doing his best in an impossible situation. Father and Mother both, hurt and betrayed by their children's desertion, looking back bewildered to the service they had rendered unstintingly to their own elderly parents. Nobody was doing for them what they had done for others. Mother looked after every sick person in the street—she laid out the dead and helped bring into the world all the babies and shopped and cooked for anyone who needed it. The words 'poor old' were always on her lips—poor old Mrs This, poor old Mrs That—and now it was poor old Mrs Trewick and she could not understand it. It was impossible to fathom how it had all gone wrong. Why, Angela pondered, why do I not want to be with my own Mother, why, speeding East, do I rejoice even while I am miserable?

At three years old, Sadie changed. The tantrums ceased as mysteriously as they had begun and Angela was delighted with the composed, rather grave little girl who emerged from the chrysalis of babyhood. Kisses and cuddles, once so freely given and clamoured for, were now bestowed as a great favour, or refused abruptly. It was extraordinary to Angela to experience the bodily hunger she had for Sadie now that her embraces were so often rejected—she found herself crushing Sadie to her and when Sadie fought to get loose she felt sad. Sadie even refused comfort. It was never any good rushing to pick up Sadie when she fell and cut her knee—she was up and wiping the tears away before her mother could get to her. Consoling Sadie was a luxury. Angela vowed not to make a fuss about it and tried to rejoice that her daughter was developing such pride and independence but instead secretly regretted the rapid passing of that animal closeness they had enjoyed. She is my daughter, Angela thought, yet already she is pushing me aside and there are things going on in her head that I know nothing about. Who caused the breach? Or was it inevitable? She could not decide, and chided herself for making too much of it.

The taxi ride home was one of barely supressed euphoria. How such happiness could come so quickly out of such depression Angela did not know, but as she hurtled through the noisy congested roads towards the street in Richmond where she lived there was a smile on her face and she felt as though she could get out and run, so overpowering was her newly discovered vitality. Nothing daunted her because once again she was temporarily released. She was young and well and happy and utterly removed from the clutching cruel hands of old age and family responsibilities whose miseries had so recently filled her with gloom. The guilt was there, but away from Mother and Father's actual presence she could push it into the furthest corner of her mind and refuse to look at it. The pain that was intolerable when confronted with their plight dulled to an ache and as quickly to a mere surface sensation.

The front door stayed resolutely shut as she paid the taxi off. No Trewicks here, breathing down the neck of time. She could not find her key and had to ring the bell, which brought a stampede. Tim fought Saul to open the door and Max tried hard to do it for both of them. They fell on her like a pack of wolves, shouting bits of news and voicing grudges and complaints. Behind them stood Ben, grey looking and crumpled. 'Thank god,' he said, 'it's been chaos.' She hugged them all, still happy through the rising chorus of demands, taking in the untidiness of the house without comment, only glad to be back. The warmth, the space, the colour, the comfort, the shouts and screams and laughter dazzled her. So quiet, at Mother's, so hushed and sepulchral. She took off her coat and made her way to the kitchen and began automatically to re-possess her territory, moving objects back to where they ought to be and organizing her domain. Ben's triumph was a meal in the oven, pizzas for all, with a salad laboriously prepared to go with it and two sorts of icecream to follow. They sat down at once and ate it and drank a bottle of wine and Angela almost wept at the bliss of it.

Sadie wasn't in. Ben said she had rarely been in. He grumbled mildly at her selfishness—no help given or offered—but did not make much of her defection. She came in much later, when the boys were all in bed, casual as ever.

'Oh, hello,' she said, in Angela's direction, throwing down the army kit bag she trailed everywhere with her. 'God, I'm exhausted—those fuckin' Munford kids want strangling.'

'Don't babysit for them then,' Angela said.

'Any tea?' Sadie said. She regarded her black nail-varnished nails closely. 'Christ,' she said, 'this stuff comes off easily.'

'I hear you haven't been around much,' Angela said.

'So?'

'Well, it would obviously have helped Dad if you had, that's all.'

'You never mentioned you wanted me to do anything.'

'No. I know. I just hoped common decency—'

'Oh god—look, you're just back—do you have to start straight away?'

It would be quite easy, Angela thought, for my eyes to fill with tears but I won't let them because that is what Mother did to me. There was such a strong temptation to take everything Sadie said at face value, to believe the worst.

'How's Grandma, anyway?' Sadie said. Angela thought how Father would have said he thought she would never ask.

'Much better,' she said.

'Oh good,' and then, brusque and irritable, 'Was it awful?'

'Yes.'

A grunt in reply. A yawn. How awful she looked in her black drainpipe trousers and the big man's V-necked sweater torn and ragged at the elbows. The afro perm was coming out leaving her hair bedraggled and wispy. There were dark smudges under her eyes, thick with blue eye shadow, and a prominent spot, much tampered with, on her chin.

In Angela's head was a fantasy of how it should have been—Sadie, bright and sparkling, apron on, coming to the door to fling her arms about her mother, ushering her in, sitting her down with the utmost solicitude, assuring her everything was under control. Sadie, stirring something on the cooker, face awash with sympathy, urging her mother to tell her everything, everything, ready with understanding words to share her ordeal. Sadie telling her not to worry, Sadie urging her to rest, Sadie in harmony with her silent wishes.

'I'm off then,' Sadie said, 'if there isn't any tea.'

'You could make some,' Angela said.

'Mm. Never mind. Bye—' and the door closed as she went to bed, lumping her bag.

Mother had got all that. In bed, Angela went over the occasions upon which Mother had come home and she and Valerie had vied with each other to make her feel like a Queen. They baked cakes and put on the best teacloth and screamed if Mother so much as moved a finger. They watched her eagerly as she ate and ran to provide her with more jam, more milk for her tea, more of anything in the world which it was within their power to give her. They removed her shoes and fetched her warmed slippers and hung about her like guard dogs. But there was never any real response, beyond a smile and a sigh. Angela turned over and tried to block out the memories of failing Mother. The time she went out to the theatre on a free ticket a friend had given her, worrying about whether she should go at all because Father was at the Club (the pub) and Tom and Harry were at Scout Camp and she and Valerie, nine and seven, would be alone. Go, go, Angela begged, I can look after Valerie, we will be all right, I can do everything, please, please—and Mother went, nervous, unsure, telling Mrs Collins next door to keep an ear open. They were so good. They read books and listened to the radio and laid the table for breakfast next morning so that Mother would not have to do it when she came in. They made their own supper— a cup of tea and cheese on toast—and then they went to bed. Valerie fell asleep straight away but Angela lay awake, listening for Mother. She wanted to hear her exclaim with pleasure and say 'Oh, they've tidied up and laid the table, the darlings.' Instead Father came in first and there was a sudden roar 'Goddam! Boiled dry!' which Angela couldn't understand, but then, a minute later, she heard Mother at the gate, laughing, thanking her friend, and the click⁄clack of her feet on the path and then Father, 'That's the last time you're going out leaving them—boiled dry— look—steam everywhere—another five minutes and there would have been a fire—we can trust Angela you said—trust Angela—' Mother crept upstairs as Angela's tears reached a new crescendo. 'You left the kettle on,' she said, dully, 'I shouldn't have left you.' Then, seeing Angela's distress, she tucked her up and kissed her and said it didn't matter. But it did. It was never forgotten.

Mother had been let down and Father had made capital out of it.

Sleepily, Angela told herself she didn't want Sadie to support her. Too tired to analyse her daughter's attitude, she knew only that it was more right to treat her, Angela, as Sadie treated her, than to be treated as Mother had treated her. Mother bred what she wanted. *She* bred what she wanted. These things did not, could not, happen on their own. It seemed, late at night, a comforting thought, though she did not know why.

Three

Teaching English part-time was not arduous, but a week away and it seemed so. With everything in her life so finely balanced, Angela found getting back into it difficult. The backlog of marking, the disruption of her classes while she was absent, the upsetting of a carefully worked out term's scheme of study—all meant that instead of slipping effortlessly into school on Monday, Wednesday and Thursday mornings she had also to stay there each afternoon in order to catch up. And if she stayed afternoons, she had to shop and cook when the children came in and everything became frantic. She felt more and more like Father, flustered these days if he was five minutes late setting off to buy a cake nobody wanted anyway.

Furthermore, it was Mother's birthday on March 1st and that event loomed over Angela with an awful intensity. Whatever she was doing, as she struggled to organize herself, she thought only of what she could buy Mother, knowing that since she had already bought everything Mother could conceivably want the task of selection was becoming impossible. Mother's instructions were not to send anything this year—she wouldn't be here long, it wasn't worth it. The same instructions had been given for the last ten years and served only to whip everyone concerned into a frenzy of worry. Mother's birthday had always been the most important day in the calendar—quite why Angela could not fathom, but it always had been, more important to the family than Christmas Day or their own birthdays. Shillings were saved for weeks and weeks beforehand by all four children and then they would all go off to trail round the same shops, often bumping into each other, in the search for the right present for Mother, an object as elusive as the Holy Grail. Mother protested every year that she wanted nothing but a kiss and didn't care for presents and didn't want them spending the little money they had on her but they refused to believe her, and vied with each other to please her most. Angela especially. She saved her shilling pocket money for many more weeks than the others and pondered how to spend the total for many more hours.

Pleasing Mother was the hardest task in the world. 'You won't please your Mother,' Father used to say, usually straight after he had displeased her himself. He said it angrily, but also triumph-antly, obscurely proud that she would not be pleased. If Mother had been good at lying, they might never have known whether she was pleased or not, but she was always unable to avoid truthful answers to their direct questions. 'But is it the *right* green?' she would be asked, of a cheap scarf bought to match a particular hat. 'Do you think it *goes*, Mother?' And the gentle reply would devastate the inquirer. 'Well, perhaps a shade darker . . . but it's perfect'—and oh the disappointment then and the rush upstairs to hide humiliation in a pillow. But if the agony of failing was bitter, the joy of occasionally succeeding was sweet indeed. There was the pearl necklace, bought in the market for seventeen shillings and sixpence, admired by Angela for months as it lay gleaming on the dark blue velvet cushion inside the box. Every week she stopped and inquired the price and fingered it lovingly under the stall keeper's watchful eye. Every week she counted her money and left it where it was, reluctantly, until the day came when the man said, 'Tell you what, I'll knock half a crown off and keep it until you've got seventeen and six, right?'

He wrapped it for her in pink tissue paper. She bought some gold thread and tied it up with a big bow on top. Her heart thudded as she gave it to Mother—who cried out with delight and fastened it immediately round her neck and rushed off to put on her one good jumper to show it off to better advantage. Mother, who had neither the taste nor the energy for deception, was ecstatic. Nothing since had ever pleased her quite as much as that pitiful strand of toy beads from a ten-year-old child.

This year, Mother was seventy-five. Once, while Angela was lovingly brushing Mother's thick auburn hair, she had asked her if it would turn white when she was an old lady. 'I might never be an old lady,' Mother had said. 'What?' Angela said, the brush still because her hand was suddenly too weak to continue, 'What?' 'I might not live long enough to be old,' Mother had repeated, it seemed with satisfaction. 'Don't say that!' Angela screamed, and broke into noisy sobs which would not be suppressed. Mother was full of remorse. She comforted Angela and said it was just that as her own mother had died young, and her father too, she had never thought of herself living to be older than they had been. And now Mother was seventy-five, and in any case her parents had not died as young as Angela, in that moment of shock, had been led to believe. Mother's conviction that she would never be old amounted only to a morbid fancy, but it remained implanted firmly in Angela's mind as a dreadful prophecy that would surely be fulfilled.

Seventy-five was not as special as seventy. On Mother's seventieth birthday Angela had sent a basket of seventy red roses. Like Hollywood, Mother had said, and the glamour of it had excited her. But that gesture could not be repeated, nor any of the others that had been successful because they were original. Clothes, however absurd in the circumstances, remained Mother's abiding love. Mother would have been a fashionplate, given the chance. She had the figure, she had the interest, she had the taste—all she lacked, quite cripplingly, was the money. Her sister Frances, a dressmaker, had done wonders for Mother in her youth, concocting dresses out of material left over from customers' orders for Mother to wear stylishly as she herself, small and fat, could not. But then later on Frances married and moved away and her departure coincided with Mother's hardest, leanest, years. There were no new clothes at all. Mother had to wear everything until it was threadbare and she hated it. The darkest day of her life was the furtive visit she made to a secondhand shop because she absolutely had to have a dress for a wedding.

Mother still loved clothes and being smart and liked to look nice whatever her health even if she went nowhere. People complimented her all the time on her appearance but the compliments infuriated her. Oh, that old thing, I've had it for years, she would say, as if that were condemnation in itself. If she had something new she would be endlessly critical of how she looked in it until Father's cry 'You can't please your Mother' took on a new meaning. She longed to be able to go shopping again, to try on lots of clothes and walk up and down in them in front of mirrors and finally select the best. Father, to Angela's relief, would not allow it any more. He said Mother would have an attack, she wasn't up to it, all that pulling on and off, all that fastening and unfastening. He said she had more than enough clothes to see her out.

A new dress for the coming summer would please Mother more than anything but the mere thought of shopping for it depressed Angela extremely. There were so many rules to remember. The dress must have long sleeves because Mother did not think any lady over forty ought to show their scraggy elbows. It must open down the front or else it would be too difficult to put on. It must be washable. It must not have anything that tied at the neck, because she could not tie things herself any more, but on the other hand it must have *some* kind of neck, some sort of collar, not just a bare neckline. It must not be too long, which Mother thought dowdy, nor too short, which she thought common. It was better that it should be patterned but not garish and colourful but not gaudy. The size was tricky. Small and thin, Mother had staggeringly large hips—'very deceiving' sales assistants used to say with pursed lips, to Mother's embarrassment. Size 12 was right on the upper half but tight on the lower. Size 14 was baggy on the upper but perfect on the lower. A decent fit could only be had if the styling of the dress lent itself to a tailored top and a loose skirt.

Angela bought a dress after much deliberation and several fruitless journeys to shops she had never before frequented. Packed in a large cardboard box and then wrapped in gold foil the package looked thrilling enough. There remained only the birthday cards, one from each of them, and these had to have verses. Mother set great store by a meaningful verse but card manufacturers did not. Mother liked the sentiments of the sender to be very exactly expressed, she liked a verse to tell her how much she was cherished and loved, she liked it to be above all else sincere, to be from the heart.

By the time Max and Saul had been born, as well as Sadie, life had become hectic and Angela looked back with nostalgia to the days when she had had only one child. More and more Sadie was pushed into the background without anyone ever meaning to do it. She was very good about it. It was her goodness that caused the accident. One day, one winter's afternoon, they all came in from the park muddy and cold with the new-born Saul yelling his head off. Max, a violent, troublesome, strong little boy, ran straight away into the kitchen and with one swipe cleared the table of three glass preserving jars left there to label. There were splinters of glass everywhere. With Saul frantically sucking at her breast, Angela tried to pick up the largest pieces, shrieking at Max to get out of the way. Sadie had meanwhile quietly disappeared. She went up to her room and there she ate a strange combination of tablets—a whole bottle of orange-flavoured Junior Aspirin, bought to give Max, who was cutting his back molars and woke every night screaming, half a bottle of Fluoride tablets because she liked the salty taste, and four iron pills because they were a pretty speckled colour. Sadie ate them all sitting on the rug in front of Max's cot, her deft fingers opening the bottles ('CHILDPROOF TOPS') with no difficulty whatsoever. Sensibly, she went backwards and forwards to the bathroom getting herself drinks of water between mouthfuls of tablets. Nor did she feel any guilt about what she had done, or even begin to realize the danger. When she had finished, when Max's hideous roars had subsided, she brought the empty containers down and asked Angela if she could have them for her doll's house. They went to the local hospital in a taxi—Ben had the car—as though on a treat outing. Sadie, so composed in her bright red crocheted beret, Sadie still and solemn, holding the glass of liquid that would make her sick. And Sadie stubborn, not drinking it, refusing mutely to try. On and on went Angela's pleading, bribing, explaining. Useless. Into a room, Angela insisting on being present much against medical advice and wishes, where they put Sadie on a table and pushed a tube down her throat and poured gallons of liquid through it. Sadie, tear-stained, vomit-streaked, pitifully trembling as Angela carried her out, refusing absolutely to leave her for the night. Sadie slept. Angela cried. At midnight, Sadie woke and screamed and did not stop until eight o'clock in the morning. Rocking her backwards and forwards all night Angela gratefully accepted the punishment. Every hour of exhaustion deepened her remorse but relieved her misery. When Sadie pummelled her with clenched fists she made no attempt to stop her. When Sadie's sharp nails scratched a long red line down her cheek she humbly allowed her to do it again. It was Ben who finally comforted the child. All next day Sadie stumbled about white-faced and whimpering until in the evening she made her peace—she climbed onto her mother's lap and there the sweetness of her embrace moved Angela to tears that threatened never to stop. She had no

36

wish ever to prise the soft, limp body from inside her own languid arms.
They had grown together again, they were wrapped into each other's
bodies like the tender new shoots of a vine wrap round each other the better
to grow. Their bodies said what their tongues could not and Angela was
afraid to move. The bond was there, as indissoluble as ever in spite of that
distant, remote look that had come so lately into her small daughter's eyes,
and the knowledge that it was there, that she had not imagined it, that it was
not all on her side, both saddened and comforted her.

Sadie recovered very quickly. She became proud of her adventure. She
lectured Max about not taking tablets, ever, and in her shrill, self-
righteous tones Angela heard herself and shivered.

Father 'phoned very early to say Mother's present had just
arrived.

'It's grand,' he bellowed, 'just the job. I've had it on her and it
fits perfect. She's not up yet of course, I haven't got her up yet,
she's been getting up later since she was took bad—but I pulled
it on over her nightie and she had a look in the mirror and she
says it's champion. And she got cards from the boys and letters—
bang on time—and she's over the moon.'

'Good,' Angela said.

'You'll be 'phoning her this evening?'

'Oh, yes.'

'Well, remember to leave it till after "Nationwide", suits her
best.'

Suited him best.

Organizing the children to do their bit was dreadful. None of
them appreciated the importance of doing things Mother's way.
Sadie groaned and said all right, all right, but what do you want
me to say, and Angela at her most scathing suggested it might not
be too difficult to answer that one herself. Surely it was not
beyond her ability, at the age of sixteen, to think of how to wish
her grandmother a happy birthday? Surely she had some natural
feeling for an old lady who had always loved her and was now ill
and housebound? Sadie flounced out, slamming the door, but
she came back and was there when the telephone call was made
and sang with the rest of them 'Happy-Birthday-Dear-Granny'
like an old-fashioned harmonizing group. Then Sadie, as the
eldest, was the first to speak and did it beautifully, so well that
no one could have known from her sweet solicitous tone that her

face was contorted as she signalled to Angela that she couldn't
think of what else to say. Max refused to say anything except
'Happy Birthday' and then rushed into the street to carry on with
a football game. Only Saul and Tim chatted freely and naturally
so that Angela blessed them from the bottom of her heart.

'When I am old,' Angela said at supper, 'don't ever force your
children to ring me when they don't want to.'

'Don't worry,' Sadie said, 'I won't.'

'But I expect I will want them to,' Angela said, her hand
poised above the soup ladle as she thought about it, 'I suppose,
when you're old, you want affection at any price, I suppose—'

'Hurry up with the soup,' Sadie said.

'When I was young—' Angela began.

'Oh Christ,' Sadie said.

'When I was young,' Angela repeated, but ladled out soup at
the same time so that everyone began eating and ignored her, 'I
thought I would always want everyone to tell me the truth, but
now I'm not so sure. The trouble is—'

'Mum,' Sadie said, 'wrap up.'

'Why? Why should I?'

'Because we don't want to hear you rambling on—do it if you
like but we won't listen.'

'Why not?'

'It's boring.'

'How do you *know* it's going to be boring? I used to love my
mother's stories about when she was young, I used to plague her
to tell me them—'

'—perhaps they were interesting—'

'—I could never get enough and—'

'—Yours aren't.'

'—I would plead with her to tell me my favourite ones over and
over again. But you, you have no interest at all in my memories.'

'You go on so,' Sadie said, 'you just wallow in them. I mean,
I don't want to hurt your feelings—'

'Don't you?'

'—but you've told us everything a million times.'

'That isn't true.'

'It is. And you don't just tell us stories either—you only tell
them to make moral points—you only tell them to get at us because
we aren't as marvellous as you think you were when you were

young.' Sadie was quite calm and unflurried and that made it worse. 'Like now—you want to tell us about your grandmother really, don't you? All this stuff about what old people must feel like is just working round to it, isn't it? You'll get on in a minute to how you used to go every day after school and read to her and all that and you think we're so thick that we can't see that you really mean how rotten we are when we even have to be persuaded to talk to our grandma on her birthday.'

'Well,' said Angela, 'if you have everything so well worked out why don't you appreciate how I feel?'

'It's sickening,' Sadie said, shrugging.

'But why?'

'It just is. Anything else—I'm starving.'

'What I don't understand—'

'Oh, Mum—bloody hell—'

'But why can't we ever discuss anything—I want to know what you think—when I was young nobody ever wanted—'

But Sadie had gone, grabbing an apple and a banana from the bowl on the table, stalking out without a backward glance.

'Never mind, Mum,' Max said, 'you can tell us about when you were young. What did you do?'

'Oh, it doesn't matter.'

'But I want to know, really, go on.'

'I don't feel like talking any more.'

Father had never permitted argument. If he said something you thought ridiculous or silly you just had to hold your tongue. If he said something you knew to be factually wrong there was no hope of contradiction. Worst of all were the occasions upon which he told you not to do something you knew he did himself. 'Don't cross the road without using the crossing,' he would say. 'You do,' Angela would flash back. 'You don't do what I do,' he would say, 'you do what I say, and that's that.' That was that, or you got a slap. 'Take your shoes off when they're muddy—take them off at the back kitchen door like I do.' 'You said we hadn't to do what you did,' Angela said, 'remember?' Another slap, harder that time. Nobody laughed. Nobody explained the difference. Explanation—reasoned argument—was something she was never honoured with. But Sadie had been. Everything she challenged was justified, defended or if necessary conceded as after all wrong. Yet somewhere the theory had gone wrong—*they* gave Sadie explanations by the bushel, they, Ben and herself, were prepared to share every thought, but Sadie gave nothing in return. She hated all talk. She suspected all conversation. They were left to guess the reasons as to why they were 'sickening' or boring or any of the other more unpleasant present participles.

There was just a slight feeling of fear in Angela when she saw Sadie again—a matter of feeling weak and suddenly old and unable to cope. Sadie's strength impressed her—not her physical strength, though the fact that she was now two inches taller than her mother was intimidating in itself—but an overall atmosphere of confidence that Sadie carried everywhere with her. It must be an illusion, of course. Angela realized that but it did not help. Sadie's power reduced her little by little every day—she was not the same sure person she had once been. To gain Sadie's respect was important and she was aware of an unhealthy desire to please growing in her. Sadie did not give an inch. She dictated the terms of their relationship mercilessly. There were rarely any rows —few shouting matches—no scenes—on the surface little friction. The tales Angela's friends and neighbours told her of their teenage daughters were not her experience, but the lack of real communication they complained of was. Whose fault? Nobody's. A fact of growing up that must be accepted. It must not be mourned over, or made too much of—that way, the way Mother had gone, lay disaster, and she was determined to avoid it. The fear would pass.

'Grandma's on the telephone,' Sadie shouted. Angela, startled, looked at the clock. Eight thirty, everyone milling around getting ready for school, herself included. Only ten yards to the telephone on the desk but long enough to visualize Father stretched flat on the floor and Mother hysterical at his side. And it was hysteria— sobs and choking sounds that went on and on while she said 'Mother, Mother whatever is wrong—Mother, can you hear me?' But then, blessedly, in the background, Father shouted, 'You'll have a turn if you go on like that.' Father had not collapsed. With indecent cheerfulness, Angela said again, 'Mother, what *is* the matter?'

'It's Sally,' Mother croaked.

Sally was Mother's youngest sister, youngest of the six in the family, all girls. Angela had always disliked and despised her.

'She's gone,' Mother said, before another spasm of grief engulfed her. Angela made soothing noises while she waited for the tears to subside. 'Sidney found her on the floor this morning, in the kitchen.' More tears, more roars of disapproval from Father.

'How awful,' Angela murmured.

'And—and,' Mother wailed, 'and—me like this—Father won't let me—can't—'

'I'll go to the funeral,' Angela said.

'Oh!' The long-drawn-out sigh of content took even Angela, used to Mother's values, by surprise.

'I can go in a day—no problem.' Angela said. 'I'll ring Uncle Sidney now and find out the details—and I'll arrange flowers from you.'

'You're very good,' Mother said, calmer. 'Oh, I feel so relieved —the shock—and it seemed so awful that I couldn't even go to my own sister's funeral—I can't believe it—Sally's never been ill, never, never had anything wrong with her—I can't believe she's gone first.'

'Was it a heart attack?'

'Yes—like our Mother—same age, too.' There was a new tone in Mother's voice. She was resentful—Sally was going to their own beloved Mother first and hadn't even suffered, not like Frances with her kidneys and Maud with her varicose veins and Agnes with lumbago and Amy with diabetes and of course Mother herself with her arthritis and strokes. Sally had never ailed a thing, had never had any troubles, had always enjoyed herself and now she had gone first.

'I know it's sad,' Angela said, 'but it's exactly the way Sally would have wanted to die, don't you think?' Mother did not reply. She clearly found even the suggestion that Sally might have welcomed a sudden death too insulting to consider.

'What on earth was all that about?' Sadie said, giving a final brush to her hair in the hall mirror.

'Grandma's sister's just died.'

'Oh. Does she mind?'

'Yes, of course she minds. People do mind when their relations die.'

Brush pushed in bag, dinner money grabbed from shelf, front door slammed.

At last the black suit was worn and there was some grim

satisfaction in having funeral apparel ready. If it had not been ready, there would have been no time, in the familiar panic of arrangements, which any day away entailed, to provide it. All Mother's sisters would flock to Norwich for the funeral and Mother would grieve more at missing the reunion than mourn at missing the funeral ceremony. To Angela, the thought of having to see the assembled clan was depressing. The only one of Mother's sisters she had ever liked was Frances, the dressmaker, who was thought to have done rather well for herself in marrying a bookie. They had a stout, ugly detached house in Solihull which Angela in her youth had enjoyed visiting, thinking it the height of luxury. Frances would admire her suit and describe it to Mother, who would be pleased, not knowing the suit was meant for her own funeral.

The whole affair was more pathetic and touching than Angela had envisaged. Protocol bothered everyone. None of the aunts, experienced though they must have been, seemed to know what to do. There was a good deal of irritable jostling when the funeral cars arrived. There were no visible signs of distress. Mother, alone at home, looking at the clock and following the funeral service in her prayer book, would be crying with all her heart, while in the crematorium every eye was dry. Angela looked round at all the faces and wondered if you could recognize internal sorrowing. When the time came, would all the Trewicks gather stoically round Mother's coffin and appear composed? Would all the Bradburys gather round her own without a flicker of emotion? She could not believe it. There was death and death.

The breakfast afterwards was embarrassing. Tea and biscuits, standing up in the front room, Sidney drunk and talking loudly of life going on. All Mother's sisters looked at him with contempt. All of them knew he had put Sally in the family way at eighteen by making her as drunk as himself. He was a let down. With Sally dead, none of them had any intention of having anything to do with him again. Only Mother would write, a note painfully scrawled but full of sympathetic endearments. Mother's forte was to feel sorry for absolutely everyone, especially the undeserving.

When the time came to go—she had felt obliged to wait and catch the last train—Angela was taken to the station by Frances and her husband in their flash car. They both seemed stiff and constrained whereas normally they were jolly and when Angela attempted to chat to them they rebuffed her attempt. She presumed they were more upset than she had imagined. They were almost at the station when Frances turned round and, looking at Angela with a sorrowful expression, absurd on her chubby, wobbling face, but so like Mother's martyred look, said, 'Oh, Angela, whatever happened?'

'What do you mean?' Angela said. She knew she was blushing and she felt that same unease that came over her whenever Mother turned accusing and soulful.

'Why don't you ever come near us now?' Frances said. 'All those years we doted on you and now you never come near. And you hardly visit your Mother, except when she's ill—and you were such a loving little girl. We never thought you'd just drop us, never.'

'I've got four children, Aunt Frances,' Angela said, 'and I teach part-time.'

Frances turned her back and stared out of the front window.

'You just don't understand,' Angela said, aware that her voice was trembling with what Frances would think was shame but was really rage. 'Your life is so different—you can't grasp what it's like to be me.'

'We treated you as a daughter,' Frances said, 'took you everywhere—gave you all the things your Mother couldn't afford, and this is all the thanks we get.'

The train ride home was frightful. Though she succeded in writing a long descriptive letter to Mother listing the floral tributes and the size of the congregation in the Chapel of Rest, Angela was pursued by Frances' idiotic accusation until it drove her frantic. Everywhere she went miracles of tolerance and understanding were expected of her—the past, her past, seemed one huge debt, burdening her with commitments she had not sought. Mother needed her, her own family needed her, relatives as remote as Frances appeared to need her. They all drained her dry. They all wished her to put herself in their position—but who put themselves in her position? Who protected her? To whom did she turn and say she needed them? Not to Mother and Father, that was certain. It seemed a million years since she had even contemplated going to them for help or comfort. Not to her children —such a thought was almost laughable. Elsewhere in the world there might be mothers who wept with exhaustion or depression

or misery, mothers around whose necks tiny arms wrapped themselves to console as best they could, but she was not one of them.
To have cast herself on her children would have horrified her.
Only her husband was any good as confidant and helper but
even Ben was often useless because he thought she magnified the
obligations she felt. She was the fulcrum upon which everything
turned and no excuses for not performing her vital function would
be accepted.

She put the letter in an envelope and addressed and stamped it,
ready to drop in the letter box at the station. None of her real
thoughts were in that letter—she never inflicted doubts or worries
upon Mother, who had to be cheered up. There was nothing
Mother could do anyway. Nothing anyone could do. If her
burdens grew too heavy she would have to collapse before anyone
noticed. Women—mothers—did it all the time and were trampled
on and despised for being feeble. But she was not feeble. She was
strong. The devastation and ruin that would follow any collapse
of hers would be truly terrible, and so there was no choice. One
struggled on, hoping one day for relief. But one thing she would
not do was pass the baton on. As the train howled its way
through the dark night she kept her tired aching body straight and
vowed to break the chain. Sadie should not feel what she felt.
Sadie should be free as air, unfettered by shame or guilt or duty.
Sadie should not have hanging over her that thick pall of
maternal expectation. To that, she pledged herself.

The house was dark and cold when she finally reached it,
neither a light nor a voice to welcome her, even Ben soundly
asleep. She knew it was foolish of her to expect anything else
when it was after midnight but in her exhausted state the absence
of any sign that she was cared about brought tears to her eyes.
She was too tired to make so much as a cup of tea. In no time at
all she would be in the middle of another morning hubbub with
everyone acting as though she had just come back from a gay
weekend in Paris instead of a dreary funeral in Norwich. She
always seemed to be going away for reasons that had nothing to
do with pleasure yet the family persisted in treating her journeys
as self-indulgences. And tomorrow she had the third form at
school—inattentive, cheeky, boisterous, the hardest of all the
groups to interest and control. She would make them write a
story called 'The Funeral'.

In the hall, she fell over Max's football gear, dropped there when he came in at four o'clock and climbed over ever since, boots and shorts and shirt and socks and the ball itself in one big heap. In the bathroom she hung all the sodden towels on the hot rail, put the top back on the bottle of cochineal which Sadie used liberally to tint her hair and rescued the soap from the plughole. Only Mothers did things like that. If she were not there, none of them would do anything. Everything—all the debris of a large family—would accumulate and block up the windows and doors before anyone either noticed or complained.

Sadie took seven or eight years to betray the truth. Every night, Angela carefully laid out Sadie's clothes for the next day without thinking she was doing anything unusual. Sadie simply got up and put them on. In an area where children wore any odd assortment of old clothes Sadie stood out, bandbox fresh, colours co-ordinated, socks startlingly white, black shoes polished till they shone, hair brushed and brushed and neatly tied back. People made fun of Angela for dressing her daughter so immaculately but she didn't care—she liked to do it. But then, as the boys were born and Sadie was left more to her own devices, it became obvious that she would not continue the tradition of Trewick cleanliness and smartness. She was quite happy to put on knickers that were dirty, socks that smelled, shirts with stains on the front. Angela shouted at her. Obediently, she would go and change without conceding that there had been anything wrong with her attire in the first place. As time went on, she stopped giving in. 'I like dirty socks,' she would say, and 'They'll only get dirty as soon as I get to the playground anyway.' It was no good Angela trying to get her to see how much more attractive it was to be clean and tidy. She just didn't see. She did not have within her any appreciation for freshness or elegance. Angela had to stop herself from saying the things Mother had said to her with such effect—'I don't like to see you scruffy, Angela'—and began instead to acknowledge Sadie's right to dress how she wanted. 'Sadie's an apprentice slut,' she would tell people cheerfully. And to Mother and Father who were appalled by their grand-daughter's slovenliness she said, 'I don't see that it matters, frankly.' Unfortunately, it still mattered to her too much and it was very hard work concealing this from Sadie.

'While I was away yesterday,' Angela said at breakfast, knowing it was quite the wrong time for such a speech, 'nobody did a thing. The dishwasher hasn't even been emptied, the dirty

45

dishes have all been left for me to do, the entire house is festooned with apple cores and clothes and god knows what and it's become a dump in less than twenty-four hours.'

'I'm off,' Sadie said, mouth jammed full of toast.

'You are *not*,' yelled Angela, 'I haven't finished—sit down.'

'I'll be late for school.'

'You won't.' Sadie didn't sit, but she stayed, hand on hip, expression vacant, as provoking as possible.

'I am not your servant,' Angela said, 'I work, I run this house, and I expect co-operation. You are all utterly spoiled and it's got to stop.'

'What put you in such a temper?' Max said. Tim began to cry.

'Coming back to a slum,' Angela said, 'coming home feeling shattered and having to start cleaning up.'

'Okay, okay,' Max said.

'It isn't okay. It's all wrong.'

'What do you want us to do then?' Max said.

'Help.'

'All right, I'll help, but don't go on about it.'

'I really will be late,' said Sadie.

'Oh, go on then. But I would have thought—'

The kitchen emptied dramatically. She dried Tim's tears and assured him she hadn't meant him. She put him in the car and drove him to school, pausing to collect some clothes from the dry cleaner's on the way. Her resentment at having to do such a small thing showed her how low she had become—she never resented doing anything for Ben, who worked so hard and for such long hours. Mother had never seemed to resent anything. She had just got on with it, seeing it as her lot in life to slave away after them all. Angela could not remember a single occasion upon which Mother had shouted at them all as she had just shouted at her children. Mother had cleared up after them and never appeared to mind. Somewhere, something had gone very wrong. Mother must possess some secret, Angela decided, to which she herself did not have access. Either that, or she was an unnatural mother. She didn't know how she was going to find out which was true but as she drove on to her job with set face and tensed shoulders it seemed the most important question in the world to answer.

Four

'Where are you going for your holidays?' Father said on the Monday evening telephone call.

'We don't know yet.'

'We don't either,' Father said, with emphasis. 'Your Mother's moaning on about it. Mrs Collins set her off—going to Newquay for a week—oh, we never go anywhere, no holidays for us, your Mother says. She says she wishes someone would give her a holiday, stuck here indoors, year in, year out. Well I said get yourself to Angela's. Here, here she is—you talk to her—she doesn't seem to like anything I say, twisting her face up at me. You tell her what's what.'

'Ignore him,' Mother whispered, then cleared her throat. 'I can't go anywhere, not in my condition, he knows that. He can go and have a holiday—he's the one that needs it. He can put me in a home and gallivant where he likes. I'm past caring.'

In the background Father shouted, 'I don't need any holiday—it's you that started on about it, lass, not me.'

'Ignore him,' Mother said again, faintly.

'I'd love you to come here for a holiday like you used to, Mother,' Angela said, striving to insert warmth and conviction into her voice, 'but I just don't think you could stand a three-hundred-mile journey, do you?'

'No, I couldn't,' Mother said, 'I can't even get half a mile to church. I'm finished, past everything.'

'You're not—you're getting better every day—but you're not up to a long tiring journey. Listen, why don't I come down for a week and let Father go to Valerie's—you both need a break—it would be the perfect solution, give you both a sort of holiday at least.'

'Your Father wouldn't hear of it,' Mother said, 'he wouldn't go off on his own, would you?' There was a confused minute while the message was relayed and then a roar as Father emphatically refused. 'There,' Mother said, 'I told you he wouldn't go, didn't I?' Angela could not tell whether she spoke with satisfaction or not.

It was easy to picture Mother hunched in her armchair in front of the fire, listening miserably to the plans of Mrs Collins and other neighbours with their weeks here and days there. An annual torture that made Mother increasingly bitter. Instead of summer sunshine making her feel happier, bringing as it did the prospect of a seat in the garden in place of a seat in one small room, it made her furious. Anyone would have thought, from the vehemence with which she spoke, that Mother had formerly had the most sumptuous and regular holidays and not the pedestrian week with one of her sisters in Exeter or Plymouth that had been the reality. But something would have to be done or the remarks would go on and on until October brought the end with 'Well, there was no holiday for me, at any rate.'

'I think,' Angela said that evening, 'we will have to spend all the Easter holidays in St Erick after all.' The protests drowned her explanation. When they were all quiet, she began to enlarge on Grandmother's unhappiness but none of then would relent. Even Ben was steadfast in his objections. She exaggerated, he said. Her mother and father were perfectly happy really, and even if they weren't why should she consider their needs more than her own family's—why shouldn't their hatred of holidays in St Erick weigh as much in her mind as her parents' need to have them here? 'They are old and feeble,' Angela said, 'we are all young and strong. We can afford to be magnanimous—is it really asking so much?'

She went to bed haunted by the little scene in her mind, Mother and Father trapped in that pokey room, Mother wretched because she never went anywhere. She could not sleep for attempting to solve the insoluble. There was nothing she could do, short of moving next door to them, to effectively make them happy. Leaving St Erick had been the ultimate betrayal, which they had seen coming a long way off. In their opinion, all would have been well if it had not been for 'that Grammar School'. It gave her big ideas, they said. 'You used to be such a nice little girl before you went to that Grammar School,' Mother used to say, sorrowfully. They said they didn't know what had got into her, that they could see how it would all end. 'You have children,' Father said, 'you look after them and work hard for them and then what do they do—they leave, the minute they're any good to you. We never did, but you, you'll be up and off, finished.'

'That's life,' Angela would say, 'children don't stay at home when they grow up unless there's something wrong with them.'

'There was nothing wrong with your Mother and I,' Father would say, 'we knew what duty was.'

'You had no choice,' Angela would say, knowing it was foolish to prolong such an argument. Whatever was said afterwards, Father always managed to finish with the same words, 'Elephants stay together, they don't leave the herd.'

They all ought to be near, Tom and Harry and Valerie and her, visiting every day, as Mother and Father had visited their parents when they were alive, a happy extended family. Except Angela could remember no happiness, only obligation and the gratification which came from it. Every Sunday after morning Sunday School Father marched all four of them down to his parents' house, down to the gloomy, solid terrace house by the river, and there they would troop in, into the dark hall smelling of damp and decay, into the back room where a big, blackened kettle hung on a hook over the hardly burning fire. Warned to be quiet and behave themselves one minute, they would be ordered to entertain their crippled grandmother the next. They would be pulled by the arm in turn to the bed in the corner where Grandma lay, propped up on pillows so that she could stare through the dusty net curtains into the yard that held nothing but a dustbin and was bound on all sides by high brick walls with pieces of broken glass on the top. Grandma was a fearful sight. Her crooked arthritic fingers made her hands into claws and her dreadfully pale emaciated face was always screwed up with pain. 'Kiss your Grandma,' Grandad would say, 'a nice big kiss, mind,' and then it was a battle between rival fears, between dreading the touch of the loathsome flaccid skin of Grandma's cheek and dreading Grandad's anger if his commandment was not enthusiastically obeyed. Angela remembered no pity for Grandma, nor any stirrings of compassion for Grandad, who was an ogre with a partiality for mental arithmetic. 'Five nines,' he would suddenly shout, pointing a poker at his victims, and the first to answer correctly got a penny. It was always Angela. Then Grandad would storm and shout at the boys because he wanted them to be cleverer. 'Letting a lass beat you,' he would roar and if Tom burst into tears of fright, as he quite often did, then Grandad would drive him with the poker to the back door and put him outside. Father never interfered. He would watch Grandad with an odd smile on his face and never lift a finger to protect poor Tom.

Sometimes, as they wailed their way home, exhausted by the tension of it all, he would say 'Now you know,' a statement so obviously incomplete and enigmatic that Angela could never fathom it. 'Why do we have to go there?' she would ask. 'Why— when Grandad's so horrible?' 'You be quiet about your Grand-father,' Father would say. Mother was no better. 'There are things I'll never forgive your Grandfather for,' she would say to Angela when plagued for enlightenment. 'Things he made your Father suffer. You don't know the half of it.' And Angela, who badly wanted to know that half and every other little scrap there might be, was left unsatisfied and wondering. She went with Mother twice a week to make Grandma's tea and watched Mother washing Grandma tenderly and making her bed expertly and heard Grandma say 'Oh, you're a blessing, Mary, a blessing. I couldn't manage without you, dear.' She saw Mother unpacking cakes and blancmanges, she heard her standing up to Grandad about the coldness of the room, she felt the whole atmosphere of the dreary house lighten and brighten when Mother was there. And there were others—elderly aunts and invalid cousins whom Mother fitted into her rounds, strange old people who lived in hidden rooms tucked away at the back of lanes and buildings, unknown to anyone else except Mother, Angela thought. Mother looked after them all and thought nothing of it and when, as she grew older, Angela complained about visiting them, Mother just said 'Poor old things' and she was silenced.

Three times a year they went to St Erick, she and the family, three times only, a week or less at Easter, Whit and during August. They crammed into her parents' house and their goodwill evaporated in a matter of hours. From the moment she went through the front door Angela felt suffocated not only by the pungent smell of lavender polish too thickly used and rose potpourris too regularly renewed but by the memories of living there. Sometimes on train journeys looking out of the window at rows and rows of featureless houses Angela would think how awful it must be to live in them and then experience a physical thrill of shock as she remembered that once she had done. When Grandad died, outliving Grandma by a mere six months, there had been some talk of moving into their house but Mother had refused to consider it. It was, she said, a horrible place with big draughty rooms and difficult stairs and no garden. It was built in Queen Victoria's time, she said, and looked it. Only Angela, aged twelve, had wanted to live there. She had wandered about the house while Mother ministered to Grandma in the one used room and it excited her. Upstairs, there were four huge bedrooms with wide bay windows, the sort of windows where you could make a seat and sit there reading a book like children did in the books themselves. They could each have a room instead of she and Valerie sharing, and Tom and Harry squashed into a box room that was like a slit. But Mother was adamant. They would sell the grandparents' house and divide the money with Father's brother and sisters. So they stayed in their council house—'at least it has modern comforts,' Mother said—and used their share of the money to decorate it from top to bottom in flowered wallpapers and cream paint. They bought a new dining room suite, though they did not have a dining room, and a greenhouse and put the rest away for a rainy day though by then it was hardly enough to buy a couple of good umbrellas. Father, who would have liked to have a car, was a little disgruntled after the whole business was over, but Mother was given a great deal of innocent pleasure.

The house was like thousands of others, literally so, one of a mass-produced lot that sprang up to deface the landscape before the war. Mother had chosen theirs herself and was proud of it. Her uncle was brother-in-law to the town planning officer and he told her to take her pick. Mother chose a two bedroom-with-boxroom and a washhouse attached. It was all they could afford at the time, she said. There was no bathroom and an outside lavatory but then bathrooms with lavatories upped the rent considerably. When, at school,' Angela studied briefly the rudiments of architecture it made her laugh to think of their council house ever being designed. Designed? Windows, doors, building materials—who ever considered anything but cost where council houses were concerned? 'We were so lucky,' Mother said, and felt guilty about using her uncle's influence. 'We got the best two-bedroom one on the estate,' she said. Nobody else's soul was seared by living in that graceless shelter, except Angela's, and she could take her fancy notions elsewhere.

She would have liked to buy Mother and Father their own house—something pretty and old—but they would have none of it. When marriage to Ben made her prosperous she offered them, with Ben's full approval, a charming cottage high up on the hill behind the town, a hill with a view of the river far below and easy access to the countryside around. They said no. They thanked her and admired the cottage and refused. They had neighbours on the estate, they had always lived there, they didn't fancy moving; not now, not if she didn't mind. So Angela put in a bathroom for the council's benefit and had a telephone installed and Mother and Father pronounced themselves well content. Only when Angela and her family came did the house suddenly seem too small, but to admit it would not have been considered. 'Plenty of room,' Father would say, even when confronted with absolute evidence that this was a lie. Angela and Ben slept in the spare double bed with Tim on a camp bed beside them. Sadie slept on another camp bed in the bathroom which had once been the box room. Max and Saul slept in Mother and Father's old room. 'Plenty of room,' Father said, and, 'Always room for your own family.'

Before Sadie was born, Ben brought home a strange and colourful toy clown that he had seen in a shop window. It was big and fat with long spindly legs and a lolling head. The stomach of this stuffed creature was yellow, the arms orange, the rest brown. Angela decorated the whole of the baby-to-be's room round it. She painted all the walls a vivid sunshine yellow except for one, above the mantelpiece, which she covered in dark brown cork. Later, children's drawings would be pinned upon it because of course her children would be given crayons as soon as they could hold them and she would know how to treasure their efforts. There was an orange rug on the shiny wooden floor and an orange blind on the window. The room was at the top of the house, on the top floor, overlooking the long, tree-filled garden. In the last stages of her pregnancy, Angela haunted it. She imagined the delight of the child who would have it. She sat at the window in a rocking chair and tears came into her eyes as she thought about it. Sadie turned out to be indifferent to her room. As soon as she was old enough, she neglected it. The cork remained brown and bare—no pictures were ever drawn for it, or if they were, Sadie immediately removed them and took them downstairs to pin in the kitchen. The many open shelves had untidy little clusters of things dumped upon them and never looked organized. The big work table was filthy with scraps of plasticine that had hardened and was allowed to collect dirt. 'You say it's my room,' Sadie said when Angela called it a dump, 'then you want it to be like your room was at my age.' Angela was wise enough not to say she had never had her own room, that that was the point, the reason for her distress. She and Valerie had shared a bed in a room so small they had to turn sideways to get between the enormous wardrobe and the bed itself. There had been no beautiful spacious room in which she could take a pride, no private place to which she could retreat to read. But then Sadie never read and wasn't private. It was clear from the beginning that Sadie was not a solitary creature destined to love a room high up and secluded. Eventually, she moved. They had the old coal cellar next to the kitchen made into a room, intending it as a study, and Sadie begged to have it. There was barely room for her bed and no room at all for clothes or belongings. Everything she owned was either crammed into a cabin trunk or draped round the walls on hangers and hooks. She maintained she liked its smallness and darkness. Angela never went into Sadie's room unless she had to, and then claustrophobia overwhelmed her to such an extent that if the door had been accidentally shut, she would have screamed.

Ben humoured her but prophesied doom, a rare thing for him to do. The children were glad only that they did not have to stay at Grandad's and be harangued for their sins. Angela merely counted the days of freedom left and worried incessantly. She knew the place, she knew the hotel, she was completely familiar with exactly what to expect in the way of weather and she had made her decision to go because it was an experiment worth trying. Neutral ground, she told herself repeatedly, might solve all their problems. They would be on display and Trewicks displayed rather well.

Already, Mother and Father had had three weeks of anticipation and whatever the outcome would have many more of enjoying their unexpected holiday in retrospect. It did not even have to be a success for them to do that. Angela could remember several shared holidays with Mother and Father—holiday homes rented on freezing beaches—which had been totally disastrous but were now gone over nostalgically. It was the going away together that mattered. They remembered that—the public exhibition of unity —and forget the arguments, forgot how rude and naughty their grandchildren had been, forgot their disapproval of how Angela and Ben brought them up. They remembered only what they wanted to remember and their version of it.

Perhaps the same would happen again. And this time, there was the hotel to consider. Mother and Father had never stayed in an hotel, not ever. Boarding houses had been the pinnacle of their achievement, and even then they had to go back thirty years or more to remember when last they had graced such an exclusive establishment. All through Angela's childhood Mother had written off inquiring prices at selected boarding houses—stayed at and vouched for by better-off folk—but they had always been too high. She never went to stay in a boarding house and was envious of those who did, until Aunt Frances told her they were only a kind of cheap hotel and not to be mentioned in the same breath as the real thing.

The things that might worry Mother and Father had been taken care of. Their bedroom would have a bathroom attached and all round would be Angela and her family forming a solid block of Trewicks. The hotel was at the seaside, near the small town of Port Point, Father's favourite place in the whole world, not that he had ever ventured far into it. For something like fifty years he had gone every Sunday to Port Point to fish and walk along the cliff. Angela alone of the children had liked to go with him, but loving the sea rather than Port Point. 'The King would have come here, you know,' Father would say, 'only there was no hotel big enough.' 'What king?' Angela would ask, suspiciously, but Father didn't know. The fact that the king—any king— almost came should have been enough for her. Father said the reason he almost came was for the air which he had rightly heard was purer in Port Point than anywhere else, but Angela thought he must have wanted to come for the quiet. Port Point was not pretty, but it was quiet. It had a green and several streets of dull terraced houses and a cobbled main road along which stretched the shops and hotels. It was high up and open and apart from a few copses of pines totally exposed to the Atlantic winds which swept across it all winter and half the summer. 'Bracing,' Father would say, 'get that in your lungs and feel the difference.'

All one usually felt was exceedingly cold, to the point of numbness. A mile past Port Point there was a headland sticking out into the Atlantic. There stood a convalescent home and two hotels, both much admired by Mother and Father, who had never been in either. Sometimes, after Father had marched them along the cliff from Port Point, they would ogle the hotels, especially the bigger and more Edwardian of the two, and Father would say something about when his boat came in. The sea was a mere hundred yards away on one side and along the other was a narrow road leading onto the estuary. If the weather was good, it was the most perfect spot imaginable. If it was bad, there was no hope, not for Mother, not for the one person the holiday had been arranged for. The real killer would be a strong cold wind, the most likely thing of all on that particular part of the north Cornish coast—cold winds and drizzle, a combination so frequent it was sheer madness not to anticipate it.

Angela did anticipate it. Her anticipatory imagination was in excellent working order. The point was, Mother and Father would still get a change of surroundings with very little effort on their part. They would have the excitement of staying in an hotel. They would have all their meals made and the novelty of choosing from a menu and the stimulus of other people around. Father could tramp into Port Point every day. The children could run wild and not be noticed. It would be better than nothing—it would prevent that coma of depression into which she herself fell under the strain of trying to cope, of trying to make Mother and Father happy. It would throw a smokescreen between her and the Angela they wanted and in it she could hide.

She grew more and more silent as the day to drive down to St Erick approached. She had nightmares in which Ben was called away and she had to manage Mother and Father herself. It could not be done, not for a week, not with the children squarely on her back too. Ben was the ideal son-in-law. Often, Angela found herself apologizing for Mother and Father and the way in which inevitably they were made his concern as well as hers, but he bore no resentment. He said they took each other's parents on—but he had none himself, a vital difference Angela harped upon. She envied him so passionately his orphan state that it frightened her. If Mother and Father had been Ben's parents how tolerant she would have been, how kind and considerate, how anxious about their welfare, how easy she would have found it to be objective about their troubles. If her parents, like Ben's parents, had been killed in a car crash when she was twenty how deeply she would have mourned them, how sincere would have been her tears. And how liberated she would have felt.

But Mother and Father were old and alive and eagerly awaiting her arrival in St Erick. Waiting for Angela to solve all their problems. She would whisk in and organize them and liven them up and they would not feel lonely and deserted and failures for a week at least. 'You will help, won't you Sadie?' Angela pleaded. Sadie grunted. 'You will talk to them and try to understand why they are as they are?' 'It's so awful,' Sadie said, 'Grandad's so stupid and Grandma just sits and we just have to sit too. It's agony.' 'I know,' Angela said, 'but look at it from their point of view.' 'I do, but you go on so—I mean, what do you expect us to actually *do*?' 'Just be cheerful. And look for ways to please them. And make them feel wanted. That's all. And don't sulk or fight with Max—just try to be a little less selfish for once.' 'It's all hypocrisy,' Sadie said.

After Tim was born, Angela was ill. Sadie was nine, Max seven, Saul six and that was meant to be that, their family complete. But Angela's doctor made her come off the pill 'for a while anyway' and she became pregnant in spite of the most careful precautions. She would not have it that Tim was a mistake—she had made no mistake. He was an accident and that was different. An abortion was available but to her own astonishment she found she could not bring herself to have it. There was a small corner in her heart that had not quite done with babies, and though it was irrational and silly, and though she had only just gone back to teaching and was enjoying it, she went ahead and had Tim. Mother and Father were shocked. Knowing they would be she did not tell them until she was six months pregnant and then when she broke the news she went to great lengths to point out that she wanted the baby and that they were not to think of it as a catastrophe. But they did. The baby was thought of by them as a disaster—'as if you didn't have enough already'—and there were so many unpleasant innuendoes in everything they said about her unexpected pregnancy that Angela felt like a criminal. They both prophesied doom and as it turned out they were nearly right. She was five days in labour and then had a Caesarean. Tim was a pitiful not-quite-five-pounds baby who had to stay in an incubator for a month. Mother and Father's concern was deep and genuine—and burdensome—but the element of 'we told you so' hard to endure. Then as soon as she came home, Angela developed glandular fever. It took her four months to climb out of the appalling listlessness and exhaustion that sapped every ounce of her already depleted strength. She did not have to be told that she needed a holiday. Valerie came, a heroine, and looked after the children and Angela was taken off to the sun, too weak to resist. With her own feebleness so apparent, she had thought the children, especially Sadie, would understand why she had to go away, but they showed no signs of doing so. Sadie in particular was resentful. 'The baby will cry for you,' she said accusingly, 'you know he will. He'll cry and cry.' When the plane took off for Greece, Sadie's hostility haunted Angela—she saw her daughter's cold, tight little face staring at her with what she imagined was hatred. The entire two weeks she was away she woke up at night sweating with terror as Sadie's shrill voice rang in her ears saying 'But what about us? What about us?' Suppose the plane crashed, suppose one of them was killed while she was away, suppose they were all wretchedly unhappy—it would be her fault for putting herself first. Mother had not gone off to the sun after an illness. Mother had carried on. She had always been there, putting them first. Though she grew tanned and put on weight and felt human again for the first time since Tim's birth, guilt tinged every day. When she went home, to find everything in perfect order, it was Sadie's smile that meant most. Ben said she was a little tyrant but Angela saw it differently. Sadie had been afraid. Sadie had estimated correctly her mother's importance in her life and shuddered at the thought of what would happen if it was removed. Sadie was nowhere near ready to go her own way and until she was— until that blissful day—the truth of her deepest fear had to be acknowledged.

'Couldn't I stay here?' Sadie said, the day before they were due to go.

'No, you could not.'

'Why not?'

'Because this is a family holiday.'

'Well, I don't like family holidays. I'm not a child any more— you're always telling me I'm not—I don't like any of the things we do on a family holiday. I hate walking. I hate touring round places.'

'It will do you good.'

'How *can* it do me good if I hate it? And what do you mean "do me good"?'

'All the fresh air—'

'—god!—'

'—and just getting away from the dirt and noise of London and having time to really relax.'

'But I like the dirt and noise—I like London—I don't want time to relax—it's boring down there with nothing to do and nowhere to go. You don't even like having me with you, you know you don't.'

'We couldn't leave you behind anyway, not alone in this huge house.'

'Why not? I could have Joanna and Sue to stay.'

'No. You're not responsible enough. Take last week when we were all out—you didn't even notice the downstairs sink was overflowing. If we hadn't come back when we did there would have been a flood.'

'Then can I stay with Sue?'

'No. You're always accepting other people's hospitality and never returning it.'

'Oh, Mum—you're so ridiculous when you say things like that. Sleeping on somebody's floor isn't hospitality.'

'And eating their food?'

'I'd get my own food.'

'You don't do that here—you're here every meal time with your tongue hanging out and if there isn't a three-course meal you're mortally offended.'

'But why are you forcing me to go?'

'Because—because I want you to—and I don't think the alternatives are acceptable—and it would disappoint Grandma and Grandpa if you didn't.'

Father had regularly forced them to do things as a family. He forced all of them to go for a family walk every Sunday evening. They hated it. They would spend the whole week trying to fabricate cast-iron excuses and when they failed they would all line up with scowls on their faces, hands thrust deep into pockets and feet ready to trail as they were marched out. Father didn't seem to care what their attitude was—all that mattered was their presence. They would walk up to the woods, strung out in a line behind Father, who alone knew their destination. If their sulking spoiled his pleasure he never mentioned it. When they got back in the house he would say 'That was grand now.' Never once did he try to explain what he got from executing this exercise.

Irritation at being cast in the role of coercer made her bad tempered on the telephone with Valerie, who rang only to express admiration for what she was about to do.

'Mother is so excited,' Valerie said, 'she can't stop talking about it.'

'Don't,' Angela said, 'I can't bear it. You know as well as I do the whole thing will be the most terrible anti-climax.'

'Oh, it might not be—it might be lovely—the sun might shine, you never know.'

'I do know.'

'Anyway, I think it's marvellous and I know Mother and Father do too. And you'll have the children to help.'

'Valerie, don't talk rubbish. Children are never a help.'

'Well, Mother just loves to be with them.'

'She doesn't. Within minutes they drive her crazy and then I have to spend all my time keeping them apart.'

'At least it will be a rest.'

'That's very unlikely.'

'Would you like me to come and help then?'

'I would hate you to come and help. It would only make the situation worse.'

'Thanks very much.'

'Don't be so touchy. You know what I mean, or you ought to. Anyway, it would be a waste—save yourself for another time when I can't manage it. They can come to you later in the summer when Mother is stronger.'

'They're always welcome,' Valerie said.

It took Angela's breath away—Valerie saying something like that—about Mother and Father being welcome, about looking forward to having them—and coming out with similar platitudes and refusing to admit they were lies. Even after Mother and Father had been to stay with her she kept up the pretence. 'They had a lovely time here,' she would say. 'Father was quite happy pottering around the town and Mother enjoyed the view.' It drove Angela mad. Father had told her how he hated Manchester where Valerie lived. 'It's a filthy big town,' he would say, 'dirt and noise, disgusting. Don't know what she wants to go and live there for—no peace, nothing.' And the only comment Mother had ever passed about the view she was reputed to enjoy was that it made her dizzy, living in a flat so high up. There were vague mumblings from both of then—quickly stifled—about not getting enough to eat because Valerie didn't eat enough herself to feed a sparrow, and about the terrible heat that stifled them in her sixth-floor flat, and of how they feared the lift. Nothing they said added up to having had the good time Valerie maintained they had had. The only explanation Angela could come up with was that either Valerie needed to keep up the myth because the truth was too distressing, or that she simply did not know what the truth was. In which case she was exceedingly lucky.

'Sadie,' Angela said, 'sit in the back please.'

'Do I have to?'

'Yes, you do.'

'I'll be sick if I sit in the back.'

'So will I,' Angela said firmly, 'and I need to be in better shape than you today.'

'There isn't even room in the back.'

'It's your fat bum,' said Max.

'Fuck yourself,' Sadie said.

'Stop that language,' Angela shouted. The whole street could hear them. 'Just get in and shut up. There's plenty of room.'

'When will the first stop be?' Tim said.

'Oh god—we haven't even started yet.'

'I just want to know, that's all.'

'In two hours' time.'

'*Two* hours? But we usually stop in one—we usually—'

'Oh shut *up*—I don't know when we're going to stop—when we need to, that's when. If only you would all be a little more grown up.'

'Listen who's talking,' Sadie said.

'Look,' Angela said, turning round to face her. 'I am tired and fed up and I don't like doing this any more than you do so it's hardly surprising I'm bad tempered—'

'Just don't take it out on us.'

'I'm *not* taking anything out on anyone—'

'Yes you are.'

'—I'm just asking for a little consideration, that's all—a little understanding—some ordinary sympathy—'

'Oh, god.'

'Thank you. Thank you very, very much.'

Sadie burst out laughing, and tears of humiliation came into Angela's eyes.

She had put herself into a ridiculous position, just as Father used to—throwing the hat out so ostentatiously that all her daughter wanted to do was be sick into it. She had whined and whimpered and begged for mercy in those sanctimonious tones that made nonsense of what she was asking for. Mother had never done that. Mother would be grey-faced with visible exhaustion yet never let out a single moan. She would be carrying all the worries of the world on her poor shoulders yet never try to unload them. It was Father who pointed out the obvious and made them all jump to help Mother and they hated him for the way in which he did it. 'She'll be dead before you notice,' he would shout, and 'you'll appreciate her when she's gone.' It had thrown them into a panic, rushing to get things for Mother, forcing her to put her feet up, swearing they would be better children. And she had just sighed and said she could manage and that had cut them to shreds.

Sadie, however, had laughed, and rightly. Angela was compelled on the long journey down to St Erick to admit that her attitude was ludicrous. It was crass and stupid to roar in a bull-like way that you were tired—nobody could believe it. It was contemptible to say she did not want to go to St Erick and to boast that she was being dutiful. Nobody ever called forth compassion in that way. She knew Sadie despised her double standards and failed to see her motives were honourable. She had always hoped that by being open about all her joys and troubles she would achieve a depth of understanding with her children that Mother had never had with them, and that when they grew up that harmony would remain. But she had been mistaken. Exposing her own anguish only severed communication.

She sat half mesmerized by the traffic on the motorway wondering what would happen if she simply abandoned all her responsibilities. Suppose she were to stay in bed and let them all get on with it? Suppose she were never to telephone or write to

Mother again? Suppose she were to do only those things she wanted to do and fret only about herself and wait for others to look after her for a change—what would happen? She did not want to be so important. She did not want to control anyone's destiny. She wanted to fade quietly into the background and have no one at all relying upon her. But she could not do that. She was a Mother, and Mothers stood like rocks, immovable and solid, while all the rest eddied around them.

'You're shivering,' Ben said.

'I know. I think I must be getting a cold.'

'That's all we need.'

He had not meant to be unkind. He never was. But in her fragile state the remark was enough to start her crying again and she had to take refuge in a fit of pretend sneezing until she had finished. Mothers did not cry in front of children.

'Filling the car with germs,' Sadie murmured, and rolled down a window. A blast of cold air whipped across Angela's neck and brought her out in goose pimples.

Five

Mother's open suitcase, put out on the bed for Angela's inspection when she arrived, was a poem. Angela told her so, said she was lost in admiration, but Mother was uncertain whether she was being mocked or not and stood frowning while Angela checked the contents at her insistence. Everything had been arranged perfectly. Every garment was wrapped in tissue paper, the sleeves and pleats of skirts and dresses interleaved with yet more, and all the jumpers and blouses were folded carefully to prevent unnecessary creasing. No wonder Father had been in a bad temper ever since they had arrived. Clumsy, except with nuts and bolts, he had been compelled to stand for hours doing exactly what Mother had said to her beloved clothes. She suddenly became a tyrant, ignoring his furious protests that he had done his best and could do no better—he *must* do better. With her one good arm she showed him how to do it and cursing and swearing he tried to obey her instructions. Shoes were wrapped in news-paper and secured with elastic bands, then wedged round the edges of the suitcase to form a wall which contained the softer things. Toilet articles were in two different waterproof bags—one for talcum powder, face cream and ointments, the other for soap, facecloth and denture powder. Mending things, without which Mother never travelled so great was her fear of snapped elastic or lost buttons, were neatly contained in a small zipped bag like a pencil case. A hair brush and comb, in a cellophane bag, nestled in one corner and a bag of curlers and hairpins in another.

'All present and correct,' Angela said, 'it would make a

customs officer cry with pleasure.' But Mother did not want her to be facetious. She was not happy with the number of stockings she was taking, nor with her decision to take only one coat, a heavy tweed coat. Suppose it turned out warm, what would she do then? Angela's airy reassurances were not reassuring. Perhaps she ought to take a light coat too. Angela agreed, readily, but Mother was annoyed by her refusal to agree that it was important to have the right clothes. Mother would have liked Angela to have been as concerned and anxious as herself. 'It really doesn't matter,' Angela kept saying, 'take anything you like—take all your coats if you want.' 'Oh, don't be silly,' Mother snapped. But in the end a decision was made and the lid of the case closed and locked and strapped with a big leather strap, even though it would only be going in the car with them for twenty miles.

Father sat in the front with Ben, ostensibly to direct him. Ben, who had driven to Port Point scores of times, had no objection to feigning ignorance. 'Turn left, turn right, keep straight,' Father loved to shout, even if every direction he gave was quite obvious. He knew shortcuts that Ben claimed put a hundred miles onto every journey but then Father liked to turn the simplest journey into a trip down memory lane. There was no road he had not ridden along on his bicycle, no village where he had not had a drink. The entire county of Cornwall was intimately known to him and his proprietorial air gave Angela great pleasure.

But it irritated Mother, who sat in the back with Angela and Sadie while all three boys squashed into the rear of the estate car with the luggage.

'Oh shut up for heaven's sake,' Mother muttered as Father reminisced, 'they've heard that a thousand times.'

'Never mind,' Angela said, 'it's a good story.'

'*Is* it? Eh? Oh, well then, sorry I spoke,' Mother said, jealous, twitching horribly, 'Oh well, if you think so.'

'It keeps him happy,' Angela whispered, disloyally, and squeezed Mother's gloved hand.

'I remember the year that pond over there was frozen solid in June,' Father was saying, pointing out of the window.

'Rubbish,' Mother said, quite sharply and loudly.

'Who's rubbish?' Father said, 'It's a fact—it was 1946—no, must have been '47—'

'There you are,' Mother said, 'can't get it right,' and she nudged both Angela and Sadie and smirked. Father for once did not rise to the bait, but went on telling Ben and anyone else who cared to listen about the great freeze-up in the middle of that summer he could not quite place. Mother's showing off had failed in its object, which was to publicly humiliate him and goad him into making a fool of himself. Angela sighed with relief at a small crisis passed but knew Sadie would be disappointed—Grandma and Grandad were to her comedy characters whose repartee she relished and looked for.

It began to rain as soon as they turned onto the main road at Camelford, hard lashing rain that had a hailstone or two in it and could not be argued away. 'Just a shower,' Ben murmured, but his windscreen wipers could barely cope with the torrent. Mother shrank from the sight and sound of it and cast beseeching looks at Angela. 'It won't last,' Angela said confidently, 'better to get it over with now, then it will be fine when we get there.' 'Oh, no bother,' Father agreed.

He must have heard Mother say, rudely, 'What do you know about it?' but he rose superbly above the taunt. Nothing was going to dim his pleasure. As they drove on the rain redoubled its efforts and they had to slow down to a crawl. A smile fixed on her face, Angela's thoughts were of instant death for them all— a sudden, merciful extinction from the face of the earth before any of them knew what was happening. Hysteria at the approaching horror of a week near Port Point in the rain began to grip her and she had to keep swallowing hard to stop herself screaming.

'What will we do if it rains all week like this?' Saul shouted from the back of the car. 'What will we do, Mum?'

'Oh, lots of things,' Angela said, 'don't you worry about it. There won't be a dull moment.' Ben smiled at her through the driving mirror.

'Like what?' shouted Max.

'We'll play games,' Angela said, 'I've brought lots with me—'

'I can't play games,' Mother interrupted, 'not with my eyes— and I can't hold cards either.'

'We'll play games that don't need good eyesight or involve holding cards,' Angela said. 'I-spy and —'

'Christ,' Sadie said, very softly.

'We can wrap up and have a blow along the cliff,' Father said. 'You'll never notice the rain once you get going.'

'I can't walk,' Mother said, 'not in this, bad enough at the best of times but I couldn't stand up to this.'

'You might not have to,' Angela said, 'let's face it when it happens.'

But Trewicks faced everything before it happened. They were frequently grieved to find that what they had suffered in advance had never actually materialized. Depression would overwhelm them at the merest hint of disaster and only begin to lift when their worst fears proved justified. That cheered them up. Trewicks were quite splendid in catastrophes, absolutely magnificent in the midst of tragedy just so long as they had predicted it. More than anything they hated people who professed to live in the present, who did not cross their bridges before they came to them, who believed the worst might never happen. Knowing all this, born and bred to this fearful philosophy, Angela sensed Mother and Father's deep disapproval of her attitude. They loathed her cheerfulness, even Father who was being so cheerful himself. The difference was that he was being cheerful *in spite of* thinking everything disastrous whereas Angela was not admitting disaster had overtaken them. Though Mother and Father appeared divided about the effect of the rain, they were united in despising their daughter's refusal to face facts. They wanted her to look at the rain and sink into deep gloom. They wanted her to say things that Trewicks said, 'Just our luck' and 'No good hoping.'

Because this was how she knew they felt, Angela did not speak again for a long time as they drove towards the sea, fearing to cause conflict when there was enough already. In the back, the boys were unnaturally quiet, as though awed by the deluge outside. Angela was lulled almost to sleep by the close atmosphere in the car and the slow pace they were driving at and the rhythmic wheezing of Mother's breathing. She made a hole in the steamed-up window and peered out at the fields, each greener than the last, a dozen or more shades from a brash emerald to the subtlest sage. She wondered if she ought to remember out loud cycling past them when she was a child, head down, off on her solitary pilgrimages to Port Point, forty miles, there and back, her legs burnt with wind and sun and weary with pedalling her Raleigh Sports up so many hills. She had made those bike rides because they were something to achieve—often, before she was even at Westdowns, she was tired and had no real desire to go on to

Port Point, where in any case she would only lean on her handle-bars for a little while before returning, but Trewicks did not give up. She had said to herself that she would cycle to Port Point and so she must.

'I used to cycle this way,' she said at last, when she felt the silence becoming deadly.

'Yes, you did,' Father said, 'many a time.'

'I always got off at this hill—' Angela said.

'How fascinating,' Sadie murmured.

'—it was the only one I couldn't get up. And then at the top you get the first view of the sea and it's downhill all the way. I used to see how far I could freewheel.'

Sadie began to hum, quietly, but Father and Mother were pleased with her.

They neared the turning for Port Point and there was a distinct lifting of spirits within the car. The children sat up straight and began pointing out things as they followed the narrow road that wound along the cliff. Even Sadie liked arriving at new places though within a very short time she might be cruelly condemning them. The rain seemed to slacken and the clouds to lift just a little and there was a suspicious brightness in the sky over to the west which might or might not turn out to be the sun. Against all reason and all Trewick training Angela began to feel optimistic.

Before she moved to comprehensive school, Sadie revealed herself to have pride. Max would come home often claiming nobody liked him and nobody would play with him and that he had had to sit all playtime by himself. But not Sadie. Angela thought at first that the contrast between Sadie and Max might be based on her daughter's greater popularity—perhaps Sadie did not come home from school with tales of woe simply because she had none to tell. Because she had so many friends she was never lonely and sad. But one day Angela had to go to see Sadie's headmistress and as she went across the playground, looking for Sadie among the gangs of shrieking girls, she saw her sitting by herself, quite alone, a dejected little figure at the end of a bench. It was hard to continue on her way but she knew instinctively that Sadie would not wish her to stop—especially not to stop and ask what was wrong. At teatime she said to Sadie, 'Do you always have someone to play with at playtime?' 'No,' Sadie said. 'What do you do when you haven't got anyone?' Angela asked. 'Oh,' Sadie said,

'*I have things to do.*' *The conversation was closed. Angela did not know whether to applaud or regret her daughter's pride, but ever afterwards she noticed endless instances of it. At a loose end, Sadie would invariably apply herself to conquering the problem—and succeed. She never let anyone see that she was bored or unhappy. She did not retreat into any shell and set her face against the world. She seemed to always be on the watch, ready to snatch her opportunities, in a way Angela had never been. And it made Angela happy to notice the rejection of the Trewick tradition she was afraid to have passed on.*

The car had barely stopped in the gravelled forecourt of the hotel before Father was out, tugging in vain at the locked rear door. 'I'll get her out,' he shouted, 'hang on, Mother, I'll have you out in a minute.'

'What's the hurry?' Angela said, from inside.

'She's been sitting long enough.'

Angela opened the door and in an instant he was grabbing Mother roughly by the arm, hauling her out like a bag of coal. He gave her contradictory instructions about what to do with her limbs—'Pull that leg up—up—put your shoulders this way—this way—down with your head now,' and she tried to obey without complaining. The only thing Angela could do was get out at the other side and ignore them. Interfering was useless—the whole pantomime of getting Mother into and out of cars simply had to be gone through in this way.

They stood in the middle of the entrance hall, an uncertain group with little coherence. Saul and Tim broke away, darting off round the corner to see what they could find, and though the noise they made ought to have been stopped, Angela was relieved that someone was behaving naturally. Ben went off to find a manager or receptionist and she was left to stem a rising tide of panic that this hotel was not perhaps what she had thought it was. They ought to have gone to the Port Point Hotel itself instead of choosing Grun House because it looked architecturally more imposing and was even nearer the sea and had ground-floor bedrooms, so vital for Mother. They had never even been inside it—she had trusted the charm of the double-fronted sandstone building and the cheerfulness of the flower-filled windows. Now that she was through the front door she sensed an air of abandon for which she had not been prepared.

'Sit down, Mother,' she said, pointing to a dusty-looking armchair in the corner.

'I've been sitting down the last hour,' Mother said, holding her head up high. 'Anyway, that chair doesn't look any too clean, and I've got my good skirt on—I'll walk about a bit.'

'Not much now,' Father said eyeing her critically, 'nice and easy.'

'Oh shut up,' Mother said, shuffling backwards and forwards across the black and white tiled floor, a distance of five or six yards at a time. Father whistled. Sadie stood looking out of a window onto the garden. Max was absorbed in a comic, slumped in the chair Mother had spurned. Angela took Mother's arm and together they went up to a large picture—a watercolour—of the sea. Mother strained to appreciate it. 'Nice colour,' she said. 'Very,' Angela said.

The appearance of Ben and a smiling manager cheered them all until the horrifying news was broken that there were no ground-floor bedrooms.

'Our ground floor is given over to sitting rooms and the dining room and so forth,' the manager said. 'We *used* to have a few ground-floor rooms—you're quite right—but we converted them into a play room last year.' He smiled with satisfaction, oblivious to the concern he was causing. He was the sort of man, Angela thought, who was oblivious to most things—his job was to serve the public, in whom he was not the slightest bit interested. Smiling was his limit.

'I can't climb stairs,' Mother said and gave a little laugh that hurt Angela so much she flinched with imagined physical pain. 'I'd better just go home. No place for me here.' With surprising strength she began to pull Angela towards the door.

'Hold on,' Ben said. He was avoiding Angela's eye. His manner, placating and easy, took some of the tension out of the air and the manager looked towards him hopefully. 'Let's just look at these stairs first—they might not be too bad. It's all my fault—I told my secretary to book ground-floor rooms and I suppose when they said they had none I just told her to get what she could without thinking. I'm sorry.'

'I won't be able to manage, no good trying.' Mother said, and such was her pitiful expression that Angela instantly forgave her. It was humiliating for Mother to have to stand there at the bottom of a flight of stairs while everyone stared at her and waited. Her left leg, broken in a bad fall five years before, had never mended properly and had left her unable to use it without difficulty. Stairs, steps, changing levels of any kind were obstacles she avoided. The doctor had said a stick would help but she would not have a stick. Father was equally adamant—'would make an invalid of her' he said, and the subject was closed.

Ben put his arm round Mother's waist and encouraged her with little jokes, quickly expressing surprise that the fiendish stairs were actually so shallow and so few in number and without any twists in them—simply ten straight stairs leading onto the first landing—and best of all carpeted so that she need not worry about slipping. Mother responded as she would not have done to either Father or Angela. She allowed Ben to help her and accepted his compliments and in no time at all the dreaded stairs had been surmounted with not the slightest trace of strain on her face. She stood at the top, only a little breathless, while Ben congratulated her. Angela felt faint with relief and as she made her own way up the stairs had to cling to the banister rail to hide her weakness.

The rooms were disappointing. There was no denying it. But Angela was aware that the disappointment was hers rather than Mother's. She found the rooms ugly but Mother noticed only the comfortable beds and thick fitted carpet and the spacious bathroom. She shuffled about fingering the counterpanes and towels—'good quality'—while Angela went over to the window and fought with the net curtains to see the view. It at least was satisfying—a clear vista of grass and sea, uninterrupted by any man-made thing. 'It's a beautiful view,' she said, 'come and look.' Mother came over to the window and stared and turned away. 'Not much to see,' she said, 'not that I can see much anyway. I daresay it will be very nice on a good day.' Outside, Angela could hear the boys running from room to room, jumping on beds and fighting over who should sleep where. She let the curtain drop. 'Put it straight,' Mother said, 'it was hanging nice and straight before you meddled with it.' 'Why don't you have a little rest after all your exertions?' Angela said, alarmed by Mother's sudden high colour.

'Oh, I'm *sick* of little rests,' Mother said, 'I want shaking up instead of resting.' She would not even sit down. 'What are we going to do now?' she said. 'What are we going to do now we're here?' 'I thought,' said Angela, weakly, without conviction, 'I thought it would be a lovely idea to go into Port Point before dinner and have a look round.'

Father was nowhere to be seen. When they had descended the stairs, three abreast, Mother half lifted down between Angela and Ben, he was nowhere to be found. No one had seen him since Mother had begun to climb the stairs. Angela sent the boys off in different directions to look for him while Mother exclaimed at his thoughtlessness. 'Just like him to wander off when he's needed,' she said, 'typical.'

'Let's wait outside,' Angela said, 'in the car—he might be outside,' but at that minute Father came into the entrance hall with Saul and Max on either side like policemen and Tim pulling him along shouting 'He went to see a man about a dog, he says.' Mother's disgust made her frightening. 'I might have known,' she said, and then again, separating each word very carefully, 'I might have known. At a time like this—to play that game.' Father said nothing—no excuses. He looked a little grey and crumpled and Angela remembered how abruptly he had turned away when Ben led Mother towards the stairs. 'Let's go into Port Point,' she said quickly. 'Who wants to walk and who wants to drive?' 'I haven't any choice,' Mother said.

Angela walked with Father and Max, leaving the others to get noisily into the car. Ben was best left with Mother anyway. With him, she was charming and dignified and tried harder to enjoy herself. He would squire her around gallantly in the old-fashioned way she liked and would involve her in little conspiracies that made her feel years younger. His manner towards her was both deferential and teasing, a combination she clearly relished. Ben was the sort of young man she felt she ought to have married— just a bit above her class, with money and brains and a certain gentleness about him that appealed to her. He looked how she liked young men to look—clean shaven, tall and straight-backed with blond hair that looked as though a nanny had brushed and combed it that very morning. She approved of his shyness, of his kindness, of his lack of 'pushiness'. His job was something of a disappointment to her. All she understood of it was that it was 'something to do with oil' and that was a pity. Mother's real cup of tea were professional people—doctors, lawyers, teachers—but she managed in Ben's case to overlook this deviation from her ideal. There was the comfort, after all, of knowing that he had been educated at a minor public school, even if he now repudiated what it had stood for. He had beautiful manners and a lovely speaking voice and she envied Angela her luck.

They walked at a terrific pace along the cliff. The noise of the waves bashing against the rocks and of the wind sweeping along from the open sea without interruption made all conversation impossible. Father, she knew, would have liked to give voice either to his conviction that the stairs were going to kill Mother or to his fears that the whole trip had been a mistake. Angela blessed the elements. She walked along with her eyes half closed, face upturned to meet the rain, enjoying the buffeting the wind was giving her. Father enjoyed it too. He looked strong and confident as he marched on, just a little ahead, his tweed overcoat buttoned to the neck and his cap pulled firmly down.

Long before they reached the end of the cliff path, Angela was anticipating the weariness of trailing Mother round the shops. They were not the sort of shops one could spend much time in— a few small food shops, a few garish, cheap tourist shops—but to Mother, deprived of all shops, they were something. She missed going into shops and looking to see what they had. She missed the simple exchange of money for goods and the satisfaction that came from a primitive love of trading. She missed the small observations one made in shops, the feeling of belonging, the casual gossip overheard. And the Port Point shops, though few in number and disappointing in content, were the sort of shops Mother had used in her youth. They were tiny, room for no more than a dozen people at a time, with highly polished windows in which goods were displayed in rows. Mother could stand and look in the windows for hours, comparing and contrasting the appearance and price of all the items, and then she enjoyed being decisive once inside. Yet when Father joined her, glowing and beaming from another blow along the front, and asked her what she had been doing, she would say 'nothing much' and look sulky. He would turn to Angela and say, 'Haven't you taken her round the shops then?' 'You can't call them shops,' Mother would spit out, and Father would say, 'Beg pardon, what would you call them then?'

If only they could walk on forever, past Port Point, past the docks where once they had embarked for Tintagel and almost capsized in the fishing boat that took them, along the sand where in summer they ate paste sandwiches crouching behind the reedy grass. Their only holiday as a family ever had been at Port Point and oh the pride of it! Angela remembered boasting at school that she was going on her holidays to the seaside, thrilled that at last she was upsides with those who regularly did, no longer obliged to toss her head and announce she *preferred* going for 'days'. The wretchedness of discovering the caravan was not a caravan as she thought of one—not a gypsy caravan pulled by a horse—but a hideous modern contraption was quickly overcome. The site, in those days, was deserted and if Romany romance was lacking the caravan was at least in a proper field and the field was ten yards from the beach. The sun shone the whole week—they were blessed, Mother said—and she ran on the sands and pretended she rode a horse called Chestnut.

They turned off the sea front at the amusement arcade and made their way across the green to where they could see the car parked in front of the church. The rain had stopped and away from the sea the wind was much less fierce. Angela could see Sadie leaning against the wall, her arms folded across her chest, the sleeves of her pullover pulled down over her hands.

'She looks frozen,' Father said, eyeing her critically from a distance. 'Hasn't she got a coat?'

'No,' Angela said, 'she doesn't like coats.'

'Ridiculous,' Father said, 'should have more sense—you always had coats, anyway.'

'Oh, it's her own fault,' Angela said, 'she'll just have to learn.'

'Can't you do anything with her?' Father said.

'I don't see the point.' Angela wanted to finish the discussion quickly before they reached Sadie.

'You're her Mother, that's the point,' Father said.

'That doesn't mean I'm a policeman. Hello, Sadie.'

'Where's your Grandma?' Father said.

'Dad's taken her round the shops.'

'Why didn't you go with her?'

'I didn't want to.'

'Oh well,' Father said, 'hoighty-toighty, eh.'

'The shops aren't very exciting, Father,' Angela said.

'You thought they were at that age.'

'At that age,' Angela said, 'I had never been out of St Erick. I thought anything was exciting.'

By the time Sadie was ten she had been to America, South Africa and New Zealand, to every European country except Denmark and Norway, and to every region of the British Isles. Sometimes living in different countries for months at a time because of her father's work, sometimes on holiday, she was familiar with aeroplanes and boats and trains and the airports and docks and stations that went with them. She travelled well, taking in her stride hold-ups and cancellations, adapting quickly to different climates and customs and picking up where she had left off when she came home. It was as though she had been born experienced—her lifestyle simply appeared to confirm her innate sophistication. And yet, though she was immensely proud of her daughter's versatility, Angela slowly began to realize that it was not matched by an equal confidence. Sadie only seemed confident. It did not matter how many times they had flown—she would not fly on her own. The truth was, she had no taste for independence and however wide her horizons had been she remained narrow in her ability to do things herself. Angela could not understand this—it did not make sense. She found it hard to accept that it was only when accompanied by her family that Sadie was blasé. With a shock, Angela realized, as Sadie reached adolescence, that unless she was buttressed by friends or parents Sadie was as timid as a girl who had never been out of a country village. Though she had travelled thousands of miles and exchanged continents several times she could not take a 5p bus ride to the local swimming baths without a companion. Directions confused her. She would say she couldn't manage without any shame, and drove Angela to say things like 'When I was your age I could go anywhere— I liked trying to get myself about.' St Erick, of course, had been different from London, but still Angela was surprised. Sadie had no taste for adventure. She was only bold if someone was with her and her opportunities had seemed wasted. Unless, Angela found herself thinking, unless it is all my fault—unless I have wrapped her in cotton wool and never exposed her to chance, unless I have been too strong and capable and dulled any spirit she had, unless we have travelled too much and killed any natural wanderlust.

Dinner at Grun House was at seven-thirty, one sitting only. Angela tried hard, from five o'clock onwards, to make an occasion of it. All four children were threatened with the most

74

dire penalties if they did not dress in a manner which would please their grandparents—clean trousers, clean white shirts for the boys and a skirt and blouse for Sadie, who referred to both garments as outlandish. Ben put on a suit and Angela herself wore the least flamboyant of her peasant dresses. When they were all ready, they lined up outside Mother and Father's door and knocked formally and were admitted with equal politeness. Mother had her best frock on, the birthday present from Angela, and earrings and necklace that Valerie had given her, and her feet, which in the last few years had become rather swollen, were somehow squashed into black patent leather court shoes. Her white hair, crimped and flattened by the hairdresser the week before, was brushed into life by Father, to the best of his ability. The scent of Devon Violets filled the room and clung even to Father, resplendent in a dark threepiece suit, white shirt with a stiff collar, and a regimental tie to which strictly speaking he was not entitled. He had run away at the age of fifteen to enlist in the army during the First World War and for one day, since he was a big heavy lad, he had belonged to the Duke of Cornwall's Light Infantry. The next day his father arrived, beat the living daylights out of him right there in front of the barracks, and dragged him home. The war ended on Father's eighteenth birthday and to his eternal regret he was too old to be immediately needed for the next. But he wore the tie on very special occasions as a reminder of what might have been and no one who knew was ever unkind enough to challenge his right to it.

'You look lovely,' Angela said to Mother, 'very smart indeed. That frock is a perfect fit and the necklace just brings out the blue in it.' Mother blinked and smiled and whatever she privately thought did not make a single self-deprecating remark. Down they all went into the bar, Mother accepting a fruit juice without making an issue of it and bravely watching Father accept a pint without flinching. Mother did not like alcohol, neither the taste nor the effect. She was afraid of it. Father never got drunk but after a few beers and chasers on a Saturday night he became truculent and unpleasant and she hated it. Any good that alcohol might do was hidden to her. When Father came into the house after his mild drinking sessions she wrinkled up her nose and shuddered and turned away. Angela and Ben confused her—they drank, she could see that they did, but it was different for them somehow. It was a different kind of drinking that fitted in with a different kind of life and Mother had a feeling it might be acceptable—just.

'No first course for me,' Mother announced when they were all seated at the big round table in the window. She seemed surprised when no one queried her decision.

'What about you, Father?' Angela said.

'Shrimp cocktail,' Father said, 'they'll be local shrimps.'

'*You* don't want shrimp cocktail,' Mother said, with a scathing little laugh. 'Do you know what it is?'

'It's shrimps,' Father said.

'Yes, but shrimps in mayonnaise dressing,' Mother said. 'That wouldn't suit you, would it? You don't like things messed up, do you?'

'He might like mayonnaise,' Angela said.

'He's never touched it,' Mother said, 'one look and that'll turn him off—I know him.'

'Tell them to leave off the dressing,' Father said, 'I'll just have them shrimps raw.'

'You can't do that,' Mother said, 'the very idea—messing people about.'

'Certainly he can,' Angela said, 'he can have the shrimps however he likes. This is an hotel, Mother—you ask for what you want.' And then, because she had spoken too sharply and had hurt Mother, she said, 'What about main courses—there's some lovely salmon trout on the menu, Mother—how about that?'

'I can't see the menu,' Mother said.

'Well, Sadie will read it out for everyone.'

Sadie read through the menu slowly and clearly. She was very willing to do so—anything to do with food usually brought out the best in her. When she had finished, with frequent recaps, there was an animated five minutes of consultation. Mother and Father found it very annoying. Trewicks did not hesitate—they made instant decisions. They never, as all four grandchildren were doing, said one thing then changed to another. The waitress, who was used to cowed children overawed by the occasion, was clearly amazed by all the shouting and discussion. She had a full page of crossed-out orders before at last everyone had finally made up their mind. 'Everyone happy now?' she asked, grimly, and Mother and Father were embarrassed by her disapproval. 'Sit nice and straight,' Mother whispered to Tim, who was slouching across the table, 'and don't fiddle with the cutlery.'

'Why not? I'm not harming it.'

'You might cut yourself—and it's just been polished—look, you're taking the shine off.'

'I don't care,' Tim said. 'Mum, can I go and play in the corridor till the first course comes?'

Angela said he could at the same time as Father said he certainly could not. The impasse was side-stepped by the immediate arrival of that first course which kept Tim firmly where Father wanted him. Ben ordered a bottle of wine but only he and Angela drank it. She realized, as she swallowed a second large glass before she had so much as tasted her smoked mackerel, that she was going to get dizzy before the meal had really begun. Already, her head swam and she did not seem to be able to hear what everyone was saying. She tried to put her hand over her glass but Ben knocked it aside firmly and looking her straight in the eye said, 'Drink up. This is a celebration.' She found herself giggling and felt Mother and Father's eye upon her. 'Grandad,' Ben said, 'how about a pint?' 'Oh no,' Father said, 'oh no, no, no,' and he shook his head.

Six

It was the last bit that rankled. 'What time is it?' Mother had asked as the dessert plates were cleared away. 'Half-eight,' Father had replied, holding his watch up to the light to be sure of absolute accuracy.

'Is that all?' Mother had said. The smile left her face, unsure that it had ever belonged there anyway. 'It's early. What do we do now, stuck here?'

They were still at the big round table in the window, slightly apart from the other guests, who looked at them with interest and a certain envy. They seemed, Angela knew, such a wonderful example of family solidarity. There had been laughter throughout the meal and the children had behaved gratifyingly well, not just by eating up every morsel on their plates, but by talking intelligently and sensibly to their grandparents. Nobody had shouted, nobody had tried to show off, nobody had sulked. It was hard to remember any other recent family gathering which had been such a success. Yet there was Mother with the air of a petulant child clamouring for the next treat, and what, after all, was that going to be? Angela did not know. The pleasant effects of the wine left her in an instant as every pair of eyes looked to her for direction.

'How about a walk round?' Ben suggested.

'Good idea,' Angela said, gratefully.

'I can't walk around,' Mother said, 'I've walked enough today. Where to, anyway? There isn't anywhere to walk, stuck here. It's pitch black. There aren't any pavements. And it's cold too—there's a wind getting up.'

'Well,' Ben said, 'I'll take the boys for a quick dash up to the beach and back.'

'I'll come,' Father said.

'You?' Mother said, 'you'll get your death going out at this time, at your age, in this weather.'

'I'll wrap up warm,' Father said. 'Shan't be long.'

'The ladies will retire for coffee,' Angela said, brightly. 'We'll have it in the sitting room and make ourselves comfortable before anyone else gets there—we'll hog the fire and stuff ourselves with chocolates.'

But there was no fire. The only sitting room was small and cheerless with no furnishings other than a two-seater sofa that had had considerable wear and a couple of new, ugly, graceless modern armchairs covered in a repellent lime green moquette. There was a centre light with a powerful bulb in it and no other lamp which could be put on in preference to the appalling and unnecessary glare. The heavily patterned curtains, when pulled together, hardly met. 'Is this where we're going to sit?' Mother said. 'God, what a dump,' Sadie said. Angela pulled the two chairs together and dragged a black leather foot stool across the shabby carpet to join them. 'I'll sit in this one,' she said, 'and you sit here with your feet up, Mother.' Sadie remained standing. 'Does anyone mind if I go and watch television?' she asked, looking at Angela. Angela returned the look steadily. Let Sadie interpret it how she liked. 'Coming, Grandma?' Sadie said. 'No, dear,' Mother said, 'I haven't come on holiday to watch television. Anyway, I get enough of that at home, can't get away from it and most of it is rubbish.'

Left alone together, Angela and her Mother sat motionless, waiting for the arrival of the promised coffee. Angela knew that the thought of a waitress appearing at any moment was the only thing that prevented Mother from expressing her keen disappointment with the room, the lack of entertainment, with life itself. She wanted the coffee to come, she wanted the distraction its arrival would bring, and yet she dreaded the moment the tray was brought through the door because it would signal the end of Mother's forbearance. 'Oh good,' she said, far too loudly, when it at last arrived. 'Oh lovely—and biscuits too—how nice—thank you so much. What pretty cups, Mother—do you see?—like those rose-covered ones Grandma had in her china cabinet—do you remember?—and the bowl and jug matching.' She poured the coffee, exclaiming at the heat of it, and fussed endlessly over the sugaring and milking of the suddenly precious liquid. She discussed the layout of the tray—such a sweet embroidered tray cloth, so rare these days didn't Mother think—and the cost of coffee in general and her own preference for brown rather than white sugar. Mother made a stab at replying but Angela knew she was only biding her time. She was letting her babble on until such time as she chose to deliver her onslaught, and though she drank and drank Angela's mouth grew dry with nervous anticipation. She prayed for the boys to burst into the room, but they did not. She longed for Sadie to drift back in, even to sit and bite her nails and look moody, but Sadie did not appear. It has to be gone through, Angela thought, and there are no shortcuts.

'I'll never sleep,' Mother said eventually when she had finished her second half cup of extremely milky coffee, 'not after coffee in the evening.'

'You can hardly call that coffee,' Angela said.

'But it *was* coffee,' Mother said, 'and it is a stimulant, I've read it is. It will keep me awake, not that I ever sleep anyway. Your Father says I do, but I don't—I lie awake hour after hour, all night sometimes.'

'Well, you don't need so much sleep now,' Angela said, comfortingly. 'You don't use up so much energy as you get older. And you can snooze any time you want during the day, can't you?'

She had meant to console Mother but saw at once that she had only infuriated her, and that all the pent-up emotion kept at bay by the ceremony of drinking the coffee she did not want would now be released.

'But I don't want to snooze,' Mother said, thumping the chair arm with her bad hand, 'that's all I do—all day—sit and doze and that's all. What's the point, that's what I want to know—I'm no good to anyone—I'm just an old nuisance—I can't do any-thing at all—isn't it terrible—don't you think it's terrible?'

The room was very quiet. Faintly, Angela could hear the wind in the trees outside. 'You were right,' she said to Mother, who was leaning forward waiting for a reply, scarlet in the face, 'there *is* a wind getting up. I can hear it.' But Mother would not be deflected. She struggled up, and began shuffling backwards and forwards between door and window, nursing her left arm, body stiff with rage. 'I'm sick of it,' she said, 'day in, day out. I've tried to think of those less well off, I've tried to think of all the young folk who are invalids, and all those people who do things even though they are crippled—but it doesn't make any difference to me. I'm just a lump in a chair.'

'Don't,' Angela said, 'you're upsetting yourself.'

'Of course I'm upsetting myself,' Mother shouted. 'You're worse than your Father—keeping me wrapped in cotton wool.'

'I just meant,' Angela said, 'you have to face facts. It's no good complaining about them.'

She was shocked herself by the coldness of her tone. Mother stopped, abruptly. She stared at Angela, and then sat down. All that was necessary was to go over and hug her and weep together for a little while. 'You could be lying in bed unable to move,' Angela said, her voice clear and level, 'you could be blind and deaf and in a home. You're surrounded by a family who love you and you want for nothing in the way of material comfort. You can't have what you really want—you can't have a new body and a new life. There's nothing I can do to help.'

'I was always useless,' Mother said, 'never had any fight.'

'It's no good looking back,' Angela said harshly, 'or forward. You just have to live in the present. You have to live from day to day and, if things are very bad, from hour to hour.'

She was sweating—sweat ran down the back of her neck and along the inside of her dress. She looked down at herself and was surprised not to find deep stains visible. Her heart pounded and her head throbbed and yet out came those clipped, unfeeling words from which Mother recoiled. She shrank back into her chair and hunched her shoulders and her face took on a wary expression which was new. 'You're very philosophical,' was all she said, but she seemed to have lost interest in any conversation. She closed her eyes. Angela closed hers. The tears forced their way through but she let them drip unheeded. Mother was beyond paying any attention. The time for tears had passed.

In hospital, after Tim's terrible birth, Angela longed to see her other children and yet she was afraid. She did not want them to see her weak and pale-faced, barely able to lift herself off the pillows. She thought it would be too frightening for them. And so she controlled her urge to tell Ben to bring them in now, this very minute, the first moment she opened her eyes after the long anaesthetic. She waited three whole days. She waited until she was strong enough to brush her hair and put some lipstick on. She arranged herself carefully in the bed, her hands clasped lightly on the smooth covers and her legs flat underneath. She was smiling in the direction of the doorway through which Ben would bring the children long before they appeared. She imagined Sadie rushing over and hugging her and exclaiming with delight and her brothers hanging back, embarrassed and bashful. But Max and Saul came straight to her. They beamed and sparkled and kissed her and began straight away to tell her what they had been doing. It was Sadie who hung back, Sadie who looked frozen and distant. Sadie plucked at the blanket and spoke in monosyllables and avoided Angela's glance. 'Sorry it wasn't a sister, Sadie,' Angela said, 'we did try.' 'Oh, I don't care,' Sadie said. 'When are you coming home?' 'Not yet.' 'Why not?' 'I'm not better yet.' 'You look perfectly all right to me.' And how it had stung, however easily explained away. All that evening Angela lay remembering Sadie's indifference to her suffering. No tenderness, no concern, only that hostile little face and the foot tapping with impatience. A sick Mother was no part of Sadie's expectations. Angela confessed her distress to Ben. 'She didn't even ask how I was feeling,' she said. 'Even Saul asked that.' But Ben said Sadie had been silent throughout the entire week. He said he had found her lying on her bed in the middle of the day with the curtains drawn and no light on and he had asked her what was wrong. 'Nothing,' she had said, 'I'm just thinking about Mummy.' That was all. It made Angela feel much worse than she had felt before.

Angela woke long before she needed to and lay listening, as if for a baby. Faint shuffling sounds came from next door where Mother and Father had spent their first hotel night in their lives. She knew from the light that it was not yet dawn but she felt alert and ready, as though waiting to go on duty. She had told them to knock if they needed anything, knowing Trewicks always managed whether they needed anything or not, but she had tried to anticipate their every want. She had procured extra pillows, checked the bedside light worked, and as a final stroke of genius had gone to the kitchen and got them to fill a flask with tea so that if Mother woke in the night she could still have the soothing drink she was used to. A cup and saucer, milk, sugar and a sweet biscuit were all laid out on a tray within easy reach.

She heard a muffled crash and at once got up, snatching her dressing gown from the end of the bed. Trying quietly to push open the door of Mother and Father's bedroom she discovered it was locked. She tapped gently but there was no reply. Slowly she swivelled the door handle backwards and forwards hoping to attract attention, but suddenly there was the same deathly hush that there had been when she first woke—that pre-dawn quiet, that still hour in which it was so easy to imagine souls departing. No lights were on. Ear to the keyhole, she could hear nothing at all. She went on standing there for a while, shivering slightly with imagined cold, and then she went back to bed. As she pulled the sheet up over her shoulders, the first bird sang.

'Damn window,' Father said next morning when Angela went in, 'got stuck—no way to close the thing. Nearly went through the pane trying.'

'Why did you want it closed?' Angela said. 'This room is stifling—the central heating was on all night, you know, not like home.'

'Your Mother was in a draught.'

'I was not,' said Mother from her bed, 'it was you.'

'All right, Mary,' Father said, 'another thing I've done wrong. All right, lass.'

He looked tired and depressed whereas Mother glowed.

'Why did you lock the door?' Angela said. 'I could have come and helped—and you shouldn't lock doors.'

'Never know who's about,' Father said. He went to the mirror and began putting on his tie to complete his dressing. From the dressing table he could see the sea and it seemed to give him new heart. 'Grand day,' he said.

'We could go and have breakfast now,' Angela said.

'Your Mother can't—not at this time—she has to get up slowly since she was took bad.'

'I know she has—and she doesn't have to get up at all—I've ordered her breakfast to be sent up.'

'She can't be left,' Father said, 'that wouldn't be right—not in a strange place with us all down below.'

'I wasn't going to leave her—mine is coming with hers so there's nothing to worry about.'

'Oh, you shouldn't have done that,' Mother said, 'you go with the children. I'll be fine on my own.'

'No, you won't,' Father said. 'I'll stay if anyone does.'

'*I'll* stay,' Angela said.

'I don't want anyone to stay,' Mother said. 'I'll get up—I should get up anyway.'

'I've already ordered our breakfasts up here for eight-thirty,' Angela shouted, 'and it's almost that now—I can't change it—and I want to have my breakfast here.'

Father went off with Ben and the family, fully suited and immaculate, his *Daily Express* sticking out of his pocket, satisfied that Mother was being well looked after, and ready to enjoy an enormous breakfast—bacon, eggs, sausage and tomato, all fried, and the likely winners ticked between mouthfuls. His breakfast was important to him and never neglected. Even on his own he went through the whole ritual every day, filling the house with greasy fumes and only afterwards opening the kitchen window a fraction to clear air that needed a gale blown through it before the smell had any chance of shifting. Mother, with her sloppy cereal messes, had always annoyed him and Angela with her cups of black coffee was an object of ridicule. It was no good giving him lectures on nutrition—he lived by the frying pan and considered himself an advertisement for healthy eating.

The breakfast that had been brought up looked attractive, though the attraction was more apparent than real—gleaming silver dishes and pretty china somehow concealed the fact that there was very little actually on the tray to eat. Mother had bran and a boiled egg and a piece of toast with marmalade, though she was careful to say that she did not really like marmalade, she was only trying it because it was there. Angela had half a grapefruit and some toast and a whole pot of coffee to herself. She sat in a chair beside the bed with the tray she was sharing with Mother perched on the beside table between them. There was something agreeable about munching away together in silence, both eyeing the contents of the tray as though afterwards they would be tested on their ability to memorize them.

Looking at Mother concentrating so happily on her food, for once relaxed and rested, Angela reflected that she was more content than she would admit, or Father allow, in bed. She often looked as though she would like to stay there forever. Her colour was always better when she was in bed and propped up on pillows her body seemed more substantial and stronger. There was an air of peace about her which disappeared the minute she was dressed and as upright as she could get, with all the strain of being mobile showing. The effort of attempting to co-ordinate the muscles that still worked, of putting into motion the limbs that still functioned, set her face twitching and protesting and destroyed the illusion of harmony that she was looking at now. Mother struggling to move around as she was required to do was a pitiful sight—back protesting, neck refusing, legs frequently giving up. Mother in bed did not tear at the heart.

'Isn't this pleasant,' Angela said, wanting to register that there was no self-sacrifice involved. A feeble shaft of sunlight came struggling through the clouds and the net curtains to light up the pink nylon eiderdown and bathe them both in a rosy glow.

'Is it?' Mother asked, her eyes fixed as usual on Angela's face, brimming with unspoken intimacy—but this morning Angela thought they held something else, something a little sharper, a residue of Mother's bitterness the night before. She was less afraid of it simply because it was the morning.

'Yes,' she said, 'I think it is—just the peace and quiet and having breakfast brought to me even if it isn't much. There's nobody yelling at me to find shoes or books, no mess to clear up afterwards. Just no noise.'

'Oh, you'll be wanting noise before long,' Mother said, 'when all the children have gone and there isn't a sound all day and nobody to speak to you. No one wants you when you're old, nobody bothers you then.'

'No,' Angela said, but she was denying Mother's first pronouncement though she knew she was intended to take up the second, 'no, I won't be wanting noise, ever. I hate noise. I don't like that part of motherhood—I don't relish being at the centre of a hubbub and I won't hanker after it when it's gone. I'll love the solitude.'

'Will you?'

'I'll be able to get on with what I want to do.'

'If you can,' Mother said, 'if you're able and not handicapped. Not that I had anything to get on with except looking after all of you. That was all I was good for even when I was well. I never had any talents or interests, not like you.'

'Yes you did,' Angela said, 'you could sing and play the piano for a start. I can't do either.'

'Oh, that,' Mother said.

'And you could embroider and make lace—look at all the lovely things you've done—that patchwork quilt you made—'

'They don't matter,' Mother said. 'I was always useless. I've had a wasted life.'

'Look,' said Angela briskly, clattering the breakfast things together ready to be collected, her voice taking over as the edges of pain blurred in her head, 'you've had a good life—you've brought up four children beautifully and you've been a pillar of the church and the community—in no sense has your life been wasted so don't talk nonsense.'

But it was not nonsense. It was not what Mother had meant and the dishonesty of pretending that it was hurt her. Mother was right. She had been wasted. She was clever and gifted and ought not to have spent her life cleaning out grates and lugging vast baskets of washing about. She had wasted her considerable energies scrubbing floors and mending clothes. Nothing in her had ever flowered. And it could not be argued that it did not matter because she had been happy as a domestic drudge—she had not been happy. She had got herself into a trap she ought to have seen and escaped. Her powers of organization were formid-able, yet what had she organized? Her ability to work quickly and deftly was plain for all to see, but who had seen outside her family? She had thought that since her lot was marked out from the beginning it was her bounden duty to endure it and make the best of it because nothing else could be done. Angela had always known Mother was a rare bird, if doomed to fly nowhere. There was not a book in the house apart from the Bible but the breadth of Mother's knowledge was astonishing. Marrying Father, that had been her mistake, and that was a wound already probed and found still deep and bleeding.

'Look at you,' Mother said, 'what you've done.' Angela laughed out loud. 'No, you needn't laugh—you've made some-thing of yourself, you aren't just a dogsbody.'

'Rubbish,' Angela said.

'No,' said Mother, 'it isn't rubbish. You've been to college and you've read books and you're a teacher and you know what's what.'

'I don't,' Angela said.

'Don't what?' said Mother, prepared to be indignant.

'I don't know what's what,' Angela said. 'I don't know it any more than you do. It's a secret to me too.'

'Don't talk daft,' Mother said, but she laughed and so when Father marched in, checking up on them, it was a scene to gladden his heart.

Angela was always there when the children came home from school—always. With a sense of virtue she turned down all jobs that would not allow her to be in the playground by three-thirty or at home slightly later. Deliberately, she took a much less interesting job teaching English part-time in a comprehensive school rather than a more stimulating one as head of drama simply because it allowed her to be free every afternoon. She felt she had no choice. She had to be there when they all came in full of woe or joy—an hour later was too late, the tide of troubles shared had been missed. Especially where Sadie was concerned. Sadie arrived at four o'clock, red-cheeked and hungry after cycling home. Tea? Angela said. Orange juice? Crackers and cheese? And Sadie would make her choice and sit at the table and blurt out a rushed catalogue of the day's events. Angela paid grave attention to each piece of trivia. She picked Sadie's coat up from where it had been dropped, she rescued her shoes from under the table, she put her bicycle away in the shed. Her own preoccupations were firmly pushed into the background. Sadie did not want to hear them. If Sadie knew she had done something special that day, she did not inquire how Angela had got on. A Mother, Angela thought, should be there when you come home to soothe and explain and support. It is the most important function there is. But often she was left with a sense of foreboding. What was she nurturing by providing such a service? She was a soft cushion, delicious to sink into—and extremely bad for the back if sat upon too long.

Mother was far more quickly bored than the children. The rain gave way on the second day to mere dullness with the occasional burst of sunshine, but it was by no means warm enough for Mother to sit about or totter around. It was agony watching her trying to be game. They played beach cricket with Mother bravely swearing she was perfectly happy to sit on a canvas chair, surrounded by blankets and windbreaks, but it did not need Father to point out the pity of it. Even he bowled and batted and almost ran, but Mother sat staring out to sea, her hair a blob of white perched on top of a mountain of rugs. They went backwards and forwards to her, scrupulously solicitous, involving her in the score and state of play, but her smile grew more desperate and her eyes closed and Father shook his head.

They did the coast run twice—crawling along from beach to beach, the windows down, urging Mother to feel the sea air and watch the waves. They parked with the car pointing at the sea and exclaimed at the huge expanse of sand across which the horses galloped as though racing the breakers. But Mother only saw the horses as a blur and the sea as a smudge. She walked a little way towards the village but the pebbles got in her shoes and even the smallest breeze made her eyes water. 'Leave me,' she said, 'go off and enjoy yourselves—I'm holding you back,' and they stayed closer than ever, clinging to her, fearful that she would see it was true.

They went to Port Point each afternoon and parked on the green and the boys ran off to the amusement arcade with Father while Mother sat on a chair in front of the church. Almost at once she complained of cold, and worse, of boredom. 'Might as well sit in the car,' she said to Angela.

'You're getting the air better here.'

'Oh, I need more than air,' Mother said, and when Angela did not reply, 'it's more than air I need.'

Angela closed her eyes and thrust her hands further into her pockets. If it had been Saul complaining she could have told him sharply not to have been so self-pitying. If it had been Max she could have told him to get outside with his football for goodness sake. If it had been Tim she could have cuddled him. But it was Mother, and her boredom was based on fact. There was nothing for her to do. Her holiday was simply an extension of what she did anyway—she sat, she stared, she suffered.

'Look,' Angela said, noticing how very often she talked to Mother as she did to her more exasperating pupils, 'at least you're sitting somewhere different and with company—isn't that better than stuck in that room at home like last week?'

'And next week,' Mother said.

After that, they sat in total silence for fully half an hour. The church clock chimed four. Mother sighed and fidgeted. Angela did not move a muscle. Her mind raced ahead to the rest of the week, a kaleidoscope jumble of outings and activities in which Mother and she sat on numerous benches waiting for a miracle. When someone said 'Good afternoon Mrs Trewick,' Angela jumped more than Mother, who was suddenly all charm. Yes, she was on a little holiday—just a few days—with Angela and her family—yes, very nice, quite good weather, lovely hotel— oh yes, Grun House, outside Port Point, good food. Out the sweetness flooded as Mother conversed with the lady from her church congregation so elegantly on all manner of everyday topics, and as the lady departed Angela heard her say to her friend, 'Such a wonderful woman—been so ill—never a murmur of complaint . . .'

It was what Mother needed. They still did not speak, but Mother's demeanour had subtly changed. She had brightened up, was now quite eager and expectant. A bit of company had put her on her mettle and brought out the best in her. Mother had always said she liked to stay at home best but it was a lie. Mother liked to go out. She blossomed in company and was popular. People in any gathering gravitated towards her, attracted by her intelligent, gentle face that looked so uncertainly in their direction, and she responded to their interest gracefully and with dignity. Afterwards, there would be an animation about her that was otherwise lacking, and all who came within her orbit benefited from it until the lustre faded. Mother on her own at home quickly became gloomy. Turned in on herself she brooded on her own character defects and sighed over her plight. Now, when she was old and ill, her determined conviction that she hated to socialize was her undoing. The church workers offered to take her to Mothers' Union meetings in a car, but she would not go. She said she was quite happy at home. Friends suggested coming to collect her to take her to this function or that but she declined with thanks.

No more members of the church congregation appeared though Angela scanned the green hopefully. There were few people about mid-April, mid-week, at Port Point. Those who had ventured forth wandered about in an aimless way, looking at the time frequently. It was the very worst place to have brought Mother. The novelty of the hotel had quickly palled and there was nothing else to look forward to. The need for some sort of action that would convince Mother she shared in it was urgent. 'We're all quite happy here,' Ben said. 'Mother isn't.' 'But she isn't happy anywhere.' 'We have to try harder.'

Angela spent a lot of time on beaches when Sadie was small. Often, Ben would take them with him to some country where he was working and they would stay in an hotel and while he went off each morning she would go to the beach with Sadie, and Max in a carrycot. She hated beaches. Lying in the sun was anathema to her. Pale-skinned and red-headed, she never grew sunburnt attractively. But Sadie did. She was a beautiful brown within days. Sadie loved the beach—loved building sand castles (Angela hated the feel of sand), loved collecting shells (they bored Angela, who knew nothing about them and could answer none of Sadie's questions) and loved searching in rock pools for crabs (Angela was afraid of crabs). She did all the things Sadie wanted her to do and it gave her pleasure to see Sadie so happy and healthy, but secretly she wished she did not have to do any of it. She wished she was at home, but never mentioned it to Ben. He would have been sad and shocked. She could see the look of utter happiness on his face as he dropped her off each day with towels and spades and buckets and picnic—it was how he wanted his family to spend their day, an idyllic image fixed forever in his mind. And Angela told herself to try harder—to take what her child was offering with both hands and make the most of it. She must not be selfish. She must not be a kill-joy. She must not be resentful.

On the third day they went off to Bodmin Moor for the whole day. Angela announced the plan at breakfast and Mother instantly perked up. It was a long time, she said, slightly accusingly, since she had been to the moor. It would be nice to see the hills. They went off with the sky blue—'too blue' Father said, suspicious—and spirits high and a picnic in the back of the car, though Mother and Father were both appalled at the thought of eating outside, at that time of the year, with the ground sodden and every surface still coated with rain—there was no sense in it. They were honour bound to go to the moor, much beloved by Father, whose memories of jaunts to it were more numerous and sharper than any others. He followed the route with pleasure, sitting bolt upright in the car the better to see both right and left.

'This is where we came off the motorbike, eh Mam?' he said, twisting round to beam at her shortly after they were through St Breward. 'This corner here—what a smack—hit a sheet of water in that dip yonder and it was head over handlebars before I could put a brake on. What a to-do, eh Mam?'

Mother said nothing. She deliberately turned away and made a face at Sadie who sat on the other side of her. Sadie made no attempt to control her giggles, but Max took up the question.

'What happened, Grandad?'

'Oh, you'll have to ask your Grandmother that—she's the one with the memory.'

'What happened, Grandma?'

'Nothing. We came off the bike, that's all.'

'Was it a real motorbike, Grandad?'

'Course it was a real un—a Sunbeam 500 cc, grand bike, took it to the Isle of Man to the T.T. races one time, came twentieth out of a hundred and thirty—was it twentieth, Mam?'

'I don't know I'm sure,' Mother said crossly, but Father would not be put off.

'Ay, twentieth,' he said, 'but then after that to-do at that corner I sold it. It was a bad accident—your Grandma damaged her knee—miles from anywhere and nobody in sight.'

'What did you do, Grandad?'

'Oh, I don't know—what did we do, Mam?'

'Nothing, as usual,' Mother said.

They all laughed, though not quite sure of the joke. Father, not caring whether the laughter was for or against him, simply glad of a response, smirked as though he had scored a point in a complicated game. 'Nothing, eh?' he said. 'Funny we aren't still lying on that road then.'

'We would have been if it had been left to you,' Mother burst out. 'Useless, you were—heaven knows what would have happened to me if that nice solicitor hadn't come along and taken me to the doctor.'

'Oh, it was a solicitor, was it?' said Father, winking at Angela, who tried not to see.

'A real gentleman,' Mother said, 'beautiful manners, and so considerate. I wrote and thanked him afterwards.'

'There you are,' said Father, 'I knew you'd remember in the end.'

'I didn't say I'd forgotten,' Mother snapped, 'I said you did nothing as usual.'

'Wasn't much I could do lying on a road with concussion.'

'You didn't have concussion,' Mother said, spitting out the word with a contempt that took Angela's breath away. 'Concussion! A knock on the head and a cut eye. It was me that was really injured—two months in plaster with that leg and never really right ever after—and all because you couldn't look where you were going.'

'Oh no,' Father said, and the teasing had gone from his voice, 'no, lass, no—I was looking where I was going all right, no doubt about that—nobody could have seen that water in that dip that night.'

'And you were going too fast.'

'I was well within the speed limit—if I hadn't been you might have been a goner.'

'Might have been as well,' Mother said.

'Look,' Angela said, 'look at those lambs—Tim, look, aren't they sweet? Ben, stop—let's get out and look at them.'

Mother's face was red and mottled and her mouth puffed out as though she were blowing air from within and refusing to let it escape. She would not get out of the car to see the lambs—would not even look at them through the car window. But Father got out and walked the length of the field with Tim and because she was so upset Angela went a few yards from the car herself, committing the unforgivable sin of leaving Mother alone.

'Why is Grandma so angry?' Sadie said to her, as they leaned on the gate. 'What was that all about?' Angela wearily went over several explanations in her head, but the story of Father's and Mother's antagonism, and yet their devotion, was too difficult to encapsulate. She could not even begin to make Sadie see why they acted as they did, nor could she describe to her daughter why it was so much worse when she herself was with them. Mother's unhappiness and discontent flowed like a poisoned stream through the clear field of Father's fond memories flooding them with ugly, brackish cynicism that polluted his nostalgia.

'It's difficult,' she began at last, 'Grandma doesn't like to admit that—'

'Look,' Sadie said, 'there's a black lamb.'

'Was that a deliberate interruption?'

'What do you mean—I just saw it, that's all—you're so touchy.'

'I thought you wanted to discuss Grandma's anger.'

'Oh, that—it doesn't matter—it's funny, isn't it?'

'Funny?'

'Oh god—forget it.'

Sadie climbed the gate and strode off towards the others. Angela stared after her. She looked round. Behind, Mother's white head peeped above the back seat of the car. She wished she could stay all day leaning on the gate in the sunshine.

Seven

They parked and had coffee and cakes at the nearest café. Mother was not going to come in but Angela assured her it was an ex-tremely tasteful café—nice crockery—no horrid plastic tables and spikey chairs that were impossible to sit on. And Mother approved. They sat at a table in the window and guzzled. and she said 'very nice' after her Danish pastry which Angela had cut into pieces for her so that she would not spill crumbs down herself through taking too large a bite. Father did not come in. He said he had an errand to do and marched off looking important. He had not been gone five minutes before Mother, who had said 'good riddance', was saying 'where do you suppose *he's* got to?' and watching the door anxiously. 'I know where he's gone,' Ben said, 'it's a surprise.'

Father had gone to inquire if there were still horses to be hired to ride on the moor. There was no need for him to have gone ahead to ask, but it was all part of the treat. He liked to hang about the stables and watch and make deductions that could have been anticipated by a simple direct question. It puzzled all Angela's children, who had not been brought up to subservience and who could not see that there was any element of nervousness in gruff, rude, domineering Grandad. 'Why don't we ask the man?' Angela would frequently hear them saying and back would come the answer, 'No need to ask—we'll just watch and see.'

He was back, beaming, just as they emerged from the café. 'Plenty of horses,' he announced. The boys went off eagerly with him while Ben drove the others round. By the time they got there, Father had selected a horse and all three boys were fighting over who was going to ride which pony.

'Do you want to ride, Mam?' Father said, with that same awful wink he had already over-employed this morning. She turned away from him in disgust, tugging at Angela's arm, but Angela made her wait, made her sit on a seat and watch them set off. Ben and Max went first with Father and then the rest behind. They were all laughing and shrieking and countermanding Ben's orders the minute they were issued. 'Silly things,' Mother muttered.

Together, they trudged along the bridle path, Angela pausing every five yards to admire something or other in order to give Mother a chance to rest. Mother worried about getting her shoes dirty but Angela pointed out that the ground was exceptionally dry. 'For you, maybe,' Mother said, 'but when you're old you have to take care.' 'I'll get you some Wellingtons,' Angela joked, 'real gumboots.' 'I can't wear Wellingtons,' Mother said, 'not with my feet.' The seat on the side of the path was occupied. As they approached Mother said, 'People on that seat—no good hanging about—nowhere to sit.'

'There are only two people,' Angela said, 'and it is a very long seat.'

'We can't intrude,' Mother said, hanging back, 'and I don't like sharing seats anyway—come on, we'll go back—I didn't want to sit down—it was your idea.'

'Yes, it was,' Angela said, 'and it still is and we're going to sit on that seat,' and she dragged Mother towards it and the two ladies already there were perfectly charming and invited Mother to share the Dunlopillo cushion they had so thoughtfully spread along the seat and Mother had an agreeable conversation with them about damp and rheumatism and Angela had ten minutes to look around and soothe herself.

The riding party was just returning as they settled themselves once again on the bench inside the stable door. They were still making a great deal of noise as Ben attempted to manoeuvre his horse into position. 'Listen to them,' Mother said, 'what a row.'

'They're enjoying themselves.'

'Should do it quietly—disturbing folk.'

'They aren't disturbing anyone, Mother.'

'They'll come off if they aren't careful. And your Father

shouldn't be on a horse at all, not at his age. Behaving like a kid.'

'He likes horses,' Angela said, thinking she had not seen Father look so jolly for a long time.

'*I* like horses,' Mother said. 'I always liked horses, better than he did. But I know when to stop. What would happen if he fell off, eh? What would he do then?'

'Mother,' Angela said, 'they are not going to fall off.'

Nor did they. Amid cheers, Ben successfully tied his horse up and helped Grandad and the children off. They were all flushed and boastful, swearing they had ridden 'almost' across the moor, each child loudly proclaiming they had ridden the furthest and best. Even Sadie joined in, and Grandad caused trouble by saying she was the best of the lot.

'What a time you've been,' Mother said, 'we've been frozen.'

'You should have come, Grandma,' Tim said.

'Grandma can't, pet.'

'Why not? Grandad did.'

'Grandma can't manage on and off horses any more.' Tim accepted the answer without interest. If Mother had hoped to earn a 'poor Grandma' she was disappointed. He did not know Mother had always found reasons for not being adventurous. 'I can't' had been Mother's stock reply to all offers of excitement. 'I can't, I won't, I don't want to.' How Father had ever got her onto a motorbike was an impenetrable mystery.

They drove round to the other side of the moor towards Kilmar Tor, looking for a place to picnic. Angela was fussy. She would not consider a lay-by, or one of the public parking places where other people had already set up tables and chairs and were busily boiling kettles. They stopped five times and each time she got out and inspected the prospective site only to reject it as unworthy. There were loud exaggerated groans from the children. 'Does it matter where we eat?' Sadie complained, 'I'm starving.'

'So am I,' Mother said, a little defiantly. 'Grandma's hungry,' Sadie said, accusingly.

'It must be perfect,' Angela said, not to be swayed, 'sheltered and warm and secluded and with a view.'

'You'll never find it,' Mother said, 'not if you look till doomsday.'

'You leave her alone,' Father said, happy to drive on forever through the countryside he did not see enough of.

'We'll just go a little further,' Angela said.

They went much further. They left the main road and went round the back of Kilmar Tor and by sacrificing a view of Brown Gelly they found a glade the shortest possible distance from the road that satisfied all the rest of Angela's stringent requirements. Then began the laying down of ground sheets and transportation of chairs and rugs for Mother and Father and the ceremonial bearing of the picnic basket itself. Three times Angela tested Mother's chair, draped all round with car rugs, until she pronounced it snug enough for a newborn baby, and then Mother sat down (as if on a throne) still maintaining she would just as soon eat in the car, and then the unpacking of the food began. It took Angela twenty minutes to set it out on a red and white checked cloth but when she had finished they all agreed it had perhaps been worth waiting.

The sun shone, the breeze was a mere murmur, and there were no flies or wasps to disturb the calm.

'You shouldn't have bothered,' Mother said, mouth full of chicken, 'a few sandwiches would have done.'

'It was no bother,' Angela said, 'I enjoyed it.'

'All that money,' Mother said, 'the expense—chicken and prawns, they're expensive to start with.'

'We don't do it every day,' Angela said, 'this is a special treat.'

'It's very nice,' Father said, the last piece of veal-and-ham pie washed down with Guinness. 'Very, very nice. I don't think we've had a picnic like this for a long time, have we Mam?'

'Don't be silly,' Mother said, 'we've *never* had a picnic like this, you know that perfectly well. When did we ever have picnics, anyway?'

'Oh, often,' Angela said, quickly, before Father could take up the cudgels. 'I remember going to Port Point in the train with a carrier bag full of food—and sitting stuffing ourselves on the sea front.'

'Biscuits and cheese,' Mother said, 'and a hard-boiled egg.'

'Delicious,' Angela said, 'it's the eating outside that matters.'

'Then you should just have done the same today,' Mother said, 'instead of rushing round exhausting yourself getting all this spread together.'

'I didn't exhaust myself,' Angela said. 'Tea? Coffee? The hotel gave me big flasks of both.'

'Mam will have tea,' Father said.

'No I will not. I'll have nothing. I'll only want the doings if I drink anything.'

'We can stop at the next village,' Angela said, 'there's bound to be somewhere you can go.'

But she refused. She closed her eyes and put her head back on the cushion behind it. Father made a face that was difficult to interpret. Angela, heavy with the knowledge she had somehow let Mother down, began to tidy up the picnic things.

When Sadie had friends to tea, Angela sat down with them and joined in the conversation, not wanting to be a remote figure in the background who dispensed food and drink and cramped everyone's style. Sadie said nobody else's mother did that. She said other mothers just left everyone to it and she said this in such an aggrieved way that Angela was left in no doubt as to what she ought to do. But she did not do it. She sat down and talked to Sadie's friends and they responded and it was really rather pleasant. She liked getting to know them. She talked to Jane about her dog and to Laura about her year in America and to Kate and Emily about their families. Sadie tended to interrupt and show off. Angela never let her get away with an exaggeration. 'Really, Sadie,' she would say, 'you know you didn't like apple picking. You said it was boring and moaned all day because there was nothing to do stuck in an orchard.' Or when Sadie condemned an outing she had clearly enjoyed Angela would put the record straight. Afterwards, Sadie would burst into tears and say her friends would laugh at her. 'You might have agreed with me,' she would burst out, 'you didn't have to spoil what I was saying and make me look stupid.' 'You didn't have to lie,' Angela would say. 'But you should be on my side,' Sadie would shout. 'You're never on my side—always against me. Other mothers are on their children's sides.' So Angela stopped having tea with Sadie and her friends. She could not bear to be a party to her daughter's more extravagant fantasies, and equally she was not willing to pay the price of spoiling them. Sadie had challenged her loyalty and left her confused as to where it lay.

On the top of the Kilmar Tor they all collapsed onto the ground, panting and groaning with the effort of rushing the climb. The children were impressed by themselves and so Angela, disparaging their achievement to tease, reeled off the list of hills she had tackled before she was twelve, all with Grandad. That amused them—they could not imagine Grandad climbing any-thing. Angela said if it had not been for Grandma he could have climbed Kilmar Tor with them all that day.

Always, it was a case of if it had not been for Father, Mother would have done this or that, and that if it had not been for Mother, Father would have done one thing or another. But they had married, not after any whirlwind courtship but after a four-year engagement at the responsible ages of thirty and thirty-four. Mother, at thirty, had married Father because she was afraid she would never have a home or children. That was what she claimed, driven into a corner by a shrill-voiced young Angela crying 'Why did you marry him?' Not for love. She never said she loved him. She said she wanted to have children and to have children you had to get married and Father asked her. Nobody else asked her. At seven, Angela was too young to feel the pain of a confession that later tormented her—a confession Mother need not and ought not to have made to her small daughter and yet a confession she was eager to offer. Angela did not even know if it was true—oh, she did not doubt nobody else had asked Mother to marry them, but had she really no feeling for Father? A woman of such honesty, a Christian who prayed so hard for guidance? Fury had raged in Angela's heart—the desire to smash and crash the house to pieces, the dreadful urge to hit Mother, to bash her and scream at her for this humiliation, this lack of expectations, this willing-ness to take second best because nothing else was available. Thoughts of what she might have said to Father, of bargains she might have made with him, were unbearable. Father should not have accepted her terms, if he knew what they were. He should have resisted Mother, who only wanted to be a mother.

From a long way off they saw Mother and Father as they descended down the path they had climbed. They were walking backwards and forwards across the small area of even ground. Father had folded up the collapsible chairs, which rested against a giant boulder, a glaring patch of artificial colour against the greens and browns. He looked up and saw them and waved. He pointed them out to Mother and Angela knew she would be saying 'I can't see them, I can't see a thing with my eyes, no good pointing anything out to me.' But she stood leaning on Father's arm, craning upwards, and then lifted her hand in a faltering fashion and waved a handkerchief. They all shouted and yelled and waved back, jumping up and down in the air the better to be seen. 'I couldn't see you,' Mother said when they were down, 'but I heard you.'

'Well,' Father said, almost as soon as they were all settled in the car and on their way back, 'that's it. A lovely day. Thank you very much, very nice. We'll soon be back in St Erick now. How many more days have we got?'

Nobody said anything. Angela yawned. Trewicks were always home in spirit by the middle of any holiday just as they thought of Christmas on the beach in August and of Easter sweeping the snow in January. The silence seemed to annoy Father. 'Home again, home again, jiggety jig,' he said loudly, and then, 'Well, have you enjoyed your holidays, Mam?'

'Very nice thank you,' Mother said, automatically, her lips hardly moving. She had retreated into herself. Angela saw how mild and benign she was feeling—she would not react, however hard Father pushed her.

'What have you liked best, then?' Father persisted.

'Oh, everything.'

'That's not much of an answer,' Father said. His tone was dangerously jocular. 'I don't think much of that.' But Mother was quiet. 'Well,' he said, 'where shall we go next year? Eh? The world's our oyster.' Mother's continued silence and the lack of response from everyone else made him restless. He fidgeted with his seat belt and fiddled with the window. 'We could turn left here and go round that way,' he said to Ben. 'I think I'd prefer going straight back,' Ben said. 'Oh well, just as you like. You're the driver. You're the boss.' He kept quiet for a few miles and then began to whistle 'It's a long way to Tipperary'.

'Do you know that song—eh?—Max? Saul? Do you know it?'

'Yes,' Max said.

'Join in then.'

'Don't want to.'

'Nobody seems to want to do anything,' Father said, 'nobody's got much crack today. Cat got all your tongues?' When nobody replied he said, 'Like riding in a bloody hearse.'

It was very rarely that Father swore, especially in front of children. That was one of Mother's more spectacular victories. So violent did Father always seem, so given to roaring and shouting throughout her childhood, that Angela had been surprised later on to discover that his supposed foul language was a figment of Mother's imagination. Mother had made damn and hell and bloody seem foul, that was all. Any of those words made her burst into horrified tears and it was her shock and distress Angela remembered. That had not changed. The moment Father came out with his bloody, Mother shivered and frowned and pressed a hand to her mouth, the way she did when she was upset and afraid of showing it. But she said nothing.

'I don't know,' Father went on, 'we had a bit more life in us when we were young, I know that. We didn't sit like dumb ducks.'

'We're tired,' Angela said, 'the children are worn out.'

'Worn out? At their age? Good god, what with? Sitting in a car? Walking up a little hill? They don't know what being tired is. Don't make me laugh.'

He was nowhere near laughing. He was truly angry. Irritation had changed into rage so rapidly it was impossible to mark the transitional stage. Rapidly Angela reviewed the day—perhaps a quick one on the way to the stables but that was so long ago it did not count, and nor did a Guinness at the picnic. It was always drink that made Father truculent. Friday and Saturday nights and Sunday dinnertime he would come home not in the least drunk— he was never drunk—but suddenly demanding entertainment from his family. They would all try to escape. Quietly, Angela would try to slip off upstairs, but most of all he wanted her to be there. 'Sit down,' he would order, 'give us your crack.' 'Haven't got any,' she would say, sullen and a little frightened. 'Then you'd better think of some,' he would say, as Mother dished up an enormous plate of food. 'Where've you been today? Who've you seen?' he would splutter between mouthfuls. 'Eh? Come on—cat got your tongue?' She would refuse to look at him. Taking care not to let open disgust show in her face she would sit meekly at the table, eyes fixed on the tablecloth, waiting for Mother to divert his attention so that she could go upstairs to bed.

But Father had not had a drink. It was simply age fuelling his temper more effectively. His outing was over and his regret that it was, that the pleasure would not be endlessly prolonged, goaded him into attacks on everything. He needed comfort, but nobody was going to give it to him.

Sadie hated Max, or said and acted as if she did. She tolerated Saul and was reasonably fond of Tim, but she hated Max, nearest in age and her permanent enemy. It was painful to Angela to see the intensity of her hatred. Whatever poor bumbling Max did, Sadie mocked—whatever he said, she imitated. She crushed him at every opportunity and in the normal course of family life there were many such opportunities. Sometimes, Max deserved it. He could be provokingly slow and stupid, doggedly hanging on to a point long since passed. But other times, at his nicest, he was concerned and shy about expressing an opinion that showed sensitivity and understanding—and it was at those times Sadie put the boot in. 'Why do you do it?' Angela asked afterwards. 'Why are you so cruel to him?' But Sadie would make a sound of irritation and flounce out. It drove Angela into being Max's defender. When he was small, it meant opening her arms for him to run into and when he grew bigger it meant replying for him and scoring off Sadie on his behalf. She learned to know the times Sadie was going to hurt him most—that look on her face, of malice and cunning, when Max, all vulnerable and dimpled, launched into one of his ponderous sagas. And when she had defended him, Angela would catch another expression of Sadie's—catch just the tail-end of jealousy and bewilderment as she ran away in defeat. She knew it was Sadie who needed help most, but was powerless to give it to her.

Mother and Father began packing to go home the night before the second-last day.

'Might as well do it now,' Mother said, 'then it's done.'

'No sense hanging about,' Father said, 'start early and we'll have plenty of time to do it. No hurry.'

'The week isn't over yet,' Angela said, exasperated into the reaction he wanted. 'We have two whole days left. Why spoil those two days packing?'

'Doesn't spoil them,' Father said.

'Of course it does—all this thinking ahead instead of enjoying the present.'

'Oh, you have to think ahead,' Father said, 'get things done in time and that. We'd be in a mess otherwise, wouldn't we Mam?'

'Would we?' Mother said, but she was as bad as he was, always hurrying on to the next thing, constantly clearing quite clear decks.

'That case could be packed in five minutes,' Angela said, 'there just isn't any need to do it now.'

'We aren't clever like you Angela,' Mother said, 'it takes us longer. We're old and slow.'

'Oh don't be so ridiculous,' Angela said angrily, 'it's got nothing to do with being either old or slow. It's an attitude to life.'

Neither of them said anything. Father gave a small, strange smile. There was no mistaking the sly look Mother gave him, nor the pressure of Father's hand upon Mother's as he passed her some stockings to put in the case. He wanted Mother to acknowledge that sometimes she identified with him against her children. Angela had ideas foreign to both of them and he longed for this to be made plain. But Mother would go no further. 'What time will we be setting off on Saturday?' he said.

'Why do you want to know?' Angela said. 'Does it matter? You aren't catching a train or anything.'

'Oh, it matters,' Father said, 'have to get organized, have to get things in for the weekend. What'll we have for Sunday lunch, Mam? A bit of ham?'

'Not if it's like that last lot,' Mother said. 'Nasty fatty gristly stuff.'

'There you are,' Father said, happily, 'hard to please as usual. No more menus anyway—back to the kitchen. What time will you be leaving for London when you've dropped us off?'

'Oh god,' Angela said, 'I don't know and I don't care.'

'I haven't sent any postcards,' Mother said suddenly.

'Who do you want to send postcards to?' Father said.

'Nobody. I can't be bothered. But they'll expect them—Mrs Collins and all that lot. She always sends me one.'

'We'll buy some this morning,' Angela said.

'You've left it a bit late,' Father said, pursing his lips.

'I know I have.'

'There is plenty of time,' Angela said.

They bought eight coloured postcards in Port Point while the others went to the putting green. Mother protested she did not care what they were like—Angela could choose any she liked—but then she proved highly critical of those selected. She worried and fretted and frowned over which card to send to which person and then dictated contradictory messages to put on them until Angela was hopelessly confused but trying to conceal her dismay. 'Put "Have had a nice—no, pleasant—week down at Port Point—weather not too bad—no, put weather mixed—have got out and about and have enjoyed some nice runs—no, that's clumsy—put, went for an interesting excursion—no, she'll think that means on a bus—put, drove to Bodmin Moor yesterday and had a delightful picnic in beautiful sunshine." That'll do. Now, what can I say to Mrs Collins?'

'The same?' suggested Angela.

'Oh no,' Mother said, 'that wouldn't do. Oh, I can't think what to say to her.'

'Does it matter?'

'You say that about everything—of course it matters—' Mother's face was turning a dark red and her eye twitched violently, 'nothing matters to you—you're always saying "does it matter" when of course it does.'

'I only meant writing a card shouldn't upset you so. When you get a card you don't scrutinize it for hidden meanings, do you? You don't judge its literary merits. You just glance at it and look to see where it's from and that's all. Don't make it into a burden.'

'It is a burden,' Mother said, the bluster gone. 'I can't be bothered to think, that's the trouble.'

'Then *don't* be bothered—don't send any cards.'

'But people expect them, and it shows I'm on my holidays.'

'Oh, Mother,' Angela said, and managed to put her arms round her and hug her. She was very near to tears at the mess she was making of a simple job. They laughed a little together and then returned to the fray, and this time it went easier.

They finished the little stack of cards after lunch back at the hotel and then Angela made an outing of going to the Post Office along the road for stamps. Father wanted her to drive Mother there, but Mother insisted she was up to walking. She clung to Angela's arm tightly but stepped out smartly enough. For once there was very little wind and no rain and they were sheltered by the thick hedgerows that grew either side of the narrow road. Angela pointed out all the flowers hidden among them—the purple vetch and white convolvulus and even a few primroses among the wet moss at the bottom. Mother showed interest and strained to see. But when they reached the tiny shop-cum-post office she was panting and breathless and looked up at Angela with panic-filled eyes.

'I don't think I can manage back,' she said, 'your Father will be angry.'

'No he won't.'

'He was right. I can't even go for a little walk now.'

'We'll sit down for a little while,' Angela said.

'Where? Where? There isn't any seat,' and Mother began to moan slightly and look around frantically.

'I'll get one from the shop,' Angela said.

'Oh, you can't do that—'

'Of course I can'—and before Mother could stop her again, she had asked the lady serving if she could bring out a chair and it was brought willingly and at once, and Mother collapsed onto it and then Angela telephoned to Ben to bring the car. 'I'm such a nuisance,' Mother said tearfully.

When they got back to Grun House, Father was waiting, standing sternly on the steps with his arms folded across his chest. Angela glared at him, willing him to keep silent, but he said, 'You shouldn't have made her walk that far. You should have known better.'

'She wanted to walk,' Angela said.

'Never mind what she wanted,' Father said, 'you shouldn't have let her—she can't do what she wants, not in her state.'

'I thought it would do her good.'

'It will make her bad again.'

'She can't sit all her life in a chair—she has to do something sometimes, take some risks.'

'Oh yes—you can talk—and who pays the price? Eh? Who looks after her when she's ill? Muggins, that's who. You don't know.'

They had raised their voices, arguing about Mother as though she were an inanimate object while behind them she remained in the car, waiting. 'For heaven's sake don't make Mother feel guilty,' Angela said, 'she's afraid of what you'll say.'

'I should think she is,' Father said, threateningly, but his first words as he opened the car door were, 'Now don't worry, lass—nice and easy does it.'

'I'm all right,' Mother said, 'no need to fuss.'

'Nobody's fussing,' he said, but he was, handling her with even greater exaggerated care. 'The sooner I get you home the better,' he said. 'Keep an eye on you. You're not used to all this gadding about, that's the trouble, too big a change.' Mother's groan only made him worse.

Yet again, they went onto the cliff top. Yet again, Mother sat smothered in rugs on a chair in a sheltered spot with the car turned sideways to the sea to act as a windbreak though there was still no wind. Yet again they played games while she slumped before them, her eyes closed. Guilt hovered in the air with the seagulls. Their cries and screeches were a melancholy accompaniment to the concern they all felt. For a long time Father would not join in any of the sport. He stood in front of the huddle of blankets that was Mother, arms akimbo, looking down at her, studying her, twitching a cover more securely round her shoulders. She did not betray by a single word or movement that she even knew he was there. When one of the children shouted loudly 'Grandad!' he put his finger to his lips and motioned them to go away. But he beckoned to Angela, who went to him reluctantly.

'What do you think of her? he asked.

'She's tired,' Angela said, 'that's all.'

'I don't like the look of her,' Father said. Angela turned abruptly away and stared out to sea. The tide had turned and the water was rushing quite fast across the mud inlets where small boats were marooned.

'I don't like the look of her at all,' Father repeated.

'Course, it's her own fault—she knows her limit, she knew I was right, she knew it was too much before she started but then she gets these ideas and thinks she's spoiling everything and there you are. And she worries about what's going to happen—that doesn't help—I keep telling her what will be will be but it's no use. She's weary all right, but she's had a hard time, no doubt about it, what with her arm and her leg and her back's playing up but she won't say anything about it to you of course, and then she gets depressed, starts talking about dying and that though I stop that one straight away—and she misses the family, that's the biggest blow—'

'I must get Tim out of that bog,' Angela said, and ran off unnecessarily fast to where Tim was quite happily up to his knees in mud searching for a ball. Ben turned round, amazed at her feigned cries of anxiety and the game of cricket came to a stop. Angela yanked Tim out, roughly, concentrating on the look of the thing. 'Don't stop,' she shouted at the others, 'just carry on—carry on, can't you—for heaven's sake—I'll look after Tim.' She made some remark about the state of his shoes and crouched down

beside him, rubbing in vain at his legs with a handful of coarse
sea grass. 'It's only mud,' Tim said. 'I know it's only mud,' Angela
said. 'What did you shout for, then? I wasn't doing any harm.' 'I
know you weren't. Sssh.'

They walked back slowly towards Father, as slowly as Angela
dared. A pulse beat still in her temple and she put a hand up to
hold it. She tried to take deep breaths, tried to lift her thoughts
away from the crumpled figure of Mother, and Father standing
guard. But no matter how hard she focused on the clouds above
or the sea in the distance she found her gaze pulled towards the
two forlorn figures. She was taking Mother home soon, to rot by
inches, plonking her down in her miserable routine, at the mercy
of Father's all-devouring solicitude, allowing her to slip further
and further into confusion and pain. She was her daughter, her
much loved daughter upon whom had been lavished unstinting
care, and now that she was needed all she did was run away.
She thought only of escape.

'What was all that about?' Sadie said, meeting her halfway,
tired of the childish game and spoiling the game by deserting.

'Nothing.'

'You would have thought he was drowning.'

'I was all right,' Tim said.

'I know. I'm sorry.'

'You gave Grandma a fright. She opened her eyes and really
sat up. What was wrong?'

'It just got too much.'

'What got too much?' Sadie frowned and stopped. 'I don't
know what you're going on about,' she said.

Angela was tempted to say 'You soon will.' It was the sort of
dark threat Trewicks were used to muttering. 'You'll know when
it's too late,' Father used to say, asked to explain some particular
piece of adult behaviour Angela did not understand. 'When it's
too late' invariably implied death, and almost always Mother's
death. They were all going to appreciate Mother when it was too
late, or all going to help her when it was too late, or most
frequently of all be sorry when it was too late. But Sadie must
never feel what she felt now. She and Ben could never be Mother
and Father, wrapped round heartstrings and impossible to loose.
She would go out of Sadie's life whenever the time came and
Sadie would have no need of subterfuges. And so she said to

Sadie, 'Don't worry—I'm not on about anything. Forget it.'

They bought icecreams in Port Point as a farewell treat, enormous cones of soft icecream with bars of chocolate flake sticking out of them. Mother loved icecream. She wolfed the whole lot down in half the time it took the children. 'That was nice,' she said, 'only thing that eases my mouth.' 'What's wrong with your mouth?' Angela said. 'Oh, nothing—it's sore, that's all—my teeth don't fit right any more—they slop about and then food gets under and rubs—oh, my mouth is just a mess, like the rest of me.'

Mother and Father didn't have a dentist. Father still had all his own teeth, or half of them, yellow or blackened stumps but teeth all the same. Mother had no teeth at all of her own. She had had them all pulled out at the age of thirteen—she couldn't remember why. She sat on an upright chair in the front parlour with her father holding her hand. They had put her into a black pinafore and covered her lap with a rubber apron and gave her a tot of whisky which made her gag and choke. Then they prised open her pretty soft little mouth and pulled out all her teeth. She said she could not remember much about it, only her father's big warm hand firmly clasping hers and his gruff voice telling her she was a good girl. For three months she went around with a scarf round her face and was embarrassed if anyone saw her without it. She ate nothing but blancmange and bread soaked in milk and she hid from strangers even more than usual. They gave her a pair of false teeth, heavy and rough, that gripped her gums like a vice. She had had two more pairs since, each worse than the last.

'We'll see about it,' Angela said, 'at once.'

'Oh, never bother,' Mother said, passing a hand over her tired face, 'it really doesn't matter. I'm used to it. I shouldn't have mentioned it.'

'Of course you should mention it,' Angela cried, 'of course you should—all this suffering in silence—I can't stand it—it's so stupid, so—'

'Now, that's enough,' Father said, and held up his finger.

Angela had always been a good nurse. She knew how to make sick people comfortable and more important she inspired confidence. Her children felt better as soon as they had told her they felt ill. But she had a sharp eye for malingerers, and nobody malingered more than Sadie. Angela could not understand her daughter's cravenness. When Sadie had a cold, she immediately said she would stay off school though she loved school. If she had a temperature she begged for aspirin, and any sort of rash had her glued to the bed. Medicine delighted her. 'I haven't had my medicine yet,' she would remind Angela. 'The doctor said every four hours.' 'Oh don't take it so seriously,' Angela would say, but she dutifully brought the medicine and a drink and straightened the bed and Sadie thrived on her attentions. Angela could not resist saying sometimes, 'I used to drag myself to school when I was far worse than you've ever been. I didn't even use to tell my mother I felt ill.' 'How silly,' Sadie said, tartly, and Angela knew she was right.

Eight

Angela changed all their plans. Ben objected she was getting carried away but she was absolutely determined not to fail Mother in this one small respect. And so instead of dropping Mother and Father off on Saturday morning and continuing to London straight away, they stayed until the evening and the very part of the holiday she had most dreaded was painfully extended. They did not dump Mother and Father on the doorstep. They did not snatch a hasty cup of coffee and go. They witnessed the whole depressing ritual of the Trewicks' return home.

The minute they entered the house, Mother rushed across the living room floor with astonishing speed and stood ripping the days off the calendar that hung above the fireplace—six savage tears across the perforated tops leaving in her hand a clutch of screwed up paper slips.

'Well, that's that,' she said, loudly, brandishing them at Angela, 'that's my holidays done. I'll be stuck in this room for another twelvemonth likely.'

'No you won't,' Angela said, 'summer is coming—you can get out into the garden.'

'It gets too hot,' Mother said, 'too hot or too cold—it's me that's the matter, not the weather. I never feel right.'

In the background Father was shouting 'I've got the case unpacked—now do you want it on top of the wardrobe or under the bed? Eh?'—and then he began the endless recitation of all the trivial things that he claimed must be decided upon without delay.

'There's the milk tokens to get—how many?—and there's the

Parish Magazine waiting to be collected and do you want Mrs Collins in tomorrow as usual?'

'Don't care,' Mother said.

'Oh, now that won't do,' Father said, 'she'll want to know—Sunday's Sunday—you can't mess people about like that just because you've been on holiday—yes or no?'

'Oh all right, if she wants to come in, though I've nothing to say to her and she talks a lot of rubbish.'

'That may be,' Father said, 'but we have to take what we can get and after Angela's gone that's not much. Mrs Collins is regular—she's a good neighbour.'

'She's boring,' Mother said.

The children began to fight, noisily and in earnest. None of them had wanted to stop—the holiday over, home had a distinct allure. Against a background of screams and yells and Father's roars to shut up or they would feel the back of his hand, Angela telephoned the dentist she used to have at St Erick and fixed up an appointment for that afternoon. It was a huge concession, obtained only by the use of that refined way of bullying that she had learned during the last decade. 'You were rude,' Mother said, as soon as she had finished. 'They need somebody to be rude,' Angela said. 'And I'm not an emergency,' Mother said, 'the very idea—what a lie.' 'Of course you are. You've been an emergency for more than fifty years, going through agonies with those bloody teeth.' 'No swearing,' Mother said, 'and you ought to feed those children, noise they're making.' 'I've no intention of feeding them,' Angela said, 'they've stuffed themselves for a week and now they can just starve. It will do them good.'

But she sent them off with Ben, to scrounge anything they could find in the town. Mother and Father had some soup, tomato, tinned, lurid orange and nauseating but eaten ravenously. Then 'It's ten to,' Father said, and Mother went off to get ready. She took the greatest care, best dress and everything clean from the skin out. She even put on some make-up, dabs of powder high on her cheek bones and a smudge of lipstick applied with her good hand to a bunched-up mouth. Father looked pleased when she reappeared. He had always liked Mother to take care of herself, to dress up in such bits of finery as she possessed, to be the elegant lady he saw her as. 'That hat's not straight,' he said, when she was quite ready. 'You look like a drunk sailor—here, more on the back of the head, that's it, that's better. I don't know what you'd look like if I didn't keep an eye on you.' Mother stood in front of him, blinking, humble, inviting remarks.

Angela helped Mother out of the car tenderly and was curt with the girl who took her time opening the door at the dentist's. 'No need to have spoken like that,' Mother said. They sat in the waiting room for twenty minutes. Angela gathered up a pile of magazines and offered them to Mother, who refused them. 'I can't see them,' she whispered, 'I'll just sit.' 'I could read something to you,' Angela said. 'No, thank you, I'm all right.' With other people in the room Mother did not want to talk at all. She eyed those other occupants furtively and tried to sit up very straight, bolt upright, gripping the arm of the chair tightly as though it might take off. Restless, Angela paced up and down the dingy room, finding things to criticize as she went, publicly refusing to be as intimidated by the surroundings and situation. 'Good god,' she exclaimed, 'you would have thought they could empty the ashtrays—ugh.' 'I think you should sit down and leave things alone,' Mother said, looking frightened. 'Are you cold?' Angela said, 'Shall I put this gas fire on?' 'No, no,' Mother said, 'I'm quite warm—do leave things alone.'

Angela finally sat down beside Mother, though she continued to tap her foot impatiently and was ready to criticize anything else that occurred to her. Years and years of this sort of thing—of waiting rooms with Mother who treated them like holy shrines. Years of awe and dread building up into a great fear of anyone at all in a white coat. 'Keep very quiet,' Mother said before they entered the clinic with Angela's septic finger. 'Sit very straight and do what you're told.' The smell of antiseptic made her sick, but she pressed her lips firmly together and obeyed Mother's instructions. The doctor was a lady, but big and heavy with short iron-grey hair and a voice like a man. 'We'll have to lance that,' she boomed, 'disgusting state it's in. Keep still now, child, no fidgeting. I hope you're going to be brave, are you? No fussing when the needle goes in?' She fainted. Mother was embarrassed and kept apologizing. The first words Angela heard were 'I'm so sorry—she's only six—I'm so sorry—she's usually very good.' They were allowed to sit in the secretary's office for a while before they went to get the bus home and although Mother cuddled her, and exclaimed at the awfulness of the operation, Angela felt wretched because she had let her down. There were too many mortifying occasions like that to remember. Doctors, medical personnel of any kind, were gods who held your fate in cool hands. You spoke of their wisdom in hushed tones and whatever they told you to do, you did, questioning not their infinite wisdom. Second opinions were things you had never heard of, doubt a sentiment out of step with gratitude.

Mother jumped when her name was called and struggled immediately to her feet, pulling at Angela's sleeve. 'Hang on,' Angela said, 'he can wait for you just like you waited for him.' 'Sssh!' Mother pleaded. The very sight of the surgery had her genuflecting. 'Good afternoon, Mrs Trewick,' the dentist said, smiling broadly and indicating the chair, 'and Angela—my goodness, you've grown—how many years is it since you sat there in your gymslip, eh?' His laughter was loud and Angela wondered why she had never thought him coarse. Quite the reverse. She and her friends had found him exciting—none of them had objected throughout their school years to the various unnecessarily tight embraces he had adopted while drilling their teeth. They loved the squeeze he gave them as he whispered 'Just a wee rinse, now,' and the grip of his hand as he consoled them if he had hurt. Angela was proud to go to him. 'I've got a dentist,' she said at home, aged thirteen, 'I'm not going to the school clinic any more.' She had arranged it all herself, benefiting from the expertise of her new-found friends at Grammar School.

'Now what's the trouble, Mrs Trewick?' He spoke in that patronizing way Angela remembered so well—that faintly insulting though always polite tone reserved for the old, the stupid, the deprived.

'My mouth's sore,' Mother said, nervously.

'Well, let's have a look. Can you take your teeth out for me, please?'

Out they came and lay on the tray provided like fossils newly unearthed. Bits of denture powder still clung round the base of the teeth. Angela's own mouth went dry at the sight. Carefully and gently the dentist poked and prodded Mother's poor mouth and then, while she sipped the pink antiseptic solution he gave her, he examined her false teeth.

'Well,' he said, giving them a disdainful look and wiping his hands fastidiously with a brilliantly white towel, 'I don't think there is much doubt that those things are causing all the trouble. They don't fit, do they?'

'No,' Mother said.

'I don't suppose they've ever fitted. They're a scandal, a disgrace to dentistry.'

Mother's eyes began to look suspiciously watery. 'The point is,' Angela interrupted sharply, 'what can be done about it? There isn't much point in telling my Mother she's had a bad job done—the point is, what can be done about it?'

Mother's tears had been arrested at the price of horror. 'Oh, *Angela*,' she said.

'No,' the dentist said, 'she's quite right. I ought to have begun by saying there is no reason why you shouldn't be one hundred per cent more comfortable—you just need new dentures. The trouble is, the gums have receded of course and the dentures will be difficult to fit—they'll need a lot of tricky measuring and that takes time and money.'

'It doesn't matter,' Mother said quickly. She snatched her teeth from the tray and put them back in, turning away from Angela and the dentist. 'These will do me,' she said, 'they'll see me out. Let's go—thank you, thank you very much.'

'Wait,' Angela said.

'I'm not up to it,' Mother said, upset, getting worked up. 'I couldn't manage backwards and forwards—I couldn't manage all that carry on—and your Father would play war.'

'How many visits exactly would it take?' Angela asked, glaring at the dentist, who appeared taken aback by her sudden antagonism.

'Oh, three or four—say four, and a final fitting to be absolutely sure.'

'Then we'll have it done the next time I'm down and I'll bring you each time, Mother. Can we make a series of appointments now, for August, so that the whole thing is arranged?'

Mother weakened and hesitated and wondered aloud whether it was worth it but Angela had spoken so decisively it was easier to go along with her. And it was not until August. The dentist shook their hands most cordially and leapt to the door to open it for them himself.

Sadie was taken to the dentist at three months old. She lay in a carrycot while Angela had her teeth drilled. Later, she sat strapped into a pushchair and laughed at the high-pitched whine of the drill. She continued to go with Angela until she went to school and then she had her own twice-yearly appointments made for her, to which she looked forward. The dentist had a box of small plastic games and toys which he invited children to delve into after he had looked into their mouths. Sadie enjoyed picking her toy and since she never had to have anything done she did not mind opening her mouth. She would rush to the tray, ignoring the dentist, and Angela would have to remonstrate and tell her to wait and to get into the chair first. Sadie was rather off-hand to the dentist. When he asked her if she had enjoyed her holidays she would say 'Yeah, I did' and when he inquired if she liked school she would say 'of course' scathingly. As she grew older she complained he was a bore. At twelve, to Angela's alarm, something seemed to happen to Sadie's teeth—in six months she had her first three fillings. They did not hurt but Sadie blamed the dentist for making her feel uncomfortable. 'He's such a clumsy fool,' she said, and Angela worried that the dentist might have heard. He wanted Sadie to have a brace to correct the shape of her upper teeth. Sadie refused. 'The dentist knows best,' Angela said. 'Oh rubbish,' Sadie said. 'You ought to listen to him and do what he says,' Angela said. 'Why?' Sadie said, 'I don't believe I need a brace—he just wants to mess about with my teeth, that's all. I don't want a brace. I don't care what my teeth look like. You can't make me have one, nor can he.' And Angela could not. The dentist had no authority in Sadie's life.

They drove back to London at high speed with Tim asleep in the back and the others nodding off. They took it in turns driving, stopping only twice for petrol and a cup of coffee.

'I hate driving in the dark,' Sadie complained.

'We all do,' Ben said.

'Then why did we have to? Why couldn't Grandma go to the dentist another day?'

'Because she wouldn't have gone,' Angela said.

'It's made us so late,' Sadie said, 'it's such a stupid time to travel.'

'Oh shut up,' Angela said, 'all you care about is yourself and your convenience.'

'I don't see why Grandma has to be put before us.'

'No, you don't. That's the really awful thing—you really do not see why a poor old lady—'

'—oh christ, not that bit, not—'

'—and her comfort had to be put before your pleasure.'

'All I don't see is why *you* have to do it just at the wrong time,' Sadie shouted.

'Be quiet—you'll waken Tim. I have to do it because she's my Mother and nobody else will do it if I don't. Do you think I like doing it? Do you think I like holding everyone up all the time? What I'd like to do is just collapse and let you all look after yourselves—I'm sick to death of looking after everyone—thinking and worrying about parents and children—I'm sick of it.'

'Heh,' Ben said, quietly, 'calm down.'

'I'm so tired.'

'We're all tired,' Sadie said, 'and no wonder.'

'I'll drive,' Ben said, 'you try to doze. And I want everyone to be quiet—is that understood? Not a sound until we stop outside our own front door.'

'Thank god,' Sadie said.

'I said not a sound. Right. Seat belts on. No pushing, no shoving and no talking.'

But Angela could not doze. She closed her eyes and put her head back and was perfectly comfortable but her brain teemed with relentless thoughts. It was a trap. She ought to have known— she *had* known—having a mother, being a mother, they were both pledges to eternity, promises to be something impossible. She had tried so hard to break the chain but it was too tough and strong. She did not know which was worse—the agonizing pain of failing to be the daughter Mother needed and wanted and had a right to expect or the misery of failing to be the mother her daughter needed and had an equal right to expect. Nobody was satisfied with her. She could no longer hug and kiss Mother and be close in heart and spirit. She could no longer embrace Sadie, who every day retreated further and further from her and yet looked to her for everything. The cars flashed past on either side, headlights blazing, and the noise of the engine vibrated through her body and straight ahead the road stretched endlessly black and murderous.

She didn't move when at last they stopped. She sat quite still, aching, while Ben got out and unlocked the front door and put the light on in the hall and gathered up the mail from the mat. Sadie followed him in, carrying only her own bag, and disappeared into her room. Angela could hear the record player being switched on immediately and the sound of pop music floated through the night air. 'Where are we?' said Max in the back. She did not reply. He yawned and groaned and said 'oh, home' and stumbled into the house. Ben went backwards and forwards alone, heaving cases and bags and junk from car to house until a great heap of paraphernalia spilled from the door to staircase. He carried Tim in and up to bed, and guided Saul on his way. Still she sat. He finished the unpacking and came round to her side and unclipped her seat belt. 'Come on, old lady,' he said. At last, she forced herself to get out, stiff and slightly sick. The house smelled of unaired rooms and paint. She wondered what on earth had just been painted and went into the kitchen with a puzzled frown on her face.

'Well,' Ben said, 'that's over.'

'It's not over,' she said, dully, 'it just goes on and on.'

'Seeing them is over. You look fagged out. Go to bed. You've done your bit—for god's sake, forget them for a while and rest. You'll make yourself ill and then what would we all do?'

Mothers couldn't be ill—it was against the rules. She lay in bed thinking how ill she felt and telling herself she could not be ill. There was nothing in the whole world as terrifying as a mother being ill. Everything seemed to stop. There were no comforts any more. Even the table set by someone else looked wrong and upsetting—nothing was done right. Mother had not intended to frighten them all when she went into hospital—it was Father. His worry turned into anger and flew in their direction, exploding when it hit its target. It caught her unawares as she stood at the back kitchen door, flushed and happy, off to practise the nativity play at Sunday School, excited about the silver foil wings she wore as Gabriel. He shouted after her 'Get off with you then—all this hurry—rushing your dinner—get out—and pray for your Mother at that church—pray she doesn't die when she goes into the infirmary next week.' Her hand froze on the steel latch of the door. She turned back and looked at Mother washing the dishes. Mother looked guilty and apologetic. 'Pay no attention, Angela,' she whispered, 'it's nothing—I won't be in long.' Father didn't contradict her. It was one of those rare times when he had shocked himself. Nobody elaborated on what had been said. 'Bye, then' Angela said.

Angela had always refused to say that she would never die. When Sadie first found out about death at nursery school when she was four and the class guinea pig died she had not been upset. She had been intrigued. She told Angela the guinea pig was asleep forever. They all buried it in the school garden and the teacher gave a good lesson about flowers dying and coming up again. Sadie was rather surprised when the guinea pig did not come up again. But later, when she realized properly that her father had no parents, that her other grandmother and grandfather were dead and that she had never seen them and was never going to see them, then death took on a new aspect. Where were those grandparents was the most insistent of her many questions—where exactly were they? Burial appalled her. Her face went white and still at the thought of the coffin and bodies and six feet of soil (Angela concealed nothing). But the fact that her grandparents had died in a car crash helped her to accept the fact of their death—a car crash was so easily understandable, so unlike normal life. Why people died continued not to bother her so much as what happened to them after they had done so. One night in the bath she sobbed endlessly and begged Angela not to put her in a box in the ground nor to burn her to cinders. 'I won't,' Angela promised, 'I won't, I won't, but you're not going to die for years and years and years.' 'I want you to keep me beside you always,' Sadie cried. 'I will,' Angela promisèd, 'I will, I will.' At the price of total truth she had temporarily relieved her little daughter. Death no longer meant maggots and wet blackness but merely a long sleep in her own bed. Sadie talked about death a lot for a while, but in a matter-of-fact way. She told Max, when his day of fear came, that it was silly to be frightened of dying. Dying was just going to sleep. Everyone died just as everyone was born—it was natural. It only happened when you were very, very old or very, very ill or very, very hurt in a car crash. Angela had serious misgivings as she heard Sadie come out with it all so pat, but she did nothing about them. Soon enough, one of Sadie's contemporaries might die and then the whole thing would have to be gone into again. Gradually, the knowledge of what death was would come to her but Angela could not bring herself to foist it upon her.

Nobody guessed. Angela was quite startled at how little any of those who loved her and were closest to her noticed about what she felt was the dramatic change in her appearance. She felt she looked ashen. Every morning for a week when she looked at herself in the bathroom mirror she was shocked by the greyness of her skin and the huge dark shadows under her eyes. Nobody commented upon it. 'I look awful,' she said to Ben, but he looked and shrugged and said he didn't think so and that he'd seen her look much worse. The children were oblivious to her looks whatever they were, and at school, because she was only part-time, there was no one she saw regularly enough or for long enough to remark on her health. She was glad to be at home and away from Mother's and Father's eagle eyes. They would have noticed. Mother would have looked at her suspiciously, and Father would have said 'You don't look right—what's up?' They would have discussed her condition gloomily and shaken their heads anxiously.

She felt as ill as she thought she looked—nothing specific, just a terrible tiredness, a feeling of being drained of all vitality. Everything she did was a superhuman effort, which she made but did not know how. When she woke up in the morning her first thought was how wonderful it would be to get to the evening and be able to go back to bed again. She went earlier and earlier each evening until she was hard on the heels of Tim. 'This can't go on,' Ben said, 'you'll have to go to the doctor—you must be anaemic or something.' 'I've always been anaemic,' she said. 'Well, you must be more anaemic than usual, that's all. It's that awful holiday we had—it's pulled you down. You just need some iron tablets or something.'

Her own doctor was away and she felt glad—she felt less foolish before a locum when her story was so weak. She was proud of her health and of her record of hardly ever coming to see the doctor and did not want it spoiled by the hysterical nature of her complaint. 'I've got a soft spot for Mrs Bradbury,' she had once overheard him saying to his receptionist, 'she's always cheerful whatever's wrong with her.' The compliment—silly, because the doctor knew perfectly well her cheerfulness had never seriously been put to the test—thrilled her. Remembering it, she did not want to hear herself say 'I'm tired, doctor.' The world was full of women who were tired. It was a whine she hated to hear on her lips.

The locum was nervous, much more nervous than she was. He was young and raw with an alarming Adam's apple and a strong frown cultivated to make his smooth pink features more acceptable in a doctor's role. He cleared his throat rather a lot and fiddled with her medical folder in front of him and took a long time to ask her what seemed to be the matter. She felt very old and experienced in front of him. 'I'm tired,' she said, and smiled. 'I know it sounds feeble but I really am absolutely exhausted— I've got no energy at all and I'm dragging myself around. It's gone on for two weeks and it's getting worse and worse. I feel I'm going to collapse any minute.' 'Let's have a look at you,' he said, and motioned towards the couch. 'Take your top things off,' he said. He sounded her chest carefully, back and front. He looked in her mouth and ears and eyes. He asked her to cough and prodded her breasts and armpits and backbone, and every, thing he did made her feel even more stupid. 'I'll be delighted if you tell me I'm a fraud and kick me out of the surgery,' she said, but he was too young to want repartee.

She dressed and sat in front of him, not wanting to laugh in case a laugh ruffled the stern calm he was so successfully achieving.

'How old are you, Mrs Bradbury?' he asked, though her folder must quite clearly have told him.

'Thirty,seven.'

'Children?'

'Four.'

'Ages?'

'Sixteen, thirteen, twelve and six,' she said impatiently.

'Mm. You've got your hands full.'

She was growing tired of his ludicrously conventional manner.

'Periods normal?' he asked, tapping his teeth with a pencil.

'Yes,' she said. She could not actually remember the date of the last one and knew he was going to ask her. 'I can't remember the last one,' she said, 'but it wasn't long ago.'

'Are you on the pill?'

'No. I have been, but Dr Burnett took me off it for a year again, six months ago. What's that got to do with anything?'

'Could you get back on the couch?' he said. 'I'll ring for the nurse.'

Faint pinpricks of alarm danced up and down her spine and her stomach felt queasy. He gave her an internal examination, working thoroughly enough to convince her that when he grew up he would make a brutal gynaecologist. 'What's this for?' she said, 'I've just had a smear.' But he ignored her. She dressed again, flustered and irritated, wishing that after all she had waited until her own doctor came back.

'I rather think,' he said, 'that you're pregnant.'

'*What?* But I can't be—I'm still menstruating—it's impossible—
I use a cap and I know I haven't made any mistake—I *can't* be
pregnant.'

'I'm sure you are, in fact I'm quite positive you're roughly
fourteen weeks pregnant. It can sometimes happen that periods do
continue, or what appear to be periods, though in fact the flow is
greatly reduced and you probably thought you were just having a
light period, or indeed . . .'

On and on he droned, pleased to have the opportunity to use
all the information he had so recently learned, pleased too—or so
it seemed to Angela—that he could put a patient in her place. She
hated him violently. She hated the necessity of having to talk to
him at all about things she would much rather not have mentioned and now she hated his objectivity, of which he was so
proud. There seemed no humanity in him at all. She could
imagine without any difficulty the way in which he would tell
someone they were going to die. Twice a day he would repeat
to himself a little homily about the importance of not getting
involved with patients and never realize he was not in any danger.

Her hatred had distracted her from what the locum was
actually saying. '. . . no difficulty,' he ended.

'What? I'm sorry—I missed what you said.'

'I said there shouldn't be much difficulty arranging an abortion,
which is what I presume you would want.' He was smiling, she
thought condescendingly. His fingertips touched as he propped
his elbows on his desk and put his hands in a praying position.

'Oh,' she said, a funny, sharp, distinct little 'oh'.

'With four children—and at thirty-seven—and I see you had a
Caesarian last time. The only thing is we do need to move rather
quickly. At fourteen weeks the foetus is getting rather big and it
becomes quite a different sort of operation if it is left much longer.
I don't think we have time to try a National Health job quite
frankly—you really ought to be done this week. Would you like
me to ring Mr John at The Royal Foundation? Dr Burnett
usually refers patients to him.'

He was waiting, his hands now rearranging the other medical
folders for that morning. He looked at his wrist-watch surreptitiously. 'I can't think,' Angela said, and he smiled again but
got to his feet. Whatever happened, he was going to have a

surgery that ran like clockwork. She knew she was fitting in with his preconceived notions about the behaviour of middle-class, middle-aged women. 'Why don't you go home and think about it?' he said, 'then you could ring me when you reach a decision. Either way, I'll support you.' It was a quaint thing to say and made her look at him again. 'Thank you,' she said, and followed him stiffly to the door, which he opened with a courtesy that added to her confusion.

She did not go home, but went straight on to school, where she sat in the staffroom and marked books, as she had planned, over the lunch hour. It was the humdrum nature of her task that anchored her firmly to the world when inside her head she floated through the window out into the summer sunshine. She taught the fourth form with her customary vigour, surprised to hear such a firm, matter-of-fact voice coming out of a throat so dry. She went home and set the table, cut the bread, put sausages into the oven, sliced tomatoes, mixed a salad, moved to the cooker, to the cupboard, to the table, to the refrigerator, to the wastebin, backwards and forwards and sideways in her kitchen, sure of touch, firm of purpose and all around her children asking for glue, for scissors, wanting to know where tennis shoes were, swimming things, racquets, telling her the date of the school fete, of the outing to Brighton, of being in teams and plays and concerts. No pause for thought and yet the thought there all the time—I am to be a mother again.

She said nothing. She supervised supper absentmindedly and hardly spoke. Of course, she would have the abortion—of course she would. There was no choice. She felt stupid and ashamed and degraded. But what would she tell the children? Her children had to be told something. She could not, like Mother, say that she was going into hospital and that would be that. They would ask why and 'for an operation, dear' would certainly not be sufficient. They would demand an explanation as any normal child would —it was she who had been abnormal, too afraid to ask why Mother was in hospital, too terrified to ask what it was. She had gone in and out of that horrible infirmary where Mother lay, white and weak, for a whole month without ever knowing what was wrong. She still did not know. Mother never told her and she never asked. Anything to do with Mother's body, sick or well, frightened her. But her children would not show the same reticence. Any information would have to be exact. If she said she was having an abortion they would want to know what that was, and told what it was the image of bloody embryo babies burning in an incinerator would without doubt haunt their dreams, and the dangers would not elude their worldly minds.

Her head ached fiercely by the time they were all in bed. She sat in the garden sipping a large glass of lemonade watching the sun burn the brown brick wall to a ruddy red. An uncomfortable, illicit excitement made her tremble and shiver. She could have this baby. She could become a mother again. And as she sat in the half-darkness of the late May evening it came back to her how magical that time was—that eerie time when she knew she carried a growing baby without being able to feel it. She had walked through life so proudly, shooting sly looks at her own belly when no one was looking, stroking herself furtively with a sense of triumph. She ought not to be seduced by the sweetness of nostalgia, and yet there stole over her a dreamy contentment that made her smile. She could start all over again. Now that she knew what it was to be a mother she could make a better job of it. It would be a girl and what would she call her? Antonia—Rosalind—Cassia—Beth—she repeated them all to herself, a litany of ghosts.

Ben came home very late and went through the house calling her name before he found her sitting in the garden on the bench under the pear tree, her empty glass lolling drunkenly in her lap. They kissed. He took off his jacket and tie and yawned and stretched and sat beside her. 'What an awful day,' he said. She didn't ask him why. Eventually her silence penetrated his fatigue. 'You went to the doctor's,' he said, 'I forgot—what happened?' His tone was not really interested and she felt irritated by his apparent lack of concern. It was all so silly and melodramatic—she couldn't bring herself to say 'Darling, I'm pregnant.' She squirmed at the thought and got up abruptly. 'Aren't you hungry?' she said, and marched into the kitchen, head erect. 'I was enjoying sitting there,' he said, 'there's no rush. It's years since you've sat in the garden waiting for me to come home—can hardly remember the last time. Do you remember that first summer, when Sadie was born? Scorching. We lived in the garden.' He rambled on, following her into the kitchen, accepting the sandwich she made and the cheese and biscuits. 'Anyway,' he said, 'how did you get on?'

'I hate the way you ask.'

'How do you want me to ask?'

'All smug. You hadn't even remembered.'

'I did in the end.'

Still she could not find the words. She knew he would latch on immediately to the part of her news that did not matter.

'There isn't anything wrong is there? Come on, for god's sake, why all this touchiness?'

'I'm pregnant.' The viciousness with which it came out relieved her. 'I know—it's ridiculous. I'm three months pregnant.'

'But *how*?' He looked incredulous and somehow fragile when she wanted him to be strong.

'The usual way, I imagine.'

'You know what I meant.' They were suddenly enemies, glaring at each other furiously when she wanted to be comforted. She knew perfectly well it was she who was dictating the terms.

'We haven't had intercourse without taking precautions.'

'Oh don't *talk* like that—I hate it—so coy—Christ—what does it matter?'

'Of course it matters.'

'Why? Do you want to pin the blame on me?'

'Blame—don't be silly—it never entered my head to—it's just reasonable—'

'I'm not reasonable, I don't feel in the least reasonable, I don't want to hear about reason. I feel terrible and all you do is carry out an inquisition.'

He came over to her and said 'I'm sorry' and tried to put his arms round her but she shook him off.

'Don't you want to know when it will be born—shall we choose a name—I thought Antonia—what do you think of Antonia?'

'Don't, Angela.'

'Of course it will be a girl. A sister for Sadie.'

'Are you serious?'

'Well, we've got enough boys, don't you think? I *hope* it will be a girl.'

'But surely you'll have an abortion—I mean, these days it's so easy, isn't it?'

'Absolutely easy,' she said, 'you just get up onto an operating table and wham bam thank you mam out with the knife and the nasty thing cut out and thrown away. No trouble. After all, I don't want to be a mother again, do I? Not when I'm such a disaster already—not when we've learnt our lesson—we've had our fill of mothers, haven't we—'

She wept a long time. Ben soothed and hugged her and cursed his own clumsiness and said if she wanted the baby it would be lovely and she was the best mother in the world. It appalled her to discover the man she loved so dearly could find it so difficult to appreciate the turmoil she was in. She allowed him to hold her, and indeed drew the comfort she needed simply from the closeness of his body, but he was for the first time no good to her. He looked after her tenderly, he said he would make all the arrangements and all she needed to do was rest, he would take care of everything.

'There's Mother and Father,' Angela said, 'I don't want them to know—they mustn't know—I really couldn't bear it.'

'You can't just disappear,' Ben said. 'What will I do if they ring—and they will, if you don't.'

'I'll tell them I'm going on a teaching course,' Angela said. 'I've done it before.'

'Christ, as if we didn't have enough worries.'

'I can't bear them to worry about me. And the children—I don't want them to know.'

'Oh now look—'

'I can't bear them to be upset, and they would be—it's too horrible—and they might think I was—I was going to die.'

'Don't be silly.' He was angry because the thought of her in danger had never occurred to him. 'Die?' he repeated. 'There's no question of that. It's a routine operation—'

'Yes,' she said, 'quite routine. Forget it.'

Nine

She walked to the Royal Foundation Hospital, briskly, though her legs were weak. She walked through the streets busy with children rushing to school and men racing along with raincoats flying in the direction of the tube. None of them knew where she was going, or cared. She was just a woman gaily dressed in a skirt of many colours, stepping out smartly in the morning sun. The day before, Sunday, it had rained and she had been pleased—the greyness of the sky, the persistent dripping of the rain on roof and windows, both had mourned for her and cloaked her misery decently. Round and round she had gone, checking clothes for the children, organizing list after list of food to be bought and meals to be made and jobs to be done until she was dizzy with the effort of it all. But it had to be gone through—mothers did not just go into hospital, not if they could help it. Mothers could not even be ill or have an operation without intense preparation.

As she approached the large double doors of the hospital slogans and lines from hymns and poems pounded through her head. Abandon hope all ye who enter here, and she smiled. Forget the little children who cannot come unto you for they will have to manage on their own and will. She told herself to be calm, but calmness was not the problem, she was very calm, seeing what lay before her with great clarity and neither weeping nor screaming. She had been a model of calmness after the first shock. But she was afraid and could not dispel her own fear. Since everything was clear to her, nothing could be evaded—the risks had been explained to her and she understood them. There was no reason at all why this abortion should not be perfectly straightforward—no reason except that sometimes it was not. She had bled profusely after Tim's birth and that was not a good sign. And the foetus was too large to make the operation routine.

Her bag was heavy. Her arm ached, but she did not regret walking—anything to avoid a funereal procession in the car with Ben gloomy at her side. She would walk in and she was determined she would walk out—unless she came out feet first in a box. And at that wonderfully Trewick thought she burst out laughing so naturally that people turned to look at her as she crashed her way through the doors and she saw that they were wondering what could send a woman so merrily into hospital on a sunny Monday morning. Still smiling, she made her way across the enormous entrance hall to a telephone and got out her purse.

'Hello, Mother,' she said, pressing the button hard then waiting for the pips to stop. 'I'm ringing from a call box just to tell you our telephone is out of order so I won't be able to ring tonight.'

'Oh dear,' Mother said, instantly brightening, 'that's a bother.'

'Yes it is,' Angela said, 'and it's going to take at least three days to mend—something to do with a fault in the street cable. The thing is, the 'phone sounds as if it is ringing normally but we can't hear it—it's the worst kind of fault.' Baffle Mother with science and you were usually all right. 'Anyway, it can't be helped—don't you try to ring me because I'll ring you as soon as I can. Now how are you?' A question she tried hard not to ask but fell into out of nervousness. She must remember she was on a timed call and that the money would run out any minute.

'Oh, not so good,' Mother said. 'I've got a bad back and a cough—you don't want to hear my moans and groans.' In the background Father shouted, 'She's proper poorly but she won't tell you.'

'I'm sorry,' Angela said, 'perhaps you'll feel a little better tomorrow—perhaps this lovely weather will clear your cough up.'

'It isn't lovely here. It's cold.'

'Oh. Well, perhaps you'll get our sun tomorrow. I think I'm going to get cut off in a minute and I haven't any more change, so don't forget, I can't ring you till our 'phone is mended, probably Friday—' and the pips went. No time for any awkward questions, not that Mother would think of them until hours later when she was made to go over the conversation for the twentieth time by Father, and then they would feel aggrieved that she could not to go out to a friend's house or a call box to maintain the regularity of the contact with them. It might, after all, have been better to say she was going away on a course, except that then they might ring 'to see how the children are' and she did not want them dragged into her own duplicity. She replaced the dead telephone receiver, relieved. If only she could be cut off in reality like that. She gathered up her things and went to find the ward she had been told to report to, her one thought to shut out Mother's need of her.

But there was no escape from the pressures she felt crushing her. Thoughts of Mother and of her own family crowded into her head and tormented her. She lay until they brought the pre-med injection, watching the shadows gather in the corners where the white walls met the white ceiling and with every minute her resolution to think only of herself grew feebler. The only alternative seemed to be to think about what was going to be done to her—they would cut and clip and search for the huge-headed slippery pink foetus with its tiny claw hands and they would prise it out of her womb and hold it between bloodstained rubber fingers and throw it into a dish to be taken away and disposed of. She would lie there, still and white-faced, unprotesting, a sacrifice on the altar of chance. Such a brave baby it must have been to struggle through the obstacles put in its way—so strong, so worthy of life. The abstract pity of it brought the first tears to her eyes.

She stayed awake until the very moment she entered the operating theatre. In the ward, other women came to talk to her but she rudely ignored them—she wanted no interest of any kind. She would choke if she had to say why she was there and the thought of all that wearisome friendliness that could be hers for the asking repelled her. 'They hardly come near you,' she heard one patient complaining about the nurses, 'hardly ever get any of them about. Scandalous.' She was glad. She relished exactly that smiling brusqueness that others found hurtful, and did not pine for a solicitous doctor who would pat her hand and dispense sympathy. Preferably, she had not wanted to see the doctor who was going to do the operation. Meeting him the week before for an exploratory examination had been painful and she had tried hard not to learn and remember his face.

All along the corridor and into the lift she gloried in that strange drugged feeling of having let go completely—a feeling of utter irresponsibility that had never been hers before. There was nothing whatsoever that she could do. Bound to the operating trolley, her limbs languid and pliant, she felt caressed by every movement. Round and round the nurses swung her, strange attendants in dark green with a great urgency in their eyes. If they spoke, it was in low, hurried voices, without acknowledging her, and yet they handled her with respect and even awe. They stood in the lift with their backs to the wall staring straight ahead, pulling themselves in so that they did not graze even the side of her stretcher. She began to feel she was not there at all. Pleasantly, disembodied, she hovered above herself and looked down and said 'How white you are Angela, how frail and pathetic, how dreadful this ordeal is for you, my dear' and she hurried to answer 'No, no—I feel nothing—I am happy—don't be afraid for me.' She knew it must be the drug making her hallucinate but she didn't care—the dialogue came and went lazily in her head and she rid herself of a lot of things she wanted to say. The sound of a baby crying as they wheeled her out of the lift and into the anaesthetic room pierced her pleasure sharply and for an instant, before the door swung to and the sound was swallowed into her memory, she felt the most acute distress. Visions of Mother, of Sadie, of all her children and of Ben appeared before her and as she tried to raise herself from the table the attendants restrained her with expressions of the greatest concern. At her side, a new face appeared, a girl who held her wrist and gazed intently through the porthole in the door opposite, concentrating on something Angela could not see. They were all waiting, all tense. 'Can you manage?' some unseen person said. Angela wondered if the question was addressed to her and struggled to think of how to say that of course, of course she could, when the girl who held her wrist said miserably, 'I don't think so—not this one—not the first.' And then some signal must have been given. She felt a needle in her hand and the last thing she saw was the doors ahead swing open and the last thing she said was 'goodbye baby,' her lips and tongue clumsily slurring the last word.

Sadie made a great fuss of Daisy Benson, the baby next door. Whenever her mother brought her in, usually to arrange some piece of domestic trivia with Angela, who was a good if cool neighbour, Sadie would swing Daisy onto her knee and bounce her up and down and make silly noises and generally thoroughly disturb the child. She babysat for Daisy and would come back with tales of how sweet she had been and how she loved her. It surprised Angela. 'I didn't know you had that side to you,' she said to Sadie after one particularly demonstrative display, 'What do you mean?' Sadie said, on the lookout for all insults. 'Well, all that kissing and cuddling—it isn't your style, is it? You never kissed or cuddled Tim.' 'Of course not,' Sadie said. 'Why of course?—he was a baby too, every bit as lovely as Daisy, and you ignored him.' 'I didn't—you wouldn't let me cuddle him—every time I tried you said I was getting him far too excited or something. You kept him to yourself.' 'What lies,' Angela said angrily. But were they lies? She thought back to the first year of Tim's life. He was so small and weak—he couldn't be thrown around like the others— she probably had protected him too much and Sadie could be forgiven for thinking it wasn't protection so much as possessiveness. But she watched Sadie with Daisy and saw her attraction was skin deep—she tired quickly of the child if it was anything but beaming and happy. She played boisterous games but had little patience. When Sadie said, 'Oh I love Daisy—I love babies,' Angela turned away in case her own cynicism showed in her face. Sadie was a million miles from being the natural baby lover she proclaimed. If Daisy interfered with anything she valued, or if looking after Daisy interrupted anything that she was doing, then she put herself first, Daisy's charms or needs forgotten. Sadie never put herself at the bottom of any pile. There was not one shred of martyrdom in her make-up. Angela marvelled at it. She saw Sadie as a mother and knew it would be a different experience. To Sadie, motherhood would be what she chose to make of it, and not what motherhood chose to make of her. And that, Angela told herself firmly, was right. Sadie was right. Daisy lay and screamed in her pram when Sadie was in charge and Angela went and looked over the wall and saw Sadie sunbathing. 'Sadie,' she said, 'Daisy is screaming.' 'Oh, she'll stop,' Sadie said, 'I'm not going to fuss.'

'Can you hear, m'dear? It's all over. Can you hear? It's safely over.' Over, over, over—echo, echo, echo. But trapped—no movement to right or left, choking, struggling, wanting to faint when she was already prone, to vomit, to escape, groaning, panic-stricken, remembering the voice, that voice that told her it was all over but failed to bring her any comfort, that dark figure at the end of her bed that spoke soothing words yet seemed to threaten her, and those other faces round about, doing things, hurrying with something, wiping her brow, turning her over, all with fuzzy edges so that she was not sure of their reality. And then the third awakening, light-hearted, silhouettes clear and firm, the earth steady, and only a lotus-eating sleepiness to trouble her. Nurses came in and out taking readings, their profiles lovely in repose as they stood quietly holding their watches pinned to the starched white fronts of their aprons. If they just left her forever cocooned in her swaddling clothes she would be quite happy. She floated along with nothing expected of her, with no decisions to make, and instead of fretting over her children and Mother she hardly thought of them. Something had cut off inside her. She was unbelievably content.

All through the weeks that followed as she recovered from an abortion that had depleted her strength much more than it ought to have done, she thought about Operation Day lovingly. She found herself going over and over the details, following herself along the corridors of the hospital, watching over herself through the night that followed. It loomed very large in her life and in her dreams. She wanted to talk about it but nobody wanted to listen. As soon as she was home—after a mere four days—they all wanted to forget that she had been ill. She came home and went to bed and within minutes she resumed office. However much Ben roared at them all to keep *out*, Mummy was resting, in they all came, one by one, full of woes and triumphs that had to be shared. And she could not bear the look in their faces of wariness and hesitation, and that large-eyed look of innocence and pathos that turned her heart over. 'Don't worry,' she found herself saying, 'I'm fine—I'm better.' So they took her at her word. They wanted her up and busy and bossy so she got up and fulfilled their expectations. She got up much too soon, bleeding heavily and horribly weak, and staggered about the house doing everything she normally did. Alone, with no commitments, how rapidly she could have recovered. If she were childless, if she were a spinster, if she were motherless, an orphan, somewhere all by herself . . .

In the afternoons when all the children were at school and Ben had dashed into his office for a few hours she went back to bed and rested. She wished someone would come to look after her. 'Let's get an au pair,' Ben had said, 'or a mother's help—just for a while.' But she had vetoed the idea. Au pairs and mother's helps brought more problems than they solved. 'Sadie ought to be made to help more,' Ben said, 'I'm going to make her.' But she vetoed that too. She didn't want Sadie to be made to do anything—she wanted her to want to do it, out of common humanity, but there was little sign of that. Sadie responded to any abnormal situation by absenting herself. She sometimes put her head round the bedroom door and said 'Hi—feeling okay?' and Angela knew she always said, 'Yes, fine,' so what could she expect? And when Mother said 'Everybody all right?' she always said 'Fine—splendid' so what could she expect there?

What she wanted was a mother. What the whole world wanted when it was sick or ill or tired or miserable or lonely was a mother —a fit, healthy mother with no problems of her own who would come and take over. Angela lay on her bed and closed her eyes and fantasized. Some kind, capable woman of mature years who would be firm with her and stand no nonsense yet not fuss. Some lady of great calmness and serenity who could organize the household and create an atmosphere of peace and goodwill. Some female helper who would fade into the background at all the right moments but always be there to lean upon. I want the moon, Angela thought, and two tears of distilled self-pity trickled down her cheeks.

When the telephone rang her fingers moved rapidly to switch off the extension beside her bed, but on the other two telephones in the house the ringing went on and on, shattering the mid-afternoon stillness. She thought it might be Ben. Sniffing, wiping away her tears, she rolled onto her side and languidly lifted the receiver.

'Hello? Angela?' Valerie said, sounding frightened.

'Hello,' Angela said, barely able to get the word out so great was her fury at having answered at all. Who wanted Valerie, at this moment, in this frame of mind?

'How are you? I thought I'd snatch time off and ring you in the afternoon so we could talk in peace.'

'How kind. I'm fine. How are you?'

Stunned, Valerie searched for a reply. 'I'm fine, of course, but how are you really? Was it awful? I've been thinking of you ever since I spoke to Ben—did he tell you?—it sounded so frightful, you must be so upset.'

'I'm not in the least upset.'

'Oh, you must be—losing a little baby—though of course it was the right decision—'

'Why?'

'Why what, Angela?'

'Why was it so definitely the right decision?'

'Well, you've got four already—'

'People have twenty.'

'But you've never really liked being a mother, have you—I mean, really liked?'

Valerie's voice trailed away as Angela's continuing silence alerted her to the fact that she had blundered badly. When still, after a minute's pause, Angela had said nothing and the telephone hummed with tension she tried to make amends. 'What I meant was,' she said, 'you're a marvellous mother—everyone says so—anyone can see it—but you don't really relish it do you—I mean you've often said being a mother crucifies you—and there are other things you'd rather be—so I thought it was fair enough to assume you'd be glad not to have to be a mother all over again. Angela? Angela? Have I offended you? I'm sorry if I have—I only meant—'

'No, you haven't offended me,' Angela said, 'you've just appalled me, that's all.'

'What have I said?'

'Oh, never mind—for god's sake, what does it matter—I was resting, as a matter of fact.'

'I'm sorry. It's just I wanted to know how you were, and I can't ask Mother because you haven't told her, have you?'

'No.'

'Don't you think you ought to?'

'No, I don't. Ought doesn't come into it.'

'How will you manage, then, if anything happens?'

'What the hell do you mean—"anything happens"?'

'If Mother had an attack again—Father says she isn't at all well—you wouldn't be able to travel in your condition and—'

'Of course I'd be able to travel—don't talk rubbish—and all this morbid predicting of attacks and stuff—I don't want to hear it.'

'No, I'm sorry, all I meant was Mother thinks you're hale and hearty and you're not and I just wondered if—if—perhaps—are you managing all right? Would you like me to come down and help? I could get compassionate leave—'

'I do not,' said Angela, 'need compassionate leave.'

She got up after that. There was no rest possible while she remembered how viciously she had slapped down Valerie, who was only offering sympathy. She never seemed capable of giving Valerie what she wanted—those intimate sisterly chats in which confidences were given and taken. Valerie would have relished details of the abortion, would have loved that description of Operation Day she had given herself so many times. Valerie, with that hangdog look, cheeks quivering, voice wavering with the weight of heartfelt thoughts, wallowing in that same sentiment, that same mawkishness that afflicted Mother. She wanted to reject the whole package as soon as it was presented. If it had been Valerie who had had an abortion how they would all have suffered as she wept and wailed her way round the family claiming her due as an invalid. Mother would have been distraught.

The children came home to find her sitting in her dressing-gown in the kitchen peeling onions. She needed the onions for supper but they were a good cover for her despicable weak tears. 'Want a cup of tea?' Sadie asked, making one for herself, but that was all, no searching looks or questions, for which Angela told herself she ought to be thankful. No secret, fearful sidelong glances to see if she was all right, none at all like the ones she had constantly given Mother, especially once, after another un-explained spell in hospital. Mother had taken to wandering up and down at night, backwards and forwards across the tiny top landing where there was barely room to move, three paces across, three paces back, shuffling along in her pink, furry, pom-pom slippers that were loose at the heel. There was no escaping her on the way to the bathroom if one was unlucky enough to waken in the night. 'Did I waken you? I'm sorry, dear—it's the pain—if I keep moving the pain isn't so bad.' She had merely grunted and dashed back to bed, horrified, offering no comfort. Many nights she heard Mother's shuffle and thought of her pain, whatever it was, and she cringed. She pulled the blankets over her head to shut out the small sounds Mother was making. She never sympathized, never extended any offers of help. Mother must have thought she did not care. Mother must have thought her callous. Mother, at that time, was looking for a mother.

'Want a cup of tea?' Sadie repeated, and Angela tried to look behind the toss of the head and studied yawn. Sadie stood waiting for the kettle to boil, tapping the edge of the cooker with a spoon, whistling until the kettle began to whistle. She did not look at Angela—it seemed many weeks since she had looked directly at her at all. Ben had told them, in the end, what their mother's operation was for—he had respected her wish to keep it secret from the parents, but not from the children. He said Sadie had been phlegmatic. He said she had asked 'Will Mum be all right?' and when he had said but of course, perfectly all right, it was nothing, she hadn't mentioned it again. While Angela was in hospital Sadie alone had visited her and been gay and cheerful and full of breezy anecdotes. There was no suggestion Sadie worried. And yet, as Angela accepted her tea, she sensed, in the quick flicker of the eyes going over her face, a certain doubt and hesitation. She did not want Sadie to cringe as she had cringed— she did not want her privately speculating on her mother's misery and retreating from it with terror only to be plagued with guilt and remorse. 'I'm perfectly all right,' Angela said loudly, 'just a bit tired and sorry for myself.'

They used to drive, three times a year at least, down the motorway to St Erick. If they could, they set off early on Sunday morning, about seven, and so avoided heavy traffic. But occasionally they were obliged for one reason or another to go on Friday afternoon as soon as Ben returned from work and then it was impossible to escape the nightmare of a crowded M4 with all the cars jostling for position between the serried ranks of gigantic lorries on their last lap before home and determined not to give an inch. They all hated it. 'Not the motorway,' the children would cry, but it was the only sensible route to take. Inevitably, because so many other people thought likewise, the heavy traffic meant accidents. They witnessed several spectacular crashes. Worst of all, when Sadie was seven, they once had to crawl past the most horrible scene on the other side of the road. The police were there but the ambulance had not yet arrived. On the road lay a man whose head was one mass of dark-red blood. It oozed onto his chest and flowed onto the road where he lay half under a car. In spite of his injuries he was attempting to raise himself up and as he levered himself up on his elbow the blood from his head wound seemed to come from a fountain so furiously did it spurt. 'Don't look, Sadie,' Angela said, 'Don't look.' She couldn't have said anything more calculated to inflame Sadie's curiosity. Sadie clawed her way to the window, pushing aside Max and Saul, who were equally determined to see, and because the thought of Sadie's terror if she saw the spectacle before them was unbearable, Angela turned in her seat and with one violent shove pushed her onto the floor of the car where she lay screaming with the pain of banging her head. 'If you'd said nothing,' Ben said, 'she wouldn't have batted an eyelid.' 'She would,' Angela said, 'it would have kept her awake all night. I don't want her ever to have to see such dreadful things.'

Mother and Father had been curiously over-excited by the story of the out-of-order telephone. Frequently, just to assure themselves that it was now mended, they made spot checks in the weeks that followed. Barely able to crawl back upstairs to bed, Angela would hear the telephone ring and it would be Father, at ten in the morning. "Phone all right then?' he would say, and when Angela allowed exasperation to show in her voice 'just making sure it would be all right for tonight when you ring— don't want your Mother sitting here waiting and nothing happening.' She did not dare take the telephone off the hook as she wanted to do. Driven to another subterfuge to escape Father's persistence, she told Ben to say she had a cold and was staying in bed for a couple of days. Naturally, they then rang night and day to see if she was better.

'I'm fine,' she said, forced to capitulate and resume talking to them, 'it was just a cold and sore throat.'

'Maybe it was tonsillitis,' Mother said hopefully, 'you don't want to take any chances with tonsillitis.'

'It was just a sore throat.'

'Valerie's *turned* into tonsillitis,' Mother said, 'it was awful— she was off all last week with it, never been so poorly she says since her appendix.'

'Really?' Angela said, yawning, quite unable to arouse any enthusiasm for Valerie's lost appendix, which had loomed large in their childhood and now had something of the status of an historical event. For a year, it had grumbled. Every now and again Valerie would be sent home from school weeping and clutching her side, and how Mother fussed and fretted over her, quite sickeningly. She would sit for hours stroking Valerie's forehead in the most stupid useless way, and was up all night refilling hot water bottles to press to the sore side. Angela was moved to a camp bed so that Mother could sleep with Valerie 'in case anything happened'. One Christmas Eve it did. The appendix burst and Mother and Valerie went off in an ambulance, half the street watching. Mother looked noble following the ambulance men, who carried Valerie wrapped in a thick red blanket. There was a little crowd of people gathered at the gate. Mother didn't speak to them. She bowed her head in a dignified way and drew her coat about her. Angela could see how she was admired for her composure.

'You want to watch a sore throat,' Mother was saying, 'don't let it go on too long—get yourself to the doctor's if it isn't better soon.'

'Oh, it will be—I don't need a doctor. I'm fine.'

'So you say,' Mother said, 'but I know you—you don't look after yourself, you won't pay any heed even if you are ill. Ridiculous. You were always the same.'

Mother might be right. She hadn't ever given in to illness. Sometimes she had forced herself out to school when the ground upon which she walked seemed to be coming up to hit her. On those days she would lurk in the cloakroom, sitting on the shoe bench half hidden in the coats hanging down, hoping nobody would discover her and see that she was shaking and send her home. Once she was indeed found and sent home with a streaming cold that had narrowed her eyes to little red slits and she had felt humiliated. 'You?' Mother had said when she opened the door. '*You* ill? Good heavens, I can't believe it.' Angela had crawled upstairs and cried with mortification. She was the strong one. She was the healthy one. It did not suit her to be ill, with all that implied.

Nothing had changed. She hung up on Mother, with promises to take care, and began at once to organize the evening meal. There was no reason at all why she should not leave them all to fend for themselves, except that she could not do it. Her stomach still ached, the tiredness had not lifted, and she felt awful.

'I might be late tomorrow,' she said when they were all eating. 'I don't know exactly when I'll be back. Take your keys. Tim, you're going to the Bensons for tea.'

'Where are you going?' Max said, preparing not to listen to the answer, but when she said, 'To the hospital,' he looked interested. 'Why?' he said. 'What for? You're not going in again are you? Bloody 'ell.'

'No, I'm not,' Angela said, 'I'm going to the clinic for a check-up.'

'What for?'

'Oh for god's sake,' Sadie said, 'what do you think for, you fool?'

'Oh yeah,' Max said, 'for your eyes, isn't it?'

'Christ,' Sadie said, 'you are so bloody thick and stupid I could strangle you.'

'I didn't know,' Max said, 'it could have been for her eyes for all I knew.'

'I have never in my life been near a hospital about my eyes,' Angela said wearily.

'He's just a cretin,' Sadie said.

'Shut up, you fuckin—'

'Max! No swearing—now stop it—'

'—she is anyway—always showing off, thinks she knows everything—'

'At least I know—'

'I am *trying* to explain arrangements for tomorrow.'

'—bye,' Sadie said, and rushed out.

'Max, you know why I was in hospital. Daddy told you. I'm going back just so they can check everything is all right, which it will be.'

'I forgot,' Max said, not so belligerent now Sadie had gone, 'it was to have that poor little baby killed, wasn't it.'

'Killed?' Tim echoed.

'You are so thoughtless,' Angela said.

'Well, it's the truth.'

'Since when have you been so keen on truth?'

'I don't see why I shouldn't say it.'

'To spare my feelings, that's why.'

'My feelings were hurt when you did it,' Max said, 'you didn't think about my feelings, did you? Oh no.'

'Shut up,' Angela said, 'just shut up.'

Plenty of time, in the clinic next day, to think about what she should have said, about how cleverly she ought to have turned the conversation, but no, she had been brusque and impatient.

Presented with an opportunity to explain how miserable she felt she had let it go. 'Can I borrow that book?' the woman next to her said. The book was a magazine Angela was not even looking at. 'Of course,' she said, and hurriedly passed it over. 'They pass the time, don't they? When you're waiting and worrying, I mean.' The woman was very thin and pale. Angela saw she had a stick at her side. 'It's mostly the time I fret about,' the woman said, 'with two little ones at home you can't help it, can you?' 'No,' Angela said, 'you can't.' 'And I worry about what they'll say when I get in there—we all do, don't we?' 'Yes,' Angela said. 'I mean, they never take into consideration that you're a mother, do they? With their "come in tomorrow" and all that. If they say that to me again I'll just say you must be joking—how *can* I go in again?' The question hung in the air and Angela did not know if the woman wanted an answer or not. 'What are you here for?' the woman suddenly said, throwing the magazine she had flicked through onto the table. 'A check-up,' Angela said. 'I had an abortion a month ago. It's just to see everything is all right.' 'Oh well then,' the woman said, 'you're sitting pretty, aren't you? Excuse me, there's a friend.'

The woman got up, with difficulty, and went over to the other side of the room where she spoke to a bright, nervous-looking girl who looked terrified as she was approached. 'Hello, Irene,' Angela heard the woman say, 'how are you, then?' 'Fine—and how about you?' 'Not so good—it's in my leg now, in my leg and my neck.' 'I'm sorry,' the girl said, clutching her bag even more tightly to her and looking desperately to right and left. At that moment, her name was called and she leapt up and almost ran down the corridor. 'Good luck,' the woman shouted after her, but Irene ignored her. The woman began to limp back to her place and Angela realized she too was afraid of her, but it would be too pointed to change her seat. 'Nice girl, Irene,' the woman said. 'Got a baby of six months and her husband ran off when all this began.' Angela smiled politely and nodded. 'We started off together,' the woman said, 'in the same ward, but she's doing better than me. I'm a goner.' I must move, Angela thought, but could not. 'It's my kids that worry me most—I mean, what will happen to them? It's not the dying of cancer worries me, it's the kids, that's the point. What happens to kids when their mum dies?' 'I'm sure—' Angela began, wetting her lips, 'I'm sure you won't die.' 'What?' the woman said, and laughed. 'Listen, I've got hardly no chance. They think I don't know. They stood at the end of my bed and one said to the other "what kind of prognosis would you care to give?" and the other said "with that secondary in the bone marrow—well you know as well as I do". They said that—to each other, mind, then they both turned to me as if I were a dummy and said, "We're sending you home, Mrs Green." It made me sick. So I know, you see. It's a matter of time, and then what about my kids?'

There were other people looking at them, frowning, with distaste, and that hostility to the crippled woman's shrill cry for help forced Angela to try to answer when she would rather not have done. 'What about your husband?' she began, but the woman interrupted her. 'I'm divorced,' she said, 'long ago. These two of mine aren't his anyway—their father didn't want to know. I've managed on my own up to now.' 'What about your mother?' Angela said, 'haven't you a mother who would help?' 'A mother?' the woman said, 'a mother? Listen, I've got a mother. My mum is around all right—every day—sounds good doesn't it —but do you know what she says to me—she says if I got up off my backside and did something, got a bit of life into me, she says I'd soon feel better. She thinks I should just buck my ideas up instead of feeling sorry for myself. It makes you laugh— there's my mum, in hysterics because her new front door doesn't fit properly, telling *me* not to moan. She doesn't understand.' 'No,' Angela said, 'but at least she's there—I mean, you can rely on her—it's better than being without any mother at all.' 'I sometimes wonder,' the woman said, and then her name was called, and as she trailed off there was such a clear lightening of everyone's spirits that Angela was ashamed of mankind.

There was an occasion so long ago that Angela, though she could remember her feelings clearly, could not place it—yet another of those times when Ben was away and she was alone with Sadie. She woke up one morning to find every bone in her body aching and her head swimming and her skin burning. Far off, though it was only in the next room, she heard Sadie crooning to herself, all alone, happy for the moment and yet not for long. Sadie needed her. Sadie could not even get out of the cot by herself. Sadie could not change her own nappy or feed herself. Soon, the crooning changed to intermittent crying and then a strong insistent bawling.

'Ma ma ma ma,' Sadie screamed and rattled the bars of the cot. Angela struggled up and instantly collapsed beside the bed, her legs giving way underneath her in the most alarming fashion. She tried to call out to Sadie to reassure her but could only cough and croak. She lay on the floor, willing herself to get upright, telling herself over and over again to come on, come on, Sadie needs you. She managed to sit up and take deep breaths and by degrees she got onto her feet again and worked her way round the furniture to the door. She staggered into Sadie's room and at the sight of her Sadie gave a great scream of delight and began to shout 'out out out out'. But Angela could not let her out. She sat at the side of the cot and clung onto the bars. Sadie pulled her hair and bounced up and down and cried harder. She knew she must force herself down the stairs and ring someone. She left Sadie, who began to wail and shriek hideously, and began the long trek down the stairs driven by the absolute necessity of getting help for Sadie. She was her mother. She could not faint or give in or cry uselessly in the baby fashion she wanted to for her own mother. There was no possibility at all that she might give in and sleep again for a while and leave Sadie to take her chance.

Ten

It was on a Saturday, midday, with Ben and the boys watching
the football preview on television, slumped stupid and passive,
gorging crisps and drinking forbidden cokes. Sadie out—parts
unknown. And Angela wandering in the garden picking up
pears full of September wasps. The holidays had been good.
They had gone to St Erick en route for the Scilly Isles and Mother's
teeth were fixed and Father helped with the garden. They had
been cunning—four days before their real holiday and three days
on the way back, tanned and refreshed after the heat. That way,
it had not seemed too bad and their excuses each time—must
leave for the Scillies, must leave for work and school—carried
conviction. It was perhaps always the way to do it.

Angela stayed in the garden. So much of the summer had
passed her by in a daze of worry about one thing or another and
now she felt rested and refreshed. She even felt philosophical.
There was nothing she could do about Sadie—Sadie was going
her own way and grieving about it, pining for the lost intimacy
and trust of childhood was no good. There was nothing she
could do about Mother either—Mother had drowned herself in
her own misery long ago and could not be rescued. Neither of
them were really her burdens and she must not convince herself
that they were. That secret contract she imagined she had
sometime signed was not after all binding. She could be herself.
She could even sometimes think of herself first without necessarily
undermining the whole edifice of motherhood.

Afterwards, the cruelty of the telephone ringing at that precise time struck her as calculated—someone, somewhere, had been watching and chortling and rubbing their hands with manic glee. The boys did not move. Ben did not move. It would be one of Sadie's friends and it could be left to ring. She stayed in the garden, dead-heading the second crop of roses, and waited for the ringing to stop. But it went on and on and began to spoil the peace of the garden. Every window was open and since they now had two extensions three telephones were shrilling away. Angrily, she marched in. 'Can't any of you answer the telephone?' she shouted and, still angry, snatching the receiver from its cradle, 'Hello, who is it?' 'Is that you, Angela?' The football commentary blared in the background. She had already spoken—she could not pretend she was not there, she was too late to disconnect Father and take the bloody, hideous, wicked telephone off the hook.

'Father, what's wrong?'

'They've taken your Mother to hospital—ay—I know—it's a shock—always the way when you think you're out of the wood, always the same. What a blow—never thought it would come to this. It started on Thursday,' he said, his voice growing stronger as he properly began the saga, 'but she wouldn't let me ring you— Angela's just got back from her holidays, she said, she doesn't want to leave home—anyways, Thursday morning damn me what a flood—oh, it was chronic—couldn't get to the bathroom in time—stuff everywhere, and of course that upset her, then with being sick on top of it—'

'Oh god,' Angela said, weakly, 'this is awful.'

'It is that. It was awful, no denying it. All the sheets and that and the eiderdown you just took to the dry cleaner's, what a business. I had to get the doctor of course when I'd cleaned the worst up—came round and examined her and gave her something and came again yesterday but she was no better and he says I'll have a specialist to her in the morning. Go and get this prescription. Well, Mrs Collins sat with her while I went for it but it did no good, tossing and turning all night, and then the bloomin' specialist chap was here before I'd had my breakfast— just got the bacon on—damn me if the bell didn't go. Anyways, they had a look at her, the both of them, ask her questions and that—though mind you when they asked her if she ever had trouble opening her bowels she says no and that was a lie—I told them—of course she does, but she pretends—and then he says, the specialist like, we'd better have you in hospital Mrs Trewick and he 'phones from here and the ambulance was round in no time—hardly had a chance to get her things together and of course she was weeping and I couldn't find the blue nightdress she wanted or the right vests—'

He paused for breath. Angela knew he would be standing up as he always did for telephone calls. She could not interrupt him and tell him she did not wish to hear all these sordid details, nor could she risk sympathizing over the lost bacon frizzling to extinction in the big black frying pan.

'I went in the ambulance with her of course and I must say they were very considerate, very, no cheek—oh, and she's in the new part not the geriatric, and that pleased her, she's in Ward Alexandra, in a little room on her own so that suits her and I spoke to the sister and put her right and now I've just got home and got a loaf on the way and now I'll ring Valerie and then I'll have a bite to eat and then get back to the hospital to sit with her.'

'Don't exhaust yourself,' Angela said, 'it's a long way to the hospital.'

'No, it isn't—I'm not tired though I admit I was yesterday. I don't want her in that hospital. She's frightened. But it gives me a break and they might be able to do something for the poor lass.'

'Did they say what they thought it was?'

'A blockage, that's all, or an obstruction—that's what they said—that's all they told *me*.'

'I'll ring up,' Angela said. 'I'll ask to speak to the specialist.'

'Good,' Father said emphatically.

'And then I'll come down.'

'Oh no, no, no, no,' Father said, 'oh dear me no—she's in hospital now—no point in you coming—no, you wait, and see what happens—I'd catch it from your Mother if you came. She won't like me ringing either—that'll be bad enough in her book—but I told her, I can't keep it secret, Angela and Valerie want to know, I can't keep it from them. You're their Mother—they're entitled to know.'

'Of course,' Angela said, dreadfully afraid that her deep longing to know nothing of any of this might show in her falling voice. She cleared her throat determinedly. '*Of course* we want to know.'

'Well then. Now I'll get on with my dinner and strip that bed and get those sheets out again—there's a good wind and they'll dry in no time.'

'You've done very well,' Angela said.

'No choice,' Father said, 'what has to be done has to be done. But I was flagging, mind.'

'It isn't surprising. You should have got help.'

'Where from?'

'Well, the social services—'

'I spit on them,' Father said, 'wouldn't let them near your Mother.'

'You liked the District Nurse.'

'That's different.'

'She's part of the social services and—'

'They pry into everything—I don't want any truck with them, I'll manage, don't you fear, there's no need to start talking about social services, no need at all, no call for it.'

She knew she would have to go down. Half blind with misery she stumbled through the sunny kitchen back into the garden, bitterly resenting the way Ben had continued to watch the football programme without appearing to notice her distress. She would have to go tomorrow or Monday—trains were bad on Sunday. Mother needed her, lying terrified in hospital, too scared even to ask for a drink of water and trying so hard to be good. She was lying there, old and wretched, dependent on others for the most trivial things, lying wondering what the point of all this suffering was, wondering why she was deserted and alone when she had freely given such vast quantities of love and affection to others. If she didn't go, she was betraying all Mother stood for.

'Lunch!' Max called. 'Come on—it's finished—it's ten past one—we have to leave in half an hour Mum.'

Angela went obediently into the kitchen and took a casserole out of the oven. She ignored all questions. In silence she served everyone and left some for Sadie to go back into the oven. She doled out baked potatoes and broccoli and her movements were abrupt and stiff.

'What's wrong?' Ben said, rushing through his meal as fast as Max, thinking only of getting to the football ground in time.

'You may not have noticed but the telephone rang. Mother is in hospital.'

'Oh, god. What's happened now?' And as he said it he looked quickly at his wristwatch.

'I can't be bothered to go through it. Anyway, I'm going down on Monday morning.'

'Not again,' Ben said.

'I have to go.'

'What about Valerie? Isn't it her turn?'

'Passing the buck—talking about turns—it disgusts me.'

'You've just had an operation—'

'Don't be *stupid*—I haven't just had it—it's two months ago since I had it and I'm perfectly well.'

'You won't be if you go tearing down to St Erick—it exhausts and depresses you—you come back in a state and you've only just got out of one.'

'You will be late for your precious match.'

'Get your coats, boys.' There was a rush from the table. Ben put his hand over hers but she snatched it away. 'Look,' he said, 'I know you're upset and I understand the reasons but I want you to wait—wait a while and see what happens—it isn't as if your Mother is at home, she's safely in hospital being looked after—'

'I'll only go for a day and a night, to show willing. I'll spend Monday at the hospital, sleep at home, then come back on Tuesday morning.'

'We'll discuss it when I get back.'

But they never did. The minute the topic was returned to in the evening, Ben gave in. He, who did not know what filial duty was, gave into her version of it. She wished he had not. She wished he had been quietly authoritative and made her stay at home. She didn't want to look after anyone. She didn't feel strong enough. Her arms ached from holding so many heavy babies for so long and she was afraid she would drop them and they would smash to the floor and crack open their pot heads.

Sadie was a great maker—give her cardboard and Sellotape and string and scissors and she concocted the most ingenious things. All on her own at the age of five she made a harp out of a shoe-box lid and elastic bands, and a kind of usherette's tray for her dolls so that when she carried them around they could sit and look at her. Angela, whose fingers were all thumbs, marvelled at her talent. She encouraged Sadie to do more things. Whenever Sadie said, "What can I do?" Angela said, 'Make something.'

Sadie grew more and more ambitious. One day she set herself to make a puppet theatre out of two large cardboard boxes in which Angela had carried groceries home from the supermarket. Coming and going through the living room Angela saw Sadie absorbed in her task and smiled. What a glow it gave her. She wanted someone to call so that she could say casually, as they passed Sadie and saw her industry, 'Oh yes—she's always doing things like that.' All morning Sadie struggled while Angela admired at frequent intervals, but then a change came over the scene. The boxes Sellotaped together, the stage decorated, a curtain made out of a J-cloth, the puppets waiting to be displayed—and Sadie's scissors slipped making the opening at the back. The cardboard tore and wrenched the Sellotape holding the top box on and it fell off. Sadie screamed and wept. 'Never mind,' Angela said, 'look—I can mend it easily—' 'The hole is wrong,' wailed Sadie. 'I can make it right,' Angela said, 'look, look—I can put this bit back here and—' 'But I don't want it like that—it isn't mine any more—I don't want you to help me.' 'But if I don't it will be all spoiled.' 'I don't care,' Sadie said. Angela withdrew. Five minutes later she heard more screaming and when she went back into the room Sadie was stamping on the broken puppet theatre with tears streaming down her blotchy face. 'But I could have helped you,' Angela said, and cuddled Sadie, who surprisingly allowed her to do so. 'Next time,' Angela said, 'I'll make you let me help you—it's no disgrace to be helped.'

Angela walked from the station to the hospital reflecting that she never seemed to be away from hospitals these sad days. At least she was no longer afraid of them—she could cope with that queasy stomach as she went in and the claustrophobia of the corridors. She knew now how the system worked. Queen Mary's Hospital in St Erick would be no different from the Royal Foundation in Richmond except that it was smaller and newer and altogether more pleasant. She had watched it being built. Every day, on her way home from primary school, she had stopped to watch the cement mixer and to talk to the man who fed it. She had seen the foundations being dug, the bricks being laid, the plate-glass windows being fixed—it had seemed to go on forever without her ever seeing the ambulances and stretchers she had longed for. Her cement-mixer friend said hospitals were places to keep away from. She wondered why, until Mother took her to the old infirmary to see Grandma, who died there a week later. Grandma was in bed, quieter and stiffer and yellower looking than ever, moaning now and again and turning her death's-head face to and fro. To one side of her an old, old woman in a torn, stained brown nightdress was clawing at the wall, licking her fingers over and over so that the saliva would make marks, and on the other side a bald creature, whose skin was the colour of chewing gum masticated too long, sat in a wheelchair beside its bed thumping the floor with a stick. Mother did not seem to notice them. She took things out of a basket, like Little Red Riding Hood, and tried to get Grandma to look at them—at the apple tart, the lemon curd, the half dozen fresh eggs brought for her tea. Angela ran out and hid behind a door. She crouched down into herself and trembled and when Mother came and was angry she cried. 'Don't be so heartless,' Mother said, 'how *could* you—running out like that—as if you didn't care about Grandma at all.'

Mother wasn't in the geriatric ward, nor in the old infirmary, and Angela put the ghosts of both behind her as she walked up the long drive of the new hospital bordered on either side by bright red geraniums. The large windows let the sun into every cranny of the place and she smiled with pleasure at the sparkling cleanliness and cheerfulness of it. Mother, surely, would feel reassured. She would admire the glossy white paint and the polished blue floor and the sprigged curtains in shades of yellow and green that separated one bed from another. Angela looked around as she followed directions to Alexandra Ward and prepared her first words. 'This is more like a hotel,' she was going to say.

But she never spoke them. Mother was lying in a coma of incomprehension when she reached her. Alone, in a small side ward with thick dark green blinds pulled down over the windows, she lay on the high bed, her eyes shut, her face screwed up into a thousand deep wrinkles. Angela's heart began to beat loudly and irregularly. She tip-toed to the side of the bed and looked down at Mother, her pretty hair unbrushed and scraped back behind her ears, and the pain was intolerable. Fearing that she might not have the courage to stay, Angela spoke quickly, 'Hello, Mother,' she said, 'guess who.' Mother kept her eyes closed. She frowned even harder and said, 'Oh, go away for heaven's sake—bothering me.' 'That's a fine thing,' Angela said, hating her own hearty tone, 'when I've come all the way from London to see you.'

'I don't care where you've come from,' Mother said, 'just go away—leave me be—I don't want anyone.'

Angela wondered how drugged Mother was to talk so insolently, to have so completely changed character. 'Don't you know who it is?' she said. 'It's me, Angela, your ever-loving daughter—Mother, can't you hear me?'

Mother opened her eyes, those large blue eyes now bloodshot and sore, and as she looked at Angela the most glorious transformation worked in her face and joy transfigured it. They both cried. Then Angela laughed and wiped away her tears on her sleeve. 'Well,' she said, 'that was touching,' and wished she hadn't.

'Oh, Angela,' Mother said, 'you don't know what it's like lying here, just a sorry old woman.'

'At least you're in a lovely hospital,' Angela said, 'more like a hotel really. And at least you have your own little room.' The easy bit was over. Mother's spontaneous reaction to the sight of her was short-lived. Happiness drained out of her face once more leaving it haggard and weary. The reproaches, the fears, the dissatisfactions that now rushed to Mother's lips must be borne.

'It's like a private room,' Angela said.

'Nobody comes near,' Mother said, 'they just leave me. I can't even lift a glass of water but nobody cares.'

'They think rest is good for you, I expect,' Angela said.

'Rest? There's no rest here. If I do fall asleep they're at me, pulling me up and making me move when I don't want to.'

'Otherwise you'd get bed sores.'

'I've got every sort of sore. If your Father didn't come they wouldn't do a thing. He doesn't neglect me like they do.'

'But he's only got you to look after.'

'Not for much longer,' Mother said.

'I'm sure this is one thing at least that can be put right,' Angela said.

'I don't care,' Mother said, 'I just want to go home.'

'Tea, Mrs Trewick?' a nurse asked, with a nice smile.

'No,' Mother said, rudely, 'it's horrible tea.'

'Come on now,' the nurse said, 'it isn't that bad. You have to keep up your fluids, you know.' Angela saw how gently she lifted the invalid cup with its fluted spout to Mother's lips, how carefully she lifted her head. Mother took a mouthful and grimaced.

'I've got to give her an injection,' the nurse said, 'so if you'd like to wait—'

'It's my daughter,' Mother said, 'she can stay. Stay, Angela. See what they're doing to me. They might do it better if you're here.' The nurse flushed.

'I want to see the sister,' Angela said, 'this is a good opportunity, Mother. And I can see this nurse anyway is looking after you beautifully. I'll come back in a minute. Just be good.'

The sister on duty was a nasty, patronizing, fat little corporal of a woman whom Angela disliked on sight. Angela was careful not to antagonize her. She was prepared to be deferential, knowing her accent and her clothes and her whole demeanour would do their work.

'Thank you for sparing time to see me,' she said, with the kind of simpering, harmless middle-class charm she had picked up and now used shamelessly.

'It's my job,' Sister said, cutting through the cant.

'I really just wanted to know what exactly is wrong with my Mother? My Father is very vague.'

'He's been told,' Sister said.

'Well, he hasn't understood.'

'All I can tell you is there's some sort of blockage. Mr Farrar will investigate tomorrow under anaesthetic, then, if need be, he'll operate.'

'Can I see Mr Farrar?'

'He's a busy man. He won't tell you any different to what I've told you.'

'I'm sure he won't, but I'd still like to see him.'

'Then you'll have to ask his secretary for an appointment. Third floor. Second blue door on the left,' and Sister got up. 'Now if you'll excuse me, there's work to be done, if that's all.'

'It isn't quite all. My Mother does seem to feel a little neglected—I'm sure it is her imagination but I was wondering if perhaps she could be put in with other people? It might make her feel better.'

'It wouldn't make them feel better though listening to her moaning and groaning. She'll go into the ward after tomorrow anyway, and then she'll be complaining she wants to be on her own.'

'I expect,' Angela said, with her most lavish smile, 'she isn't feeling very well and that makes her irritable.'

'Oh, we all don't feel well sometimes,' Sister said, with a frown, 'and we don't all behave the same. The trouble is, your Mother is spoiled. We get old folk in here that have come from bed-sitting rooms and nobody to care for them and they weep with gratitude for how we treat them—they can't believe such kindness exists. But your Mother has been pampered—plain as a pikestaff. She's been spoiled by your Father and she expects us to spoil her too. She's forgotten how to do anything for herself.

'My Mother,' said Angela, tiring of the silly game, ready for a little rudeness if it would deflate Sister's overwhelming pride, 'has spent her whole life doing things for other people. She's never once put herself first, never even thought of herself, and now that she's old and ill and in pain I would have thought she was entitled to a little compassion instead of lectures on being spoiled.' She had spoken louder than she had intended, but Sister was not put out.

'Oh, you're another,' she said with a short bark of a laugh, 'just like your Father, wanting me to treat Mrs Trewick like royalty. Well, we can't do that but you shouldn't believe all she tells you—illness makes the old a bit funny in the head. My mother is the same, always thinking nobody cares. Off you get back to her and let us do the worrying.'

Angela went back, dutifully, knowing Sister had somehow won in spite of the stand she hoped she had made. She would not go, yet, to see Mr Farrar. Sitting in the semi-gloom, watching over Mother, who only opened her eyes now and again, she waited uneasily for Father to arrive. She had not told him she was coming, dreading the production he would make of her flying visit. She heard his footsteps right at the other end of the long corridor. When she was very young she had tried to copy Father's impressive walk. He walked like a policeman, feet slightly turned out, gait ponderous and slow. His shoes were always highly polished and very heavy with thick leather soles into which he hammered clinkers to make them last longer. Getting up to go to work in the steam laundry one Christmas holiday, Angela had been stunned to find that Father polished his shoes and everyone else's while he waited for the fire to draw properly and the kettle to boil at half past six in the morning. He sat on a little wooden stool in his boiler suit with a row of shoes in front of him and worked away at them with brushes and rags. 'You're mad,' Angela said, barely able to keep upright or open her eyes. 'Fancy doing that before a day's work.' 'Nothing wrong with it,' Father said, keeping on with the polishing, appearing quite content and even happy. Shoes were vital indicators of caring. Their shine, their whole look, told people everything you needed to know about them.

She heard his unmistakably authoritative feet and smiled slightly—the smile played about her mouth and she could not control it. 'Sssh,' she said to Mother who was making no sound, and watched the door intently. She knew what she wanted to catch—the same split-second thrill Mother had experienced. But Father was a tougher nut. He hardly gave a start, only the merest flicker of shock, and then he was saying, without any change of expression, 'I thought you'd come—I said to Mother yesterday I wouldn't be surprised if we had a visitor today when the weekend's over.'

'She shouldn't have come,' Mother muttered, 'all that way.'

'That's right,' Father said, 'play war with her.'

'Oh, she's not,' Angela said, resisting his attempt to start that awful squabbling they both indulged in, 'don't pretend she is. She's only concerned for me and I'm fine.'

'Good,' Father said. 'What do you think of her then?'

They discussed Mother's condition amicably. Angela said she had spoken to Sister and Father said 'A real bitch' and Angela agreed. She said she would see Mr Farrar if she could before she left the next day and Father was relieved. 'Once they know what's what your Mother gets treated right,' Father said, 'no doubt about it.' Angela said she was going to go to their house and eat and have a bath. Father approved. He gave her long, complicated instructions about the immersion heater and which bread to use and he handed over the front door key with dire warnings not to lose it. 'Now,' he said, as she was about to go, 'Valerie will ring. She'll be cross, mind, that you've stolen a march but it can't be helped—tell her you never told me.' 'I'll tell her,' Angela said, grimly, hating the fact that she and Valerie were always going to be assumed rivals. Father would not let them be anything else even though at their age rivalry was unseemly.

Sadie was good to Max until he was four and then she decided to hate him. 'I hate Max' she would tell strangers and when, looking at the then angelic, sweet, waif-like Max, they said it was impossible, nobody could hate him, she was emphatic. 'Yes I do,' she would say, 'I hate him. He fights all the time. He spoils everything I do and makes Mummy tired because he wakes up and cries all night.' Angela, hearing her, dreaded the outcome. She wanted her children to love each other. She tried hard to combat Sadie's antagonism but she could make no headway against the daily list of Max's crimes. The situation grew worse as Sadie and Max grew older. Sadie no longer said she hated him, but treated him with contempt. Angela did not want to become Max's champion. She wanted Sadie to love him. One Saturday when Sadie was twelve and Max ten they were going out for lunch. Everyone had been warned to be ready by twelve-thirty. At one o'clock Max still had not found his shoes and was roaring round the house looking for them while the rest of the family had been sitting in the car for half an hour. 'Right,' Ben said, 'I've had enough. He can stay at home,' and he started the car. They pulled away from the pavement and suddenly Sadie shouted, 'No—don't leave him.' 'He deserves it,' Angela said, 'he knew perfectly well he had to be ready half an hour ago—he's done this kind of thoughtless thing once too often.' 'No,' Sadie said, 'don't leave him on his own—he's scared, even in daylight. I'll find his shoes.' Which she did. Max snarled at her and accused her of hiding them in the first place and refused to be grateful but Angela went to lunch reading into Sadie's abstracted silence the deepest significance. The link was there. Nothing else mattered.

Angela felt she could be coming home from school, so exactly did she follow the same route. Always on her own. Sometimes she found herself drifting along in a group, but she was never happy about it. She walked alone but talked to herself all the way, reasoning out things that had disturbed her, selecting what was suitable for Mother to hear. Mother was always at home, knee deep in steaming clothes draped on a clothes horse round the fire, moving the dry ones to one side and the thicker, wetter towels to the middle. When they all came in from school she made a hole so that they could see the fire as they sat listening to Children's Hour. By the time Father came in, the clothes horse would be removed and the glory of the blazing fire in the black range exposed to welcome him home. Angela always felt welcomed herself. Mother kissed her and gave her milk and a scone and in the quick absorption of the homecoming atmosphere she would feel happy for a while—there was a hiatus, a hiccup in the day, as she transferred from one world to another. When the readjustment was complete, happiness fled. She was not the same girl at home. At school she was alert and willing, at home she was often sullen and disobedient. Except for Mother, there wasn't anything about home that she liked for long. She wished there were no weekends or holidays to interrupt school.

Father had left the house immaculately tidy. His stamp was on the place from the moment she opened the door. All the windows were tightly closed in spite of the beautiful weather—Father feared burglars constantly—and the curtains were half drawn. The guard was on the fire in the living room, a low fire heavily banked with small loose coals and dust to keep it smouldering until such time as Father wished to call it into life. His slippers lay in front of it, turned sideways on to catch the heat. In the kitchen, her eye saw the tray set for his supper when he came back—plate, knife, salt, pepper, cup and saucer, sugar and milk. On the grill were one and a half slices of toast already cut and spread with cheese. She opened the cupboard doors at random—all the supplies she and Valerie had bought six months ago used, only sad packets of blancmange and cheap tins of tapioca left. Former glories— row upon row of Mother's beautifully preserved fruits and jams— were nowhere to be seen and the thought of them hurt.

But nothing was scruffy or neglected. She took sheets from the airing cupboard and though they had been badly ironed and folded they were clean. She made up her old bed, noting the hot water bottles, stone cold, against the mattress—Mother kept them aired by heating them once a week. The house was very quiet except for odd ticks and creaks that had once been familiar but now were not. She used to conspire to have the house empty but now she wished that it was not—she wanted someone, even Father, to talk and break the dangerous hold of memories. There was nothing to be nostalgic about, that was the worst admission to herself. There was no time in this house she had always hated that she wanted back. Her feelings were those of misery and dread and she remembered them as she went into the bathroom. She opened the window and put the taps on and thought there was nothing she would put the clock back for except Mother's arms round her when she was small.

Whenever they came back from one of their many spells away Sadie would rush to her room and re-emerge looking pleased and relieved a long time later. 'What have you been doing?' Angela would say, annoyed that she had been struggling alone to carry in luggage or unpack bags. 'Nothing —just seeing everything was there,' Sadie would say, non-committal, almost shame-faced. Her room meant more than she was prepared to admit. It puzzled Angela that Sadie could neglect it and yet secretly care for it. Whenever she and Ben had discussions about moving as they did from time to time Sadie would protest violently. 'This is our house,' she would say, 'you can't just leave it.' 'Why not?' Angela said, pushing for the answer she wanted, 'a house is just a house.' 'It isn't,' Sadie would say. 'Why not?' 'I just don't want to leave it—it makes me feel ill to think about it.' And that was as far as Angela could get her to go, but it was far enough.

She was in her nightdress and dressing-gown when Father came in at nine o'clock.

'Nice to see a light on,' he said, 'it gets lonely on your own, very.' Since it was Father making the statement the effect was not pathetic.

'Can I get you anything?' she said.

'Oh no, no, no—I left my supper ready—no bother—a bit of toast and cheese does me in the evening these days—Valerie rung?'

'No.'

'That's strange.' He paused in the act of taking his coat off to consider it. 'I wonder what's up—she usually rings before nine because I'm usually back before then. That's odd.'

'You can hardly call it "usually" after two days,' Angela said, but Father ignored her. He went to hang his coat up and then came back to poke the fire, which sprang at once into sheets of flame, and put his slippers on.

'Why don't *you* ring her?' Angela said.

'Oh no—she said she would ring—it isn't up to me to ring her, not after she said that.' Slippers on, he put his shoes in the cupboard next to the fire, first inspecting them critically for wear and blemishes.

'You're the only person I know who puts shoe trees in shoes every time you take them off,' Angela said.

'You don't anyway,' Father said, 'anyone can see that—treat them terrible—easy come, easy go.'

'I wouldn't have the energy,' Angela said.

'Doesn't take any energy—just common sense to look after what you've got. Now if the phone rings when I'm making my supper, leave it—it'll be Valerie—I'll dash and answer it. Though mind you, her not ringing might mean she's on her way.'

She forced herself to stay while he ate his miserable snack. 'It's the anaesthetic worries me,' he said at the end of it, 'if they operate, like. I don't know if she'll be strong enough to stand it.'

'If they don't think she is, they won't do it.'

'Oh, it's all right for you to talk—shows what you know—there's more goes on in hospitals than meets the eye.'

She took it as her thought for the night. Father put the news on and did not seem to mind when she said she was going to bed. Everywhere, he saw deviousness, but how happy it made him. Unlike Mother, he kept himself occupied with the millions of possibilities people's wickedness laid open to them and he never ran out of ideas. He had always played Machiavelli to Mother's Hope, Faith and Charity. Angela remembered rushing home one day just before she left school and describing in the most graphic detail an accident she had seen in which a perfectly innocent driver had knocked down and injured a reckless cyclist. 'I must offer to be a witness,' she said excitedly, 'the driver never had a chance but nobody will believe him.' 'You do that, poor man,' Mother said, 'stand by him and tell the truth.' 'Keep away,' Father said, 'never get mixed up with the police—never volunteer to go anywhere near one of them courts.' She followed Mother's advice and her own inclination and regretted it. She had to keep going back to the police station to make statements and lost her holiday job by appearing in court weeks later and the driver she was so determined to help turned out not to have a licence so he could not be saved from trouble. And as Father had predicted she felt mixed up with the police, who looked at her too carefully and with a hostility that frightened her.

She slept well and woke late to Father already banging about. He ignored her and could not get her out of the house quick enough, which suited her very well. Though the weather had changed and it was raining she walked to the hospital again and sat with Mother before they came to take her down to the operating theatre for her investigation. When she arrived, Mother was out of bed, slumped in a chair, all huddled up with her head lolling to one side. 'They've had me here hours,' she whispered, 'not even put my slippers on and my feet are frozen.' Angela put her slippers on for her and went in search of a nurse. 'My Mother would like to get back into bed,' she said. 'Sister said eleven o'clock,' the nurse said 'and it's only quarter to.' 'But she's uncomfortable,' Angela said. 'Oh well,' the nurse said, 'we'll risk it. But Sister will be cross.'

Once she was back in bed, Mother looked better. Angela talked to her until she was hoarse. She told her things about the children, tales of her teaching experiences, anecdotes about Ben's work. Mother made no response. When Angela paused, exhausted, she said, 'May you never come to this, Angela.' 'I would be quite pleased to,' Angela said, 'if it meant I'd got to seventy-five with all my children grown up and happy and a long healthy life behind me.' Little tears began to run down Mother's cheeks.

Hardly able to cope with the nausea and trembling that had suddenly come over her, Angela bent over Mother and said, 'Mother can you hear me? I'm sorry. I didn't mean to be cruel—it's just—' she stopped. What was it 'just'? She patted Mother's hand pointlessly. 'They'll make it better soon,' she said.

She watched them wheel Mother away. Sister was brisk and sharp. 'It's only a minor job,' she said, 'won't take long. He isn't going to operate now you know, even if it is anything—he's far too busy—his list is full of major surgery today—go and get yourself a cup of tea and come back in an hour.' Obediently, Angela went, but not to the cafeteria. She went and found the river and walked along it getting soaked to the skin. Now and again she turned to look back at the hospital where Mother was being poked and prodded. It would be such a relief if she died quietly, in a tidy Trewick way, on Mr Farrar's table. She picked up a stone and stood holding it for a minute. If she could throw it to the other side, Mother would die. If she failed and the stone fell into the river, she would live. She shut her eyes and got ready to throw with all her might but her might was nothing—her arm was weak, her strength vanished. She did not throw the stone at all.

Eleven

Father was waiting for her, beaming. 'Nothing wrong,' he said, and then his face changed as he saw Angela's condition. 'Damn,' he said, 'you've gone and soaked yourself.' 'It doesn't matter,' Angela said, dully. 'Of course it matters—coming into a hospital soaked—anyways, the surgeon says it isn't what he thought and he's put her right and she'll be home in no time.' 'What does that mean?' Angela said. 'What it says,' Father said, irritable. She was robbing him of his pleasure by her dripping clothes and doubting Thomas questions.

'And Sadie rang,' Father said.

'What for?' It was uncanny how far away her own family seemed whenever she was with Mother.

'They've all been invited out after school today—says you needn't hurry back. You could get a later train.'

'No,' Angela said, 'I'll get the one I planned.'

'I just thought you could sit with your Mother longer, that's all, that's all I was meaning.'

'She'll be tired after the anaesthetic,' Angela said, 'and now she is going to be all right I can go.'

'Suit yourself,' Father said, shaking his head at the folly of a world in which his way was not seen as the best way by everyone. 'Anyway,' he said, 'Valerie's coming tomorrow.'

'Good,' Angela said. It made going much easier if Father thought her jealous.

She went up to the ward and said goodbye to Mother, who had only just come round and was sleepy. Father walked to the end of the hospital drive with her. 'It will be another long haul,' he said, 'but I'll manage somehow.'

'Yes,' Angela said.

'You'll ring this evening?'

'Of course.'

'We'll just have to keep our fingers crossed. She's had a bad time, no doubt about that.'

'Yes,' Angela said again.

They walked the rest of the way in silence. Angela shifted her overnight bag from her right to her left shoulder. Embracing him was out of the question—no physical gestures of any kind came naturally, not even the brush of her hand. 'Remember,' she said, 'I can always come again at any time if you need me. Don't hesitate.' 'I'll get the bedroom decorated while she's still in,' Father said, 'needs doing.'

'It would be better if you had a rest.'

'I can't rest, not with her in here, it will keep me busy. What shall I do it in—same again?'

'A change might be nice for her,' Angela said, 'she spends a lot of time in there. How about a pretty wallpaper?'

'Can't wash wallpaper. Emulsion's best.'

'Pink, then, the very palest pink you can find. I'll get a Dulux card on the way to the station and ring you tonight.'

'But the eiderdown's blue,' Father said, pursing his lips, 'and the counterpane. You know what she's like—will pink go?'

'Yes,' Angela said, 'the pink I'm thinking of will—it'll give the room some warmth and dark blue goes very well with it. That bright yellow is awful.'

Father walked back up the drive quite jauntily. Their hearts were full of worry and gloom about Mother and they found refuge in Dulux paint charts and discussions on shades of pink. She waved before she turned the corner and he waved back, strongly, a salute made with enthusiasm and vigour. She had done none of the things for him that she ought to have done but he was so much easier to deal with than Mother. He found comfort in euphemisms whereas she despised them. He allowed himself to be distracted from his misery whereas she clung to hers. When the time came, she would be able to deal quite easily with Father. He would reap what he had sown.

Angela knew that in so many ways she had always been too strict. She expected a great deal of Sadie in some respects. She tried to instill into her daughter habits of carefulness that went against the grain. 'Don't lose this,' she would say to Sadie, 'keep it in your pocket at school and don't lose it.' And when Sadie came home and had lost the purse and admitted taking it out of her pocket to show a friend in the playground, then Angela was angry out of all proportion to the crime. 'How could you be so stupid,' she stormed, 'when I told you—when I warned you,' and she went on and on, far too long. Gradually, Sadie became secretive. She tried to hide the fact that she had lost anything. One day, her teacher rang Angela up and said did Sadie have to dry herself with a handkerchief after swimming every week? Angela was horrified. She could not wait to meet six-year-old Sadie out of school. 'What on earth have you been doing?' she said. 'Where is your towel?' Sadie burst into tears. She cried all the way home. She cried for an hour after she had got there. Finally, in a voice thick with tears, she said, 'I knew you'd be angry—you said it was a special towel—I knew you'd be cross and shout.' The shame made Angela blush. 'Oh Sadie,' she said, and held her tight, 'it was just that it was a specially big, thick, lovely orange towel—I didn't mean—' but her voice trailed away. She had meant it, and Sadie knew she meant it, and the misery of inflicting such anxiety upon her child depressed her for weeks. Children heard what they heard and that was all.

'I'm glad your Mother is better,' her neighbour said. 'What a relief.'

'Yes,' Angela lied, 'a great relief.'

'It is amazing how well she pulls through each time.'

'Amazing,' Angela said.

'I expect you'll be going down again when she comes out?'

'No,' Angela said, 'I don't think I will.'

'I don't want to be rude—but don't you think you ought?'

'Ought?' Angela echoed, 'of course I ought, but I've my own family to think of. I seem to have been going backwards and forwards all year. I can't go on doing it.'

'But it's never for long, is it?'

No, it was never for long, but Daisy Benson's young and pretty mother who herself still had a youngish and pretty mother did not yet know how long time spent with an aged, ill relative was. Time measured out in sighs and groans, in guilt and distress, time heavy with unspoken reproaches and unconfessed regrets. Nobody realized. In the local train coming back, before she changed at Exeter, Angela had got into conversation with a woman she vaguely knew—a woman called Olive Wyatt who once lived in their street and had since moved away. She recognized Angela and asked how her mother was. She took Angela's breath away by expressing surprise that she came back so often to see her mother. 'There is no alternative,' Angela said, 'don't you find you worry about your mother all the time?' 'Good god no,' Olive Wyatt said. 'I go to see her once a year for the day and that's it— out of sight, out of mind.' 'But they're so pathetic,' Angela said, repelled by such coldness, 'and it seems so sad to treat someone who has loved you and taken care of you—' 'Sentimental rubbish,' Olive Wyatt said, and buried herself in her book.

'You didn't stay long,' Sadie said as soon as Angela got in.

'By the look of this house I stayed long enough,' Angela said, sending her anger in a direction that would be understood. 'Has nobody washed a single dish? Have none of you put a single thing away? Do I have to come back exhausted to clear up the mess?'

'Don't start as soon as you get in,' Sadie said.

'What do you expect me to do? Say thank you Sadie for looking after everything so well?'

'Okay, okay.'

'But it is *not* okay—you say okay and carry on in exactly the same selfish way and then you're annoyed when I criticize you.'

'You never do anything else,' Sadie muttered.

'That isn't true,' Angela shouted, and then she sat down suddenly and put her face in her hands, knowing such dramatic gestures only alienated Sadie more. There was silence in the messy kitchen, strewn with all manner of dishes and half eaten pieces of food. After a minute, she got up and began clearing the table. She tied an apron round her waist and began running hot water and stacking all the dirty things on the draining board. Sadie stood up and walked off.

'Sadie!' Angela shrieked.

'What?'

'Where the hell do you think you're going?'

'To do my homework of course.'

'Your homework can wait. Just come straight back in here and at least dry these dishes. The dishwasher is full.'

'Why should I? Max is—'

'I don't want any discussion—just do it—here's a cloth—stand there and dry them quickly and properly before I collapse.'

The steam rose from the sink of hot soapsuds and inflamed Angela's cheeks. She plunged her rubber-gloved hands into the water and washed the dishes methodically, finding the routine task something that soothed her, as she always did. Sadie took hold of saucers she had just washed and ignored plates that had been done first and Angela imprisoned the rest of the saucers with one hand and said, 'It is only common sense to dry things that have already drained a little.' Sadie took the plates, four at a time. 'Nobody,' Angela said, 'can dry four plates at a time—take them one at a time please.' Eventually, they were finished. Sadie put the cloth down and began to walk out of the kitchen. 'Those dishes,' Angela said, 'do not stay in a heap there. They need to be put in their places.' Sulkily, Sadie put them away, crashing them against each other as much as she safely could. 'Is that all?' she said.

'Do you think it is?' Angela said. 'Looking round this kitchen would you say that was all?'

'You're so bloody sarcastic.'

'And you're so bloody inconsiderate.'

'Thanks,' Sadie said, and went.

The mystery of how she could moved Angela to despair. She worked away cleaning the kitchen, reflecting all the time that in wishing to free Sadie from the stifling constraints of duty, she had let loose a creature who was so selfish nothing could arouse her pity—nothing, at least, about her mother. With everything that was bad Angela felt she had also thrown out everything that was good. She had not wanted to be her daughter's responsibility as Mother had been hers—and she was not. Her daughter saw her as strong and independent. She had not wanted to live through her daughter as Mother had lived through her—and she did not. She had wanted her daughter to treat her as an equal, and she did, but for the life of her Angela could not see that this was a victory. She felt defeated, driven into the ground. And it must be her fault.

Unhappiness made her silent. She welcomed the boys back mournfully and Ben with a listless smile. Throughout the evening meal she had eyes only for Sadie, who seemed oblivious to any tension. She ate and drank and warned herself not to accuse by implication—not to shoot reproachful glances at Sadie as Mother had done at her, not to use pathos as a weapon.

'Can I have a party?' Sadie said, with no preamble.

'A fine time to ask,' Ben said, 'when your mother has just got back from an exhausting trip.'

'That's all right.' Angela said quickly: 'Of course you can have a party. I've always loved your parties.' And she had—for years she had given Sadie wonderful parties, imaginative and well organized, the envy of the neighbourhood. Sadie winced. 'The only thing is,' she said, 'I'd like to do it myself this time—I mean, I wouldn't want you there.'

'That sounds like a good idea,' Angela said carefully.

'I don't want the boys either. I'd like the house empty. I couldn't have the sort of party I want with the boys here—it spoils it.'

'How does it spoil it?'

'I don't want to go on about it—I just want the house empty. Can't you take them away somewhere?'

'For your convenience?'

'Okay, okay. Forget it. I won't have a party. It doesn't matter.'

'Don't be petty—of course you can have one—it's just I don't see how I can get rid of three boys without a great deal of bother. Couldn't I just guarantee that they all stay on the top floor?'

'For god's sake don't try and persuade her,' Ben said.

'I suppose so,' Sadie said, grudgingly. 'But there'll be a lot of noise—they might not sleep—it wouldn't be any good them complaining. And you're not going to say no drinking or smoking are you?'

'Certainly I am,' Ben said.

'What kind of party is this?' Angela said.

'Just the kind everyone has. I'd clear up the mess and everything. You wouldn't have to do anything. But I need the house.'

'How many people are you thinking of inviting?' Angela said.

'I want to see the invitations,' Ben said.

'There won't *be* invitations—it isn't that sort of party—you just tell people and they come.'

'I could cook pizzas,' Angela offered.

'No,' Sadie said, 'it would be a waste of time. They'd only get stood on. I don't want any proper food.'

'And I don't want any proper drink,' Ben said.

'Beer's harmless,' Sadie said, 'and cider and a fruit punch—I can have that can't I?'

'I suppose so,' Angela said.

'I'll clear the ground floor,' Sadie said, 'and we won't let anyone go upstairs. Where can I put the lampshades and pictures and big things like rugs?'

'But why do you have to move lampshades?'

'They might get broken—it's best to have as little stuff about as possible. It's for your sake, you know—it's your things I'm protecting.'

'What are you bothering with a party for?' Mother said on the telephone, 'you spoil that girl.' Mother, newly out of hospital, was peevish. For the last two weeks Angela had filled out the minutes with details of Sadie's approaching party, hoping it would entertain Mother but it did not—it annoyed her.

'I won't be doing anything so it's no bother,' Angela said.

'You never had parties,' Mother said, accusingly, 'not at that age.'

'No,' said Angela, 'but Sadie isn't me. She likes parties.'

'With boys?'

'Oh yes—that's the point.'

'I think it's scandalous,' Mother said emphatically, 'carrying on like that—at her age—with boys and that—you never bothered. I just hope nothing happens, that's all. Your Father says something is sure to happen.'

'What does he mean?' Angela said, knowing perfectly well, knowing Mother would never let the words past her lips.

'Oh, something, likely,' Mother said, 'bound to be something with boys around.'

They meant Sadie might become pregnant. Something Will Happen had always meant that. Now that she had been respectably married for so long they had forgotten it was the prophecy they had made to her. They were sure, now, that she had never been interested in 'that kind of thing' but they had not been so sure when she was eighteen. Mother lived in mortal terror of anything, never mind something, happening. Every time Angela came home from the most innocent of outings Mother's worried face spoiled the day. By the time she had a real boyfriend and they had something to worry about she was conducting her experiments so far from home and with such secrecy that they had little hope of ever keeping track of her. All they knew was that she came in late on Friday and Saturday nights and would not say where she had been. When she told them about Sadie she knew she was only telling them decades too late about herself.

'It's only fun,' she said. 'She's at the age for big noisy parties. There's no harm in it.'

'But the house,' Mother said.

'Oh, she'll clear it up. I don't mind a few marks and spillages—they can't be helped.'

'No need for it,' Mother grumbled. 'You're just aiding and abetting her. None of these young folk have any respect for property these days.'

'How do you know?'

'I've seen the things they do on television—and your Father reads terrible things out of the newspapers.'

'I don't call that evidence.'

'Don't you? Eh?' Mother soon grew nervous if her opinion was challenged. 'Anyway, I hope you don't have cause to regret letting her have this party.'

'I'm sure I won't,' Angela said.

'What,' said Sadie, 'was all that about?'

'What?'

'All that spiel on the phone to Grandma about me—what business is it of hers whether I have a party or not?'

'I have to talk about something—I try to involve her in whatever is going on—she likes to know.'

'She likes to moan.'

'No, she doesn't—it's just it's hard for her to understand the attraction of the sort of thing you want.'

'So of course you explain it all to her beautifully.'

'I try.'

'So modest.'

'What are you getting at—that edge to your voice—?'

'Oh, forget it.'

'I'd like to, but I can't—you're always sneering and you won't ever explain why.'

'Well, you make up for it.'

'You're so unfair, Sadie—you do nothing but knock me all the time and then the next minute it's "can I have a party?" and I'm supposed to fall over myself arranging it and I do and—'

'Oh God, I was waiting for that—you always want thanks all the time—you pretend to be all casual and it's yes of course and then you whine if you don't get thanked and told how kind you are.'

'Well, if that's true—'

'It *is* true.'

'—then it's very sad and I'm ashamed but—'

'Not *that* attitude, please.'

'—I don't actually think it is true. You force those kind of remarks—'

'Nothing needs to be forced out of you—it just pours out all the bloody time, endless speeches all the time.'

'—out of me, you drive me to them, you don't know what it's like to have somebody telling you you haven't been grateful enough.'

Like Father. 'You'll realize,' he used to shout, 'you'll realize what's been done for you when your Mother and I are ten feet underground—then you'll be sorry you didn't appreciate us, you'll see.' She had mimicked his silly posturing and laughed as loud as she dared and openly despised his crude, ludicrous attempts at moral blackmail. What, anyway, had he ever done for her? He talked as though he had showered her with worldly goods. But Sadie had been showered with worldly goods and, more important, with tolerance and reason. It had made no difference.

'Oh, I give up,' Angela said, 'think what you like.' She almost said, 'I try my best,' but remembered just in time that that was Father's feeble parting shot.

Everyone had always commented on how amenable Sadie was. Right from nursery school she was beloved by teachers because, they said, she was 'so biddable'. Other children had tantrums, wouldn't do what they were told, but Sadie always did. 'It's just a question of explaining everything to her,' Angela boasted. Some of Angela's neighbours found it suspect. They said such sweet reasonableness was unnatural. Sometimes Sadie came home in tears because she had been mocked. 'Josie says I'm a goody-goody,' she wailed, 'and her mother did too.' All because Sadie obediently did not go into puddles with her plimsolls on. Angela had told her not to go into puddles unless she had her Wellingtons on. She had explained that if you went into them with plimsolls on you (a) got your feet very wet which was (b) uncomfortable when you were a long way from home and (c) it ruined the plimsolls because plimsolls were only made of canvas. Sadie had understood. Sadie had seen the sense in the argument, and she had not gone into the puddles. 'Tell Josie,' Angela said, 'that she's silly and that there is nothing wrong with being sensible.' Dutifully, comforted, Sadie had gone off with the message, only to return in greater despair with the cry, 'Josie says I do whatever you tell me.' 'Well,' said Angela, 'that's exactly what you should do.' But was it?

Angela left the house soon after eight o'clock on the Sunday morning after Sadie's party. There was broken glass inside the gate, lots of it. She paused to kick it to one side. Opening the gate she found her hands covered with something sticky and examining them saw it was egg. There were eggshells and blotches of running yolk on the pavement in front of the house.

Richmond Park was almost deserted, the early morning athletes and dog walkers put off by the hard rain. She trudged along to the Round Pound and then veered off left, following the line of trees that stretched in a rough line towards the river. That way, it was more like real country whereas down beside the road the frustrating feeling of a municipal park persisted. The rain was harsh and coldly cleansing, the air sharp and icy fresh, stinging her face, hurting her throat as she gulped it down, eager to drive out the muggy, beery, disgusting stench of the house she had just left—an overall smell of decay that had made her feel sick. No possibility today of flinging open doors and windows to let the wind blow through the rooms. For days the cigarette smoke would cling to curtains and the odd hidden stub would reek until she tracked it down and got rid of it.

She ought to have brought the boys with her, away from that contaminated place, but they were still asleep. The noise had been so tremendous—music so loud that people had rung from several streets away to complain—that they had taken refuge in her bed, all three of them, frightened by it. Language unbelievably foul and vicious had floated up the staircase as little gangs of louts forced their way past the flimsy barrier, and the laughter from those others who jammed the hall swept upstairs in great threatening waves. She had lain there, one arm round Tim, remembering that somewhere down there was Sadie, in a gold lurex tee shirt that was far too tight and a pair of black satin jeans that followed every contour. Mother would have had a fit, yet she, she said nothing. At eleven, Ben had had enough. He had gone down and ordered them all out, and they had gone with none of the fuss or trouble he had anticipated. He came to bed angry, telling Angela it was her fault, that she ought never to have allowed such unsupervised chaos, saying that she had only agreed to please Sadie.

He was right, but was it a crime to want to please one's daughter? Angela had gone on lying awake long after the boys had been taken back to bed and the house was quiet. To want to please—she did not want to force Sadie in any particular direction, she did not want Sadie to have to hide her way of life because it was different from that of her parents. She had heard Sadie going to bed with her two chosen girlfriends who were staying the night and as smothered giggles and hasty sssh's emerged from her room Angela had smiled, a little happier. At least Sadie *had* been pleased. But now, walking in the park, purging herself of her house's unpleasant atmosphere, depression returned. Her Wellingtons squelched in the muddy leaves as she plodded on, wishing she did not have to go back to the kind of scene there was bound to be at lunch when Sadie emerged without the protective covering of those friends, who would have gone. She walked down towards the gate that led into their road, wondering how long she could manage to stay out—but it was mean to leave Ben to begin clearing up the mess, mean to let the boys get up to pools of vomit still lying in corners of the living room.

Lunch was a tense meal, with Sadie sitting opposite white-faced, hollow eyed and speechless. Nobody spoke much, except Max, who complained constantly about the smell which lingered everywhere.

'It will wear off,' Angela said.

'You shouldn't have let them smoke,' Max said, 'it isn't healthy—it gives you lung cancer—just breathing it in gives you it—I'm probably getting it now—'

'Good,' Sadie said.

'You shut up—it's all your horrible friends—they kept me awake half the night with their swearing.'

'Baby,' Sadie said.

'There's glass outside to clean up,' Ben said. 'It's dangerous—somebody deliberately smashed milk bottles on their way out.'

'How do you know it was deliberate?' Sadie said.

'Because six milk bottles standing in a wooden holder do not take themselves out onto the doorstep and break themselves into extremely tiny pieces.'

'Okay, okay.'

'And there are two banisters broken,' Ben said. 'I hope somebody is going to mend them.'

'They were wobbly already,' Sadie said.

'So?'

'Well, all this fuss about two broken banisters,' Sadie said, lips curling with contempt, 'you'd think it was the end of the world.'

'They cleared up quite well in here,' Angela said, nervous.

'*Quite* well?' Sadie said, glaring. 'We spent bloody hours washing the floor.'

'You missed the sick,' Ben said.

'Oh, what a fuss,' Sadie said, pushing her chair back, ready to go back to her room, aggrieved.

'I hardly think you can claim we've made a fuss,' Angela said, 'I think we've been very good considering—'

'I knew it!' Sadie shouted, her eyes closed, one fist pounding her forehead. 'I just knew it—I was waiting for the self congratulation to start—okay—so you're both heroes letting me have a party—thank you very very very much—*thank you*—great. Now can we just forget it?'

They let her go. 'She didn't mean to sound like that,' Angela said quickly, 'it's just how it comes out. She's exhausted—she can't really hear how she sounds.'

'You're always on her side,' Max said. 'Of course, if it was me it would be different—you'd shout then.'

'I'm really fed up with Sadie,' Ben said, 'you do seem to make rather a lot of excuses for her.'

'Because nobody made them for me.'

'That was different. You aren't to Sadie as your Mother was to you.'

'How do you know?'

'Obviously you aren't—it's quite a different situation—your Mother was weak and you were strong. Sadie is as strong as you—you don't have to handle her like china. I'm really bored with the whole business—if you're not handling your Mother carefully you're handling Sadie carefully. Neither of them are worth it—

I don't know why you waste your time—all this putting them first—I mean, what is this? Some kind of charity you're running?'

It was rare for him to be angry, and even then Ben's anger was not a frightening thing, nor did it last. The children knew it too and counted upon it, whereas her own temper was something they dreaded. 'Don't put her in a temper,' was a warning Angela often heard one child beg to another and though it made her ashamed it also made her smile at their naïvety. She was never 'put into' tempers—they just came, like the wind, and startled her by their violence. But now, when she ought to be angry and raging, it was she who was calm and quiet and Ben who temporarily shouted and grew red in the face. She sat in the empty kitchen and thought about what he had said. She saw herself as caught in the crossfire between Sadie and Mother—she saw herself as being shot at by both of them from different angles—but Ben saw her as deliberately setting herself up as a target. While she was ill in the summer she had thought for a short time that he might be right—there she had been, wounded and withdrawn from battle, her thoughts turned inwards and away from Sadie and Mother, and they had survived her detachment. Perhaps she ought to resolve to be detached all the time—to cut out of her heart those feelings of pity and sorrow and guilt that made her melt in their hands though they never guessed it.

'The party went very well,' she said that evening on the telephone to Mother, knowing that Sadie, who was eating left-over trifle behind her in the kitchen, could hear every word. 'Sadie and her friends cleared up beautifully afterwards.' She heard Sadie scrape the plate unnecessarily hard. 'No,' she said, 'there was no damage to speak of.'

'That's good,' Mother said. Now that the event was over and no disasters had occurred, she had lost interest in the topic. But to Angela, practising her new coolness, it seemed Mother was more cheerful.

'I went to the doctor's today,' Mother said.

'Oh, really?' Angela said, casual, determined not to probe further than she needed to.

'Yes, to be checked over you know—it's six weeks since I was in hospital—' Father in the background shouted 'six weeks and three days'—'and they said to go to my own doctor after six weeks so your Father made the appointment and we got a taxi—'

'Well done.'

'—and down we went. He says my heart is sound and my lungs clear and my blood pressure lower than it has been for years and my insides as good as new.' Mother sounded excited and happy. 'Of course, it's all nonsense—I'm an old woman—everything's wrong with me—but the doctor thinks I'm better than I am so I suppose I have to listen to him.'

'Yes,' Angela said emphatically, 'you do.'

'He even said a change would do me good.' Father was shouting again. 'What?' Mother said, pretending to Angela she could not hear. 'Your Father's shouting—oh, I'm not going to tell her that.' Fearfully, Angela struggled not to fall into the trap she sensed—she did not have to press Mother to tell her what Father was shouting. She waited for Mother to go on, saying nothing and hating herself for cowardice. 'Your Father says I have to tell you that the doctor was asking when I was off to visit my daughters now I am so much better—says a little trip would be just the job before the winter sets in.'

It was cruel to pause for even a second. 'Well,' Angela said, voice croaky and thick, 'when are you? You know you're always welcome.'

'Eh?' Mother said, with a deprecating little laugh. 'No, I'd never manage it—if you were nearer—and I'd only be a nuisance.'

'Of course you wouldn't,' Angela said. 'If you think you can stand the journey—I could come and get you in the car.' The offer had to be made—in the name of common decency it had to be made.

'Eh?' Mother said again, and the telephone receiver went blank for a moment as she turned aside from it to confer with Father. 'Your Father says that would be grand.'

'Well then,' Angela said, 'that's settled. Let's make it as soon as possible, before the clocks go back. I'll discuss it with Ben and ring you back.'

She found, as she put the receiver carefully down, that she was trembling. She went into the kitchen, where Sadie had moved onto cake, and sat down, trying to compose herself, waiting for Sadie to notice her distress and ask what was the matter, but no inquiry came.

'Grandma is coming to stay,' she blurted out.

'Oh yes,' Sadie said, neither shocked nor surprised. 'When?'

'I don't know. Soon.'

'Will Grandad come with her?'

'I don't know. I haven't even thought about it.' Which would be worse—Mother alone or Mother with Father? Hard to decide.

'You don't look very happy about it,' Sadie said, licking her spoon, which still had cream from the cake on it.

'So you do notice,' Angela said, 'you're not made of stone.'

'Ha ha.'

'It wasn't a joke.'

'What's so awful about Grandma coming anyway?'

'If you can't see, I can't tell you.'

'Well, that's a relief.'

Angela knew she could not afford to say 'Sadie, have you no compassion?' or anything else emotive that would have her daughter out of the house in one minute, and it seemed important for reasons she only dimly comprehended that Sadie should do no such thing. So instead she said, 'I don't think Grandma will be able to get up all those stairs, not even as far as my bedroom.'

'That's no problem,' Sadie said, 'she can have my room. I don't mind. How long will it be for?'

'I don't know,' Angela said, almost weeping, 'oh, I don't know.'

'Okay, okay, sorry I asked,' Sadie said.

It was eight years since Mother had been, the year before her fall, two years before the first heart attack. She and Father had come for three weeks in the long summer holidays, every day an eternity. Windsor Castle, Whipsnade Zoo, Greenwich, Hampton Court—every day an outing somewhere just to keep things moving, just to prevent that awful plummeting of the stomach when Mother sighed and said, 'Well, what can I do?' Evenings at the theatre—Sadlers Wells, D'Oyly Carte Opera, 'The Mousetrap'— anything suitable. Mountains of food of a kind they never ate— puddings galore—snacks slipped in with home-made scones and cakes and late-night suppers with gallons of tea. Sudden devotion to television programmes they had never watched, and all the time that overpowering feeling of unease, of failing Mother at every turn no matter how hard she tried.

'It's too much,' Ben said when finally she roused herself to tell him, 'you're just not up to it—and it isn't even the holidays.'

'Half term is next week. Ideal.'

'Agony,' Ben said, 'you can't possibly have her.'

'Don't be ridiculous,' Angela said, hearing the hysteria in her voice but powerless to control it. 'Can't possibly have my own Mother who is coming to stay for the first time in eight years? Are you listening to yourself? You're being absurd—it's my own Mother—how could I ever not want the poor soul if she wanted to come? The world would be a rotten place if daughters had to look for excuses not to have their own mother—when she's a mother like mine—so good and gentle—who did so much for me—when she isn't a harridan or a busybody—'

'She's a martyr,' Ben said, 'and that's worse. And anyway the point isn't what your Mother is like, it's what you are like when she is around. That's the point.'

'Oh, I don't want to hear your points. There's no argument. Mother is coming and I'm going to welcome her. It's the least I can do—and I *do* welcome her, I really do, it's just that—that—'

'The strain kills you,' finished Ben.

'Strain? It's so shameful to even mention the word—I ought to be thrilled—elated—'

'Well, you're not.'

She went and sat in Sadie's room. It was very small indeed, smaller than she had realized. Angela gazed round her dismally. Mother would not like the rush blind on the window, she wouldn't be comfortable without thick curtains, but then there were old curtains galore in the house. She would not be comfortable either with stained floorboards underfoot but one rug lifted from any of the rooms upstairs would easily cover the entire floor space. The bed was out of the question. Sadie slept on a mattress— the base of the bed was somewhere in the garage swathed in polythene because Sadie said divans were suburban. There was nowhere at all for clothes—except for an old restaurant hat-stand over which Sadie flung everything. Mother would need a chest of drawers, if they could get it in. All the cut-out pictures, mostly of naked bodies, would have to come off the walls and the bare bulb dangling in the corner would have to have that other suburban touch, a lampshade. The room, for Mother, was totally unsuitable, but it was on the ground floor next to the downstairs bathroom with no steps of any kind to be negotiated. It could with little effort be made presentable.

Father did not after all intend to come, though it was a delicate matter finding out. Mother, he said, would enjoy it more if it was just her treat, and after triumphantly decorating the bedroom he could now move onto the living room while Mother was out of his way. 'There's plenty of you to look after her,' he said. Valerie said the same. 'You've got enough on your plate, heaven knows,' Valerie said when she rang, 'but then Sadie is there to help.'

'Help?' Angela said, 'Sadie? She's given up her room and that will be that.'

'Won't she help Mother?' Valerie said. 'A big girl like that? Can't she help her get dressed and that kind of thing?'

'Valerie,' said Angela, 'how often did we help our grandmother get dressed or undressed?'

'But Mother isn't Grandma,' Valerie said, 'it isn't the same at all, Angela.'

'She is to Sadie.'

'How *can* you say that?' Valerie said. 'Oh no, you're wrong—Mother is quite different—I'm sure Sadie will be only too glad to help her—anyone would be.'

'It isn't worth arguing about,' Angela said.

It had taken Sadie a long time to accept that Mother was Angela's mother. The idea amused her, but she didn't believe it. 'But she's so old,' Sadie said, 'she can't be your mother.' 'When I was little like you,' Angela said, 'she wasn't old. She was like I am now.' Sadie still was not satisfied. She would stand in front of Mother and question her—was she really Angela's mummy? Driven finally to accept the relationship, she was never quite happy about it. She whispered 'I wish Grandma wasn't your mummy,' into Angela's ear. 'But why? You like Grandma—she's a lovely lady.' 'Yes,' Sadie whispered, 'but she's old—her legs without her stockings are all withered and the veins stick out.'

Twelve

Angela tried, bravely, to turn it into a treat. Ben would not let her drive all the way there and back on her own, nor would she let him fetch Mother by himself, and so, the usual complicated domestic arrangements complete, they set off together on Monday morning as soon as all the children were at school. 'It will be rather nice,' Angela said, 'driving on our own.' Ben said nothing. They were going to stay at an hotel near Dartmoor that night and pick up Mother the next day before driving back again. 'It's ages since we had a night in an hotel on our own,' Angela said. 'Don't you think it was a brilliant idea of mine?' 'Brilliant,' Ben said, flatly.

There was always the thought that they might crash or get miraculously lost or delayed in some perfectly acceptable way. The ordeal ahead might never happen, though being a Trewick by birth Angela could draw no comfort from such an idea. Looking out of the car window as mile after mile of motorway flashed safely by, worrying silently about whether the Bensons' au pair girl was really reliable enough to hold the fort for one night, she tried to imagine an accident in which she would not be hurt but somehow immobilized—obliged to spend months lying in a white room with soft music in the background and kind nurses hovering over her to say, with a smile, at intervals, that she was not to worry, everyone at home was fine, she was fine too, everything in the whole world was fine, all she had to do was lie there and not move and not think. Occasionally one of the children would appear at her side, looking wonderfully well and happy, and even Mother took part in this curious ritual, wishing Angela well and assuring her that she was perfectly all right herself.

There were tears in her eyes when Ben broke her reverie by stopping for petrol. Hastily, she blinked them away. How terrible to be so self-pitying, how disgusting to fantasize an escape from a quite ordinary predicament. The noise of the filling station, with lorries grinding their way in and out, was a relief. She could not afford to slip into a trough of gloom and depression. She got out of the car and stood up straight and walked briskly up and down. The anticipation was by far the worst part—once Mother was in the car and the visit had begun the fear would fade a little, she would be too busy to torture-herself. She began to hum as she got back into the car and smiled brightly at Ben when he returned from paying for the petrol. 'That's better,' he said, and began to whistle himself, sitting at ease in that totally relaxed way she so envied, even his face quite calm and almost un-furrowed. Her own was never calm. Surprised by mirrors or shop windows, hers was taut and anxious. Tension ruined her looks. She had that dark-eyed look that made women old before their time.

They arrived at Drewsteignton on the edge of Dartmoor before three in the afternoon and immediately drove to the beginning of the footpath that led up to the moor. The path rose steeply so that very quickly there were views of the countryside below. Angela raced ahead of Ben, who was no climber. She paused a good hundred yards ahead of him and turned and cupped her hands and shouted. The sheep scattered in fright and Ben sat down holding his side. She ran back down and pulled him up and pointed towards the top of the moor. 'All around me eagles were yelling,' she said, laughing, teasing him with her sudden energy and vitality. 'No, that isn't right—"All was still, save by fits the eagle was yelling and starting around him the echoes replied."'

'Oh yes,' Ben said, 'First prize, no doubt.'

'No, runner up in the Schools' Verse-speaking Competition. I only got a medal. The winner got a cup.'

'The good old days,' Ben said.

'No, now are the good days.'

'You weren't saying that this morning.'

It was too late to attempt to climb further. They followed a stream down, black and murky in the fading light, pausing to look at the subtler browns and greys of ground and sky. It was so still that they heard the grass crunch under their feet and every pebble they loosened crashed like a boulder in their path. Yet Angela was not quite separate. Visions of the children mingled with the clouds and an image of Mother sitting waiting in her chair hung between them. But she did not speak of them. She did not mention them as they got into the car and drove to the hotel. She did not refer to them as they bathed and dressed for dinner and sat in front of the fire sipping sherry. Ben said 'Happy?' and she said 'Yes' very firmly. They ate a delicious meal and had two bottles of wine and she told herself to savour the bliss.

Mother had never had this. Sadie could not be sure that she would have it. Mother, in her depressions, whatever and when-ever they were, never had anyone to understand and support her and tell her that was better when she managed to smile. Mother had to go it alone. Wheeling his bicycle up the side passage, peering in at the kitchen window, grimy and tired in his boiler suit, Father would see Mother looking mournful and come in and say, 'Now what's up? What's the tale of woe this time?' and he would say it furiously. Mother never replied. With set face and perhaps a tear or two, she would put out his meal and Father, who could get nothing out of her, would say, 'I don't know— you try your best—you work hard—and then you get this at the end of the day.' This provoked Mother to come out with whatever it was. Invariably, Father would say, 'Well, I can do nothing about that, lass,' and sink at once into his own much gloomier and more threatening misery, from which Mother in turn rescued him. Mother knew if she went on being sad Father would shout at everyone else, 'Look at your Mother,' he would yell, 'she's had enough of you lot—now leave her alone—give her a rest.' It was Father she wanted a rest from.

'At least,' Angela said, 'it will be a rest from Father. For Mother, I mean.'

'Spare me,' Ben said, 'don't spoil a lovely day.'

'No,' Angela said, 'no, I won't.'

'Why don't we go away for a couple of weeks and do this all the time?' Ben said. 'We could go off somewhere to the sun, just the two of us—'

'The children,' Angela said, 'who would look after them?'

'We could get someone.'

'Who?'

'I don't know—but somebody—someone's au pair—the Bensons go off all the time—half the neighbourhood do. I mean, Tim's six—none of them are babies any more.'

'They hate me going,' Angela said, 'and then if we flew—both of us—the worry—'

'I knew you'd say no.'

'I haven't said no. There are so many problems—you talk as if it was an easy thing to do—it's worse than arranging an Everest expedition—just the thought—'

'Forget it.'

'Now *you're* spoiling the day. I won't forget it. It would be lovely. I'll think about it. It would be marvellous to be just us, like in the beginning.'

'And at the end.'

'What?'

'It will be just us in the end—when your parents are dead and the children grown up and gone.'

She stared at him, shocked. 'What an odd way to put it,' she said.

They prolonged the evening, prolonged the night, prolonged breakfast next morning, relished every scrap of time, but eventually they were there, outside the house in St Erick. The more pathetic it became, the more Angela smiled. The harder she wanted to cry, the harder she laughed. Feelings of panic, of wanting to run away, were matched by an external casualness that astonished her. Her one object was to soothe Mother and reassure Father and her own fears could not be allowed even the most mild expression.

They had made a bed up in the back of the long estate car in spite of Mother's protests that she would most certainly not use it, that her back would not permit her to even consider it, that she would never get upright again, that the motion of the car would make her sick if she was lying down. 'Don't worry,' Ben said, 'you don't have to lie there if you don't want to but it's there if you need to.' The thought of needing to worried Mother even more. 'I hope I'll be all right—eh?' she kept saying, as though one of them had queried her hope. The longer they took about going, the more agitated she became and yet they could not just put her in the car and depart because Father kept shouting, 'Don't hurry her—plenty of time lass—no need to hurry now.' 'Oh shut up for goodness sake,' Mother said. 'There you are,' Father said, 'you've got her flustered.'

But there was an air of triumph about their final leave-taking. Mother sat in the front looking pretty in her new feathered hat, bought after much searching by Valerie. Father stood at the gate, leaning on it, looking slightly debonair so that there seemed not the slightest need to worry about him. They all waved and Mrs Collins came out and waved too and the postman paused before going to the next-door house and waved. The car started smoothly and off they went and really it could not have been easier. Ben sang and was attentive to Mother's needs without fussing and Angela in the back allowed herself to relax just a little until, as they joined the motorway, Mother said, 'I knew I should have gone to the bathroom again,' and gave her little laugh.

'No problem,' Angela said, far too quickly, 'pull in at the next garage Ben.'

'Can't we just stop by the road?' Ben said, not thinking, not seeing Angela's glare through the driving mirror.

'Sorry to be a bother,' Mother said.

'No bother,' Angela said, 'Ben was daydreaming.'

'What I meant was—' Ben began, but Angela cut him short. 'There,' she said, 'services one mile. Stop there.'

They stopped there, and ten minutes later, and twenty minutes after that with Mother becoming increasingly distressed at her inability to control her bladder. She grew more rather than less embarrassed however nonchalant Angela tried to be. They tried hard to reassure her that they stopped just as regularly with the children, but her own feebleness depressed her. Gradually, one problem overcome, another took its place. Mother started to doze off and then brought herself to with frightening jerks of her frail neck every few minutes, but though this showed her exhaustion she would not give in to it. The bed in the back was resisted. That was being an invalid. Moreover, it was somehow indecent to stretch out in the back of a motor car. It showed faint-heartedness and Mother was determined to be resolute. She agreed to sit in the back with Angela and to have cushions at her head and to put her feet up sideways but that was all. 'Good job your Father isn't here,' she said occasionally.

'Why?'

'Well—you know,' Mother said significantly, 'me being like this—watching me—if anything should happen.'

Angela did not say, 'if it happens, it happens'. She was proud of managing to resist a platitude Mother would find so abhorrent. But the more she thought about what Mother had just said, the more it disgusted her. She wanted to tell Ben to put his foot down and roar along at eighty miles an hour and not consider Mother so carefully—foot down, fast as possible and never mind upsetting Mother. Nothing was ever going to please her for more than a minute. Nothing was ever going to reassure her. She was seventy-five and incurably ill of worry and doubt about every kind of future. 'Go a little faster, Ben,' she said. 'Mother doesn't mind, do you Mother?' Mother didn't hear—she had fallen into one of her snatched sleeps. Ben gradually increased speed until they were going at over seventy miles an hour and Angela felt a small thrill of satisfaction. She was beating Mother without Mother knowing it.

There was a long period—two, three years—when Sadie invented unreasonable worries for herself. Usually, they were to do with school. In the evening, after supper, she would torture herself with the memory of something she had or had not done. 'Miss Newton told me to put away the crayons in the drawer in her desk and I forgot and she'll be angry.' 'Don't be silly,' Angela would say, 'she won't be angry at all.' 'You don't know—she'll never ask me to do anything again,' and Sadie began to cry. 'For god's sake, Sadie, don't be so stupid.' 'It isn't stupid—she asked me— she said I was the only one she could trust—she'll never trust me again.' 'Sadie, stop it,' Angela said sharply, 'this is ridiculous—you're in a state over nothing—and anyway you can't do anything about it.' 'I know, I know,' and Sadie cried harder. Angela got up. She went to the telephone. She lifted the receiver and made a pretence of dialling. 'Hello?' she said, 'Miss Newton? This is Sadie Bradbury's mother—Sadie has forgotten to put some crayons in your drawer and she's so worried. Yes, I told her that. Yes, thank you—that's very kind—good night.' Angela came back to the table. Sadie was absolutely silent, staring at her with awe. 'Miss Newton says it doesn't matter in the least,' she said. The shock tactic cured Sadie every time. Somehow, Angela's bluff was never called, her deception never revealed. And gradually Sadie grew out of her obsession with trivial duties she knew were of no importance.

They rang Father as soon as they got in, even before they properly greeted the children or unpacked the car. 'Just a quick ring,' Angela said, 'just to say we've arrived safely and that's all.'

'Good. How's your Mother? How did she stand up to it?'

'Very well.'

'You went nice and slow, eh?'

'Oh yes. I'm going to make Mother some tea now so I'll ring off.' And she did, at once. Unless the limits of her tolerance were outlined Father would never be off the telephone.

Mother was sitting on the sofa at the end of the big ground-floor living room looking overwhelmed and reduced in size to a mere dot of crumpled clothes. The sofa would not do for her. Fifteen years of children bouncing on it had taken out of sides, seat and back any support they had ever been able to give. She sent Max upstairs to bring down the one proper chair they possessed, an upright wing chair that stood in the corner of her bedroom and had clothes thrown over it. 'You shouldn't have,' Mother said, moving gratefully into it nevertheless, 'you should just ignore me.'

But Angela could see she said it in hopes of being contradicted. She was waiting for her life to be transformed now that she was at her beloved daughter's. Already, sitting in a chair watching other people do things, the difference was not as great as it ought to have been.

'Which would you rather,' Angela said, 'eat now with the children or later with Ben and me?'

'I don't eat much,' Mother said.

'Well,' Angela said, 'when would you rather not eat much?'

'It doesn't matter. I don't mind. Whichever is easiest,' Mother said. She did not like to be teased.

'Then eat with us,' Angela said, afraid eating with the children might after all seem insulting.

Mother sat and watched the children eat. 'They haven't washed their hands,' she said, 'none of them, not even Sadie.'

'Ooooh, Grandma,' Sadie said, 'tell tale tit.'

'She's a liar anyway,' Tim said, 'I've washed mine.'

'Tim,' Angela said, 'you do not call Grandma a liar. Ever.'

'Why not? She told a lie.'

'She didn't—she just looked at your hands and saw they were filthy so even if you have washed them you haven't washed them properly.'

'Bloody hell,' Tim shouted.

'Tim, you do not swear in this house.'

'*You* do—everyone does.'

'I do not.'

'Shouting at your mother,' Mother said, 'naughty boy. My little boys never shouted at me.'

Nobody, Angela remembered, ever had shouted at Mother, neither the boys nor Valerie nor her, but then Mother had not shouted at them. For twenty odd years she had been a mother who had brought up her children without shouting at them.

'I don't know,' Angela said when the children had left the table and scattered round the house, 'how you managed not to shout at us.'

'I don't like shouting,' Mother said, 'it's horrible. And I don't like violence, especially in families.'

'Neither do I,' said Angela, 'but I shout all the time—and I'm violent—well, I slap the boys often and thump them when I'm angry. No wonder my children shout back, I suppose. I just get so furious with them.'

'They're difficult children,' Mother said. Angela, watching her closely, thought she was blushing slightly.

'How are they difficult?'

'Well, they aren't quiet, are they—they're very strong personalities—you let them do what they want—treat you like an equal.' Mother's blush deepened with the excitement of daring to criticize.

'But I don't let them do what they want—that's the point— that's where all the trouble starts.'

'Oh well then,' Mother said, 'never mind. Is Sadie to do the dishes?'

'No,' Angela said, but she did not want the subject changed. 'It must be,' she said, 'it can't be how they were born—I've made them argumentative.'

'You can't do everything right,' Mother said. 'Where is Sadie? She isn't helping you.'

'She's gone out, I expect.'

'But she didn't tell you—'

'She doesn't have to tell me every time she goes in or out.'

'—and it's dark—at this time of night—'

'It's only seven o'clock.'

'Still, you should know where she is.'

'No,' Angela said, 'I don't think so. She's capable of looking after herself. I don't want to live in her pocket or have her living in mine. She has her own life to lead.'

'Oh Angela,' Mother said.

'What?'

'You're her Mother—she's only fifteen—dear me—'

It was the fashion, in their area, to send children to holiday camps on their own as soon as they were eligible. Not as Angela had been sent on holiday on her own, put on the train to a relative's and collected at the other end, but really on their own from the beginning. It was said to be good for them but Angela privately wondered. All the same, she found herself saying to Sadie when she was eight, 'Would you like to go to a children's holiday camp for a week?' 'Who with?' 'Just yourself.' 'No,' Sadie said, decisively. 'Why should I?' 'I just thought it would give you something exciting to do one of the weeks we're at home in the summer holidays— you'd enjoy it—there would be lots of children of your own age—you'd have a great time.' 'I don't want to go,' Sadie said. 'I would have loved it at your age,' Angela said. Afterwards, she chided herself for her foolishness. Sadie sulked, aware that she had somehow been feeble and clinging and unadventurous and that Angela might despise her.

Angela was standing staring into the dark garden, where she could see nothing at all, when Sadie came in and put the light on.

'Why on earth wasn't the light on?' Sadie said. 'Where's Grandma? Where's Dad?'

'I didn't feel like having a light on.'

'Oh, the moody blues,' Sadie said, humming. She picked up the newspaper and turned to the television programmes.

'Grandma is in bed,' Angela said. 'Dad's gone for a walk in the park.' But Sadie was not listening. Her queries had been mere conversation and were not expected to be given answers.

'Do you think,' Angela said, trying to make her tone light and free from any kind of whine, 'that you could help Grandma while she is here?'

'Yeah, okay,' Sadie said. 'Don't forget I've given her my room.'

'But that's a negative sort of helping,' Angela said. 'I was thinking of something a little more positive.'

'Like what?' Sadie looked up, that aggrieved expression she assumed at any mention of help already settled on her face.

'Talking to her—involving her in what you're doing—just to make her feel she belongs. She's so pathetic sitting there all day—can't read because of her eyes—can't do anything really and she's so bored and—'

'Yeah, okay,' Sadie said. 'Goodnight then.'

'Don't go,' Angela pleaded.

'I'm going to bed—right?'

'No—every time we even begin to talk about anything that matters you run away.'

'Oh *god*,' Sadie said and sat down again, eyes closed, hands gripping the sides of the chair. 'Get *on* with it then. What do you want to say?'

'Don't you feel sorry for Grandma?'

'Christ—that again—of course I feel sorry for her—but I mean, that's life isn't it? You make such a sob story of it, carrying on and moaning around—so Grandma's old and a bit handicapped and everyone's sorry but nobody can do anything about it, can they?'

'We can be considerate and affectionate.'

'Okay—I'll be considerate, but it won't make much difference. Old is old.'

'And when you're old,' Angela said, 'you'll just accept it, will you? You won't be bitter or expect anything from anyone—you'll just sit in your wheelchair and wave your white stick and say old is old, that's life, folks.'

'You're so bloody sarcastic,' Sadie said.

'Well, you talk such rubbish. You *know* you could make a huge difference to Grandma if you made the effort—like I have to make it—'

'Good old you. I thought we would get onto that pretty soon.'

'Sadie, I try.'

'Humble now. Touching.'

'I *try*,' Angela shouted. 'I know I'm not what she wants—I won't ever ask you to do it, to be something you're not—'

'Don't worry,' Sadie said, 'there's no danger.'

'No. I don't suppose there is. You don't feel any obligation do you—to me, I mean.'

'No. Why should I?'

'No reason at all. It's exactly as I wanted it to be.'

'Good. Can I go now?'

It had been a beginning which Angela knew she had wrecked. Sadie had at least stayed, she had at least begun to express her feelings and Angela knew she had stamped on them. She would have to learn to tread cautiously. She would have to learn also to be cheerful and not make the rest of the family feel guilty. Each day, she must set her face into a look of benign good humour and keep it that way until she went to bed at night—cheerfulness, at all costs.

'You look worn out,' Mother said one evening.

'Nonsense,' Angela said, springing up to do something convincingly energetic. 'I'm perfectly all right.'

'You work too hard,' Mother said accusingly, 'on the go all the time, morning, noon and night.'

'So were you,' Angela said, 'you never stopped.'

'But I didn't have a big house or a job,' Mother said.

'Or a washing machine or a car,' Angela said, 'or any of the other labour-saving things I have. You were just a slave.'

'Was I?' Mother said. It was hard to interpret her tone. 'Well, even if I was, my life was easier than yours.'

'Oh what a lie,' Angela said, forgetting forcefulness only put Mother off and stopped interesting discussions in their tracks, 'mine is *much* easier than yours. When have you seen me standing in a freezing washhouse with my arms up to the elbows in a dolly tub? When have you seen me blackleading a huge filthy grate—'

'My grate was never filthy.'

'You know what I mean—and all that scrubbing stone floors till your hands bled—'

'They never bled—what nonsense—'

'I *saw* them bleed—'

'I probably had a little cut one day.'

'Mother, you aren't listening properly—you're still pretending you don't know what I mean.'

'All I know,' Mother said with surprising firmness, 'is that for all your fine house and car and so-called modern conveniences you seem more worn out and rushed than I ever was. I had time for a cup of tea with my neighbours anyway.'

'I don't want cups of tea with my neighbours,' Angela said.

Mother was lying back in the wing chair, her white hair spread in fuzzy little clumps against the dark green brocade. Throughout the conversation she had had her eyes shut and her hands clasped neatly on her lap. She seemed to be asleep. Away from Father's meticulous attentions Angela could not help but see how neglected she looked—her hair was not done properly, nor were her clothes fastened as they ought to be fastened. It was hard to get her dressed, so easy to encourage her to stay in her dressing gown or to put on things in which she did not look or feel her best but which were simple to haul on and off. Angela hated to humiliate her, and her garments were humiliating—the endless layers of vests, some night, some day, some warm weather, some cold weather, all to be changed at regular intervals revealing Mother's shrunken flesh, of which she was painfully aware. 'Look at me,' she would say, 'just look at me—what a sight,' and Angela, who longed to lie or find refuge in heartiness, was reduced to platitudes. There was, in particular, the horror of the corset, pink and padded, forcibly strapped in a ludicrous way round Mother's middle. Angela suggested every day that she should leave it off but Mother insisted—she could not do without it, she would feel cold and undressed and insecure. Suspenders dangled from it like thin strips of healthier skin against Mother's white, white thighs where varicose veins stood out in sharp relief. Two pairs of knickers, under and over, cotton and silk, and the worst of the business was over at the end of an exhausting half hour.

Quietly, as eager not to waken Mother as she had once been not to disturb sleeping babies, Angela went on chopping vegetables to make soup and tried to think ahead to what could be done tomorrow. Over the last four days, ever since they had arrived, she had tried desperately to entertain Mother but with only partial success. Shopping had proved too arduous and Mother had ended up sitting in the car as she sat at home. They went to a nice coffee shop in Richmond High Street and had coffee and a pastry and Angela tried to make an event of it but Mother proved remarkably uninterested in either her surroundings or the other customers and was the first to suggest that they should go. Collecting and delivering Tim from school was hardly the diversion Angela thought it might become—she could sit for hours watching the children come out but Mother found it dull. None of the bright faces or the cavortings of Tim and his friends fascinated her. 'That,' said Angela, 'is the school swimming pool.' 'Oh yes,' Mother said, 'very nice.' No questions, no curiosity. There seemed little point in hanging about.

Hardly breathing in case Mother woke from her snooze and the blessed respite was over, Angela scolded herself for unworthy thoughts. She was a woman of intelligence and resourcefulness. The problem of how to please Mother and how to enliven her days ought not to be beyond her. What she needed was entertainment, something different but not tiring, and people about her who would bring out that vitality so long extinguished. She sliced through carrots very carefully so as not to make the smallest sound and looked at Mother again and suddenly she was overwhelmed with remorse. Mother could not help her apathy. She could not become animated at will—she was too old and tired and ill. She was just a poor exhausted soul who needed love, who needed reassurance that she still had a part to play in the world. But what part? Where was Mother's part, now that she was old and finished, now that the work of bringing them all up was done? Every day, Angela had given Mother little tasks to do, things that they both knew were unnecessary, or which could be easily done in a second by Angela herself, and the play acting that this game called for was insulting to Mother's dignity. There was nothing useful that she could do and she wanted to do something useful.

Sadie loved to cook. Flour, butter, sugar, cocoa—all were materials her podgy little hands loved to pound and squeeze and mix. Angela, starved in a wartime rationing childhood, was indulgent to her little daughter. Every rainy November afternoon before Sadie started full-time school she let her 'help' to cook. They made cakes, they made pastry. Sadie's messes went in the oven alongside Angela's more competent efforts. At supper, they would taste what they had made and compliment each other and Ben would say Sadie's cake or biscuit or pastry was just that bit better. Until suddenly Sadie became dissatisfied. She watched her buns come out of the oven flatter and less round and altogether inferior to Angela's. She saw her pastry was grey while Angela's was golden brown. 'I want,' she said, 'to do proper cooking.' 'You are doing proper cooking,' Angela said. 'No,' Sadie said, 'mine doesn't look proper—I want to do what you do.' Then the cooking afternoons became a different experience. Bravely, tears in her eyes, Sadie struggled to do everything exactly like Angela—and failed. The results were only a little better. Angela tried to assist her without

her seeing that assistance was being given, but Sadie roared with fury.
'You're helping me—I don't want you to help me—I want to do cooking
all by myself.' But she couldn't. She stopped trying. Until she was seven
years old and able to cope properly she never took part in cooking again.
It made Angela sad. 'What does it matter,' she pleaded, 'as long as it's
fun?' 'No,' Sadie said, glaring, her beautiful mouth distorted into a fierce
pout.

Valerie came for the day at the end of the first week, just as the children broke up for their half-term holiday. She came, she said, 'to help out'.

'I had to get up at six,' she said as soon as Angela picked her up at the station, 'the train was freezing.'

'How noble,' Angela murmured. 'Mother will appreciate it.'

'Is she getting on all right?' Valerie said, rubbing her large red hands together to warm them up, to emphasize the extreme cold to which she wished Angela to know they had been exposed.

'I think so. It's hard to tell—you know Mother.'

'She's no bother really though, is she?' Valerie said.

'It depends how you define bother.'

'Well, she's easy to please.'

'I find her almost impossible to please.'

'We just have nice chats,' Valerie said, 'and I make her rest in the afternoons.'

'When is this?'

'What do you mean?'

'These cosy chats and jolly rests—you haven't had Mother to stay for centuries.'

'It isn't my fault, I—'

'Nobody said it *was* your fault, Valerie. I simply pointed out that you make these assertions and they're based on history as far as I can see. You don't know what it's like to have Mother to stay as she is now and it just annoys me that you pretend you do.'

'I don't know why you're angry.'

'I'm not angry. It just irritates me that everything I say you think you can cap. Don't let's talk about it anyway—Mother is the last thing I want to discuss. How's life?'

'Oh, all right. We've been having staffing problems.'

'But how is *your* life?'

'It just ticks over the same old way. I'm quite happy with my flat and my cat and the church choir—you wouldn't understand, being a Londoner, being so busy. I'm like Mother—I like peace and quiet and nothing much happening.'

There were always in Valerie's words twin rebukes—Angela should not be the one with a husband and four children and Angela should not be solicitous towards Valerie. Those were, by rights, Valerie's roles. It was Valerie who had spent her entire childhood peering into prams and begging to be allowed to hold babies—Angela had scorned them. It was Valerie, too, who sat with Mother by the fire and drank tea and listened to her dispensing sympathy to friends and neighbours. It was Valerie who adopted a concerned look and asked people how they were. Angela had no time for anyone. She was going to be a career girl and live for herself and openly despise the maternal, caring role. Now that Valerie had turned out to be the spinster on the way to being openly pitied she found the strain intolerable.

'You shouldn't have bothered,' Mother said to Valerie as soon as she saw her, 'really, all this way.' She was happy, all the same, that Valerie should see her in this different setting, in the midst of a bevy of children, looking as though she belonged for those with an eye ready to be deceived. Tim, for the first time in a long week, though Valerie had no way of knowing it, had shown himself in the light of a small boy devoted to his Grandma. When Valerie arrived, they were sitting playing snap together and Mother was laughing out loud. Tim's hand, indeed, rested on Mother's and his face turned upwards with an expression of the greatest affection. 'She needs to be with children,' Valerie whispered, 'that's the secret,' and she smiled fondly at her nephew. Later, while they prepared lunch together out of Mother's earshot, she returned to the topic. 'How lovely,' she said, 'to see Mother with her grandchildren—just what she always wanted—she just loves being with children.'

'Oh, don't be so stupid,' Angela said in that cruel way she kept for Valerie at her most slushy, 'being with children doesn't make the slightest difference to Mother. She's not even remotely interested in them—she finds them noisy, dirty, rude and a constant disappointment and she compares them constantly with the angels she now imagines we were.'

'Oh, I'm sure you're wrong—Mother adores children.'

'She does not. She only adores the theory of children—she only loves them when they can't speak and they're lying clean and cooing in their prams. She can't put up with real children.'

'Well,' Valerie sighed, 'I suppose we'll all feel like that when we get to Mother's age. We'll all be fed up with everything.'

'I won't,' Angela said contemptuously.

'How do you know? You never can tell.'

'Certainly you can,' Angela snapped. 'Pass me that knife will you—thanks—no, I won't get like Mother. Mother's not just pulled down by age and illness and her own temperament—it's just she's had nothing to do since we all left home. When we went, that was it—one big blank and she's felt cheated ever since. I won't be like that. My children aren't my life. When they've gone, I'll get on with all the other parts of it.'

'Oh well,' Valerie said, resentful and sulky, 'that's nice for you then. But you'll still need looking after when you're old and feeble—you'll still want Sadie to help you.'

'Sadie?' Angela said, 'don't be silly. Sadie won't help me. I don't want her to. I've deliberately brought her up not to think that she has to.'

'Oh good,' Sadie said, coming into the kitchen. 'When is lunch? I'm starving.'

'How are you enjoying having Grandma?' Valerie said. Angela saw Sadie register and recoil from the unctuous tone.

'Fine,' Sadie said, picking at the cheese Valerie had been given to grate, 'it's nice having her around really.'

'Is it?' said Angela, sharply.

'Mm,' said Sadie, suddenly wary, ready to refuse to be drawn. 'Where's the newspaper?'

'I don't know,' Angela said. 'I haven't had the luxury of looking at it yet.'

'Hasn't she grown?' Valerie said as Sadie slouched off. 'She's taller than you already. Isn't she helping with the lunch? You should make her help, Angela, you really should. If I had had a daughter I would have brought her up just as Mother brought us up.'

'I don't want her help unless it's freely given,' Angela said, 'she isn't my drudge.'

'Mother made us help and we never regretted it.'

'She did *not* make us help—your memory is failing you Valerie—we helped because she was too pathetic not to help.'

'But it doesn't seem right,' Valerie insisted. 'I mean, to let a grown girl do nothing in the house when you're wearing yourself out doing things for her.'

'I choose to do things for her. I like it.'

'But what will she do when she has her own house? What would we have done without Mother's training?'

'We wouldn't have imitated her,' Angela said, 'and that might have been a good thing.'

'Well, I don't know,' Valerie said, retreating into some inner world of her own just as Mother did when she could no longer cope with Angela's startling announcements. Angela longed for Valerie to attack her, to be equally strong and forthright, and to leave her in no doubt that she was wrong. She would have relished a battle instead of her sister's withdrawal. 'Anyway,' said Valerie, brightening, 'I came to help. I've finished the cheese—what can I do next? I want to be really useful.'

'Just stay with Mother,' Angela said despairingly, 'just concentrate on her. I'd rather make four thousand lunches and wash up after them all on my own than sit with Mother for half an hour.'

'Oh, *Angela*,' Valerie said, and trailed off, shaking her head.

Thirteen

All the rest of the day Angela watched Valerie with Mother and saw herself in every action. When Valerie carefully helped Mother to her unsteady feet—arm round her ample waist, legs braced in an exaggerated fashion to take her weight, face set in an expression of extreme concern—Angela saw how unbearable this solicitous behaviour was to Mother. It underlined Mother's difficulties. Everything Valerie did was a grotesque parody of what it should have been—all that was needed to get Mother up was the simple offer of a hand to pull on. There was in the inclination of Valerie's head as she bent towards Mother something offensive—it was as though Valerie was following stage directions of a crude and over-colourful variety. Nothing was spontaneous. Even Valerie's conversation smacked of condescension with its little set pieces topped and tailed for Mother's benefit. She sat there, opposite Mother, chattering away with great vivacity, putting in little laughs at the right places and sighing heavily when dismay was called for. There was no sign at all in this thirty-five-year-old woman of the child who had sucked her thumb and spent half her time on her mother's knee confiding all manner of secrets, no sign of the spotty, fat teenager who had clung to her mother's arm to and from church on Sundays rather than walk with girls of her own age. Nor was there any indication that it was to Mother that Valerie had gone when, as a young social worker straight out of college, her fiancé had broken off their engagement. Whatever there had been between Valerie and Mother had gone as surely as it had between herself and Mother.

Dispirited, Angela took herself away from a spectacle she found so distasteful. Lunch over, she said she was going upstairs for a rest. Valerie and Mother eagerly encouraged her. On the way to her bedroom she passed Ben's study where Sadie was sprawled on the floor using the telephone. She paused, hand on the banister, attracted by the grace and comfort of Sadie's reclining figure, vivid in scarlet jeans and brilliant blue shirt, as she lay eating an apple, one hand propping her up and clutching the telephone receiver at the same time. Angela smiled at her, not quite stepping into the room but about to do so. 'Wait a sec,' Sadie said into the receiver, and then, to Angela, 'Want something?' Angela shook her head. She had nothing but the usual things to say—what she wanted was indefinable. Lazily, it might have been unintentionally, Sadie gently tipped the open door with her toe and as it swung towards her Angela backed away and it closed with the smallest of clicks in her face.

Alone in her bedroom, which looked obliquely into Ben's study at the side of the house, Angela was obliged to draw the curtains in order to obliterate the sight of Sadie still engaged in her private conversation. She did not want to see her daughter, however distantly. She cared that Sadie did not care, that her daughter was indifferent to her misery. It was the trap she had always been so proud of avoiding but now she felt the cloying wraps of self-pity and resentment ensnaring her. It was no good boasting to Valerie that she had brought up Sadie differently— it was no good lying to herself—it was simply that she now found she wanted what Mother had wanted.

Ben had jaundice soon after Sadie moved to comprehensive school. He was in bed for six weeks. After that he staggered about for another three, thin and pinched and still yellow looking. Expert as she was at nursing, Angela could not help but find it a strain. Sadie, aged eleven and full of energy, did not seem to notice. 'I cannot,' Angela said, 'run up and down stairs looking after Ben and then run around down here looking after all of you. Can't you see that?' 'It isn't my fault,' Sadie said, 'I can't help Dad being ill. You're always moaning at me.' 'I am not moaning at you. I'm simply asking for some consideration. Is that too much? Don't you care that Daddy is ill?'

Apparently she did not. It was quite extraordinary how she could go out in the morning and return from school in the afternoon and never once ask how he was. Later, when he was downstairs in his dressing gown, Sadie would say 'Oh—hi' and then turn to other matters. Yet she was very fond of Ben, she liked him, got on well with him, did things with him, and at that stage never fought or quarrelled—it was just that she appeared to be lacking in common or garden sympathy. But was that the trouble? Angela remained unsure. One day, she overheard Sadie talking over the garden wall to the Carriers, their neighbours on the other side. 'Oh how awful,' Sadie was saying, 'oh that is dreadful—poor you—if there is anything I can do—let me go to the shops for you—no, please, I would be glad to— it would be no bother, no bother at all.'

All Mrs Carrier had done was strain a ligament in her foot.

Valerie, before she left, served a function more useful than she knew. It was nice of her, Angela thought, to ask the question she herself could not ask but which hung in the air all the time. 'When are you going home, Mother?' she said as she put her coat on. 'Oh, soon,' Mother said, stealing a sidelong look at Angela. 'I can't bother Angela much longer—she's fed up with having a poor old woman to look after.'

'Don't,' Angela said, 'I hate to hear you say that and you know it isn't true.'

'Your Father's been complaining anyway,' said Mother. 'I'll have to go back soon, see what he's been up to without me.' It was at least an attempt at a joke, if a feeble and bitter one, and they all seized the opportunity to make others, equally poor.

'I'll write as usual,' Valerie said finally, 'and I'll telephone. Now take care.' Mother kissed her. As always, partings of any kind reminded her of the perilous nature of life.

'Well, she's gone, that's that,' Mother said, sitting down heavily in her chair the minute Ben had taken Valerie off. 'That's that,' she repeated. 'When will I see her again? And what a long journey back—the expense—hardly worth it when you think.'

'Oh, don't look at it like that,' Angela said, 'of course it was worth it. She had a good day and enjoyed herself.'

'But what a long journey back,' Mother said again, 'and to what? Nobody at the other end. Oh, I don't like to think about it—that awful flat of hers—nobody to welcome her—empty and quiet—whatever will she do when she's old and ill without a husband and a family? It makes me ill to think about it, it does really. Sometimes I lie awake at night and wonder what will happen to poor Valerie, all on her own—oh it's awful, awful.'

'Only because you wouldn't like it,' Angela said. 'You're seeing yourself in her situation and she isn't you.'

'But she always loved children—why ever didn't she marry—she was a pretty girl—'

'She wasn't,' Angela said.

'Well, she was prettier than many and a good girl and friendly—I can't understand it—why didn't she marry?'

'Nobody ever asked her after that first time.'

'All on her own—'

'She likes it. She has her work and she knows everyone in the area and she drives to all her societies in her car and some people might envy her her freedom.'

'They couldn't—I couldn't live like that.'

'But you aren't Valerie—she isn't like you.'

'Neither of you are, neither of you.'

'Well then, don't worry yourself about it.'

'I worry all the time,' Mother said, 'you don't know half the things I worry about—round and round in my head until I'm dizzy with it.'

'It doesn't do any good,' Angela said, 'you must train yourself to blot out all these worries when you know they are useless.'

'Oh, it's all right for you,' Mother said, with one of those sudden flashes of spirit she always regretted, 'you don't worry about anything. You don't know what worry is. You've never worried.'

Angela found herself smiling, idiotically, a broad grin to hide her confusion. Mother believed what she had said. She saw Angela as confident and fearless, she accepted without question the façade so laboriously constructed. It would be cruel to disillusion her—if that was what Mother wanted, and she did, then that is what she must be given.

'That's right,' Angela said, 'I don't believe in it.'

'I can't help it,' Mother said, almost proudly, 'I was born like that—always a worrier and always with plenty to worry about. Nothing ever went right.'

'Nothing ever went really wrong either,' Angela said. 'Your husband didn't die, your children all grew up healthy and strong—'

'You've said all that before,' Mother interrupted.

'I know.'

'Well, don't keep on about it.'

'You just tell her, Grandma,' Sadie said, coming into the room and overhearing the last few remarks Mother had made. 'She's always going on about things but she doesn't believe it. She's so boring.'

'I didn't mean that,' Mother said. Solidarity among adults was very important to her. 'Your mother is never boring, Sadie, you can't say that.'

'Yes I can,' and smiling directly at Angela, a smirk of a smile, 'Mum, you're boring.'

'Thanks,' Angela said, 'I can see I must be.'

'All mothers are boring,' Sadie said.

'My Mother is very interesting,' Angela said.

'Oh, I am *not*,' Mother protested.

'You are to me.'

'Compliments, compliments,' Sadie said. 'Anything to eat?'

'If you make it yourself, and leave the kitchen tidy.'

'Okay,' Sadie said and went off.

'You let her be very cheeky, Angela,' Mother said, 'speaking to you like that—it isn't right.'

'I'd rather she said what she was thinking to my face.'

'But she's so rude.'

'I don't think so.'

'I don't know why you stick up for her.'

'Mothers do,' Angela said, 'don't you remember sticking up for me?'

Especially against Aunt Frances, Mother's dressmaker sister, who doted on Angela as a small girl but fought with her as an adolescent. Angela remembered Aunt Frances visiting them and how the criticism would begin straight away. 'What a way to tie a scarf—tie it in the front—tie it like Princess Margaret Rose,' and Aunt Frances would attempt to do so only to have her interfering fingers pushed away. 'Oh, she's naughty,' Aunt Frances would say, 'you should make her behave, Mary.' 'Leave her,' Mother would say, 'it doesn't really matter how she ties her scarf.' But Aunt Frances would not take the hint. Mercilessly, she attacked Angela's hair—'That vulgar crop'—and her language—'so coarse'—and everything about her niece that did not meet with her approval. Only once did Mother give in. 'When you come in from school,' she said to Angela, 'please say "Good afternoon, Aunt Frances." It's only a little thing and easily done.' 'How silly,' Angela said. 'What's wrong with hello?' 'Nothing,' Mother said, 'for most people, but Frances likes to be formally addressed by young people and it does no harm to give in to her on that one.' So Angela complied, going as near as she dared to a parody of what Aunt Frances wanted. It gave her great comfort and pleasure to feel that Mother was secretly on *her* side.

'Well then,' Mother was saying, and Angela was startled to realize she had been speaking for some time, 'that's that. Another day over.' and she sighed heavily. 'Next week,' Angela said, 'we'll go on some outings.'

She had saved them up especially for the half-term holidays—a series of small expeditions to please Mother at one end and Tim at the other. The first was to Woburn Safari Park, an hour's drive and then a winter picnic in the park when they had been through the animal reserve. She announced the trip at supper with all the enthusiasm she could muster, but there were no shrieks of joy. Nobody wanted to go. 'I'm not coming,' Sadie said straight out, 'and you needn't think you're going to make me.' 'We've been there already,' Max said, 'and it's boring.' 'Did you say animals?' Mother said, 'I'm not keen on animals.' 'This is different,' Angela said firmly, 'you'll enjoy it. It will be a lovely day out in the country—midweek, nice and quiet in October— we'll have a lovely day.'

It was a disaster, even before the final penalty afterwards. Foolishly, against Ben's advice, she compelled Sadie to go, claiming her help was necessary, and Sadie's resentment and fury expressed itself in vicious attacks on Max which led to screams and quarrels in the car that distressed Mother deeply. Though the sun shone brightly and the sky was a clear, sharp blue, the atmosphere was wrong from the start. No matter how much Angela smiled and hummed and tried to arouse some holiday spirit nobody would respond, except Tim, who was still young enough to like going anywhere any time. Very quickly, they were there. Very quickly the animals had been looked at and lunch eaten. In no time at all there was nothing to do and it was only half past one. Angela produced a ball and suggested a game, but nobody would take part. One by one she took her children aside and begged them to try to enjoy themselves 'for Grandma's sake', but her pleading only irritated them. It was all her fault, they said. They had told her they did not want to come, she had forced them, why could they not just go home?

By the time she drove back, Angela could no longer remember why she had ever imagined taking everyone out for the day would be either enjoyable or easier than having them all at home. Mother had got very little out of it. All day she had been quiet and nervous, even more so than usual. Surrounded by such noisy children, she had seemed to feel she was menaced, or so Angela deduced from the way in which she looked from one to another during the many arguments that raged. Who could she be sure of? Who had her interests at heart? Only Angela, and Angela, she saw, could not give her complete attention. She did not say so but Angela thought Mother was missing Father. Instead of blossoming without him, she was fading away to nothing.

Helping her from the car when they got home, Angela was struck all over again by Mother's frailty. How often, watching Father and Valerie fuss and fret, had she wanted to tell them to leave Mother alone, she could manage perfectly well, but now that she was in sole charge herself she was appalled by Mother's weakness. Twice on the short trip from car to front door Mother swayed and lost her balance and would have fallen if Angela's supporting arm had not been there. There was a dreadful inertness about her body that could only be appreciated by contact with it.

'That was a nice day out,' Mother said, safely seated in her wing chair and wheezing slightly. The children rushed upstairs to watch television and the sudden silence and calm was healing.

'It wasn't much fun for you,' Angela said, depressed and tired and unable for a while at least to maintain her outward poise.

'Oh, don't worry about me,' Mother said, 'nothing's fun for me.'

'Mother,' Angela said, eyes tight shut with the effort of keeping control, 'don't—don't say things like that. Please.'

'But it's true.'

'Especially if it is true. Don't say it.'

Mother didn't speak after that. She drank the tea Angela had given her—greedily, quickly—and then she appeared to doze.

Angela lifted her legs onto a stool and tenderly put her slippers on and covered her with a rug. Then she sat at the kitchen table, bowed down with it all, a teacup in her hand long after it was empty. Sadie, coming in search of her, radiated energy and strength. The enforced day in the bracing autumn air had given her cheeks a glow—she was bright eyed and beautiful in spite of the ugly, torn man's pullover and the too-tight, soiled trousers.

'I'm going to stay the night with Sue—just telling you—okay?'

Angela said nothing. She sat and stared at Mother and said nothing.

'I'm taking my things and going,' Sadie said, impatiently drumming her green nail-varnished fingers on the table.

'Okay?'

Angela shrugged. Mother's face seemed to have collapsed.

'Well, can I go?'

'I can't imagine why you're asking,' Angela said, 'you don't usually.'

'So I can go?'

'Go where you like. There isn't much point in me keeping you here is there? I've made that mistake once today already and paid the penalty.'

'What penalty? I thought I was very good with Grandma. What am I supposed to have done wrong?'

'There's no point in going over it.'

'Well, don't get at me. I'll be back some time tomorrow—as it's the holidays it doesn't matter when, does it?'

'No. Nothing matters.'

'For heaven's sake.'

'Go on—go. You aren't doing much good here—you may as well go.'

'What do you *want* me to do?'

'Help.'

'All right then—what?'

'Just in general. Help me.'

'I don't know what you're on about.'

Still she lingered. Angela watched her fiddling about, picking things up and putting them down, pacing the floor, walking round the table, never quite making up her mind to leave. She knew her own blatant misery had made Sadie uneasy. It was against the rules. Sadie did not quite know whether she was free or not, and uncertainty kept her close.

'Oh, off you go,' Angela said. 'I'm just fed up and ready to take it out on anyone. Have a good time.'

Sadie's face brightened immediately. 'Bye.' she said.

'Don't bang the front door on your way out,' Angela said, 'you'll waken Grandma.'

But when Father 'phoned, Mother was still asleep, two hours later.

'We've been out all day at Woburn,' Angela said, 'and Mother's having a little nap.'

'Tired her out, have you?' Father said suspiciously.

'Not really.'

'Walked her too far, I'll bet—how far did you make her walk, eh?—she can't walk far without tiring, you should know that, you've seen what happens.'

'She hardly walked at all.'

'You didn't keep her sitting in that car all day did you? It's bad for her back.'

'No, I didn't. She sat a little and walked a little.'

'What's she asleep for at this time then?'

'She was just sleepy.'

'Seems queer.'

'I could sleep myself after all that fresh air.'

'Have you covered her with a blanket?'

'Yes.'

'I'll ring back later, just to check she's all right.'

'There's no need for that, Father.'

'I'll say whether there's need or not—I'm the best judge of that,' and he put the receiver down with a crash.

At nine o'clock, just after Ben had come home, Father rang again.

'No,' Angela said, 'she's still sleeping peacefully and I don't want to waken her.'

'You shouldn't let her sleep like that,' Father said, 'sleeping all crunched up in a chair is bad for her—she has to be kept flat.'

'She looks very comfortable,' Angela said.

'You wake her up,' Father said, beginning to shout. 'Wake her up and get her walking about and then put her to bed—do you hear?—that's the thing to do.'

'I will,' Angela said.

'I'll ring before I go to bed myself just to make sure. Now mind —you get her going and then put her to bed properly—you shouldn't let her sleep in chairs—and she'll be awake all night now, her routine will be all to pot.'

'I'm sorry.'

'It's easy being sorry.'

'There isn't anything else I can be.'

'You can be a damned sight more careful, that's what you can be, my lass.'

They stood on top of a cliff, she and Sadie, right on the very edge where the grass began to disappear into cracks. Below, the sea pounded the great black jagged rocks, sending up clouds of spray so high that they imagined they could feel the wetness on their faces hundreds of feet above. Hand in hand they peered down, drawing in their breaths, trying not to be dizzy, laughing at the cries of the boys behind them, all too afraid to stand with them. Sadie was proud to be the daring one but her hand in Angela's was damp and quivered slightly and her eyes were narrow with fear. She wanted to draw back. Angela sensed this, knew although not a word was uttered that Sadie wished her to be the first to draw back but she chose to stay where she was, trying to communicate her own confidence to her daughter. She squeezed Sadie's hand and smiled and nodded at her and took another very small step towards the brink, but it was too much for Sadie, and suddenly her hand was withdrawn from her mother's, snatched away in an instant as Sadie stumbled back shouting 'You made me! You made me! You knew I was frightened and you made me!' She flew to Ben and cried and when Angela came back he said 'That was ridiculous. What were you trying to prove?' Angela smiled and shrugged. 'Nothing,' she said, 'she knew nothing could happen to her with me there.' 'I don't think,' Ben said, 'that she knew anything of the kind.'

Mother seemed confused when finally they shook her awake. Her eyes swivelled round and her mouth drooped open and seemed out of control. She was grumpy and tearful and did not take kindly to the joint efforts of Ben and Angela to get her on her feet as Father had ordered. 'Oh leave me alone,' she kept saying, 'let me be.' They half dragged her to her room and because she could not face the intricacies of removing underclothes Angela left them on, content to have taken off skirt and jumper and corset.

Then they tucked her up and left her with a small lamp on so that she could see where she was when she woke up properly.

'It was what she dreaded,' Angela said, 'being ill here.'

'We all dreaded it,' Ben said, gloomily. 'God, what a drag.'

'She can't help it—imagine how you would feel if—'

'You sound like Valerie.'

'I feel like Valerie—all morbid and depressed and it wasn't my faultish and why does this have to happen to me.'

Her misery grew as the night wore on. Twice she went to peer at Mother, shocked by the greyness of her face and the harshness of her breathing. Tenderness was useless—it was too late, it ought to have been given sixty years ago when Mother was still a young, large-eyed girl singing so sweetly in the church choir, always put on the front row because she was spick and span in a white collar that sparkled. Someone else should have given it then, before melancholy seeped into Mother's fragile soul and poisoned it for life. Gently, Angela straightened the covers on the bed. She was halfway herself to this sad state. She climbed slowly back upstairs, the carpet cold and rough on her bare feet, plodding away with limbs that felt stiff and painful. Fearful, worried, weighed down by responsibilities it was impossible to evade, she felt she was crawling through each day waiting for the next blow. Being a mother seemed to consist of seeing danger everywhere—seeing it and trying to ward it off and passing the smell of it on to one's children. She slept curled up, finding comfort in the touch of her limbs, and when morning came she was reluctant to straighten them out.

Mother woke up, hoarse and clammy with perspiration, as soon as Angela drew her curtains, determined to smile and be relaxed and sustain Mother all she could. All Mother could do was pass her dry tongue over her cracked lips. She could not, or would not, speak but answered all queries with a shake of her head. Angela telephoned for her doctor, who was reluctant to come. 'You must come,' she said, hysterical at the thought of Father's next call, 'please—I'm so worried—I must have a proper medical opinion.' He came, late in the morning when she had almost given up expecting him, and said Mother simply had a chill and was exhausted. A few days in bed—a light diet—warmth—that was all. Relayed to Father it sounded feeble and ominous, however carefully phrased.

'Damn,' he said, 'damn and blast—knew this would happen—I told you to look after her—just like the thing.'

'She only has a chill,' Angela said.

'Not so much of the only,' Father said furiously, 'at her age. I don't like that. She can be real poorly with a chill, no doubt about it. And how did she get a chill, that's what I want to know—'

'Anyone can get a chill.'

'If they're not looked after they can—if they sit too long in damp places and that.'

'Chills come from germs—'

'And from damp,' Father said.

'She doesn't look too bad anyway.'

'*You* don't know how she looks,' Father said. 'I can tell, you can't. I'd better come up anyways. Can't mess about like this.'

'There really isn't any need,' Angela said. 'I can look after her perfectly well—it would only upset her if you came, make her think she's more ill than she really is. Why not wait, see how she gets on?'

'I might,' Father said with a speed that took Angela by surprise. Was he play acting? Had he said he was coming only to keep up appearances? She felt in a strange way disappointed, though the relief was intense.

She sat with Mother most of the day, ignoring the comings and goings of the children who slammed every door in the house at five-minute intervals, endlessly on their way somewhere. Mother seemed undisturbed by the background noise. The autumn sun, diffused rather than blocked out by the orange curtains, hypno-tized Angela but Mother did not seem perturbed by the brightness. Sometimes she opened her eyes and turned towards Angela, but there was no animation in her expression. She accepted drinks of water but that was all. She slept a great deal, leaving Angela to fret over trivial but essential details such as whether she should make Mother get up to go to the lavatory. Which was preferable—dragging wet sheets and clothes off, or prodding Mother's carcass into action? They needed a bedpan and they did not have one. The local shops would not have one. She would have to leave Sadie in charge and go out in search of one. She would have to learn to do necessary things like putting Mother on a bedpan—things other people did so casually in a sensible matter-of-fact way but from which she shrank. No good muttering about getting a nurse as Ben had muttered—nurses could not be so easily got, and even if found and employed they were in this situation a coward's way out.

'How is Grandma?' Sadie asked, helping herself to orange juice, into which she mixed lemonade and ice cubes with great vigour.

'Not too good,' Angela said. She had come into the kitchen for five minutes to escape the relentless concentration of her thoughts on Mother and stood more dismayed and distracted than ever, unable to do a thing though the lunch dishes were still strewn everywhere and a cake remained half mixed on the worktop.

'Poor Grandma,' Sadie said.

'Indeed, poor Grandma,' Angela said. It was wrong, she knew it was wrong and silly and petty, but she allowed herself to add 'And poor me, don't you think?'

'Why?' said Sadie, 'what's wrong with you?' The note of irritation lacerated Angela's already torn and bruised feelings.

'I have to nurse Grandma,' Angela said.

'You like nursing.'

'When it's something that is going to get better I do—when it's someone basically healthy—'

'Isn't Grandma going to get better?'

'Yes, but—'

'Well then. I don't see why it's any different, frankly.'

'I'm tired,' Angela said, 'and worried and it's all awful.'

'Does Grandad know?'

'Of course.'

'What does he think?'

'He wants to come up.'

'Well, that's good.'

'Good? What on earth do you mean?' said Angela, finding the strength to be suddenly savage. 'How is it good? Do you ever really think—or put yourself in my position—you're being kind now, aren't you, making cosy inquiries when you don't give a damn—you won't or you can't imagine what it is like to be me. I don't want Grandad fussing about—that will be two of them to look after, won't it—two of them on my back.'

'You don't love either of them, do you,' Sadie said. She put her empty glass down and stood up. 'It's all just duty. It's horrible.'

'You don't know anything about it,' Angela said. 'It's all much too complicated. You can't talk glibly about love and duty just like that—I don't know what I feel, except guilty and responsible.'

'But you don't *care*,' Sadie said, 'you're always moaning about them—about having to ring them up and go there—you never stop moaning about it. I don't know why you bother pretending —why don't you just cut off—that's what you'd like to do, isn't it? Just never see them except once a year for a day or something.'

'Yes, yes, yes,' Angela shrieked, 'that is exactly what I would like—I'd like to be in Australia with my brothers and never know a thing except by a two-week-old airmail—I'd like to be free of the whole business—I can't stand it another minute—it goes on and on and on and I don't know what to do.'

'For christ's sake,' Sadie said.

'What?' Angela shouted. 'What? What do you mean with your sneers—no, don't go—DO NOT GO—you twist everything I say—I give you honest answers and you despise me—you attack me when—'

'You're doing the attacking, not me.'

'—all I want is sympathy and a little understanding and— and—and a feeling of not being on my own in this.'

'Well, you are on your own,' Sadie said. 'There isn't anything I can do—oh don't say I can do the dishes—I *will* do the bloody dishes and the shopping and anything you like—but it won't make it any better.'

'I feel terrible,' Angela said.

'I thought Grandma only had a cold?'

'You seemed determined to miss the point.'

'I'm going out anyway—up to Oxford Street—I suppose this is a bad time to ask if I can have the money for those boots you agreed on?'

'Get my purse.'

'I could wait until another day—it's just as it's half term—and Sue is going anyway—'

'Here—take it.'

'Thanks.'

Still she stood, money in her hand, waiting for that signal Angela knew she must give, then she would be out of the house in a flash, coatless on a cold day, putting the boredom of home behind her. Mother had never let Angela go—never gave the signal. Crouched over the fire in some private misery, or trudging up and down the windy garden unhappily pegging clothes out as the rain threatened to begin, she had remained silent. 'I'm off then,' Angela would say. Mother would say nothing. 'I'm going —back this evening.' Silence, except occasionally for 'Off you go then, enjoying yourself,' spoken dismally. It had always spoiled the first half of any expedition and when afterwards it had been time to return the memory of Mother's depression had slowed her footsteps right down.

'Have a good time,' Angela said, trying hard to smile, 'don't worry about me. I'm just fed up—I'll get over it—don't let it affect you.'

'Are you sure? Sadie said, eagerly.

'Yes, I'm sure. Buy some lovely boots and come back and cheer me up—okay?'

'Okay.'

Bribery and corruption, Ben would say, but already Angela felt better. She did not want to pass her gloom on—better, far better, to contain her anguish instead of letting it spill out as she had just done with Sadie. Her way was no improvement on Mother's—explaining and justifying her problems was as disastrous as concealing them. Mother had lost her that way. She was determined not to lose Sadie.

Sadie at six, long before she had settled down with Sue and Joanna, her two close friends by the time she was an adolescent, used to taunt her playmates. She seemed to have them home only to torture them. 'Say everything I say,' she would order Alison, one of her constant victims. 'All right, Sadie.' 'No, dumbhead, say everything—say, say everything I say.' When at last Alison had sorted out what Sadie wanted Sadie would then think up inspired insults. 'Alison is a fat spotty pooh' and Alison would repeat it, only just beginning to realize the joke was somehow on her. 'Why,' Angela would say afterwards, 'why were you so cruel to Alison? Why do you make a fool of her like that? And every time she wanted to play something you wouldn't do it.' 'I don't care,' Sadie would say. 'But you will care,' Angela said, 'when you've lost her as a friend. If you want to keep your friends you must be kind to them.' Sadie glared at her, her face closed and full of spite. 'You don't be kind to me,' she said, 'saying that.'

Mother took a little soup in the evening, and a small piece of dry toast taken into her on a tray laid out invitingly by Angela. The tray was tin, of the kind Mother despised, but out of a drawer Angela had dug a white cloth she had once embroidered, scalloped at the edges with a pattern of blue forget-me-nots round them. Mother appreciated that. Ill though she was, she fingered the cloth and said how pretty, nobody did things like that any more, and she liked the pink linen napkin in its silver ring and the delicate china teapot Angela had almost forgotten she owned. Her weary eyes ran over the tray and rested on the white rose in glass jug and she said, 'Now isn't that nice—a rose—at this time of year,' and then, after a pause, 'I like things to be nice. Your Father just throws things on a tray, never has any appearance—cuts the bread all anyhow and never thinks to match the cup and saucer with the plate.' 'But he does very well—for him—doing it every day,' Angela said. 'Oh yes,' Mother said, 'very well, when you think what he has to do, a man like him.' Her gaze moved from the tray to the window where a branch of the pear tree tapped against it. 'Pretty,' Mother said, 'that tree—pretty shapes, those branches, even bare. It reminds me of the country. I always loved the country.'

Angela kept quiet. Mother knew nothing about the country. Whenever they took her into the countryside around St Erick she was given to exclaiming over the views and the peace and quiet and then, if there was no village shop in sight, she was bored. But the country, or so she imagined, was clean and pretty and safe and therefore it had her approval. She had never, to Angela's knowledge, put a pair of Wellingtons on and walked through a muddy field. She had hardly ever accompanied the rest of the family to Bodmin Moor, and when she did, she stayed in the nearest village while they went and climbed or walked. It was Father who really loved the country. 'We used to have lovely runs,' Mother was saying, 'out all day among the fields and hills.' But 'runs' were motorbike rides, roaring through the quiet they were supposed to relish, polluting the atmosphere they liked to think they savoured. 'I'm a trouble to you,' Mother suddenly said, her voice now sharp and firm whereas before it had wavered. 'I should never have come—and now I'm ill it's more work for you—I prayed and prayed I'd be all right and no bother to anyone and now look.'

'You are no trouble,' Angela said. 'In fact, you being in bed makes me sit down and that's a good thing. And you picked the right week—no teaching and the children just come and go as they please.'

'All this waiting on me,' Mother said.

'Well, I *should* wait on you. You're my mother. If I can't wait on my mother who can I wait on?'

'I never waited on mine. I would have done, but she died so suddenly, so young, just like Aunt Sally. She was never old, my mother, she never came to this—she was spared this.'

'Yes, I know,' Angela said, 'but then she missed a lot too—you have to look at it that way.'

'Do I?' Mother said, lower lip trembling.

'Yes, you do,' Angela said emphatically, 'your mother never had the pleasure of seeing her grandchildren—not your children anyway. She never saw me. She never saw you bring up a healthy, happy family.'

Mother was silent. She closed her eyes and then said, 'Have you told your Father about me being like this?'

'Of course—I had to—he's cross with me for not looking after you better—for trailing you off to Woburn that day.'

'I felt ill before we ever set off.'

'Then why didn't you say?'

'Oh, I'm always feeling ill—it might have been nothing, just the usual—and I'm always being a spoilsport, I'm sick of it.'

'It was a rotten outing anyway—and Father is right—I should have looked after you better.'

'You look after me beautifully—you've been so good—so—' Angela jumped up. Mother's eyes were full of tears.

'Will you speak to Father this evening on the telephone?' she said.

But when evening came, after a day in which she had been much brighter and stayed awake and reasonably alert, Mother was asleep again, heavily, her mouth open and snores trumpeting forth. Father did not take the news kindly.

'You're sure she's just asleep?' he said accusingly. 'You've had a good look at her, eh?'

'Father, the doctor has been and she's been sitting up this afternoon and talking and she's had some food.'

'Good. I'll have her home the minute she's fit though. Told her

208

this racketing round would do her no good but she's that stubborn and then that doctor of ours encouraged her. Tell her Mrs Collins is asking after her, and Mrs Graham and everyone at the ladies' circle—and there's a letter from Tom, now what shall I do with it? That's the point.'

'Send it here, of course,' Angela said. At least he was back to his old fussing ways. He knew perfectly well what to do with the letter.

'Tell her I've finished the sitting room—come up nice and fresh—and I've cleaned the mirror and put it back—the duster was filthy when I'd done, she should have seen it—and the pictures, I've hung them back where they were and everything's shipshape. Next I'll have a go at the bathroom—ask her if it's to be the same colour—she's the boss.'

'I'll ask her,' Angela said, yawning.

'At least,' Father said, 'she'll have plenty of company at your place, plenty of you visiting her.'

'Yes,' Angela said, 'we're all in and out all the time.'

'And you've got Sadie to help,' Father said.

'Yes. I've got Sadie.'

Sadie was not even in. Half term was a time for long days trailing round shops and stalls, sifting junk and coming home with rubbish, and for lying listening to records in each other's houses. Morning and evening Sadie said hello to her grandmother and that was that. The boys were better, frequently rushing in to ask something or show something, completely uninhibited by the sickroom atmosphere. All Sadie had done to help was open the door to the doctor.

Fourteen

'I'm thinking,' Sadie said when finally she was home again, 'of going Youth Hostelling this weekend with Sue and Joanna. Okay?'

'In October?' Angela said.

'What's wrong with October—you said the weather was perfect when you dragged us off to Woburn—lovely healthy bracing air, you said.'

'That was for the day—you were coming back to a warm house and bed.'

'I'm really not worried about houses and beds.'

'But what would you *do* all day—you hate walking—and what if the weather suddenly changed?'

'Look, that's our problem.'

'Where would you go? You know nothing about Youth Hostelling.'

'You don't *have* to know about it to do it. We haven't decided where to go yet.'

'It all sounds very vague.'

'But can I go?'

'Yes, I suppose so.'

'I mean, you don't mind? It will be one less to look after anyway, won't it.'

'How very thoughtful,' Angela said.

'But you don't mind?'

'Why should I?'

'You always say that but you always sound as if you do.'

'Well I don't. I just haven't the energy to sound enthusiastic.

And I'm probably a bit jealous—I wish I was fifteen and going off on mad weekends instead of nearly forty and stuck at home looking after a sick mother. I expect that's why I sound gloomy. But you know I like you to enjoy yourself.'

'Thanks,' Sadie said, and then, as she drifted off, 'I just wish you would enjoy yourself too.'

Angela paused in her dreary task of sorting out the washing to go in the machine. She had wanted Mother to enjoy herself too, but she hardly ever did. Tom used to make her laugh and even got her to be silly, to fool around with them, but that was on very rare occasions and other memories of Mother in high spirits were dim and unconvincing. Mother lacked gaiety. She had no exuberance. And now Sadie thought she was in the same mould —someone apparently incapable of enjoyment. Angela shoved dirty socks and trousers into the machine, sickened by this glimpse of how her daughter saw her—and rightly. Not for months and months had she been carefree and her own laughter sounded strange to her when she heard it. It was dismal. It was an indictment of her whole way of life. Worse, really, than Mother's melancholy had been to them because whereas Mother had been plainly sad, even if none of her children knew why, she herself was strident and bad tempered and plainly nothing except unpleasant.

'Don't be depressed about being depressed,' Ben said, 'that would be the end. What do you expect anyway—how could you be a bundle of fun at the moment? You worry about your Mother, with reason, and you worry about Sadie with less reason but still with some cause. It's only common sense that you're not exactly cracking a joke a minute.'

'Sadie thinks I never enjoy myself—it isn't just that I'm not jolly. She thinks I have no pleasures.'

'All adolescents think that—at fifteen you can't understand that pleasure isn't necessarily noise and crowds and action. You can't even imagine work could be a pleasure.'

'I can't see any way out. I can't abandon Mother.'

'You don't have to abandon her. She'll be better soon and then she'll go home and you've more than done your bit—you can take it easy then.'

'I already take it easy for most of the time—hardly ever going to see them—hiding behind letters and telephone calls.'

'Most people,' Ben said, 'do not ring their mothers up every day, write every week and spend at least four weeks' precious holiday with them.'

'Most people don't have mothers like mine.'

Sadie began having a friend to stay the night when she was very young. Because she had never in her whole childhood and adolescence been able to have a friend to stay the night Angela encouraged the habit. She realized the excitement and fun and though it quite often ended in disaster—Sadie fell out with the friend at two in the morning—she knew it was worth it. The best part was talking before they fell asleep. Sadie and the friend would drone on for hours and it amused Angela, as she put Max and Saul to bed, to hear their chatter. Often they would talk until ten or eleven when she herself was going to bed and then she had to go up and be severe. One night they were talking so loudly they did not hear her as she mounted the stairs. Angela heard the friend say, 'Sadie, do you hate your mother?' She paused, knowing she ought not to listen but wanting to hear the reply so desperately that she overcame her scruples. 'Sometimes,' Sadie said, cautiously. 'I love my dad,' the friend said, 'I love him best. Do you love your dad best?' 'Sometimes,' Sadie said. 'My mother,' the friend said, 'is the most horrible woman in the whole wide world. She's mean and nasty to me—she doesn't love me at all. Does your mother love you?' 'I think so,' Sadie said. 'I wish my mother wasn't my mother,' the friend said. 'I wish Susie Barker's mother was my mother, don't you? Don't you wish Susie's mother was your mother? She's so pretty and gentle and lovely— don't you wish she was your mother?' There was a long pause. Angela began rationalizing Sadie's 'sometimes' before it was said. 'No,' Sadie said, firmly, 'no, I don't.' 'Do you like your mother better than Susie's?' the friend said, shocked. 'Yes,' Sadie said, 'I do. I like my mother better than anyone's mother because she's mine, isn't she?'

Angela was so relieved and glad she crept back down the stairs without saying a word and for weeks and months afterwards that sentence of Sadie's thrilled her and brought ridiculous tears to her eyes whenever she thought of it.

Sadie was up early. Hearing the muffled bangs so early in the morning Angela thought first of Mother and half rose with alarm thinking that Mother had fallen out of bed—until she remembered Sadie was going Youth Hostelling. She lay back down again, relishing the feeling of well-being which had come to her after an unexpectedly good night's sleep. She had gone to bed so depressed and miserable, racked with fears for them all, her head full of absurd images in which she saw herself as a lightning conductor for all that might come to harm them and did not know how long she could go on standing tall and straight and strong. She had screwed her eyes up tight to get herself to sleep and had thought that when it came it would be full of nightmares in which her wailing children would extend their pitiful arms towards her as she sank into a deep and black grave where Mother already lay. But no. She had slept deeply, without dreams of any kind, and now in the morning half light she was able to smile at her bedtime hysteria. She put out a hand to touch Ben, still sleeping fast, and then she got up and put on her dressing-gown and left the bedroom quietly so as not to disturb him.

Down in the hall, Sadie struggled with her borrowed rucksack, desperately trying to pull the straps over the top.

'I can't get the fucking thing closed,' she said.

'Language,' Angela said automatically, but not feeling that usual sense of impotence.

'I'm going to be late—bloody thing,' Sadie said, kicking the rucksack. She looked even more unkempt than was normal and the black stuff she had plastered round her eyes made them look horrific and evil.

'Have you had anything to eat?' Angela said, kneeling down and beginning to empty the entire rucksack in spite of Sadie's restraining arm.

'I don't *want* anything to eat.'

'Go and have some toast and a hot drink and I promise by the time you're finished this will be ready.'

'Oh *god*,' Sadie said, but she went and Angela heard the kettle being put on and the clink of the stone lid as the bread bin was opened.

The child had no idea. There was not a Trewick gene in her. Out they came, the awful muddle of already soiled clothes that ought not to have been put in at all, the enormous mud-encrusted Kickers shoes that ought to have been on her feet, the jumble of maps and packets of biscuits, crushed and unappetizing before she had even set off, the waterproof anorak she had taken without Max knowing and ought to have had on the top ready for use, and a sequined waistcoat for which Angela could not account. But she would confront Sadie about nothing. Quickly, efficiently, she repacked the rucksack and had it ready and waiting when Sadie came back, still clutching a mug of tea and ramming toast into her mouth.

'There,' Angela said, 'that's better.'

'Thanks.'

'Have a good time. Ring if you get lost. Have you enough money?'

'Yeah.'

'And don't hitchhike—not in any circumstances. Understood?'

She stood on the doorstep for a minute, watching Sadie lumber off down the street, fidgeting with the straps of the rucksack before she had gone twenty yards. It was a slightly misty autumn morning, still cold and damp at seven o'clock, but Angela could tell that by midday the sun would have broken through. She would have given anything to be going off to walk in the New Forest, though how much walking Sadie would do remained to be seen. Half way down the street, Sadie turned and waved and made a funny face and then she was gone, turning the corner to Sue's house. Angela picked up a milk bottle that had fallen down and set it neatly with the others on the doorstep. God knew where Sadie would end up for the night since organization was another absent talent, but she had managed to refrain from cross-examining her. Sadie was on her own. She refused to agonize over her prospects the way Mother had spoiled everything by agonizing over hers. When she eventually came back she must be greeted with a smile and her bedraggled appearance must not be criticized.

Quietly, her new mood of resolution making her feel almost light-hearted, her rested body ready for another difficult day, Angela went down the passage to the little end room where Mother was and gently opened the door. A whole night was a very long time not to have looked at an invalid and slight twinges of apprehension stirred in her stomach. But Mother looked comfortable and was still asleep. Carefully, taking care not to disturb her, Angela felt the bedclothes but they were quite dry. Pulling the curtain to one side she took a good look at Mother— her colour was gone, but then she had been ill, and her expression was stone-like, as it often was, but there was no harsh breathing. In a little while, when she had savoured the peace of the early morning house a little longer, she would wake Mother up if she was still asleep and wash her and perhaps today she would be strong enough to get up for a little while and even to talk to Father, who otherwise would become impatient and suspicious.

There was time to go through the ritual of making real coffee, to grind the beans and heat the pot and warm the milk and best, most luxurious of all, to sit at the kitchen table drinking it without being either hurried or disturbed. Being alone was something she had never had enough of. She had never been alone. At training college from the beginning she had shared a flat, and then she had married Ben straight away without that intervening few years in a bedsitter so many of her contemporaries had experienced. Often, she fantasized the state of being alone and wondered what difference it would have made to her. She imagined an immaculately tidy flat and meals when she liked them and long walks at strange times. Then she thought of Valerie once saying, a hectic weekend with them behind her, 'Really Angela, I wouldn't have your life for anything—you haven't a minute to call your own.'

Mother of course thought the opposite. Mother used to say repeatedly, 'And then you'll all grow up and go away and I'll be on my own.' She even said it if they were all out on a Saturday. 'I've been on my own all day,' she said pathetically. Solitude put Mother in a panic. Mother had never in her life made coffee and sat drinking it alone, daydreaming. She had snatched cups of tea between tasks that demanded her full attention and if she saw a break in the heavy routine coming up she had automatically filled it. Not to think, that was Mother's object—only to do, and by doing exorcize that jealous devil inside her that told her life was never meant to be like this.

Sounds of the boys stirring upstairs brought Angela to her feet. What rubbish to foist such thoughts onto Mother. 'I'm not clever,' Mother would say, forced to comment on anything upon which she did not wish to give an opinion, 'I'm not clever like you—it's no good asking me what I think.' No talk, no real talk, just a string of platitudes linked together with sighs and exclamations, but perhaps that was something to be grateful for. If Mother ever chose to unburden herself properly it might be too much to bear. Angela set out cereal bowls, put milk and marmalade on the table, and wondered if that self-consciousness between parents and grown-up children might not after all be a good thing. The inhibiting factor might be a good thing. All these years she had regretted Mother's reticence she had perhaps been making a big mistake and ought instead to have welcomed it—perhaps reticence, on both sides, was the only thing that made the mother-daughter relationship bearable. Perhaps, now that she felt the same thing happening with Sadie even though she thought she had laid quite different foundations, perhaps she should simply let it happen and not fight it, not see it as a measure of her own failure. Perhaps she ought to recognize that a wall had gone up and instead of beating her fists against it, just lean thankfully on it. Why, after all, admire those families where mother and daughter wept openly on each other's shoulders and bore daily witness to each other's more personal distress?

'You're looking very cheerful,' Ben said when he came down to breakfast, 'and real coffee—this is my lucky day.'

'And Sadie's gone,' Max said, 'good riddance.'

'How unkind,' Angela said, 'she doesn't say that when you go.'

'I never go,' Max said.

'Too true, too true,' Ben said, 'you love us too much to tear yourself away.'

'Do you want me to go away?'

'The odd hour of absence might not be grieved over,' Ben said.

'Thanks.'

'Oh, can't you take a joke?' Angela said.

'It wasn't a very nice joke.'

'I'm off,' Ben said. He kissed Angela on top of her head. 'Keep it up,' he said, 'there'll be a special prize if you look the same this evening when I come home as you do this morning.'

'I'll try.'

She sat a little while longer chatting to the boys, listening to their plans for the day, lazily trying to analyse why there should be such a complete lack of restraint with the boys and yet not with Sadie. They did not worry her. She was confident and sure in all her dealings with them. She could show her affection easily and felt close and secure in their company. Sadie, who was shrewd and highly sensitive to atmospheres, probably saw this, but how did she interpret it? Did she see herself as different, or Angela as different to her? Or perhaps she never thought about it at all.

Angela had never met Tom's wife—none of them had. Tom met her in Brisbane two years after he emigrated. She was called Jo-Ellen, which Mother thought outlandish. There was not much correspondence—a card at Christmas, the occasional brief, badly written letter, and a photograph of each child as it was born. Jo-Ellen had four girls in a row, exactly two years in between each. Angela, who had Sadie the same month Jo-Ellen had her second daughter, used to show Sadie the photographs of her cousins and tried to make them mean something to her. With Ben an only child, Valerie unmarried and Harry, from whom nobody ever heard, childless, Tom's children were Sadie's only cousins. When the last of Tom's girls arrived Sadie was six years old. Angela opened the envelope with the Australian stamp and without thinking said, 'Oh how awful— poor Jo-Ellen has had another girl.' 'Why is it awful?' Sadie said, looking at the photograph of the anonymous baby. 'Well, she has three already— four girls—an all-girl family without any boys.' 'So?' Sadie said, eyes beady, frown ferocious. 'It's nice to have both,' Angela said, beginning to be ashamed. 'I wouldn't like all girls or all boys.' 'Why does it matter?' Sadie said, with one of those sophisticated looks for which she was already famous in the family ('she was born old,' Mother said). 'It doesn't really,' Angela said, weakly, and then, 'anyway, I'm glad I've got both.' 'You nearly didn't,' Sadie said, 'with three boys and only one girl. You nearly had all boys.' 'Yes,' Angela said, 'Wasn't I lucky to have you first? Daddy always said let's have a girl first to be sure. It would have been dreadful to be a mother without a daughter.' Sadie smiled, a small satisfied smile. Angela was relieved, but knew that if Sadie had been just a little older, she would have found her out.

'Mother,' Angela whispered, laying a cool hand on Mother's even cooler arm. 'Mother, can you hear me? I've brought you some tea.' She put the rose-covered china tea cup and saucer to which Mother had taken a fancy down on the bedside table and crossed the room to open the curtains. The last leaves had fallen off the pear tree. She stood looking at it for a moment, wishing the leaves were golden and brown instead of a shrivelled, dried-out black. Pear trees were sad in autumn. Here and there underneath the tree she could see the odd wasp-eaten fruit, rotting in the soil, an ugly, slimy thing. The tree was still beautiful in spring, thick with white blossom, each flower upon it perfect in every detail, some as huge as roses, but the fruit always began to fall before it was ripe because the tree, old as the house, was stricken by some mysterious disease that made the fruit useless year after year. Ben said they ought to chop it down and plant another but she would not hear of it. The tree to her was lovely.

'Mother,' she said, louder, injecting a note of brisk authority into her voice, her teacher's voice, 'Mother, come on, wake up, you're like Rip Van Winkle. Have this tea before it gets cold. It's the most beautiful morning—look, slightly misty, but the sun is going to come through any minute. Sadie has gone off already—you should have seen her with that rucksack—I can't imagine her walking more than a hundred yards from café to café.' On and on she chattered, tidying the table with Mother's things on it, picking out the dead flowers from the vase on the window sill, twitching the bed covers, straightening them, waiting for Mother to make some sign. She made none. Standing at the end of the bed Angela studied her. Her eyes were still closed, the eyelids heavily veined and the grey lashes at the end stubby and bedraggled. Under each of Mother's nostrils there was a single blob of blood, thick and clotted, entirely blocking her nose. Making a small sound of annoyance at her own neglect, Angela moved to the head of the bed, handkerchief in hand, and wiped the spots of blood away. Through the thin fabric of the handkerchief they felt hard and obstinate. She wiped more firmly, stifling the repugnance that threatened to overwhelm her, and all at once a great stream of dark, thick blood poured out, soaking the handkerchief, running down into Mother's half-open mouth, draining into it, draining ludicrously into the pink crevices where her teeth should have been and into the wrinkles round the corner of her mouth, and then like some poisonous brackish stream flowing onwards down her neck and onto the white coverlet where a stain, wide and long, spread rapidly across sheets and blankets.

Mesmerized, her own hand holding the sodden handkerchief sticky and wet, Angela watched Mother's blood soak the bed. Nervously, knowing it was no good, she dabbed and dabbed at Mother's nose, looking to see if the bleeding had stopped, pulling at the stained sheets to take their appalling redness away from Mother, who did not like mess. Somewhere, a long way off, she heard the boys thundering about. There was no one to whom she could shout for help even if any sound would come from her dry mouth. A memory came to her of a diagram in a first-aid book—

a person with a nose bleed ought to be flat on their back, their head only slightly raised, and a cold compress should be applied to their forehead. She pulled the three pillows from behind Mother's head one by one and let Mother fall back, and then she grabbed a towel and managed to move her shaking legs in the direction of the little downstairs bathroom where she soaked the towel in cold water and squeezed it out and returned to lie it across Mother's head. The bleeding stopped. Cautiously, afraid to be mistaken, she began wiping the blood away with the towel, stroking Mother's face with the thick bulky material, watching drops of water slide across the sticky surface of her skin. It had stopped. Nothing more was coming from Mother's nose. Relieved, Angela returned to the bathroom and filled a basin with warm water and took soap and a fresh towel and went back to Mother. She began to wash her tenderly. How had Mother come to have a nose bleed? It seemed so strange, and strange that all the fuss had not wakened her. Slowly, her hands still in the basin of warm water where bubbles of soap burst on the surface, Angela felt doubt. She turned the soap over and over with her hands until the water was cloudy. She dried her hands carefully. A pulse began to throb in her head as she forced herself to lift Mother's eyelids. A hard, dull, creamy whiteness looked back at her. Lips bitten between her teeth she slid a hand down Mother's side. Nothing seemed to be beating. She put her ear down on Mother's chest, suffocated by the warm sweet smell of the blood, but there was no sound. 'Milkman!' Max shouted in the background. She heard the clatter of milk bottles. Stiffly, holding herself very erect, she walked to the end of the hall and took her purse off the shelf. 'Cut yourself?' the milkman said as she handed him the money. She tried to say no, but could not manage the simple word. She smiled and shook her head. 'Max,' she said, 'take these into the kitchen.' 'Ugh,' Max said, 'they're all over blood.' She looked at the milk bottles, bloody fingerprints smearing the glass, matching the red tinfoil top, and carried them herself into the kitchen. 'Max,' she said, 'ring Dad at the office. Tell him to come home quickly.' She was sick into the sink where cereal bowls still floated, seeping left-over porridge into the water. 'Dad,' she heard Max say, 'can you come home—Mum's sick.'

Mother had died, around five that morning they said, peacefully they said. Mother had felt nothing, no pain, no strokes, her heart had simply packed up. The doctor was matter-of-fact. To all Angela's tearful questions he replied either with a shrug or monosyllables. He seemed to think it was very good of him to have come at all, to a dead person who was not even his patient. She did not dare blame him. He said there had been nothing the matter with Mother's heart when he listened to it three days ago. These things happened. He left after making out a death certificate and giving them instructions about what to do with the body as if it were a fallen tree.

The body was a problem. Angela had a great dread of ever going near it again, of ever even seeing that body to which the doctor referred as though it were an inanimate object. She could not go into the room. The things that needed doing she could not do. It was Ben who went in with the doctor, Ben who later closed the curtains and found a clean nightdress and sheets for the undertaker who was soon to come. They waited two hours for the undertaker's men to come and when they did Angela was embarrassed and ashamed. They were kind and solemn but they gave her no relief. She sat at the foot of the stairs, crouching, listening to their low voices, imagining what they were doing with their expert hands. She could not bear to watch Mother's body leave the house and hid upstairs until the click of the front door and the sound of a car moving off told her they had gone. It seemed the worst of a series of betrayals. At home in St Erick bodies lay in the house until they were taken away for burial. The whole street came to pay their respects, tip-toeing into front bedrooms murky with drawn blinds, peering at the body and whispering over it and leaving the bereaved household to its tears. To send Mother to a parlour of repose was hideous. It ought not to have been allowed. Father would have a fit at the thought.

Over everything hung the dark cloud of Father's innocence. Mother had been dead for six hours and Father did not know. At eleven o'clock on a Friday morning he would be going for his weekend shopping, walking purposefully to the butcher's with a string bag to buy half a pound of mince. The longer she waited to tell him, the worse the delay would seem, the more unforgivable and heinous her crime. She had tried, waiting for Ben to come home, to ring Father but her hand resisted moving towards the telephone and stayed limp and lifeless in her lap. She had tried again, waiting for the doctor—Ben had brought the telephone to her—but she shook and trembled and Ben had said she would feel better when the body was out of the house and that she would be able to do it then. But she felt no better. She was still horribly afraid. Speechless, she stared at Ben, willing him to make this awful call for her though she knew quite well he could not.

'Come on,' he said gently, 'get it over. I'll dial for you.'

'I can't, I can't.'

'You must. I'll ring now.'

'No—I don't know what to say—how to say it—what shall I say?'

'The words will come when you start to speak.'

'They won't—he'll be so angry—he'll shout—'

'No, no, he won't—of course he won't—how can he be angry? —it wasn't your fault.'

'He'll say I should have known how ill she was—he'll think I neglected her, didn't realize how serious it was, and I didn't did I?'

'Nobody did—the doctor said your Mother's heart was perfectly sound three days ago—these things happen.'

'Father doesn't believe things happen. He'll think I tricked him—he'll feel so cheated that he wasn't there.'

'He couldn't have done any good.'

'Oh I know, I know, but he's watched over her all these years and seen her through all her illnesses and then not to be there when it actually happened—it will paralyse him—I just can't bear the thought—'

'Well,' Ben said, a little grimly, pacing around the room, 'you have to bear it. Nobody else can do it for you.'

'Couldn't you—?' But her voice faltered and the question hung in the air. Ben came and sat beside her. He tried to put his arm round her but she pushed it away.

'Look,' he said, 'you know it would be unforgivable that your Father heard your Mother had died from anyone else except you. When he'd got over the shock he would think back over it and hold it against you. I'll ring if you like, but I don't think I should.'

He helped her to compose herself and brought her a cup of coffee so hot and strong she scalded her lip at the first mouthful. The small pain was pleasant—she touched and rubbed the tiny burn with pleasure as it helped her focus on what she must do. Ben closed the door so that none of the boys would come rushing in unexpectedly from the Bensons' where they had been hastily dumped, and carried the telephone over to her. 'Two minutes,' he said encouragingly, 'and then it will be all over. I'll carry on when you've told him the actual news.' He dialled the number and handed her the receiver and she sat in a daze listening to the ringing tone. She saw in her mind's eye the cluttered living room and the green armchair with its back to the light where Mother would sit no more and at that mawkish thought tears came yet again from that inexhaustible source inside her. They felt cool on her hot cheeks as they spilled down her face. Thoughts like that must not come into her head—she could safely leave them to Valerie. As the telephone rang and rang she began to feel curiously hopeful—perhaps Father would never answer. 'He must be out,' she said to Ben, and began to put the receiver down but Ben said, 'Keep ringing. He may be out in the garden.'

'Hello,' Father bellowed.

Her heart raced but she managed to say 'Hello, Father.'

'What's up?' he said at once. 'I was in the garden—got it all straight for the winter now. What's the trouble then? How is she?'

The words Ben had promised her would come had not materialized. She listened abstractedly to Father's breathing—he always pressed the receiver far too close to his mouth—and to the noise in the background of a police siren wailing. She could have sat forever saying nothing, merely absorbing other sounds, as though waiting for them to form a sentence on her behalf.

'Are you there, Angela?' Father said, impatiently.

'Well, come on then—I haven't got all morning—I've got my pension to collect and there's a gas bill to pay, just come in this morning but your Mother doesn't like them to lie. Did she have a good night?'

'Yes,' Angela said, 'she had a good night.'

'Slept well, eh, that's the ticket. How is she this morning then? Brighter?'

'No,' Angela said.

'Damn,' Father said, 'that's like her—up one minute, down the next. Always the same when she's been ill—two steps forward, three steps back. What's wrong this morning then?'

'She had a nose bleed,' Angela said. If only she could cry, if only the tears would tell the tale for her, but now, when she needed them, they deserted her.

'A nose bleed?' echoed Father, entranced by the novelty, 'that's queer—she's never had a nose bleed before. What caused that then? She didn't get up and fall did she—I told you to watch her—she's that unsteady on her feet even when she's only been in bed a day—did she fall and bang her face?'

'No,' Angela said. Ben had begun to walk restlessly up and down the room again.

'Well, then,' Father said, 'how did she come to have one? That's what I want to know. Have you had the doctor?'

'Yes.'

'Good. What did he think of it then? What did he say?'

'He said—' Again, her voice trailed away. There was a sudden and complete cessation of any sound at all from her throat as though the vocal chords had been severed at one blow.

'Come on lass—has she had a turn?'

When the silence continued,

'Well then? Eh?'

'Father, there isn't any way I can break this easily—' and now Father was silent, just when she most wanted him to bluster and nag. He would be standing at the window, keeping an eye on the street in case so much as a dustbin was out of place, standing in his stocking feet with his massive Wellingtons left on the doormat. Most likely he would be wearing his old brown tweed sports jacket and underneath a grey Marks and Spencer's cardigan that kept him particularly warm. He would be scowling, disliking the turn the conversation was taking. 'Father,' she said, closing her eyes but unable to shut the image of him out, 'Mother is dead. She died in her sleep, peacefully. There was nothing anyone could have done. The doctor said her heart was sound three days ago. I'm sorry—Father?'

She had never, in all her dreadful imaginings, thought he might hang up. The shock made her tremble. Prepared for the violence of his anger and grief she did not know how to cope with his abrupt withdrawal.

'He's hung up,' she said, staring stupidly into the receiver as though it might at any moment spring into life again.

'What shall I do?'

'Wait a while, and then I'll ring back,' Ben said. 'You've done very well—it's all over.'

'All over? Done well? He's all on his own in that house—'

'As he would want to be.'

'There's nobody for him to talk to—'

'He wouldn't want anyone.'

'He may have collapsed—he might be lying on the floor—'

'Your Father? Never. And if he had, he couldn't have rung off. He just doesn't want to talk. I'll ring Valerie now and get her to go straight there. That's the best thing.'

She went to the glass doors that opened into the garden and stood flattened against the cold glass staring out at the table they ate from in the summer, still faintly covered with frost. She could hear Ben's soothing tones and could tell from what he said that Valerie must be crying. Why should Valerie cry—why should she cry herself—only Father, who had loved Mother unreservedly to the very end, had any need to cry, as she was sure he would not. He would have gone into the garden. He would be stalking up and down the rigidly straight paths made from cinders taken from the fire—up and down, patrolling, arms folded across his chest, frowning at the last of the cabbages. Mother always said Father's face told no one anything whereas she, she wore her heart on her sleeve. Angela spread her hands against the glass, steadying herself. There was no escape from the dreadfulness of the immediate future but she must be brave this one last time. For Mother's sake, she must do it.

Angela had always been afraid of cats—any cat, all cats. She could not bear to be touched by them and if one jumped onto her lap she would scream with fright however public the place where it happened. The house she and Ben bought a little while before Sadie was born had belonged to an old couple who loved cats—not just their own three but everyone else's. The first month of living in this house was spent chasing away cat after cat— they came jumping over the garden walls all day long and if the kitchen door was open they ran in, expecting their former welcome. Angela chased them away and did not leave the door open unless she was in that room. Gradually, the cats stopped coming. But one day Angela went up to her bedroom to rest after lunch and as she walked into the room, closing the door behind her, she turned round to take off her shoes and saw on her bed a large black tom cat with blazing green eyes. It was vast. It stood there, on the quilt, back arched, tail stiff, claws digging into the material, and Angela clutched at her throat in an exaggerated gesture of terror. But she did not scream. She backed towards the door, slowly, not wanting to make the hideous cat jump, and felt for the knob, watching it all the time. She told herself to be brave. She said to herself be calm, be calm, think of the baby. And she found, because of that need, the courage to open the door and turn her back on the cat and make a gesture of dismissal. The cat was out in a flash. She followed it downstairs and watched it run into the garden and returned triumphant to bed. She had managed to overcome her fear for the sake of the baby. Was there anything, she wondered, that could make her quail now she was to be a mother and had a duty to someone else?

When the last arrangement had been made, the last exhausting timetable gone over, they remembered Sadie. 'I don't even know where exactly she has gone,' Angela said, 'just somewhere in the New Forest.' There would be nobody at home when she returned the following night. Angela and Ben were travelling on the train with the coffin and the boys had been scattered among long-suffering friends. 'Father will want Sadie at the funeral,' Angela said.

'Oh, I don't think so.'

'Of course he will,' Angela said, shouting, contemptuous, 'he will expect it.'

They had not spoken again to Father. Ben rang repeatedly but there was no reply. They had to wait until Valerie got there to hear that he was all right but did not want to talk to anyone. He was, said Valerie, anxious to have Mother home—that was what was upsetting him most, the thought of her body among strangers. Once told the coffin would arrive the next day he was mollified. The funeral arrangements were of no interest to him. He had said they were to do what they liked—to do what Mother would have wanted.

And what was that? Neither of them had any excuse for not knowing. For more than ten years Mother's funeral had been an imminent event. Her eye had held a loving light whenever she had talked of it but nobody could remember any precise instructions except that there were to be no flowers. Of hymns, they knew nothing, and even burial or cremation was a choice they hardly knew how to make. Angela was determined Valerie should decide—it would give her something to do as she wailed her way through each day.

The boys would not come, of course. Even Father could see that, though there would be a part of him that would expect them to pay the necessary hundreds of pounds to fly over for Mother's funeral. Telegrams had been sent and replies received but Tom and Harry were lost causes.

It was to his daughters Father would look—to his daughters and to his grand-daughter, and as she thought of the performance to be gone through Angela shuddered and passed a weary hand over her eyes and wondered if, after all, she was capable of it.

Fifteen

Valerie never seemed to have been off the telephone. Her tenth call in twenty-four hours almost made them miss the train.

'I can't believe it,' she said, as she had already said many times, 'I just can't believe that Mother has passed on.'

'Oh for God's sake,' Angela said, not bothering to keep her irritation out of her voice, 'don't be so ridiculous—and don't use those awful euphemisms—all this passing on stuff. Mother is dead. She was old and ill and she was expected to die—stop acting as though it was completely unexpected.'

'But it was,' said Valerie, 'I didn't expect it—I had no idea—you didn't even tell me she was ill. It was so sudden—the shock—'

'Oh Christ,' Angela said, 'the only one who has any right to talk about being shocked is me. I got the only shock going when I found her dead. That's what the word shock means.'

'It must have been awful for you but—'

'Yes, it was awful, and I didn't enjoy the rest of it either.'

'I can see that—I mean, I do realize how terrible it must have been for you but all the same—'

'Good,' Angela cut in, 'I'm glad you do.'

'But she was my Mother too, and I would like to have been there at the end,' Valerie said and started to sob in earnest once more.

'Shut up,' shouted Angela. 'I'm sick of all this crying—nobody was there at the end.'

'I know, I know, I just meant I was so far away—'

'Then lucky you.'

'I wish you wouldn't be so horrible to me just because I'm upset,' Valerie said. 'I can't help weeping—I'm like Mother,' and she went off into another fit of hysterical crying.

'What was it you rang about anyway,' Angela said, sharply, 'we're going to miss our train—can't it wait a few hours till we see you?'

Valerie said it could and Angela put the telephone receiver down, seething at her feebleness. She resented too this claim to be like Mother. Valerie was not like Mother and never had been. She was not even a pale imitation of Mother but something quite different. All her childhood she had claimed to be like Mother and the claim had never been denied—she was cuddled and kissed and allowed to go on thinking that it was true. Angrily slamming out of the house to get into the taxi with Ben, Angela was glad that at least all pretence was now over. She did not have Mother to protect—she could say what she liked to Valerie, she could shout if she was in a rage with her and laugh at her and not worry that Mother would say 'Oh, Angela,' in that sad voice that made her suffer. Driving to the station a great tiredness overcame her at the thought of such a loosening of bonds. There was no need any more to dread telling Mother any truth, no need to torture herself with images of Mother's misery.

'I wonder if I should have stayed behind,' Ben said, 'until Sadie came home. That note you left was a bit brutal. It will be a shock for her finding it.'

'Oh don't *you* start talking about shock—Sadie won't be shocked anyway—she won't be the least bit interested—it will all be just a bore.'

'Don't be nasty. I think she was very fond of her grandmother.'

'Very fond? And how do you deduce that? She never went near her—she never did a thing for her.'

'You don't have to do things for people to be fond of them.'

'I don't think Sadie was, anyway, except in a sort of obvious hypocritical way.'

The note had said, 'Grandma died on Saturday—please ring us at St Erick at once. The boys are at the Bensons' and the Carriers' and we want you to come down for the funeral.' She had packed a case full of suitable garments and put it on the kitchen table with the note on top. She had written to Sadie's headmistress and booked a mini-cab for her—all she had to do was confirm the time she wanted to be picked up. It was all organized. If Sadie was back by seven, as she ought to be, she could catch a train that night. If she was not, she could stay with her friend Sue and join them in time for the funeral in the afternoon. Sadie didn't need to think at all, simply obey clear instructions.

Angela looked at herself in the mirror nailed up in the back of the taxi. At last, the black suit was donned for its original purpose. Mother would have been proud of her. She looked both elegant and feminine. With the suit she wore a grey silk blouse with a collar that came out over the neck of the jacket and round her neck she had a heavy gold locket with a picture of Mother on one side and Sadie as a baby on the other. She wore black shoes and very fine, light-grey tights and in her buttonhole she had a white rose. She even had a hat—a simple grey felt hat that shaped itself to her head in a way that both looked and felt entirely natural, and she wore gloves for the first time in decades.

The coffin was already there. They followed it as it was taken down the platform and stood beside it while it was loaded onto the train. The procedure she had dreaded turned out to be easy and relaxed and perfectly matter-of-fact, without any awkwardness at all because the men who were doing the job had obviously done it so many times before. The blinds were drawn in the compartment containing the coffin—a first-class compartment—and she and Ben sat next door. They left their blinds open but nobody got in beside them. Looking out of the window as she waited for the train to begin, Angela wished she had thought of having a veil to protect her from stares. A veil would have been a little ridiculous but Mother would have liked it. She realized, even as the thought came to her, that she was falling into that habit much beloved by recently bereaved people—the habit of automatically registering what the deceased would or would not have liked and wanting to pay attention to these wishes. It was as though the dead left a clearly defined trail behind them, like a slug leaves a trail of slime, and there was pleasure in following it, however gruesome.

Ben did not approve of people who gloried in grief. He was watching her anxiously, waiting for the tears and sentiment as they began this most sentimentally tearful journey. To please him, to earn his approval and also to reassure him that she herself wished to act as he would wish her to act, she suggested they had lunch and forget about the sandwiches she had brought. They had a bottle of best British Rail wine before they changed trains—a nerve-wracking experience with the coffin to think of—and were comparatively merry until St Erick, where Father and Valerie were seen waiting on the platform. They were both dressed in deepest mourning from head to toe. Angela saw them before the train had stopped—they flashed past like black dots, merging into each other to form one gritty blob. She looked at Ben, speechless, and he sighed. Together they went into the corridor, ready to open the door the instant the train was stationary. 'I wish,' Angela said, clutching at Ben's sleeve, 'I wish it was this time tomorrow and it was all over.' 'It will pass in a flash,' Ben said. 'It's the last lap—don't forget.'

She tried hard to remember. The last lap. Father's ashen face, so much worse than she had expected, so grey that her smile froze on her lips. The forlornness of the coffin on its trolley and Father's hand resting briefly on it and his fury when one of the porters shouted hello to a friend over the coffin itself. He might almost have said, Don't upset Mother. He avoided her eyes, more concerned with the progress of the coffin to the hearse than greeting her. The last lap. Home to that dreary house and the official installing of the coffin on Mother's bed. 'It isn't nailed down, is it?' were Father's first words. 'Eh? They haven't gone and nailed her down?' Silently, Ben showed him where the catches were temporarily fixed. Together they lifted the lid, Valerie crying before she saw a thing, and Father said, 'She looks very peaceful, very.' Angela, who had not seen Mother since that terrible morning, looked too. Mother did not look peaceful. She had no expression at all. She was nothing.

They closed the bedroom door and trooped into the sitting-room. Valerie, hideously red-eyed and hiccuping with so much crying, went to put on the kettle. Father sat down and leaned forward, his hands on his knees. 'Well, then,' he said, 'there's some explaining to be done.' He paused, staring at Angela, who could think of nothing to say.

'There's a lot of things I want to know,' he said.

'What do you want to know?' Angela said, not bothering to object. His pound of flesh was precious to him.

'I want to know it all,' Father said, 'from start to finish. I'm entitled to that.'

'There isn't really anything to say,' Angela said.

'There'd better be,' Father said.

'Mother just seemed tired,' Ben said hurriedly. 'Angela looked after her wonderfully—you mustn't think she didn't. But after their day at Woburn she was tired and went to bed and when she wasn't herself the next day we had the doctor. He said she was fine.'

'Stupid bugger,' Father said.

'Then she seemed to get better and—well—she just died in her sleep when we thought she was better. It was a dreadful shock for Angela to find her.'

'Worse for me,' Father said. 'I sent her off with you right as rain and look what happens. I should never have let her out of my sight, never. I knew something like this would happen.'

'It had to happen sometime,' Angela said, only wanting to console him but realizing immediately she had said the wrong thing.

'What? What's that? Eh? It wouldn't have happened if I'd been with her I can tell you that, not by a long chalk.'

'I couldn't help Mother dying, Father.'

'I don't know about that. Any road, what did she say?'

'She was asleep when she died.'

'Before that—what were her last words? Come on.'

'I can't remember.'

'Her last words and you can't remember—that's the sort of thing I mean—no consideration.'

'She didn't *have* any last words—I didn't know they were going to be last words, did I? I didn't know she was going to die.'

'Neither did I.'

Mercifully Valerie came in with cups of tea. They all drank gratefully.

'There are so many people coming to the funeral,' Valerie said. 'The Vicar thinks the church will be crowded.'

'As it should be,' Father said, 'she'd want plenty. If they can all sing it will be all right.'

'Just the family at the house of course,' Valerie said, blotchy face momentarily animated. 'I've made that clear. It will be all we can do to feed relatives without coping with friends and neighbours.'

'Your Mother liked a good funeral tea,' Father said sternly, 'nothing shabby—no bought cakes or anything.'

'It won't be shabby,' Valerie said, 'I've baked non-stop since I arrived.'

'I was only saying,' Father said.

They sat in silence for a while, sipping tea, Father slurping his noisily. The light had faded and it was completely dark outside but nobody drew the curtains. They were all watching Father, afraid to start any conversation of which he might not approve. Suddenly he put down his cup. 'Here,' he said, 'what about Sadie? Eh?'

'We can't get hold of her,' Ben said, 'she's gone Youth Hostelling. But she'll be back tonight and we've left messages. She'll ring any minute I expect. She'll come tomorrow.'

'Good,' Father said, 'and where's all them boys?'

'Staying with friends,' Angela said. 'We thought they were too young for a funeral.'

'They should be here,' Father said fiercely, 'showing some respect. Nobody shows any respect any more, that's what. Mother doted on them and they aren't even going to be at her funeral. Scandalous.' He shook his head. Nobody dared to say a word. One half of Angela's brain was registering disgust and the other shame. 'She was too good for this world,' Father was saying, 'always was. She suffered, oh she suffered all right.'

'Not too much.' Angela said, timidly, meaning to console.

'What do you know about it?' Father asked, suddenly getting to his feet, snapping the glaring overhead light on and pulling the curtains together so roughly that the runners screeched. 'Thought the world of you, your Mother did, and what did you do—went away, that's what. No eyes for anyone else, only you—what's Angela doing, what's Angela thinking—and what did you care—nothing.'

'I did care,' Angela managed to say, though it was much too painful to say anything.

'Well you didn't show it. Funny way of caring. It upset her something chronic. What's it all mean, she used to say many a time—what do we have children for? No good saying now you cared.'

'No,' Angela said, 'no good at all. But I hope she knew.' Valerie began to cry. 'Would anyone like anything to eat?'

'Yes,' Father said, 'I've had nothing but tea and biscuits all day.'

They were once in the cinema in Leicester Square, when Tim was six months old and still a delicate, difficult baby. They had not been to the theatre or the pictures for about a year and the children had forgotten that they ever used to go out. Getting a babysitter was difficult. Angela had lost touch with the group of sixth formers she used before and when she tried to contact them they had all gone on to universities. She could not bring herself to use the thirteen and fourteen year olds who had taken their place—they all looked too young to be able to cope with the million crises that loomed ahead in her imagination. In the end she asked a neighbour who had once offered, a Miss Jenkins who was a retired nurse and still did some occasional private nursing. Sadie sulked when told Miss Jenkins was coming. 'She doesn't know us,' Sadie said, 'she won't be able to deal with the baby if he wakens.' 'She's a nurse,' Angela said, but Sadie would not be reassured. 'You don't care,' she said, 'you just want to go out.' 'Then I won't go,' Angela said. But Ben insisted. And then, in the middle of the film, the cinema manager walked up the aisle shouting 'Will Mr and Mrs Bradbury please come to the foyer.' Angela went with thunderously beating heart. 'Your babysitter has telephoned,' the manager said, 'she says there seems to be something wrong with the baby. There was certainly a lot of yelling down the line.' They drove home full of calamitous thoughts. There was very little wrong with Tim. Angela merely picked him up and he stopped screaming instantly. Ben walked an embarrassed Miss Jenkins home. 'I told you,' Sadie said, her face miserable and worried. 'I'm sorry, Sadie,' Angela said. 'She wouldn't let me touch him,' Sadie said, 'I could have got him quiet. She held him so awkwardly. He knew she didn't care—he could tell.' 'I'm sorry,' Angela said again, 'it won't ever happen again I promise.' But she promised not because of what the incident had done to Tim but what it had done to Sadie.

Nobody stayed in bed the morning of the funeral—indeed, there was a competitive air about the whole process of getting up. They all moved about extremely quietly, conscious of Mother's body in the house. They turned taps on and off with exaggerated care, not letting the water gush out but controlling the flow to a slow, seemly trickle. They walked up and down stairs without talking or coughing, trying not to step on certain well-known creaking ones. Frequently they bumped into each other—so successfully had ordinary noises been subdued that none of them could hear each other approaching. They would apologize in a whisper when this happened and assure each other it did not matter and for a little while afterwards behave more normally. They each breakfasted alone. Father for once did not have bacon and egg, which upset them all, knowing as they did how significant such a self-sacrifice was. He had a boiled egg instead and Valerie seemed to find this even more upsetting. 'A boiled egg?' she said, 'but you never have boiled eggs.' 'Well I am today,' Father said furiously.

By eleven o'clock they were all ready, the dishes washed, the beds made, the floors swept. Father would not allow Valerie to put the hoover on. When she pointed out the crumbs under the table he got down on his hands and knees and swept them up with a dustpan and brush. Valerie beseeched him not to. 'I don't think it's right,' she said, 'today of all days—on your hands and knees—crawling about like that—' but she tailed off. Father was out of sympathy with her insinuations. 'Out of the way,' he said, 'let me get this into the dustbin and then we're all shipshape.' He did a score of similar jobs and yet was ready in his good clothes when the first mourner arrived at the house. He stood in his black suit by the fireplace, stern and unsmiling, his eyes missing nothing about either the dress or demeanour of each arrival. Those who were wearing a light-coloured suit, or a bright dress—those who had followed modern custom and had not bothered about mourning clothes—earned an up-and-down look so dismissive that they visibly flinched and pawed at their attire with frantic gestures as though trying to rub out the blue or red or green that had offended. Those who tried to be bright and breezy in their greetings, whether out of nervousness or a genuine desire to cheer, were instantly rebuked. 'Cold again today, eh?' said one uncle, smiling and rubbing his hands together vigorously. 'Doesn't matter to Mother whether it's cold or not,' Father said, and the hands came slowly to a halt. Hearing this and similar comments speech dried up in everyone's throats. They all stood awkwardly in the small room waiting for the funeral cars to release them from this misery.

Father looked at his watch often. That the hearse might be late was a disaster so terrible that Angela could not bear to contemplate it. But Father was looking at the time for another

reason—he was awaiting the arrival of Sadie. Angela dreaded it.
Sadie had telephoned the night before from her friend's house
and though she had obeyed instructions and agreed to come up
there had been nothing in her voice to indicate that she appreciated the importance of behaving well. To everything Angela
had said she had replied 'Yeah, okay, okay,' and what kind of
guarantee could that be regarded as? Any distress she might have
been feeling was not in evidence—curiosity about the details of
Mother's death yes, but concern no. But Sadie was to be the sole
representative of the next generation and was needed as a symbol
by Father.

'She's cutting it close,' Father said, inspecting his watch yet
again, holding it near to his eyes though he was not in the least
short-sighted. 'Very close,' and he pursed his thin cracked lips
and shook his head. 'No need for it,' he said.

'She can hardly help the train being late,' Angela murmured,
smiling at Mother's cousin who had come from Truro and was
standing between Father and her, uncertain what the conversation was about and afraid to ask.

'Could have caught an earlier train,' Father growled.

'There isn't an earlier train,' Angela said quietly, feeling that
she ought not to contradict Father however wrong he was, 'this
was the first train of the day with the right connection.' If Father
said anything else she must let it go however provocative it turned
out to be. But he said nothing, only clicked his tongue with
annoyance, and she turned to doing her duty by the Truro
cousin.

None of it seemed to have anything to do with Mother. The
longer she stood there making fatuous remarks the more Angela
was seized by an insane and almost irresistible desire to go into the
little downstairs bedroom to sit with the coffin. It would make
more sense to sit quietly beside it than it did going through with
this pointless ritual. And yet to Father it was clearly not pointless.
He gave the lie to her every thought on the subject, demonstrating
as he did the way in which an obsession with the details of the
funeral could successfully opiate grief. There he stood, implacable,
working himself into a rage over times and clothes and expressions
in voices, unable to let loose his anguish except in complaint.
Watching him Angela saw how vital Sadie's presence was
becoming. He was building it up into a big thing. If she did not

arrive in time to go to the church in the family car, or if she arrived wearing her dirty jeans and torn shirt and with black nail varnish on her nails, then she would deflect the whole course of Father's grief until it poured down upon her in an avalanche of abuse.

But any chance of that happening—and she could not decide whether it would have been a good or bad thing—was averted by the arrival of Sadie a quarter of an hour before the procession was due to leave. 'Taxi,' Father shouted, and everyone crowded to the window as though none of them had themselves arrived by taxi. Angela found herself shrinking back instead of moving forward as all the relatives craned to see who Father was getting so excited about. 'It's my grand-daughter,' Father said loudly, with the most obvious satisfaction. 'I'll get the door,' and he pushed past Valerie, whom he had left to open it all the other times. Angela was unable to hear or see how Sadie was greeted. She stayed at the other side of the crowded room and was the last to see her daughter. 'Isn't she like her grandmother,' she heard someone say, and as Sadie's face emerged from between so many others Angela saw that this was true. It was the first time in fifteen years of studying her daughter's face minutely that she had ever seen it, but then it was the first time she had ever seen Sadie with her hair severely drawn back from her forehead and tied into a tight bunch at the back of her neck. It was the first time she had ever seen that thick tangled mess smooth and shining after what must have been hours of brushing. The transformation was startlingly complete. Sadie was wearing a plain, dark-grey dress that had been bought for her by Angela and shoved immediately to the back of a cupboard. Until she saw her in this dress Angela realized she had never known Sadie's shape. That was Mother's too—slim, but broad-hipped and long-legged with a softness about her whole outline that was normally entirely concealed by her masculine clothing. She did not recognize the shoes, nor the necklace, nor the cameo brooch worn as Mother would have worn it on the collar of the dress.

Ben went over and kissed Sadie but Angela still stayed where she was, nodding a greeting that Sadie acknowledged with the faintest of smiles and a slightly mocking gesture of her hand. Angela wondered if they were being offered a parody—Sadie was pleased to be doing it their way and might later guy her own performance. But even if that were so there was no hint of it for anyone else to see. Sadie stayed beside Father those last few minutes, her radiance casting some light over him so that he seemed less gnarled and grey beside her. She spoke gravely and with deference to all who addressed her and by doing so lifted from everyone that sense of oppression created by Father's unyielding mood. They were all almost light-hearted by the time the cars came and they got into them in a way which Father, before Sadie's arrival, would have condemned as being offensively jolly.

Angela had expected the journey to be made in complete silence but to her surprise Father began straight away to question Sadie about her Youth Hostelling. Sadie gave an exact itinerary, which pleased him, and added details about the weather and the journey by train there and back which normally it would have been quite impossible to get from her. Only as they swung through the gates of the church did Father say 'No talking now,' very severely and they all sat up straight and still. The tears began to flow down Valerie's face at the sight of Mother's beloved church and the deepest gloom settled upon Angela. The church was so personal—it had meant so much to Mother all through her life. She hated any Sunday when she could not go to church and there had been too many of them in the last few years. Father raged against what 'that place' did to her. He swore that it was all that damned sitting and standing and kneeling, forever bobbing up and down, that exhausted her and was even responsible for her illness. Sometimes he went with her to supervise her actions and as he forced Mother to sit throughout the singing of any hymn that had more than two verses he would mouth 'She's disabled' at the congregation around him. They would smile with embarrassment and nod and bury themselves in their hymn books.

The Vicar was waiting on the steps. Father detested him as he detested all clerics. The very sight of a dog collar enraged him. He thought clerics were hypocrites and soft and above themselves and he scorned them—yet Angela noticed how quickly he hid his scorn in subservient gestures. 'A true servant of our Lord,' the Vicar murmured, 'a real Christian.' Father merely nodded and busied himself organizing his little party into a procession to follow the coffin. Mother had said there were to be no flowers but Angela had disobeyed her. She watched Father's face closely. The coffin had gone into the hearse with nothing on top of the dark wood. It came out with a dozen white roses on top. 'Right,' Father said impatiently, 'come on—let's after it.'

The church was packed, every row full almost to the end. When they sang Mother's favourite hymn—or the one she and Valerie had chosen to remember as her favourite—the singing rose and swelled and filled the church gloriously with a rich, vibrant sound—nothing thin or reedy but a full-bodied chorus so vigorous that Angela looked about her in awe. Father must surely be gratified. He would dwell upon it afterwards and say 'She would have been pleased' without admitting he was also pleased. She noted the awkward way in which he was standing—the way that had always irritated Mother—clutching at the back of the pew in front not for support but because he did not know what to do with his hands. Valerie, in a state of near convulsion at his side, clearly annoyed him, but even as she saw this Angela also saw him frowning at her too and knew that her calmness and detachment annoyed him no less. Only Sadie succeeded in combining dignity with a slightly tremulous air, which was how Mother would have borne herself.

The Vicar's talk was flatteringly long. He dwelt at length on the service Mother had given to the church. He spoke of how she had once run Bible Class and of her work for the Women's Guild and the Sunday School and her long association with the League of Friends and the help she had given to support missionaries and of her steady contributions to the Parish Magazine and he thanked her for the thousands of flowers she had regularly donated from her garden to fill the church Sunday after Sunday. (Father flinched slightly at that. He had begrudged every bloom.) The Vicar said nobody would ever forget Mother's kindness and willingness to help others. He said she left a devoted husband and family and many, many friends, all of whom admired the courage with which she had faced a long series of illnesses. Valerie had to sit down. Father looked surreptitiously at his watch. At last it was all over and they prepared themselves to go to the cemetery. Angela caught Sadie's eye and was surprised to see how shaken her daughter was.

They once took Mother shopping to Biba, the South Kensington department store that at the time offered a kind of theatre of shopping, a place where the look of the interior, all purple and black and silver, matched the absurdity of most of the things for sale. Sadie, aged eight, loved it. She ran across the acres of thick carpet and up and down the staircases exclaiming at the wonderful treasures she saw, heaped up in brilliant piles of colour on the floor. Mother, who thought it all silly, and could not for the life of her see that it evoked any nineteen-thirties that she had known, worried that Sadie might get lost. They had lunch in the restaurant, Mother tense with disapproval. 'It's just fun Mother,' Angela said, 'there's nothing wrong with that.' 'The waste,' Mother muttered, 'you can't buy anything real—it isn't a real shop at all.' They went down in the lift. At the ground floor when they all got out Sadie got left behind—they turned just in time to see Sadie trapped at the back behind some people who were not getting out. The doors closed. Mother panicked. Angela was nonchalant. 'She'll just go up and come down again,' she said. But the lift reappeared without Sadie. Mother became hysterical. 'Sadie is perfectly sensible,' Angela said, 'she's simply got out at the wrong floor and she'll realize in a minute and come down. She won't be in the least bothered.' Five minutes went by and at last out came Sadie—but trembling, tearful with fright. 'For goodness sake,' Angela said as Sadie catapulted into her arms and clung to her, 'I wouldn't have thought a little thing like that would upset you.' 'Oh you,' was all Mother said, but she made a great fuss of Sadie and throughout the rest of the day referred frequently to her ordeal. That night, relating the incident to Ben when he came home, Mother said, 'And of course Angela would have it that Sadie would be enjoying herself— the idea—she doesn't know the half that poor child suffers.'

The crematorium, a new building up at the top of the old cemetery, was hideous. Angela could not understand why anyone could prefer cremation if these were the circumstances in which it had to take place. She wished, as they all packed into the soulless chapel that was not even remotely like a chapel, that they were instead winding their way up through the cypress trees in the adjoining cemetery. She wished, as Mother's coffin glided silently through two open velvet curtains, that it was instead being lowered into a dark and deep hole. She wished that in place of central heating fumes—gusts of warm, cloying air that rose up from the floor—she could feel the wind on her face. She wished the words 'dust to dust, ashes to ashes' could be given some meaning, as would have happened if they had been surrounded by the evidence of it. She wished most of all that this was not Sadie's first funeral, inevitably imprinted on her mind forever more as what a funeral was—two parts, church and crematorium, not coming together in any grand emotional finale but staying forever separate, the one real and moving, the other false and tawdry.

They stood at the door afterwards waiting for their cars while the next party unpacked themselves from theirs. 'Damn,' Father said, 'hanging about like this,' and before anyone could restrain him he had set off down the main path, head bent, arms flaying his sides. They all watched, obediently continuing to wait for the cars Father had spurned, knowing that they would have to endure his contempt later. Before he was at the gates that led onto the main road, the cars had arrived and they all piled hurriedly in. 'If you could stop just past the gates,' Angela said, 'to pick up my Father.' But she knew he would not be picked up. As their car slowed down he waved it on, his arms working agitatedly like a bookie's on a racecourse, and crossed defiantly to the other side of the street. 'Wait,' Sadie said, 'stop.' 'It's no good,' Angela said, 'he won't come.' But she had misunderstood. Sadie did not want to persuade Father to join them—she wanted to join him. Out she jumped and ran after him leaving them all open-mouthed.

They were home in two minutes. For the first time in three days Valerie stopped crying and hurled herself into the kitchen, expecting Angela to do likewise. An amazing array of food was put on the table in a short time but nobody would touch it until Father appeared. The sight of so much pastry—pies and tarts and vol-au-vents galore—nauseated Angela but everyone else eyed the spread hungrily including Ben, whom she would have liked to be above such things. She positioned herself at the window to watch her Father and Sadie, who could not be long. She knew she could not have got out, as her daughter had done, to walk with Father. She would have been too afraid. Why had Sadie done it? Sadie, who did nothing out of pity, or not for her mother at least. Again, thinking about it as she craned to see Father and Sadie turn the corner, Angela was forcibly reminded that her daughter was not her, and she was not to her daughter as Mother had been unto her. It seemed to her as she stood there that to think otherwise had been the source of all her confusion. Relationships did not repeat themselves and she had deluded herself that they must and that she therefore had a duty to prevent this happening.

Leaning listlessly against the window frame—Father would tell her off for creasing the curtains—Angela listened to the conversations around her. There was not much talk of Mother. There had somehow not been any talk of Mother since her death. She had imagined endless reminiscing, had even looked forward to it, but none was forthcoming. She looked towards Aunt Frances, the sister closest to Mother, and wished she would speak openly and tenderly of Mother but Frances talked to everyone about her sciatica and nothing else. Listening to all the drivel around her disgust rose like bile in Angela's throat—a thick phlegm of disgust that they could all be so callous and insensitive. Though she knew it was Father's theme she found herself thinking 'nobody appreciated her' and the maudlin thought carried her away until an image of Mother's sweet face filled her vision and brought the first tears of the day to her eyes.

She wiped them away quickly as Father and Sadie came in at the gate. Father stopped on the garden path and pointed out something growing to Sadie, who stooped obligingly to look at it. Then, as though the house were empty, Father took out his key and opened the door. Loudly, he scraped his feet on the mat. There was a trailing off of words—sentences were left suspended in mid-air while Father made his entrance. A few people decided they had trains to catch, trains never mentioned before as leaving so early. 'Nobody eating?' Father said, perfectly amiable, and a relieved crowd thronged round the food. For half an hour the company was solid and convivial and then it began to melt away. 'Going already?' Father said to each departing coward, staring straight at them. None dared prevaricate. They nodded and he said with emphasis, 'Well, thanks for sparing the time. All the best now.' Within less than an hour there were only five of them left. Sadie sat at the table eating cake after cake while Valerie trudged backwards and forwards clearing plates. The noise she made ostentatiously gathering together knives and teaspoons seemed ear splitting. Father stood, arms folded across his chest, looking into the garden. Angela wished he would put on his gardening clothes and get out there but according to his own invented code that was impossible. He would not work in the garden for a week, nor would he put on the television though the radio was permissible.

'I was thinking,' Angela said, 'why don't you come back with us tomorrow—it would take your mind off things.' She knew even before Father said 'No, no, no,' that it was a stupid thing to have said. Trewicks did not want their minds taken off things—they approved of minds clinging to whatever tragedy was in hand and distraction from it was not something they desired. Father would sit it out. He would wilfully remove from his daily existence any crumbs of comfort. There could be no possibility of helping him.

They sat in a circle round the fireplace drinking cups of tea. At nine o'clock Angela said, 'I'm going to bed early.'

'Oh you'll do that,' Father said sarcastically, 'oh yes, you'll do that.'

'Why shouldn't I? I'm tired. It's been a long hard day.'

'For some,' Father said.

'For all of us.'

'Some more than others.'

'All right then—some more than others. But I'm tired. I can't see what's wrong in going to bed early.'

'You never could,' Father said bitterly, 'you'd never sit, always going off. Mother used to be very hurt by it, very hurt.'

Angela said nothing. She knew better. She sat very still and started to count to a hundred in her head.

'Very hurt sometimes,' Father said, as though abstracted, but plainly tense and determined. 'Well, it's over now. She's out of it. Nobody can let her down now, none of you.'

'I think I'll have another cup of tea,' Ben said, getting up, 'anyone else want one?' Everyone shook their heads.

'There's her things,' Father said, 'they'll need sorted.'

'Oh, just send them to the church jumble,' Angela said.

'What?' said Valerie. 'Send Mother's things to the jumble? Oh, how awful.'

'They're only clothes,' Angela said.

'Stacks of them,' Father said, 'cartloads—I don't care what you do with them—just get them out of the way.'

'Well, I do care,' Valerie said, flushed with indignation. 'I won't have Mother's clothes shoved in a heap and put in that awful church hall for anyone to finger.'

'Do you want them?' Angela asked.

'No—except one or two cardigans perhaps—I'm not sure.'

'Get yourselves in her room and do the job now,' Father said.

'It seems wrong,' said Valerie, 'with Mother buried only hours ago—interfering with her things so soon.'

'It won't get any less wrong,' Father said, 'just get in.'

They sat on the bed and faced the wardrobe, its double doors open to reveal Mother's clothes. Valerie took them all out one by one and in spite of her tender sensibilities tried several on. She was pleased when Angela told her Mother's good tweed coat suited her admirably and that several dresses only need the hems let down to be the height of chic. They stacked everything in piles—one for Valerie, one for the jumble—and then turned their attention to the chest of drawers. There were multitudes of underclothes all of which they bundled into a bag, in haste not to examine them. Valerie took all the scarves—Mother always had a little scarf in the neck of a coat or dress—and the four pathetic items of jewellery.

'We'll take all this down to the church hall tomorrow,' Valerie said, 'then Father won't have to bother. It won't worry him.'

'I don't think it would anyway,' Angela said, 'he's sensible about things like that.'

'Hard, you mean,' Valerie said, 'like you. Mother and I were the soft ones. Oh dear,' and she slumped on the bed and began to cry again. 'I shall miss her so much. I can't bear to think of her dead.'

'I can,' Angela said. 'I can bear it very well.'

'Oh, you're wicked—if Mother could hear you—'

'Well, she can't. She never could hear me. We never said anything to each other that mattered in all our grown-up lives.'

'Finished?' said Father looking in at the door.

'Yes,' Angela said.

Sixteen

Angela finally went to bed an hour later than she had intended, hoping that Father would be mollified. She thought it might be the last time she would ever sleep in this ugly house where she was born. Father would not care if they said, next holiday, that they were going to rent a cottage and come in each day to visit him. He would approve. He would have their company but the house would stay tidy.

Years of claustrophobia in the narrow, little, distempered bedroom rolled off her as she lay on her back looking at the ceiling. The cheap cotton, flowered curtains had never fitted and let in too much light even on a dark night. Father had secured them with drawing pins down each side but even so the draughts came in down her neck. There was a knock on the door. 'Come in,' Angela said, wearily, sure it was Valerie with another lugubrious speech to make. But it was Sadie, bringing her cocoa though she had not asked for any. Unexpectedly, Sadie sat on the bed. Angela sipped the hot sweet liquid, faintly revolted by it, but grateful for the thought. She saw Sadie was watching her, as she used to watch Mother, and resolved to speak. 'I'm tired,' she said, 'and depressed. My Mother's life depressed me. It ought to be a relief she's dead but I must say I don't feel much relieved yet.'

'I don't know why Grandma depressed you,' Sadie said.

'She was never really happy and a lot of it was my fault. I was never the daughter she wanted—I couldn't give her what she really wanted. At least you won't have that problem Sadie—I don't want anything from you. I promised myself before you were ever born that I wouldn't want anything from you.'

'You do,' Sadie said. 'You're always telling me that, but it's a lie.'

'I don't. I'm perfectly self-sufficient and happy and always will be. I don't look to you for anything.'

'Yes you do.'

'What? For what?'

'I don't know. I annoy you. I'm not what you want.'

'But annoying me is trivial—it's a stage—all adolescent girls annoy their mothers—'

'Oh, forget it,' Sadie said and got up. 'Grandad's gone to bed and Dad too. Do you think it would be all right if I watched a film on tele, if I kept it very low?

'I should think so,' Angela said, 'but if Grandad comes down and objects, give in straight away.'

That brief feeling of intimacy had gone—frightened away, as usual, by words. Angela closed her eyes and tried to sleep. Real closeness was silent. Often, she and Ben lay in bed and just held each other after they had made love and that closeness was the most comforting thing in the world. It was ten years since she had had it with Sadie, thirty since she had had it with Mother. Nothing seemed to have taken the place of that physical touch through which there passed to the other person love and trust and confidence. Sadie needed it and stuck between childhood and later passion nobody gave it to her.

Sadie had always wanted a dog. She would plead and plead to be allowed to have one—any kind, any breed. Patiently, Angela had gone over the reasons why she could not allow her to have a dog. Gently she probed to discover why Sadie thought she wanted one. To look after? She was bad at looking after anything. Plants died in her room from lack of water, fish died in smelly tanks she forgot to clean out, even a tortoise was run over because Sadie left the garden gate open. To take for walks? Sadie hated walks. To love? She had her family. 'But that's different,' Sadie said, 'a dog would be just mine, it would just want me—oh please—I'd do everything for it—please.' Angela had almost given in, the need seemed so strong. She had said to Ben that Sadie seemed to need this outlet for her affections. But Ben pointed out that they went abroad too often for a dog to

*be feasible. Sadie had cried bitterly. Later, several years later, when Saul
wanted a dog Sadie had laughed and said, 'Do you remember when I
wanted a dog? Thank god you didn't let me have one—what a pest they are.'
But Angela always imagined some secret damage had been done by
thwarting Sadie's instinct.*

They caught a late-morning train to Exeter and then another for
London the next day. Father did not come to the station—it
would not be right to be seen in the town the day after the
funeral. He thanked them for coming, which made Angela
wince. He said he would be all right on his own. 'But it will be
empty,' he said, 'there won't be much to do with Mother gone.'
There seemed no hint of tears in either eyes or voice. 'But I'll keep
busy,' he said, 'I'll find something to do, don't you worry.' No
one was worried. Angela thought how fortunate it was that
Mother had not exacted death-bed promises to look after Father.
They would, of course, but without anguish. Mother could never
have been put in a home. Father, if it became necessary, though
Angela was absolutely sure it never would be, could be consigned
to some carefully vetted establishment without any broken hearts.
    They said goodbye to Valerie at the barrier. 'Will you write?'
she asked Angela at the last minute.
    'If you like. But not regularly. If I have news—yes.'
    'Just to keep in touch,' Valerie said, 'now Mother's gone. She
would like to think of us keeping in touch. She wouldn't like to
think of the family falling apart.'
    'Yes, I'll write then,' Angela said.
    'And I'll come and see you sometimes.'
    'Of course, whenever you like.'
    Angela laid her head against the seat of the train. Relief, she
was discovering, was such a negative emotion. She felt nothing.
She wished Sadie was not sitting opposite so that she and Ben
could dredge over the last few days—not that she had anything to
say but going over and sharing thoughts and feelings in that
leisurely way they had perfected over the years always helped.
Sadie's presence inhibited her.
    'You did very well,' Ben said suddenly as the train drew out of
the station. Sadie looked astonished.
    'You didn't cry at the funeral after all.'
    'No,' Angela said.

'Mother doesn't cry,' Sadie said, rapidly turning the pages of the magazine she had bought. 'Why should she? She wanted Grandma to die.'

'Don't be silly,' Ben said, 'you're twisting her words—you're making it sound horrible when you know perfectly well what Angela meant when she said that, if she said it.'

'Grandma was frightened of her,' Sadie said, 'and I don't blame her.'

'Stop it, Sadie,' Ben said, sharply, 'it isn't funny.'

'You know nothing about it, Sadie,' Angela said in a flat, emotionless voice, 'don't try to make me feel guilty. Mother was never frightened of me, she was frightened of dying and frightened that I knew she was frightened. She wanted me to make everything all right and I couldn't.'

'She told me last week,' Sadie said, 'she said, "she's a terror, your Mother, she scares the life out of me."'

'Oh grow up,' Ben said, disgustedly, 'surely you can see—'

'She can't see anything,' Angela said, 'but anyway I don't want to discuss it. Let's just be quiet. It will be hectic enough when we get home and I'm exhausted.'

'I'll move with pleasure,' Sadie said, and in spite of their protests she went into the next carriage.

'Oh let her go,' Angela said when Ben tried to restrain her, 'she'll feel she's won then. Who cares.'

'So strange,' Ben said, 'after being so good at the funeral.'

'Very good. Quite startlingly good. I used to be good in that sort of way,' Angela said, watching the familiar landscape slip by. 'I'd decide for no particular reason to behave like Mother really wanted me to behave, just to show I could, and then I'd revert to type straight afterwards and they would all forget how nice I'd been just for them. They only like me when I do what they want, I used to think.'

'Pass that paper,' Ben said, 'I haven't read one for days.'

Sadie's pride was not tough enough for her to resist joining them for lunch. They talked in fits and starts, the three of them, throughout the meal. As long as they confined themselves to impersonal topics Angela saw how well they could be said to get on together. Gradually, her tiredness began to lift. She thought of things to look forward to and said, 'It will be nice to be home again.'

'At least you won't have to rush down to St Erick any more,' Sadie said, 'unless Grandad gets ill.'

'He won't get ill,' Ben said, firmly, 'not for a long time anyway.'

'It was so awful,' Sadie said, 'you rushing off like that.' Angela looked at her carefully. She distrusted Sadie in this reassuring mood.

'Awful for whom?' she asked.

'For us of course,' Sadie said. 'It was awful without you—looking after ourselves—Dad's rotten meals—Tim crying half the time and Max and Saul fighting.'

'You all managed perfectly well,' Angela said, 'don't pretend just to flatter me.'

'I'm not pretending. It was horrible. And when you were in hospital it was even worse.'

'Then I don't want to hear about it,' Angela said. She saw Mother's face when they had said the same sort of things to her and she contrasted her own dismay with Mother's pleasure.

'You should be pleased,' said Sadie, 'thinking how we all depend on you. You're always saying nobody helps or appreciates you.'

'I *never* say that.'

'Well, you imply it.'

'I do not. I don't want to be depended on. I don't want to be missed. I haven't brought you up to cling. You should all be independent—there shouldn't be any apron strings for you to cut yourself off from—'

'Oh god,' Sadie said, 'it was just a remark. You always take everything so bloody seriously.'

Every night, Angela read Sadie a bedtime story. She loved the ritual. First, the bath and then the glass of milk in pyjamas and dressing-gown and then the story with Sadie and Max in their beds and Saul already asleep in his cot. She set the scene carefully, loving the creation of an idyll Sadie would remember all her life. Ben found it all unnatural and a bit boring. The ritual took longer and longer every evening, he said, and it could not be deviated from. This could be a nuisance. Sometimes he had to wait an hour for Angela until she was ready to come down and welcome him home. If they were going out it ruined their departure as no babysitter could effectively take over Angela's role. Sometimes Angela secretly regretted it herself—she wished she just had to say 'off to bed' and Sadie and Max would go—but it was worth it, for Sadie's memories. She knew she was creating something precious. When Tim was born she fought to keep the ritual going. One night she had to give in. 'You'll have to put yourselves to bed,' she said to the other three, 'I'm too tired to read bedtime stories these days.' 'Oh good,' Sadie said, 'I never did like it anyway.'

Until Aunt Frances came to visit her Angela was surprised at how quickly life became balanced once more. She returned to her part-time teaching and felt a deep satisfaction in the momentum of each day now she could depend on its rhythm. She drove off with everything tidily organized behind her, carrying shopping lists all neatly made out to which she would turn her attention on the return journey. Her thoughts were together. That great lifting of weight which she had waited for since Mother had died had at last happened. She was a free agent—free from guilt and anxiety and that dreadful crippling sense of responsibility. She felt better and looked years younger. Valerie on the telephone said, 'Isn't it awful the way there's no pleasure in anything now Mother has gone?' and gasped when Angela said, 'On the contrary—there seems pleasure in so many things I dreaded before.'

It was perhaps this cheerfulness, this new vitality so evident in Angela that annoyed Aunt Frances and made her seek to deflate it. She rang up, some two months after Mother's death, to say that she was going to be in London the following week and would like to come and see Angela. 'We don't want to lose touch,' she said in that same unctuous way Valerie had, 'your Mother would have liked us to see more of each other again now that she's gone.' Smiling because they had never been in any kind of touch since she had grown up, Angela said she would be delighted. She invited Aunt Frances to lunch and was glad to—gestures like that were easy to make now that her energies were renewed. She went to some trouble to make sure the lunch was delicious and cleaned the house thoroughly the day before the better to impress her aunt.

'Mary always said it was a big house,' Frances said, and then rummaged in her bag for a tissue. She had not been there five minutes before she had made plain that her grief was continuous and now, as they sat down to the meal, the tears were again squeezed out. 'Oh dear, I still can't say her name without wanting to weep.' Angela, busy at the cooker, said nothing. She gave what she hoped Frances would interpret as a sympathetic smile. 'You're looking well,' Frances said. 'I don't know why your Mother ever worried about you doing too much, I must say.'

'I feel very well,' Angela said.

'You would have thought your Mother's death would pull you down,' Frances said. 'You're lucky. Things like that have always affected me dreadfully. I've felt awful ever since Mary's death—aches and pains everywhere—and then I feel so depressed, I can't seem to get out of it.'

'What a shame,' Angela said, knowing she must stop all this smiling that Aunt Frances would think inappropriate.

'Don't you feel depressed?' Frances asked.

'No.'

'Not with your own poor Mother passing over?'

'No. Mother was ill for years and years. She didn't enjoy life much—no, I don't feel depressed.'

'Well, I wish I could take it like that,' Frances said. 'She was always my favourite sister, your Mother. Poor Mary, she had a hard time of it.'

Angela, who had learned her lesson many times over but could not nevertheless leave well alone said, 'Oh, I don't know. I don't think Mother did have such a hard time of it, not when you compare her life to some other people's.'

'But you don't know the half of it,' Frances said eagerly, and from the way she suddenly perked up and put her tissues to one side and leaned across the table Angela could tell this was really why she had come. 'There are so many things you don't know—Mary was wonderful at keeping things from all you children—you've no idea. "I don't want them to worry," she used to say, "they're only young once, they'll have troubles enough in their own lives soon, I don't want to load them with mine." So she wouldn't tell you anything—just struggled on, protecting you, doting on you. It was ridiculous.'

'It sounds sensible to me,' Angela said, passing Frances a blue and white patterned plate upon which there rested a neatly filleted trout.

'Oh, but what a time of it the poor dear had and you knowing nothing of it and going your own sweet way.'

Angela could see Frances' lips trembling with the effort of choosing her words with care. Her fat, pink tongue, slivers of white fish clinging to it, darted in and out licking them as she tried to control her excitement. She kept pulling in her chins and burying them in the collar of her jumper, shaking her head slightly and even closing her eyes with suppressed ecstasy. Angela knew what she wanted. Mother would have sworn Frances to secrecy but now Mother was dead and Frances longed to be questioned, to be encouraged to let fly with the hundred and one vicious little tales she had to tell. She could be ignored. Unless pressed, she had just enough conscience not to voluntarily impart her confidences. She could be left to finish her trout and eat her salad and wolf two helpings of the chocolate gateau to which she was most partial. She could be sent away with her poisonous information still not given. There was a decision to be made and Angela congratulated herself as she made it.

'Help yourself to some salad,' she said, brightly, beaming.

'A lovely meal,' Frances said, sniffing a little, 'you shouldn't have gone to so much bother—I didn't expect it—I just thought we ought to make it up though I'm not sure what I ever did to have you never come near all these years but never mind.' She dabbed at her lips with her napkin and coughed. 'This is a lovely house,' she said. 'Very nice. It pleased your Mother to think you had a nice house. More than she ever did, poor soul. She never really had anything much after she married your Father. That was that—scrimp and save from then on and she wasn't used to it. It was her undoing. She could have had anyone and she chose him.'

'That's a lie,' Angela said, calmly, she hoped inoffensively.

'I *beg* your pardon,' Frances said.

'Mother couldn't have had anyone. She married Father because no one else ever asked her and she was thirty. She wanted a home and children and thought she wasn't going to get them. She told me herself.'

Frances had blushed a deep, purply red. Her chins wobbled as she took deep breaths. 'The fact remains,' she said, 'that marriage was a disaster.'

'How do you know?'

'Mary ended up hating your Father. You don't know anything about it. You never knew she left him once—he drove her near to doing herself in—you never knew that. There, you see.'

It was out, or part of it. Foolishly, she had provoked Frances when she had resolved to placate her.

'Well, that's interesting,' Angela said, determined to remain equable, 'have some more gateau.'

'No *thank* you. It was dreadful. You were only two and Valerie on the way—that was what brought it on—finding herself expecting again, she was disgusted, she hated all that—"Oh Frances," she told me, "I can't stand it." But of course he wouldn't leave her alone. So she left him. Said she was sorry and it was her fault—as if it was—but she wasn't coming back unless he promised not to touch her. Of course, he wouldn't. You came to me for six months while it was all sorted out, then—'

'I don't want to hear any more,' Angela said, 'and I think it's despicable of you to have told me this much.'

'It isn't right that you don't know what your Mother went through—the sacrifices she made for you. She was a saint, poor Mary, no doubt about it—what she suffered on your behalf.'

Slowly, a great anger built up in Angela as she sat opposite this vindictive woman, whose silly face was smeared with chocolate, whose eyes gleamed with an almost evangelical fervour as she spread her gospel of hate. But there was no stopping her.

'It was for your sake she went back,' Frances said, 'she sacrificed her freedom and her peace of mind for you. We all begged her not to go back—she could have lived with any of us—but she said she had to, for you children's sake, and she did. She gave up any chance of being happy for you children, more than any woman I ever know. You were her pride and joy, couldn't do enough for you, nothing else mattered.'

'Well, she's dead,' Angela said, loudly.

'Yes, and you don't seem to care.'

'Aunt Frances, you couldn't tell whether I cared or not. You don't know the first thing about me—you never have done. I'm sure you've got lots more things to shock me with but I don't want to hear them—go and tell Valerie instead.'

'Oh, I wouldn't upset Valerie—she's too like your Mother, too tender-hearted. No, it's you that ought to know—I've thought that for a long time—it made me ill to see how you treated your Mother after what she'd done for you and that's why I had to speak up. You wait until it happens to you and then you'll know how your Mother felt—wait until that Sadie of yours just cuts herself off and starts treating you like a charity.'

'Sadie doesn't need to cut herself off. She's never been tied to me since she was born. I expect nothing from her.'

'Oh, that's what you say now—you wait until you're old and ill—you'll want her soon enough then—you'll look for some repayment and you'll be disappointed if you find there's nothing there—no love, no thanks, nothing.'

Frances was growing redder and redder with each minute. They were both on their feet, shouting at each other across the kitchen table where the remnants of their meal lay neglected. It was distressing for both of them and the absurdity of it made Angela laugh.

'Aunt Frances,' she said, 'this is stupid. I don't know why you're upsetting yourself. I don't know what makes you think I didn't love Mother anyway.' It was painful to talk with Frances about love at all—the word was hard to use.

'I didn't say that, now.'

'You implied it—more than implied it.'

'I only said you let her down in the end. It didn't turn out how she thought it would when you were such a loving little girl.'

'Of course it didn't. How could it? I don't think it's fair to attack me because it didn't.'

'We always got on well, your Mother and I.'

'Oh yes.'

'We did. We were the closest in the family. I looked up to her, I'd have done anything for her.'

Angela cleared away the plates and made coffee. The time to be charitable had arrived. But after Frances had left, docile and even apologetic by late afternoon, she found it hard to get Mother's face out of her head. It was what she had expected to happen when Mother was lying in her coffin, when her body was still in the house, but no haunting images had troubled her then. Frances had bequeathed her this spectre long after the event. She went about her normal tasks explaining and pleading before this ever-present mask, which remained blank. None of Mother's real expressions passed across it—neither sorrow nor resignation, no shadow of joy or grief, only the same bland look, with the large eyes open, unblinking, staring at and through her. Angela wore herself out pleading for some response but there was none—she found her own lips moving as she began whispering out loud to Mother.

'What's wrong with you?' Sadie said, coming in from school, as usual hardly pausing for an answer. 'There's going to be a school trip to Greece in April. Can I go?' She prowled round the kitchen looking for something to eat and only turned to consider Angela when no answer was forthcoming. 'I'd pay my own spending money out of babysitting,' she said.

'I can't seem to think about it,' Angela said, 'not now.'

'When, then? We have to know tomorrow—first come first served.'

'I'll think about it tonight.'

'But *will* you? I'd be away all the Easter holidays—off your hands for three weeks—well, two.'

'That's an attraction, is it?'

'Of course it is—you like us going away—'

'Only to enjoy yourselves.'

'I *know* only to enjoy ourselves—but you get some peace and quiet too if you get rid of us.'

'I don't want to get rid of you—'

'Oh, you know what I mean—why be so touchy about it—of course you want us off your hands, anyone would.'

'I want you to feel free but—'

'Well, we do.'

'—but I don't want you to think you're not wanted.'

'I don't think that, even when it's true.'

'What does that mean?'

'Oh forget it—just a joke—anyway, I'd like to go to Greece if you'd let me.'

There was no point trying to detain her—distracted by Aunt Frances' visit she lacked the energy to pursue Sadie. The turmoil she had thought settled forever boiled up again inside her head as she dwelt upon the picture her aunt had painted. She thought she had cleared her conscience of anything to do with Mother the day after the funeral but now the agony seemed worse than ever—the foundations of her new-found serenity were shallower than she could have guessed. She did not know how to cast out Mother from her mind, accusing her, suffering for her, pathetic and good and unbearably sorrowful.

Angela hesitated on the threshold of Sadie's room after she had put Tim to bed. She peeped round the door and saw Sadie, books spread out, writing industriously. Quietly, she withdrew.

Later, when she heard records being put on and knew Sadie had finished her homework, she thought about interrupting. She thought about going into Sadie's room and sitting on the bed and confessing her distress and asking for help, but it was not something she ever did and the idea was embarrassing. She was grasping at a hope so insubstantial it slid out of her grasp at once. Instead, she wandered from room to room, wishing Ben was not going to be as late as he had said he would be, and though she did not wring her hands she took care to avoid mirrors which would reveal too clearly her anguish. She knew she was doing what Mother had done, feeling as Mother had often felt, looking for what Mother had looked for— support, companionship, shared responsibility. If only Sadie would appear and put an arm about her shoulders . . .

'No,' she said out loud, and walked with determination towards the television which she put on, not caring about the programme she might get. She drew up her chair and concentrated on 'The Body in Question', seeking to divert the hysterical meanderings of her tired brain into a more sensible direction. But the fear remained. Once, Mother had been such a comfort. When she was a child, lying awake miserable or ill, Mother had come to her and laid a gentle hand on her forehead and soothed her with endearments. 'It will be all right,' Mother had said, without knowing what was wrong, 'now don't worry,' and even when she was older and her reason told her it would not be all right and there was everything to worry about—even then, the magic had worked. She had faith because Mother was a mother. Later, she had done for her children what Mother had done for her. The same reassurance had sent them into a blissful coma of trust. She had seen small fists unclench at her words and brows miraculously smoothed and she had marvelled at her own power. But now she dreaded the thought of Mother.

She found herself on the top floor where the boys slept without being able to remember climbing the stairs. Tim was sleeping soundly, his arms flung over his head, legs spread out above the covers. To him, she was still everything. She turned away, unable to bear the sight of her youngest child who reminded her so forcibly of her own importance. 'They soon grow up,' Mother used to say wistfully but Angela could not share her regret. To be so needed was heartbreaking. She looked at Max and Saul and immediately felt better—they were through that imaginary barrier of total independence. She was beyond being everything to them and it made her glad. Yet Mother had spoken so bitterly of her sons. 'You get nothing from boys,' she had said, 'they grow apart and it's never the same.'

She was now exhausted and weeping in that way she despised —that spineless, mawkish way that the real Angela rejected. Downstairs again she made tea she did not want and sat clutching the hot liquid. Her misery had become so physical that her whole body ached. Any movement pained her. She crouched in her chair thinking that the next day she must go to her doctor and allow him to prescribe those shaming tranquillizers she had always been proud of not needing. She would fill herself up with them until time passed.

She slept where she was, in her chair, until Ben came home and covered her with a blanket, mystified, and put a pillow behind her head and a stool under her feet and left her.

She woke up as soon as the first light came through the yellow living room curtains. Her first thought was relief that she had slept at all. She went quietly upstairs and slipped into bed with Ben, who stirred in his sleep but did not waken. Her head ached and she was stiff all over but that demented racing of her brain had stopped. She saw clearly how she had worked herself into a state, how she had allowed the mischievous gossiping of Aunt Frances to upset her. It was something that could quite easily happen again—the past, cunningly reported, would always have that power over her.

'Interfering bitch,' Father said on the telephone that night, 'never liked her—wouldn't give her house room—what did she want anyways?'

'Just calling,' Angela said, 'just wanting to keep in touch for Mother's sake.'

'A likely story,' Father said, 'you watch out—she's a meddler. Your Mother went off her years ago.'

'Why?'

'Never you mind. What's done is done—wouldn't look after her own mother even though she had that big house and money to go with it. It was us took her in—were going to, anyways, if she hadn't dropped dead unexpected—and we hadn't room to swing a cat.'

'I didn't know that.'

'There's a lot you don't know.'

'That's what Aunt Frances said.'

'I wouldn't trust her to tell you the time of day. She turned Catholic, you know.'

'Father, really—'

'What?'

'Well, what a thing to say—as if becoming a Catholic was something to hold against Aunt Frances, as if it had anything to do with trusting her.'

'Course it has—once the church gets a hold on them, that's that. Them priests can do anything with them—do what they like, say what they like, and into confession and bob's your uncle.'

Defeated, Angela was silent. In the right mood Father's manic logic was funny but in the wrong one it was deeply depressing and made her see all over again what Mother had been up against.

'Valerie isn't well,' Father said.

'Oh, what's wrong?'

'Women's troubles. Same as your Mother at that age.' Again, Angela was silent. She could think of nothing to say that wouldn't embarrass them both.

'You should ring her,' Father said, 'nobody else to do it now.'

'I will.'

'In place of your Mother.'

'Yes.'

But she put it off. She did not want to be Mother to anyone else, especially not to Valerie, and in any case it was ludicrous to imagine she could take on Mother's role. First Father set them against each other, then he expected them to feel for each other that same overwhelming affection Mother had felt.

Sadie had all the fun, and Max, aged three, bitterly resented it. She was allowed at last to cross the road by herself. She was allowed to go and post a letter, straining on tip-toes to put it safely through the slit in the box. Best of all, she was allowed to go to the corner shop on errands, list and money tucked inside her pocket, shopping basket on the crook of her arm like Little Red Riding Hood. Max would stand at the gate and scream while Angela came out with the standard comforts. 'When you are old enough you can go too,' she told him, knowing it was no good. In his own eyes he would never be as old as Sadie, never enjoy her status. 'Please, Sadie,' Angela said, 'take Max with you to the shop. Hold his hand when you cross the road.' But Sadie did not want to take him. She found every excuse. 'He will only hold my hand until we are out of sight,' she said, 'and then he will snatch it away and run across the road and get knocked over and it will be my fault.' Angela swore Max would be obedient. She pleaded and cajoled Sadie, who at last reluctantly agreed. She ran upstairs to the landing window the minute they had gone and watched them all the way down the street and across the road until they safely turned the corner. How sweet they looked—brother and sister, hand in hand, the one looking after the other. On the way back, Max tried to wrestle the basket from Sadie's grasp. Sadie hit him. Max dropped the basket and ran home screaming. When Sadie arrived crying with mortification it was to her Angela gave her attention and comfort. She had foisted upon Sadie her own illusion and it was no good.

'Father says you're ill,' Angela said when finally she got round to ringing Valerie.

'I need an operation,' Valerie said, 'the doctor's been on at me for months so I'll have to have it.' She paused, and Angela knew she was meant to ask what the operation was going to be for.

'Is it serious?' she asked instead.

'A hysterectomy. Like Mother.'

'I never knew Mother had a hysterectomy.'

'You never wanted to know—Mother said she couldn't talk to you about anything, you just changed the subject.'

'How long will you be in?'

'Two weeks and then of course I have to convalesce, like poor Mother—don't you remember how washed out she was, couldn't lift anything?'

'No,' Angela said. Valerie might as well have maximum satisfaction.

'You're lucky,' Valerie said, 'you haven't inherited any of Mother's problems. I mean, you don't have heavy periods, do you, or any pain? Perhaps they've bypassed you and gone to Sadie.'

'For christ's sake, Valerie.'

'What?'

'I don't want to discuss my periods or yours or anyone's—

anything more boring—I can't stand women who make such a thing of it—it's a purely private matter.'

'What a Victorian attitude.'

'Then I'm delighted to be Victorian.'

'You shouldn't be ashamed of your natural functions. I have girls in care with mothers like you and it leads to a lot of trouble. Mother always said you were a bit funny about menstruation and—'

'Valerie, I rang you up to say how sorry I was that you had to go into hospital and to ask if there is anything I can do to help. I don't want a lecture on how I handle my personal life and I don't want to know what Mother or anyone else thought of my attitudes. So can I help? Would you like to come here to convalesce? You're very welcome.'

'No—I'm all fixed up—I'm going off for three weeks to a friend's house in the Cotswolds—Joan Simpson's—remember, I was at college with her and we've always kept in touch. She asked me ages ago, and it will be nice and quiet.'

'That sounds good. I hope everything goes well. I'm sure it will. I expect things have improved since Mother's day.'

'It's still a very serious operation. I'm glad Mother was spared knowing I had to have it, anyway.'

Angela's irritation was so great she crashed the receiver down when she had said goodbye with unnecessary vigour. At every turn she was being accused of being a stranger to Mother, somebody on the fringe of her existence who, unlike Father and Valerie and Aunt Frances and heaven knew how many more people, was not privy to her innermost secrets. What she could not decide was whether it made any difference—whether there was a lesson to be learned from this discovery which might vitally affect her determined attempt to mould her relationship with Sadie differently.

Seventeen

Angela received a letter from Aunt Frances the following week, shrieking guilty conscience in every line. She had only meant well, Frances said, but on second thoughts she realized she might have gone about it the wrong way—she hoped Angela had not taken offence—she hoped she had not upset her and trusted that they would soon meet again and be friends for her Mother's sake. Mary had always been proud of Angela, Frances said, and really she had done very well and she had not meant to imply otherwise. In a postscript she asked if she might have any photographs of *her* mother that Angela might find among Mary's things. Mary, being the only one left in St Erick, had kept them all when their parents' house and contents were sold.

It was a job Angela had meant to do but had put off, not through any feelings of distress but because it needed time she had not been able to spare. She and Valerie, sorting through all the stuff in Mother's double-fronted mahogany wardrobe, had come across two shoe boxes full of letters and cards, all crammed in without any regard for order or tidiness, which was hardly Mother's way. 'You take them,' Valerie said, 'take them home with you and sort them out—you never know what you might find—Father would only burn them without looking at them. I don't want to do it—it would only upset me to see Mother's writing. It wouldn't upset you, would it?' 'No,' Angela had said, and she had emptied the contents of both boxes into a plastic carrier bag and put it at the bottom of her suitcase and brought it home. It had stayed in the suitcase, under her bed, ever since, untouched.

Untouched, but not unthought of. Every day, when she made the bed, Angela invariably stubbed her toe on the suitcase, which stuck out a fraction from underneath. It was a silly place to keep it, but she could never be bothered to carry it up to the loft where the other trunks and boxes were kept. It was handy where it was at the rate she had been using it. She would curse the suitcase as she kicked against it and then think of Mother's papers still inside. They were unlikely to contain anything of interest—Mother's hoarding instincts had lost out years ago to Father's stronger urge to tear and destroy all communications as they were received. 'Clutter,' he would say, and into the ever-burning fire would go the postcards and wedding announcements and newspaper cuttings which Mother would rather like to have kept. Against such odds it was unlikely much could have been accumulated—but then that made the little that had been secreted all the more valuable. Angela was intrigued and yet, in spite of the assurance she had given Valerie, apprehensive. The sight of Mother's things *did* upset her, against all reason. It was not that she feared intimate revelations so much as pathos, an inescapable pathos which might be even more unbearable than Aunt Frances' mischievous gossip.

She wanted none of that. The shabby mementoes were dangerous to her peace of mind and yet when Aunt Frances requested the photographs she was almost glad to be forced to overcome her reluctance. She waited for a particularly sunny, hot Sunday afternoon to go into her bedroom and retrieve the carrier bag and then she deliberately went out into the garden where almost the entire family were doing different things and the noise—from which she was usually so keen to escape—was considerable. The last thing she wanted to do was open the bag on a cold, rainy day when she was alone and the atmosphere conducive to melancholy.

Tim was playing in a paddling pool long since too small for him. Angela could not look at the yellow inflatable plastic pool, a mere three feet in diameter, without remembering Sadie sitting in it, aged one, half scared of the extremely shallow water in it. It was on its last legs. Tim only dragged it out of the garage each year to wreck it further. He filled it to the brim and then jumped into it from the garden wall sending spray everywhere. Max was out, but Saul and one of the next door Benson boys were perched high up in the big elm tree at the bottom of the garden firing arrows at all the shed roofs they could see. Ben was cutting down an apple tree that had suddenly rotted and the high-pitched whine of the electric saw he had borrowed to do the job would normally have irritated Angela into rushing inside.

It was beside Sadie that Angela sat. Sadie lay sunbathing, as far away from all the juvenile activity as it was possible to get. She was lying on a bright orange towel, on her stomach, some books propped up in front of her in a desperate last-minute attempt to revise for 'O' levels. Angela did not sit beside her without hesitation. She placed the wickerwork chair she had brought out with her beside the end of Sadie's towel and did not sit down upon it until Sadie had looked up. If she had turned and looked and saw it was her mother and looked away again without comment then Angela, respecter of privacy above all else, would have moved at least a few feet away. But Sadie said 'Oh hello,' and actually smiled and Angela was gratified to feel welcome.

She made a business of settling down, of arranging the cushions on the rather uncomfortable chair properly, of divesting herself of her jacket, of putting cream on her shoulders. It was really very hot. Sadie, in her skimpy bikini, and Tim, in his bathing shorts, were the only ones sensibly clad. Later, they might all go and swim. Fretfully, she fidgeted with the string she had tied round the bag, aware of the scene around her. Too aware. Each and every sound seemed magnified and important, creating an effective barrier against the past contained on her lap. She found herself looking round all the members of her family as though seeking reassurance, as though challenging any ghosts that might arise from that threatening livid green Marks and Spencer's plastic bag.

'What are you doing?' Sadie asked, raising herself up onto one elbow as she half turned to look at Angela, sucking a piece of grass, her sunglasses on her forehead in imitation of girls in magazines.

'Sorting out Grandma's papers,' Angela said.

'Anything interesting?'

'I don't suppose so. I haven't started yet. I've been meaning to do it for months. It's probably just boring rubbish.'

'Can't be more boring than this,' Sadie said, and turned back to her book.

'What is it?' Angela said, knowing she was seeking any diversion.

' "Great Expectations". '

'That's not boring—it's a wonderful book.'

'To you maybe. He just rambles on—acres and acres of stuff—he's so long-winded—I wouldn't mind the story if he'd stop padding it out. It sends me to sleep.'

Angela looked down at Sadie as she feigned sleep. Her back was beautifully brown, her skin as dark as a Spaniard's on her body and yet as fair as Mother's had been on her face. The combination was curious—such pink cheeks and soft golden tanned brow against the deep dark colour of the rest of her. Angela, who burned easily, envied her.

Cautiously, she emptied the contents of the bag into her lap. The pile of papers was heavy, causing her gingham skirt to sag between her knees. She put her knees together and roughly organized the heap upon them into some sort of order. Packets first, of which there were several, done up with elastic bands. The first contained Mother's reports, from the Higher Grade School, three of them, for forms I, II and III. Conduct 100 out of 100, Punctuality 100 out of 100, Algebra 100 out of 100, Scripture 100 out of 100, Cookery 100 out of 100. Angela smiled—such a student Mother had been. But Needlework was only 60 out of 100 and Drawing 45 out of 100—the weaknesses had remained the same, to mortify her. Position in the class was first out of forty-three every time. The headmaster, Mr R. C. Wolfe, B.Sc., could not speak too highly of this talented pupil's industry, application and intelligence. She was a pleasure to teach. She would go far. Angela folded up the reports. Mother had gone nowhere at all.

'Here,' she said, tossing the reports to Sadie, 'read these.' Sadie read them and laughed, betraying more interest than Angela would have thought possible.

'Incredible,' she said. 'I mean, Grandma was so brilliant—I never realized.'

'Brilliant and wasted.'

'Why wasted?'

'She never made any use of her brains. There were no opportunities. Her father died and she left school at fourteen and went into an office and that was that.'

'You're a snob,' Sadie said, 'People can be quite happy in offices—we don't all want to be blue stockings. Anyway, she got married and left the office so it came right in the end.'

'Did it?'

'Aw, Mum—don't go all enigmatic. I can't stand it. Look at the rest of the stuff, go on.'

Angela picked up the next bundle. Music exam cards. National College of Music, London, Feb. 13 and 14 1920, Reg. no. 9511. Subject of Examination—Piano. Solo 39 out of 40, Studies 23 out of 25, Scales 20 out of 20, Viva Voce 14 out of 15. Result—Distinction, Grade—4. Year after year Mother gained a Distinction and never after the day she married Father touched a piano again. It regularly upset her that neither Angela nor Valerie had ever had a single lesson in their lives. 'Where,' she would say, face wretched, 'where could we put a piano even if we had one?' Only years later had Angela wondered why they could not have used Grandmother's piano, stuck unused in the front parlour their entire visiting childhood.

The next packet contained receipts. From P. Jones, Painter, Decorator, Paperhanger Etc. Estimates free—jobbing work promptly attended to—high class pattern books. 1 Quart Gloss Brown 9s 6d, 1 Gill Gloss White Enamel 3s 6d, 67 yards Bordering @ 9d a yard, Three Large Packets of Whiting 1s 6d. Total for said decoration £3. 3s 5d. Yours and oblige. Five pounds for settee, deliver Friday. All paid and stamped and kept. Evidence of halcyon days—decorators in and new items of furniture before the decades of doing it themselves and never buying so much as a bench began. Angela did not finish looking at them. She bundled them up hastily.

'I really can't bear to look at these,' she said, 'they're too pathetic.'

'They're just bills,' Sadie said, looking at a few. 'What's pathetic about prices for things?'

'It isn't that. It's the image it gives me—like a little girl playing at houses—such a good little girl too, who wasn't going to make her world how she wanted it to be. She soon gave up, anyway. She used to say the money just went and there was never enough of it for even small luxuries so why bother keeping trace of where it went—but I knew she wanted to really. She wanted to be the sort of lady who had an account at the local grocer's and another at the butcher's and a nice, shiny, hard-backed red book to write her expenditure down in. Instead of that it was trailing round for bargains and cheap offers, hating it.'

'Plenty of rich people do that,' Sadie said.

'That's not the point.'

'You're always saying that—you're so sure you've got the point and nobody else can have any other that could possibly be right. You're so determined Grandma was always miserable and unlucky and we all had to feel sorry for her all the time. Maybe you had it all wrong.'

'I only wish I had,' Angela said.

She picked up the next bundle—certificates of one sort or another—a baptism card, a confirmation certificate signed by the Bishop, wedding and birth certificates, death certificates, all rapidly discolouring. The last packet was a heavy manilla envelope, Sellotaped across the top. Inside was a collection of greetings cards, from herself to Mother—cards sent on her birthday and her wedding anniversary, garish cards of country cottages with roses round the door, of vases of impossibly grouped flowers, of highly made-up ladies in old-fashioned crinolines. Sometimes they had satin ribbons threaded through them, or bits of embroidery in the corners. They all had extravagant verses—

> 'I'm counting my blessings and they're without number
> I know that I owe them to you
> You've taught the meaning of true love and kindness
> Of real joy and happiness too.
> If I tried to tell you of my deep affection
> I never could make myself clear
> So I pray that God's blessings be upon you
> My own Sweetest Mother Dear.'

They were all signed in her own large, slightly backhand writing that had stayed with her until hand-writing lessons at the Grammar School had changed it into a neater italic style. 'To Mummy, with best wishes for a *very* happy birthday with *all* my love and *deep* affection from Angela.' Angela smiled slightly at the underlining and the 'deep affection'. How old had she been? Seven or eight. The messages got more suffocating still later on, rising to a crescendo on the last card of all when she supposed she was twelve—'To the most wonderful Mummy, with every nice fragment that makes the world.' She stared at that incomprehensible inscription—what had she meant? She must have thought such a high-flown mysterious sentiment very sophisticated. The card it was written on—'To Wish You Every Joy'—had a tiny notebook pinned onto the front which said, 'A Special Prayer for You Today'. Angela opened it, a smile already on her lips.

> 'What memories this day will hold
> For you and me dear Mother
> Of the many moments we have been
> So close to one another
> And through them all you've shown a love,
> So patient and so kind;
> You gave me all the happiness
> That one could ever find
> And though I can't repay you
> In full for all you've done
> I can but try to make this day
> A truly happy one.
> So let me pray for perfect peace
> Good health for us to share
> A future of contentment
> For Mother dear so fair.'

She cried. That deprecating smile still on her lips, she wept as she had known that at some time she would, silently, copiously, in the middle of a bright summer's afternoon.

'Oh, Mum,' Sadie said, noticing, sitting up, 'for heaven's sake.'

Angela passed the cards to her and lay back on her chair, her eyes dazzled by the sun on her tears. Sadie looked through them all and laughed. 'But these are just *funny*,' she said, 'they're priceless—hysterical—you had such awful taste.'

'They're painful,' Angela said, 'all that exaggerated passion—hurling myself at her—so hungry for her affection.'

'Didn't she give it?'

'Yes, yes of course she did—she was always warm and loving— I spent hours on her knee being cuddled—so gentle, always—but it was never enough—and then look what happened—it stopped and nothing took its place until I met Ben—no wonder she was sad.'

'But that's natural—people don't drool over their mother when they grow up, do they? You don't get grown women sitting on their mother's knee, now do you?'

'No, but it should change into friendship. You can still be close and intimate—'

'Sounds dreadful to me.' Sadie stretched and yawned. Angela had stopped crying. 'I must get my front brown now.' She lay on her back and closed her eyes and smiled. 'At least I won't sit with all my cards to you crying over them in twenty years' time. Never sent any, did I?'

'One or two homemade ones, when you were small.'

'You haven't kept them, have you?'

'Of course. The drawings were good.'

'Well I'm amazed. I would have guessed I'd never sent a single one—I don't go in for that sort of thing.'

'No.'

'Did you mind? I mean, did you feel disappointed when you didn't get cards from me?'

'Not really.'

'That means you did. Well, I'll send you one next year—remind me,' and Sadie laughed at her own wit. She flicked a fly off her face. 'Thank god we're not like that in this family.'

No good asking her what she meant. Already their conversation had been longer and more amiable than it had been for months. Sadie was mellowing. The rudeness, the curtness, the restless rushing from place to place with never more than an hour at home was giving way to an easier and altogether more likeable pattern. The day before she had actually asked if there was anything she could do. It made Angela ridiculously happy. As she lay back in her chair that feeling of happiness came over her as strong as wine flowing through her veins and she felt a little drunk with it. Sadie's compliments were obscure but nevertheless unmistakable. When she had said 'thank god we aren't like that in this family' Angela knew she was intended to feel flattered. Sadie condemned her relationship with Mother only to approve her own relationship with Angela.

Neither of them spoke. The boys' shouts and screams and the shrill singing of Ben's saw still filled the air but it seemed very peaceful to Angela. She looked down at Sadie through half-open eyes, furtively, and saw that she was lying prone, quite calm, neither foot nor hand moving and her face blank of all expression. But she might not feel as relaxed as she looked. Perhaps during the last half hour she had dealt with Angela's distress more cunningly than it appeared. I was crying, Angela remembered, and visibly upset, and with the slightest encouragement—a single misplaced word or look—I would have run into the house and locked myself into my room. Sadie had coped. She had helped. It was too easy to dismiss her handling of the situation as an accident. She had for so long now assumed that there was no bond between herself and her daughter—that she had failed in that relationship as surely as her own mother had, if for different reasons—that it was a shock to realize that there was any feeling there at all. Sadie had just congratulated her on not creating the conditions Mother had created. She had said 'thank god we aren't like that in this family' and whichever way she interpreted it Angela could only conclude that Sadie was glad and that she thought credit was due.

Slowly, Angela gathered up all the different documents and put them back in the bag. She would find a box somewhere in the house and put them inside it and label it and put it in the loft for posterity. She looked through them all once more to check that there were no photographs. Aunt Frances would have to ask Father about that. Photographs were the only things Father did not throw away—he liked them, saved every one however bad and even put them in albums, glue smeared all round the corners so that the pages frequently stuck together. It was unlikely that he would let Frances have the photograph she wanted—he would say he couldn't spoil the album, dear me no. Often, he brought them out on rainy holiday afternoons and, amazingly, their charm never failed.

Angela tied the string and got up to go into the house. She would bring out some ice-cold drinks for everyone and a cake she had baked in the morning before the sun made the kitchen too hot. She liked to do things for her family, even things much more servile than bringing out refreshments into the garden—it made her feel motherly. As she picked up her jacket and walked up the path into the house, carrying Mother's mementoes, she reflected upon how she had created a different image from Mother's and yet how deep the roots were that went back to that other view of maternity. She had not quite broken free—she had not quite been able to reject so many of Mother's standards. It was impossible to measure either the loss or the gain. Later, much later when Sadie was grown up and a mother herself, she might be able to see their whole relationship in a different perspective. Now, she was full of doubts still and all that cheered her was the smallest show of concern upon Sadie's part towards her. Would the concern turn into guilt? In spite of her protestations, would Sadie suffer with an aged mother exactly as she herself had suffered? Was pain the inescapable price for that unstinting love mothers gave to their young children in such abundance?

'Are you going to get some drinks?' Sadie called after her.

'Yes.'

'About time.'

'You should get your own,' Angela said, but without resentment.